YEAR OF THE RAM

A Space-Faring Gay Romance

BY
DELLA VAN HISE

YEAR OF THE RAM
by Della Van Hise

Available on Kindle or in print from
http://www.amazon.com

Also available on our website at:
www.eyescrypublications.com

If you like gay romance, you may also enjoy...
http://www.fanzinesplus.com

For my teachers,
my masters,
and the characters who inspired me.

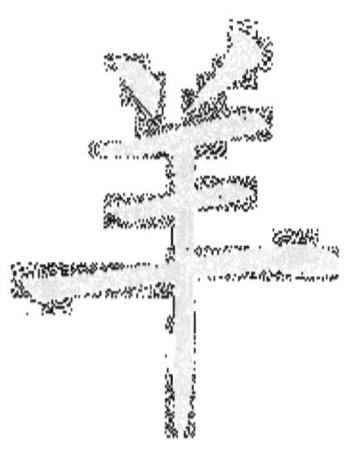

CHAPTER ONE

The spaceport hugged the ground like a dirty brown fungus on the otherwise lush green landscape of Sirius XII. Rockets stood erect and proud against the purple hue of a twilight sky, and dozens of small landing craft dotted the concrete and steel lift-off pads. The air was heavy with antiquated rocket fuel and smog, the humid atmosphere amplifying the scent of technology. Just what the terraformers ordered. The place looked, sounded and stunk just like any spacer-city back on Earth.

The single building which served the spaceport was round in shape, designed without angles to more effectively disperse the noise which thundered without warning as rockets lifted off, causing the ground to tremble in response. Sun-tinted windows blackened the entire surface of the structure, giving it the appearance of some 'flying saucer' as it stood on six chroma-steel columns at a height of more than thirty feet from the ground. Under the building were several ground cars, assorted storage bins filled with baggage headed for out-bound craft, and a plethora of air-conditioning ducts, electrical generators, and various and sundry gadgets designed to supply power, synthesize food, and otherwise service the massive structure above. Chaos incarnate. Pandemonium made manifest.

On several of the lift-off pads, blue-suited technicians scurried to and fro, each busy with a multitude of assigned duties as they prepared private, commercial or military craft for departure. Voices filtered through the afternoon heat and dirty air, creating a din of shouted orders, snapped commands and the occasional, ever-present human curse.

Morgan Diego watched the hustle and bustle with an odd feeling in the pit of his stomach – a sensation he had come to recognize as hunger. And yet, as he glanced around, he realized with a pang that, this time, the food bins had been carefully locked and coded. Barring the unlikely capture of some passing rat, he would not eat tonight.

Resigning himself, he closed his eyes for a moment, lifting one hand to his chin to scratch the two day growth of stubble. A subtle breeze plucked at his civilian attire, snapping the red flannel shirt and causing the thread-bare blue jeans to tremble as he shivered against the sudden cold.

Looking up, he studied the ceiling – which, in reality, was the under-flooring of the spaceport building. There was a time, he recalled, when he would have been safely *inside* that sanctuary, a time when his very presence would have created a commotion of pomp and circumstance as the officials at this remote port struggled to show respect to the commander of Galaxy Corps' most notorious vessel, the *Starling*.

Not now.

Now, as he looked down at himself, as he imagined his hair dirty with rocket soot and his face in need of a shave, he saw what he had become – another displaced "spacie" lingering about the bowels of a spaceport in the hopes of selling his skills to some desperate freighter commander or stowing away in the baggage compartment of some outbound ore rig.

With no money in his pocket, with the braid stripped ruthlessly from his shoulder, with only inaccurate memories to remind him of the past, he leaned against the massive pillar of stone and steel and slid to the cold concrete ground.

It would be night soon, he realized, hazarding a glance over his shoulder toward the other hapless souls who wandered without purpose under the building. Soon, the stars would be out. Soon, the others would sleep, or would make their attempt to illegally board a departing ship. Some, he knew, would die. They would hide themselves in amongst the baggage and be processed like any other article, only to find themselves in an airless chamber when the vessel achieved orbit and eventually hurtled itself toward the unforgiving stars.

He stared once more at the rockets on their pads. Most were antiquated private crafts used for short-hops within the star group, or for transport to nearby neighboring systems. Others were pleasure vessels owned by the very rich of a thousand different worlds – designed for speed and comfort as well as to transport their owners and guests to far-flung resorts bordering with dangerous excitement near the Nel-fen Neutral Zone. Still others were short-range military exploration vessels, a few were Galaxy Corps short-hoppers, and at the far end of the pad was a single star cruiser shuttle.

Straining his eyes in the approaching darkness, he felt his heart jump, wondering briefly if the shuttle belonged to his former mistress, the *ESC Starling*. And yet, closer inspection revealed the markings to be those of the *Daedelus* . He would find no sympathy there, he reminded himself. Not that he wanted any. He didn't belong anymore – not to Galaxy Corps, not to the Empire, maybe not even to himself. For all intents and purposes, Morgan Diego, Star Commander, no longer existed.

It was a sobering thought. Maybe even a little bit freeing.

Closing his eyes, he leaned his head against the cool stone beam, willing sleep to come. More than once, he became aware of feet shuffling near, of curious or desperate humans and aliens alike touching him, searching his empty pockets, deciding ultimately that he was hardly worth assaulting. He had nothing left to steal, no more riches to be taken.

He slept at last, re-living the nightmare from its onset…

~

He hadn't liked the mission from the beginning; it was one of those exercises in subterfuge best left to a team of experts specializing in covert operations, but with the budget cuts and the corruption inside the Empire reaching to the highest levels, he shouldn't have been surprised when the order came down. Simple enough. Or so it seemed. Wasn't even the first time he'd been asked to break every law known to man for the sake of allegedly preserving the domestic well-being of Earth and Empire – though even he would have been hard-pressed to see how snatching some alien plasma cocoon would make the golf courses in Palm Springs greener, or the vineyards on Marsport any more lucrative. As far as *he* was concerned, it was just another game the Empire liked to play – though he had come to wonder of late if the players were even aware of the game or the play or the fact that none of it would matter in a million years.

His instincts had warned against the whole charade from the start. But although he made his feelings on the matter clear to the brass, he was rather condescendingly reminded that he was a tool of the Empire and not the hand that turned it.

As commanding officer, it was his orders to direct the *Starling* into the Mizarian Sector, using essentially the same worn-out charade he'd played so many times before: computer error resulting in navigational inaccuracy. Translated: we're lost and oh so sorry about trespassing into your territory, but now that we're here, could you please hand over that nifty plasma cocoon or meet my little friend, Mr. Laser Cannon.

You're becoming a cynic, Cap'n Morgan, his inner critic observed. He didn't disagree.

In the half-awake quasi-dreamstate, he simply reviewed the facts, as he'd done a thousand times since everything went so dreadfully wrong.

Perhaps the biggest mistake the Empire made was insisting that even the *Starling's* second-in-command be kept in the dark as to the nature of the ship's mission. The Brass's reasoning was that, should something go wrong, the ship's two top officers couldn't both be at risk. If he were caught, Lucien could honestly claim ignorance on behalf of the *Starling* and the Empire. The Brass, it seemed, also knew that, sooner or later, their luck would run out.

And though Lucien's keen Alfarian senses had rapidly deduced the truth behind Morgan's secret orders, the commander had held his silence, distancing his mysterious friend from him in accordance with Galaxy Corps's instructions. That was the hardest part in so many ways. If an Alfarian called you his friend, as Lucien had called him many times, it was a commitment more binding than human marriage, a connection in Spirit which the Alfarian people considered sacrosanct, and which transcended even the disciplines and demands of the Galaxy Corps oaths and utterances.

Lucien was his *friend*. And yet Morgan had stood there and lied to him, the very act defiling the sanctity of the thing itself. For that, he did not like himself much.

A lot of it was a blur, happening so quickly that no one had time to think about it. The *Starling* ventured into Mizarian space, was fired upon by five Mizarian vessels, disabled – or so it appeared to the unknowing Mizarians – and subsequently captured in a field of electromagnetic stasis – the technology behind which they had been sent in to steal.

Within two days, the EM cocoon surrounding the *Starling* weakened sufficiently that a well-placed laser strike was successful in blasting a hole through it. From there, with reserve power completely intact, and the damages to the *Starling* being minimal in reality, it had been a simple matter to throw a catcher's mitt on the lead Mizarian ship, drag it into the *Starling's* cargo bay, and efficiently engage the invisibility-shielding long enough to confuse the remaining Mizarians.

No fuss, no muss. Just another day in the Corps. With a completely intact Mizarian vessel in the bay, four Mizarian androids in the brig, and barely a scratch to themselves, the *Starling* headed back for Empire territory.

It was easy. *Too* easy, Morgan had thought.

Military secrets. Alien technology. Spy vs. spy. It wasn't what he signed on for when he joined Galaxy Corps, but it was what he had become: little more than a glorified thief plundering alien ships for the techno-treasures they might yield. The *Starling* – once considered the finest exploration ship in the Corps – had even earned the nickname *Old Oxford*, a reference to a well-known pirate ship from Earth's 1600's – and more often than not, Diego himself was slapped with the title of Cap'n Morgan – the *Oxford's* commander, the infamous pirate, Henry Morgan. What it all boiled down to in the end was that the *Starling* had become the Empire's doer of dirty deeds, and Morgan was the unorthodox, unrelentingly handsome rogue at the helm. In some dark corners of the galaxy, they were almost a legend.

In hindsight, maybe it made some warped kind of sense. If the *Starling* were involved in some bit of intrigue and happened to get caught in the act behind enemy lines, Empire officials could always claim Diego and his merry band of misfits were operating outside Empire sanctions. Pirates. The secretary would disavow all knowledge of their actions… some bullshit like that. Having a seemingly rogue ship in their arsenal certainly changed the playing field and rewrote a plethora of unwritten rules. And to the Empire's top Brass, it made little difference that the sacrifices required to keep the game afoot were often human.

But his thoughts returned to the mission, to the series of events which had brought him from respectable commander to questionable pirate to starving transient.

Just as the *Starling* had been prepared to cross back to the safety of their own Empire, they'd found themselves surrounded – by a single ship. What Galaxy Corps hadn't bargained for was the fact that the Mizarian vessels they'd encountered previously had been nothing more than patrol-drones – long-range cruisers with pseudo-biological crews; their sole purpose was policing the Mizarians' self-proclaimed borders.

The Mizarian mother-ship, however, dwarfed the *Starling*. A star cruiser's lasers would be like bows and arrows against a destroyer.

Ultimatums were issued from both sides. And this time, when all was said and done, when the dust settled and the bony finger of guilt was found pointing squarely at Morgan Diego alone, Galaxy Corps couldn't – *wouldn't* – help.

Days passed while the long-range negotiations continued. Galaxy Corps maintained that Morgan acted on his own. And, eventually, the Mizarians swallowed the story hook, line and sinker. They were willing, it seemed, to release the *Starling* and her crew, but as records were examined and reviewed concerning the nefarious deeds of the ship's commander, they opted to keep Morgan himself – for "debriefing," they said.

At first, the Brass had fought the bargain for obvious reasons. A star commander held in his head more covert information than even the computers at Earthbase One. And Morgan had *believed* that fact would save him from being released to the Mizarians.

When an agreement was finally reached, however, he faced it with some degree of shock. He was to be traded, along with the captured Mizarian vessel and its android crew, for the safety of the *Starling*; and while that fact alleviated a portion of his concern, he couldn't deny the sense of foreboding it elicited from the deepest part of himself. The Empire knew little – almost nothing, he amended – about the Mizarians. For all anyone knew, they might not even breathe the same air, they could well consider humans a source of food, they could–.

He had little time to ponder it, for the agreement stated that he be turned over to the Mizarian vessel within the hour.

During that hour, he'd talked mostly with Lucien, entrusting his second-in-command and his best friend with information known only to the commanding officer of a star cruiser. In the sanctuary of the alien's darkly-appointed suite, where candles dusted the air with smoke reminiscent of the mists of the Alfarian homeworld, Lucien had seemed remarkably calm, outwardly accepting. And yet, as time drew shorter, Morgan had witnessed a building rage within his friend – a low, smoldering flame waiting to explode into destruction.

That was the common misconception humans had about Alfarians – believing them to be the cool and emotionally distant creatures who had once been referred to as "elvens" back on Earth. The reality, of course, was somewhat different, as it usually was. The Alfarians had been a space-faring race for thousands of years and had occasionally visited Earth to study human culture. As fate would have it, a few perceptive humans became aware of the scrutiny and so the legends began of a race of tall, dark beings with silken hair, black eyes and certain mystical and "animalistic" features which some humans found frightening, others found intriguing, and still others found downright captivating.

Secretly, Morgan considered himself somewhere between intrigued and captivated, though he had carefully kept those feelings to himself, for one thing was certain: Lucien was an ultimately private being, an alien among a predominantly human crew, and the last thing Morgan wanted was to overwhelm him with his own foolish human male fantasies. What*ever* they were. He wasn't sure himself. Legend said elvens perplexed and confused the senses of humans, and that was *one* legend Morgan considered to be a fact. In the three years he'd served with Lucien, he could never seem to figure the guy out, despite the fact that he had always prided himself on being able to read people more or less at first glance.

With Lucien, he was never sure what to think. And that alone intrigued Morgan Diego more than he cared to admit. Nothing more alluring than a good, solid mystery – and Lucien was definitely that. But with the disaster of the Mizarian mission and Morgan himself on the verge of being turned over to the rival aliens probably forever, all of that was ending right before his eyes. His command. His career. His friendship with Lucien. All of it.

In the blink of an eye, kingdoms will fall...

He'd tried to smile. "The *Starling* is all that matters now, Lucien," he'd said, choosing the politically correct words, the emotionally correct priorities. "Take her to safety. I'm sure you've already analyzed the Mizarian vessel, so Galaxy Corps will have their EM shield even if they don't have the Mizarian ship itself."

Lucien hadn't responded directly to that statement. "Some things cannot be considered fodder for a bargain, Morgan," he had murmured. "Lives cannot be traded so lightly for military secrets."

Silently, Morgan agreed. But he'd also accepted the mission despite his intuition to the contrary. He'd attempted to make the best of it, watching the clock swallow his remaining time with red digital numbers. "I'll find a way out," he said with an unconvincing shrug.

Lucien's brows had lifted. "Unlikely," the Alfarian commented realistically. "You're undoubtedly aware of what the Mizarians want. And I dare say they are obviously capable of extracting information."

In his own way, Lucien was saying, *'You're a dead man, Commander'*. Morgan chewed his lip, attempting without much success to remain the 'commander' for a few minutes longer. And yet, the stress of the past few days eventually had its way with him, breaking the facade of bravado down to its individual components. And each of those components cracked to reveal the core.

He reached out impulsively, his eyes clenching tightly shut as he fairly hurled himself into the Alfarian's arms. It didn't particularly surprise him that Lucien held on, too, shielding him in a fierce bear-hug that left him breathless. While it was the last thing Morgan might have expected of himself, he had to admit it was probably the most human thing he had done since assuming command of a Galaxy Corp star cruiser some five years in the past. Commander or not, he was scared. And Lucien was the only person in the known worlds to whom he could admit that fear without concern for the consequences.

For a single, terrifying instant, he almost begged Lucien to end his life, to snap his neck or seal off the flow of blood to the brain with some secret elven magick. And yet, as he felt Lucien trembling against him, he sensed the Alfarian's reverence for life surging above all else. Tears glistened in alien eyes, and when Morgan looked up to the other man's face, neither spoke for a very long time.

Lucien was both a mystery and a comfort to him – alpha and omega. With thin, angular features framed by a silken curtain of blue-black hair which cascaded over the lean but powerful shoulders, and eyes the shade of black found only between the stars, he seemed in that moment more human than any human he had ever known. More beautiful than the glint of moonlight on the still waters of the sea back home. More comforting than a half-remembered blanket from his childhood room. More dangerous than a Jovian leopard.

Time stopped, as if it, too, had been caught in the awe and wonder of that single moment, that unlikely embrace.

Alfarian telepathy was no secret. Morgan had even been the recipient of it a few times throughout the years – though always under the guise of some mission, and always like a feather-light touch of hummingbird wings. But now, without warning, the Knowing as it was called in elven lore flared open between them – dark wings taking flight, wings of the archangels and the fallen angels, wings of the warrior shielding a beloved comrade, wings of an Alfarian prince closing possessively around his chosen mate.

Morgan experienced the Embrace in a way that caused the breath to catch in his throat. For that single moment, the sensation of those wings closing around him was real, as if his own dark imaginings had manifested the reality. It mattered not in the least that the image cast in the mirror on the wall would have revealed only two men sharing an embrace. What mattered was that suddenly Morgan was overwhelmed by the abject and cruel

Knowing that he not only admired and respected Lucien, but was – whether he liked it or not – undeniably and irrevocably in love with his elven second-in-command.

So. That's how the world ends.

Not so much as a by-your-leave.

For a moment, he couldn't breathe, couldn't even think. In the next moment, he was cursing Fate and damning all the gods for their role in choosing *that* moment to make him aware of feelings which had undoubtedly been hiding in plain sight for years. Probably since the first time he shook Lucien's cooler-than-human hand and welcomed him aboard the *Starling*. Maybe even before that. In some past life. In some otherworld where duty and responsibility were nothing more than ugly words and not the obstacles they had become in the immeasurable distance between one second and the next.

And now, when there were agreements to honor and worlds to save by sacrificing himself, there was nothing in all the worlds either of them could do about it. Not. One. Thing.

Morgan Diego was property of the Mizarian Federation, and nothing could alter that.

The real horror was knowing that Lucien felt it, too. At least that's what Morgan *had* to believe, how he *had* to interpret the look in those unfathomable black eyes, the power in the ruthless Embrace.

Say something, one of the little voices whispered.

But there was not a goddamn thing to be said. Nothing to be done. Time had run out.

Finally, taking a deep breath to steady shattered nerves, Morgan retreated from the embrace, placing his hand in the center of the Alfarian's chest when Lucien moved to follow him toward the door.

"No," he said quietly. "Stay here, Lucien... or go back to the command deck." He couldn't bear the thought of having his friend accompany him to the shuttle bay. He couldn't bear the thought that he would never see this man again. And he didn't want his last memory of his friend to be one of them both dissolving away from one another.

He didn't wait for a reply. Instead, reaching out, he grasped the fine-boned elven hand, bringing it to his lips. Then, turning it palm-up, he kissed the softly-thrumming artery of the wrist in an ancient Alfarian gesture of parting normally reserved for elven princes bidding farewell to a condemned paramour – though Morgan wholly acknowledged that it was himself who was condemned.

Lucien trembled at the intimacy of the gesture, a small breath catching in his throat.

Their eyes met one last time. No words were spoken. Then, without looking back, Morgan turned sharply and fairly ran all the way to the shuttle bay. There was nothing else to be done.

Within the hour, he learned of the Mizarians.

~

Surprisingly, he was not ill-treated. The Mizarian ship was fast and reached their base-planet with five solar days, to the best of his ability to calculate time. To his dismay, he saw very little of the planet itself, being confined instead to what amounted to the Mizarian version of a starport, where he was assigned to an interior suite of rooms with no view of the landscape itself. During the landing procedure, he had noted that Mizar II was a green and blue world, not unlike Earth in many respects, and the Mizarians themselves a humanoid species barely distinguishable from their Terran counterparts. Undoubtedly, Morgan surmised, the Mizarians had probably been seeded by the whatever "master race" had also seeded Earth, Alfar, Betelgeuse 9, and a host of other planets scattered throughout the known galaxy. Same basic DNA structure, with variations in the species being determined by the local environment, differences in gravity, availability of compatible nutrition, and the like.

What further astonished him was that the interrogation procedure was remarkably simple – and remarkably effective. Galaxy Corps hadn't counted on the ability of certain Mizarian women to mind-probe, to seek and find information with ease. One of those variations within species, it seemed. It wasn't even painful. Humans had no ability to shield; in fact, without discomfort, he was often unaware that he was being probed whatsoever. It came in his dreams – drug-induced, he reminded himself – or it came during times of intense physical exercise, something the Mizarians seemed to feel was important to his well-being.

By the end of the first week, he'd revealed everything to the 'seer' that was of interest to the Mizarians.

And within another six months, he was unceremoniously released back to the Empire in exchange for the expansion of their territory to include a lifeless solar system adjacent to the 4th Quadrant of their existing Federation. The territory being of little value to the Empire, it was a treaty which was quickly signed by both parties without the necessity of face-to-face meetings between stuffy ambassadors.

Morgan Diego, it seemed, was little more than a commodity at that point. His return to Empire territory was negotiated matter-of-factly, and arranged in such a manner than neither side would be at risk during his exchange. He was unceremoniously placed in a life-suspension unit that would withstand the pressures of space, transported to the Mizarian/Empire boundary, and subsequently ejected and left to be picked up by a non-military craft hired for the job.

Within another two weeks, he was at Earthbase One, awake and aware even if somewhat disoriented, facing the debriefing team of Galaxy Corps admirals and Empire representatives.

It was at that meeting that he learned the further terms of his return to the Empire.

The Mizarians had obviously discovered that he *hadn't* acted alone. And yet, in accordance with their traditions, they ordered punishment for one man alone. As he understood it from his 'visit' in their Empire, it was a matter of honor – make an example of one rather than attempting to discipline several. In the end, one outcast made a more effective symbol than a dozen slain martyrs. Mizarian honor was strict and unbending. When all was said and done, he *had* been the one in the command chair. He'd given the orders and executed the scenario down to the last detail.

The Mizarians seemed scarcely concerned whether he'd acted alone or on the orders of his superiors. In the end, he was the one *caught* – a disgrace punishable by public banishment. Those who had ordered him, according to Mizarian thinking, would be best served to live with the guilt, the knowledge that *their* foolhardiness had resulted in another's life-long anguish.

Never again would he command a star cruiser. By the Mizarian Code of Honor, he was to be viewed as an outcast, set apart from friends, cast away from all remnants of his previous life. And the Mizarians had made certain their agreements would be met. Through the telepathic abilities of the Mizarian seer, they could read his every thought at random at any given moment. Deviation from their terms would result in immediate Mizarian attack of a neighboring star-system – an attack against which even Galaxy Corps would be hard-pressed to defend.

The Mizarians, it turned out, were by nature a peaceful race, yet perfectly capable of defending themselves against the intrusion of hostile invaders or undermining philosophies which might clash with the society they'd established. They valued order, honor, discipline. They had no wars among themselves, yet had no desire to enter normalized relations between themselves and the Empire. Self-sufficient and existing in a sector of the galaxy with a multitude of workable planets, they had no need for the laws or the lawlessness of Empire ways. Put another way, they did not choose to be governed, and in the end, who could blame them?

In essence, Morgan surmised, his release had been one primarily of compassion coupled with psychological implications. Throughout his imprisonment, he had never once been mistreated, never abused or tortured as he had believed he would be. Rather, his needs and even his comforts had been seen to with remarkable diligence.

Now, his punishment came from a distance – an effective banishment from the life he had known, the friends he had made in the course of his career, the star cruiser he had taken for a bride. And, far more important, he now realized, the real punishment was that he would never see Lucien again.

His heart ached with that knowledge, for in those final few minutes before he had turned himself over to the Mizarians, something had passed between them that could no longer be denied. He wanted to call it love, but didn't dare. The word hurt too goddamn much when he juxtaposed it against the uncertain future. And in all likelihood, the Mizarians had known even that through the eyes of their seer. The one thing in all the worlds he valued was the one thing he would now never have.

Clean. Cold. Effective.

And, in essence, the Mizarian Empire had kicked Galaxy Corps's butt without ever firing a shot, creating a treaty which the Empire dared not break.

What surprised him was that the Brass hardly seemed affected by the Mizarians' decision. Either they were stupidly plotting some additional covert action, or they'd finally acknowledged encountering a vastly technologically superior race. Morgan himself was merely informed of the terms, stripped of his rank, and ushered without ceremony from the Council Chambers.

In the sterile gray corridor with its garish fluorescent lighting, however, Galaxy Corps Admiral Bryse confronted him – the only man to meet his eyes since his return from the Mizarian Empire. The fact that Bryse was born offworld in the Martian colony may have had something to do with it. The taint of Earth was one step removed from the aging bureaucrat who could have passed for a kindly grandfather or a weekend golfer had it not been for the keen aura of authority that surrounded the man like a tangible forcefield.

"You have to understand, Morgan, this isn't a Galaxy Corps decision," Bryse had said.

Morgan didn't speak. He had nothing to say. His days of making high-sounding speeches were over.

"Okay, I know what you're thinking, and you're probably right. We *are* afraid of the Mizarians. Hell, we never anticipated that they could out-gun our entire military force with a single ship!" the admiral said as if to himself. "We're just lucky that they don't *want* a war, or we'd all be speaking Mizarian Standard by the end of the week."

Morgan was barely listening. He was numb and cold and feeling decidedly naked standing in the middle of Galaxy Corps Headquarters in civilian attire. It was the first time he realized just how much of a shield the braid on his sleeves had been.

"What about the *Starling*?" he asked at last. "My crew? Are they at least safe?"

Bryse's eyes closed and he sighed heavily. "Lucien's been in temporary command of the *Starling* since your capture by the Mizarians. He says he doesn't want to be posted as her commander permanently, but we're hoping he'll change his mind."

At that, Morgan stiffened noticeably. "Tell him that *I* want him to take her," he said quietly.

Bryse was silent for a moment, then nodded his agreement. "I'll see to it that he gets the message."

Morgan shook his head. "*You* tell him yourself," he said. "Or let me do it."

Bryse frowned. "You know that's impossible by the terms of the agreement. Hell, this whole conversation shouldn't even be happening. If that mind-link or whatever it is they have on you is anything like you claim it is, I could have just single-handedly caused a war for talking to you at all."

Morgan's lips pressed tightly together, well aware that even he couldn't always sense the mind-link when it was being enforced. "Just... tell him," he said, then turned and walked away.

"Morgan?"

He stopped, but did not turn to face the other man.

"Where will you be? I mean, if something *does* change...." Bryse's voice quavered; they'd been friends for a long time.

Morgan, on the other hand, remained numb, cold, his emotions non-existent following the devastating turn of events. "I'll be somewhere in the galaxy, old friend," was all he said. There was, after all, no place else to go.

Then, feeling like a disembodied spirit, he strode through the front door of Galaxy Corps Headquarters and into the noisy street. Members of the media hovered close-by, their remote cameras filming the fallen commander as he moved toward the anonymity of Chinatown.

No one questioned him.

The agreement between the Mizarians and the Empire had been well-publicized. And no one wanted to be the cause of a war that Galaxy Corps admittedly couldn't win. Technically, in the eyes of the Law of two different peoples, Morgan Diego no longer existed.

And, for a reason he didn't comprehend, that fact didn't trouble him. For the first time in his adult life, he was free. Without money, without responsibility, he felt freer than he'd ever been.

It also occurred to him that he had no alternative. And, for the moment, he was too numb to care. The shock of what happened shielded him from an obvious possibility.

Regardless of what had happened, he still clung to life. It was all he had left. And so, without a backward glance, he had accepted transport on an outbound salvage vessel that very afternoon, worked his way as far from Earth as he could get, and eventually ended up at Calipri-port where, ultimately, his new life was destined to begin.

~

A foot nudged him and, opening his eyes, he glanced up to see a wooden walking stick poking at his thigh.

"You there!" a voice said, breaking into his dreams and returning him to wakefulness. The tone was deep, and laced with a thick Chinese accent.

Morgan looked up to confront a man whose stature was relatively small in comparison to his voice. The round Asian face was lined with wrinkles which cut deep into the void-paled skin and it was easy to discern that this man had served in the darkness of space most of his life, but without the luxuries of a star cruiser's artificial sun. Morgan blinked, dragging himself back to full awareness, though he made no effort to stand. It occurred to him that the Mizarians had once again been probing his mind as he slept, perhaps even causing the nightmare to relive itself in his dreams. But as he squinted against the glare of bright lights on the lift-off pads, he sensed the probe slip quickly away.

"Yes?" was all he said.

The small man bowed graciously from the waist, his wrinkled lips puckering to what Morgan took to be a smile. "Your pardon for awakening you, sir," he said above the howl of retro-thrusters as a

20

Galaxy Corps shuttle settled on a distant landing pad, "but as a normal man does not usually sleep among this chaos, I am to presume you seek employment."

Morgan blinked again; his mind felt dulled. His stomach growled hungrily and, drawing a deep breath, he nodded slowly. "Uh... yes," he managed, battling vertigo as he got to his feet. Standing, he was almost six inches taller than his potential employer.

The other man wore modest attire – a faded blue cotton-gauze shirt which hung loosely about his small frame, and draw-string black pants that stopped two inches above the ankles. His feet were bare, and despite the brisk evening winds, he seemed impervious to the cold. His hair had once been black, but was now streaked with threads of white and silver which glinted in the glare of the spaceport's brilliant lights. His manner was aloof and cool, yet inoffensive, with an air of humbleness that emanated from his subdued mannerisms.

The little man sized Morgan up, seemed to come to some unspoken conclusion, then nodded to himself. His eyes were dark and intense despite his obvious age, and when he spoke it was with confidence and directness. "I seek to gather a small crew of men who are not afraid to fight." Again, the dark eyes perused Morgan hopefully. "You are a wary sleeper, I have noted while watching you."

Morgan wondered absently what one had to do with the other. But he couldn't deny his interest in the old man's offer. Already, he'd spent too long at Calipri-port with no offers of work. Already, it had been three days since he'd eaten, and though he'd been offered a position in one of the infamous brothels of Calipri's largest city, his last remaining pride forced him to decline the position.

"You are a contemplative man, given to silence," the old man observed when Morgan didn't respond immediately.

Blinking back the uncharacteristic vertigo and trying to chase the fuzziness from his mind, Morgan tried to smile. "My apologies," he murmured, barely hearing his own voice above the late-night roar of departing rockets. "May I ask what this 'fighting' entails?"

The old man's face never altered, though his eyes seemed to

brighten in the fiery tail of an outbound freighter. "You have heard of the Dagger of Zilphoron?"

Morgan's brows knotted as he searched his memory. "It's supposedly the most ornate dagger ever forged," he recalled vaguely, "the symbol of power of the ruling family of the planet."

The little man seemed surprised. "You know much for one in the streets," he observed, impressed. "Then do you also know that the Dagger was stolen by Nel-fen pirates while on display in San Francisco at the Museum of Culture?"

Morgan's heart quickened just a little, though he would have been hard-pressed to say whether it was from surprise or physical depletion due to lack of food and proper rest. "I wasn't aware of that."

Once more, the old man studied him with seeming interest, looking him up and down from head to toe, causing him to squirm as he realized how unkempt he actually appeared. His clothes were old and thread-bare, his sandals ragged and worn. His hair was longer than he would have preferred, his face darkened by several days' growth of stubble. In the back of his mind, he realized abstractly that it had taken less than two months for him to fall to this level. With his personal properties and bank accounts frozen by the terms of the treaty, he had no reserves upon which to draw other than his own knack for survival. And, realizing that he *would* survive, he lifted his chin just a little.

"Why is this Dagger of importance to you, if I may ask?" he inquired as the silence lengthened between them.

The old man smiled faintly. "Does it matter?"

Morgan shrugged. "If I'm going to fight for something, I prefer to know why," he offered, hoping he wasn't automatically talking himself out of a meal if not a job.

The little man considered that for a very long moment, his dark stare never breaking from Morgan's lingering gaze. "For myself, the knife holds no value," he said at last. Then, lifting both graying brows, he added, "We are mercenaries, my friend. The ruling family of Zilphoron has little use for protocol, and the Empire has refused assistance, claiming there is no proof that Nel-fen thieves were indeed responsible. Obviously, they wish to avoid political implications should any counter-plan to retrieve the Dagger fail." He paused as if to let that sink in. "Are you interested or not?"

Morgan frowned thoughtfully, yet he couldn't deny his interest. The Dagger was of vital importance to the ruling family of Zilphoron, he recalled. Without it, the symbol of their power was weakened, leaving their benign rule open to the possibility of overthrow by malignant guerilla forces who also sought to govern the planet. He held his silence, however, not revealing his entire knowledge to the unnamed man standing before him.

"Who hired you?" he asked bluntly.

The little man smiled again, revealing straight white teeth. "I have heard that you are a ram. It is comforting to know my sources were correct."

For a moment, the statement didn't register with Morgan, but as it gradually worked its way past the physical discomfort of cold and hunger, he looked more closely at the odd little fellow standing before him. "Just who do you think I am?" he inquired quietly.

The thin brows lifted once more. "Are you not the exiled commander who has courted the favor of kings and lords?" he asked with an all-knowing smile.

Morgan stiffened. "If you know that," he warned, "then you also know that any involvement you have with me could potentially start a war between the Empire and the Mizarian Empire." Unconsciously, he took a step back; despite his own needs, he had no desire to further endanger old friends in an unwanted war.

At that, the little man laughed aloud, his voice a deep, throaty chuckle. "Your honor serves you well, Morgan," he commented presently. "But rest assured that my people have no fear of Mizarian threats. Come," he offered, gesturing toward a passenger shuttle waiting at the far end of the lift-pads. "After you have eaten and bathed, Myrddin will teach you to shield both body and mind from danger. Within the month it will take us to reach the Nel-fen Empire, you will no longer have to fear unwanted invasions either of your spirit or your flesh."

For a reason Morgan couldn't immediately pinpoint, he found himself trusting the old man at an almost instinctual level. He glanced away for just a moment, and when he returned his gaze, he saw the other striding purposefully toward the waiting ship. Not knowing what else to do, he trotted the few steps to catch up, placing one hand on the old man's arm and raising his voice to shout above the scream of an inbound rocket.

"Who are you?" he asked, watching the wrinkles of the other's face shift to a grin in the glare of the rocket's retro-fire. "How do you know about me?"

"My name will hold no meaning for you, Morgan," the other replied, "but if it is important for you to know, I am Kim Le. Come now," he urged, once again indicating the rocket with a gesture of an aged hand. "We must depart soon, and our journey is a long one. You have much to learn."

But Morgan held his ground, his grip firming to hold the elusive Kim Le in place for a moment longer. "Wait a minute," he protested, speaking in a more normal tone as the rocket settled into its berth and its engines quieted. "How did you find me? And what makes you think I'd be interested in working as a mercenary?"

Kim Le smiled once more, reaching out to place his other hand on top of Morgan's. "Who is to say, my friend, whether I found you or you found me?" he asked philosophically. "A wise man realizes that his path crosses another's at the appointed time and place. And as for your second question," he added, once again perusing Morgan's appearance, "you have nothing more to lose. You may either work as a mercenary for our cause, or you will eventually sell yourself to the brothels." He shook his head with a genuine reflection of sadness in his eyes. "Your skills are worth more than that, and your honor will lead you down the correct path."

For a very long moment, Morgan stood staring at the pretentious little fellow with his jaw just a fraction slackened. Then, when Kim Le once again started off across the launch area toward the waiting shuttle, Morgan fell in step behind him.

The old man was right. The brothels would be his last desperate step toward an early death. Kim Le was also right about something else. He had nothing more to lose.

That was how he came to be a mercenary.

CHAPTER TWO

"What would you have me do, Vanya?" Lucien inquired for what felt like the hundredth time in less than an hour. His patience was wearing dangerously thin, and the ship's chief psychiatrist was doing nothing to improve that situation and everything to make it worse. Lucien wondered fleetingly where and how – let alone *why* – Vanya had chosen the field of psychiatry, since he was, by definition, at least half-mad himself.

Dr. Liam Vanya stared at the *Starling's* new commander, his ice-blue eyes flaming hotter than the Alfarian incense cauldron which glowed in one corner of the command suite. "I can't believe you're just going to abandon Morgan! When he was behind enemy lines in the Mizarian Sector, I could understand it a *little*," he stressed. "But now that he's back in Empire territory – a free man! – I can't believe you're just going to sit there spouting the terms of some treaty as if it's the Gospel of Gotholomon!"

Lucien's eyes closed for a moment, and he made a concentrated effort to seclude his own rising emotions behind a facade of normalcy. Whereas most humans were pleasant enough to deal with, Vanya could be a noticeable exception – largely, Lucien conceded, because the man was brutal and direct when compared to the vast majority of humans who tried to disguise their real feelings behind polite masks and social niceties. Vanya had no such agendas – which made him a valuable ally, but also an unmitigated pain in Lucien's ass. Adding to that was the well-known truth that Vanya had no regard for protocols and decorum, and had, in fact, been essentially pressed into Galaxy Corps service as an alternative to avoid certain legal charges brought against him by a long line of ex-wives.

Lucien didn't know all the details. Didn't want to know.

When he looked up to meet the intense stare of the ship's resident shrink, Lucien took a deep, cleansing breath. "Apparently you do not understand the implications of the Mizarian Treaty. That being the case, I will attempt *again* to explain them to you in the simplistic terms which your limited ability to comprehend should be able to grasp." He was surprised at his own sarcasm, and made

25

an effort to curb it.

Seeing Vanya's mouth opening to speak, he waved the remark aside. "According to the terms of the Treaty, Commander Diego is to be considered an exile by all members of the Empire. *Particularly*, he is to have no contact with former friends, acquaintances or fellow officers. Considering your predilection for reading ancient texts, I'm fairly certain you have availed yourself of *The Man Without A Country*, and if nothing else, that should give you a general understanding of what we are up against."

Lucien paused only long enough breathe, well aware that he was dangerously close to curling his upper lip in a gesture which would reveal the discreet but dangerous incisors which some humans liked to compare to mythical vampire fangs. Two little secrets in that realization caused Lucien a small amount of amusement. One: elvens were perhaps more closely related to Earth's mythical vampires than either the humans *or* the vampires suspected. And two: Lucien experienced the urge to bare his fangs *only* in the presence of Liam Vanya.

"While I fail to see the rationale of such a form of punishment, those are nonetheless the terms of the agreement." Lucien stopped to let that sink through Vanya's obviously thick skull. "Should any of us attempt to contact Commander Diego, we would be in direct violation of said Treaty, and would theoretically open ourselves up to the possibility of war with the Mizarians."

"Horse shit," Vanya pronounced.

Lucien failed to comprehend what equine manure had to do with the conversation, so chose to ignore the outburst, mentally reviewing the Treaty he'd read more times than the Tenets of Alfarian Discipline. "At any rate," he continued more calmly, "my formal acceptance of command of the *Starling* further complicates matters –."

"Spare me, Lucien," Vanya interrupted miserably, sinking down into a vacant chair and rubbing his eyes with the palms of his hands. Then, looking up, he made the point he'd come to make. "Don't you even *care*?" he asked with remarkable control of his anger. "You and Morgan were friends. And now he's been made the victim of a Galaxy Corps blunder, cast out from everything that ever mattered to him, wandering god-knows-where in filthiest parts of this galaxy.... Don't you *care*?"

Lucien stared at the other man for longer than he cared to admit, his internal conflict churning like some potent brew that left him feeling weak and ill. "My personal feelings are not a matter for discussion," he replied coldly, remembering the fierce embrace he had shared with his friend just before his former commander had surrendered himself to the Mizarians. More than any physical embrace, it was the embrace of Knowledge, of commitment. And though he had tried to convince himself otherwise for months now, Lucien also knew it was the embrace of love – a universal gesture which could never be mistaken or denied.

And though a considerable amount of time had passed since that embrace, it was a moment which had become frozen in time, held fast in the capture of his memory, held in stasis there like some unlikely diamond cast into an eternal setting of pure gold.

Put simply: Morgan Diego had captured his elven heart as easily as some miscreant spider might capture the hapless fly.

Whatever Lucien had believed about himself, whatever dreams or fantasies he may have held for his future – returning to Alfar to take a mate and father children, just for example – flew right out the airlock in the heat of that embrace, and in the moment which had followed when the human touched his lips to the throbbing artery in Lucien's wrist.

That's when his heart started to beat, Lucien knew. That was the One Moment In All Time when his soul was born out of the Nethernothing and burst to life.

Elven lore spoke of such things, but only in myth, in the old texts normally reserved for the mystics and the madmen of Homeworld Alfar. In the Olde times, the kiss was indeed as Morgan had suspected: a gesture of parting normally reserved for bidding farewell to a companion who had been sentenced to death for some crime or another. And yet, what no human knew (and few Alfarians, Lucien conceded) was that such a kiss was also far more than it appeared on the surface. When performed with a pure heart and a committed spirit, it was a kiss which might bind souls from one life to the next – literally a lifeline between the Here and the

Hereafter.

Somehow, in their innocence which both had believed to be a 'simple' friendship, they had tied their souls together in a faerie knot which not even deft elven magick would ever be able to undo.

And that was simply that.

Lucien had wondered as the months passed if Morgan were even aware of the depth of the thing which had passed between them. The human's passions ran so deep that Lucien had to concede he might very well believe himself to be enamored, but may have no real idea as to *just* how much had passed between them in that single definitive moment which had – without their immediate knowledge or consent – altered the course of both their lives forever.

"Are you even listening to me, Lucien?"

Vanya's direct question cut into his reverie and brought him tumbling back to the immediacy of his surroundings. He noted abstractly that the room felt too warm - an ever-present consequence of the fact that his own biology was designed for cooler climes. The scent of incense from the cauldron filled the air with a essence of rattlecone pine resin, the scent of homeworld which unexpectedly filled him with a pang of nostalgia, an ache that could not be soothed.

He said nothing of what he had been thinking to Vanya, but instead met the other man's eyes with a black gaze which some said had the mystical power to mesmerize or to kill in an instant if that should ever be the intent of an Alfarian male. But Lucien wasn't interested in killing Vanya. Not yet anyway.

"My apologies, Liam," he murmured softly, choosing a gentler demeanor. "I was lost in thought."

But Vanya didn't back down, didn't fall under Lucien's spell as Lucien had hoped he might.

"I don't believe what I'm hearing!" the shrink snapped. "The way you're acting, you'd think you never even *knew* Morgan! And we're not talking about professional ethics, Lucien. We're talking about right and wrong, personal honor and the duty one man owes to another." He glared at the Alfarian with the full force of his anger burning in his eyes. "Or is it possible that 'honor' on your

28

world is nothing more than a bunch of words strung together to *sound* good!"

At that, Lucien felt his patience tested. The duties required of him since Morgan's capture by the Mizarians had left him drained physically and spiritually. Time for meditation was sparse, and when he *was* able to achieve the meditative state, his thoughts inevitably wandered into dangerous territory – schemes and plans which, if enacted, could endanger the lives of trillions of innocent people.

And yet, as he gazed at Vanya through the haze of his own weariness, he could easily understand the doctor's human feelings. "It is my understanding that the Empire is attempting to have the terms of the Treaty amended," he offered, recalling Bryse's communiqué earlier in the week. "And as the Mizarians appear to be a reasonable people, it is possible that–."

"Bullshit!" Vanya interrupted hotly, shifting from equine to bovine excrement. "That's just the Brass's way of giving lip service to you and me. Hell, they're all shaking in their boots and with good reason! The Mizarians probably *could* wipe us out in record time. Bryse and his buddies back at Headquarters are just damned glad they *didn't*. They aren't going to rock the boat for the sake of one man – even if that man *is* Morgan Diego."

Sighing silently to himself, Lucien nodded wearily. "I know," he murmured. "I *do* know."

Vanya was silent for a moment, then looked up expectantly. "What about this 'Mizarian mind link'?" he asked then, his tone becoming more quizzical than accusatory. "*Can* they keep tabs on Morgan at all times? *Can* they really tell across all that distance what's going on? I mean... what if it's all just a bluff?"

Lucien's answer was succinct. "Do you want to risk that?"

Vanya shrugged. "Can we afford not to risk it?" he asked hypothetically. But he waved Lucien's answer aside with a gesture. "I know, I know. Don't give me the same old speech again." But the anger had left his voice to be replaced with solemnity. "I guess what I'm wondering is how we'll ever *know* whether any of this mind-link-monitoring is for real, or if it's just a lot of Mizarian hocus-pocus to keep us scared into submission. And, speaking of submission, just how long do you think Galaxy Corps's going to *let* those Mizarian bastards intimidate us?"

Lucien considered his reply cautiously. "It is a known fact that the military mind does not easily tolerate subjugation, even when that subjugation is benign and arrived at through peaceful means."

"Meaning that this whole mess is going to stick in somebody's craw somewhere," Vanya translated.

Lucien inclined his head in agreement, too weary to play his customary semantics-game with the other man. "As for the Mizarian's mind-trace on the commander, there is no way to confirm or disprove it without risking war. Obviously," he explained, "if the Mizarians' claims *are* correct, it is conceivable that they would sense another mind exploring the commander's should an Alfarian healer, for example, attempt to confirm the link's existence."

Vanya's brows knitted to a deeply etched frown. "Okay," he conceded, "assuming that it *is* more than just an elaborate bluff, what about trying to... I dunno... *break* whatever link the Mizarians have on Morgan?"

"If it were possible, the Mizarians would undoubtedly view the breaking of the link as violation of the Treaty; war would possibly be the result."

Slapping his open palm down against the desk, Vanya swore silently to himself. "The little bastards are clever," he conceded, "but I'm not ready to admit defeat, Lucien. We *have* to do *something*!"

Lucien's eyes closed wearily, then re-opened once more. "What would you have me do?" he inquired, tired to the bone of the dead-end roads his mind continued to encounter. Once more, their conversation had come full circle. Humans, unlike Alfarians, seemed to enjoy the pointless art of speculation, the game of what-if which never had any real conclusion.

Vanya shook his head, sighing heavily as he looked up to the pained dark gaze. "I know it's not your fault, Lucien," he said quietly. "It's just that... I've never felt so damned helpless."

"Nor I," Lucien agreed, recalling the feeling of dread which had resided deep within him since he had first learned that Diego was to be taken by the Mizarians. *That*, he reminded himself, was eight months, one week and three days ago.

But with an effort, he tore his thoughts away from those memories, reminding himself dutifully of the dangers involved in scrutinizing the past too closely.

His attention was diverted by Vanya rising at last from the chair and as Lucien looked up, it was to find the blue eyes somewhat moister than atmospheric conditions on the ship could explain.

The doctor shrugged, shaking his head just a little. "I wonder where he is," he said as if to himself.

Lucien ignored the inexplicable lump which rose in his throat and tightened his voice as he spoke. "I... do not know," he murmured. "We must hope, however, that he is... well." It sounded lame, even to his own ears.

Vanya nodded thoughtfully, turning toward the door. He stopped just before tripping the sensor, but didn't turn back to the Alfarian. "I don't really expect you to understand my feelings, Lucien," he said very quietly. "It's just that... I miss Morgan." He laughed – a bitter, lonely sound which sent shivers down the Alfarian's spine. "Just for the record, I'd feel the same about you if you were in Morgan's shoes right now."

Lucien had no answer. "Goodnight, Liam," he said, grateful to be alone when the other man disappeared into the corridor.

Then, rising from the chair and leaving the day's paper-work untouched, he went to stand before the dark cauldron. *Where are you, my friend?* he wondered, the pain rising once more in his thoughts and choking off his reason.

The cauldron gave no answer. Instead, a grain of incense popped noisily, and the once-bright flame burned low, exhausting itself of fuel.

Unremarkably, Lucien felt precisely the same – weary, exhausted of the fuel of ideas, alone. He knelt on the floor, closed his eyes, and drifted into an uncomfortable, dream-filled sleep.

CHAPTER THREE

After eating, bathing and shaving, Morgan slept a full solar day. He awakened to find himself disoriented and cramped in the crew compartment of the *Dreaming Bird*, and wasn't terribly surprised to discover Kim Le's face gazing down at him when his eyes opened.

Reality returned slowly, and as he recalled his conversation with the elderly gentleman at the Calipri spaceport, he sat up straight in the stacked bunk, wincing and cursing when his head impacted with the bottom of the bed directly above him.

The rising knot on his head served to remind him that he was no longer on board the *Starling*. His instincts alone told him this was a small vessel, maybe big enough to house a crew of 20, maybe not. A vague scent of engine oil filled the air – common on smaller vessels that lacked the sophisticated processing systems of a star cruiser – and though the floors were clean and shone with pride, their age was revealed by paths worn into the metal over decades of use.

Kim Le frowned. "You have much to learn, my friend," he observed quietly. "As soon as you are ready, your teacher awaits you."

Rubbing his forehead, Morgan bit back the automatic response that sprang to his lips, reminding himself that this old man had quite possibly salvaged what was left of his life. As the pain in his head subsided a little, he sat up again – more slowly – and draped his legs over the edge of the bed to find Kim Le sitting on the floor-level bunk directly across the narrow corridor.

A thousand questions sprang to mind, but he settled for the most obvious. "Where am I?" But then, hearing the absurdity of that, he clarified. "I mean... I remember taking the shuttle up to this ship, but after that everything's a little fuzzy."

Kim Le smiled compassionately. "Your flesh and spirit were weak, Morgan," he explained, then responded more directly to the question. "As for where you are, you are in the sleeping chambers of the *Dreaming Bird* – my humble ship. We are bound, as I have told you, for the Nel-fin Neutral Zone."

32

The brief explanation returned a few more memories to Morgan's aching head and, digesting the implications, he met the old man's eyes. "I don't suppose it would serve any purpose to remind you that it's not going to be easy to just walk right in to the Nel-fen Empire – even assuming that you *do* know where the Dagger's been taken."

Kim Le glanced away for just a moment, seemed to consider some unspoken fact, then raised his eyes to Morgan's once more. "It is best not to question at this time," he said very gently. "Let us simply say that there is more at stake here than the material concerns of one lost dagger." But he quickly waved his own words aside. "Come," he urged. "Jones has prepared a light breakfast for your pleasure. Then, after you have meditated, Myrddin will begin your training."

Morgan blinked, wondering if he'd heard correctly. He offered a faint smile, liking Kim Le despite the old man's mastery of the art of evasion. "I'm afraid I'm not much on meditation," he said, recalling with a dangerous pang the numerous times Lucien had tried to instruct him in the art. He drew his thoughts away from his friend, however, recognizing the awful ache which reached out to touch him. Perhaps what surprised him most was that the memory of their parting hadn't faded, as he'd hoped it might. Instead, the images were sharp as the fang of a laser, and seemed to grow stronger as the days, weeks, months passed. Whoever said time heals all wounds was an unparalleled liar.

But Kim Le dismissed his argument with a gentle smile. "Meditation is not a mystery, Morgan," he said softly. "It is simply the focusing of the mind on a single subject – any subject you choose." He paused, then leaned closer to rest one hand on his arm in a gesture of compassion. "Many times, it is helpful to select a subject which bears fond memories."

At that, Morgan stiffened, wondering if the old man could actually read his thoughts with the same ease as the Mizarian seer. Nothing seemed private anymore. The past was the one thing he didn't want to deal with; and his only 'fond memories' were housed in that long, lost corridor of his mind. Lucien. Vanya. Other members of the *Starling's* crew. Abruptly, he turned away.

"Ta ta ta!" Kim Le scolded, tightening his grip just a little as Morgan maneuvered his arm to escape. "The first step toward spiritual freedom is to liberate the pain and internalize the rage. Once that is accomplished, your strength will return."

Suddenly angry, Morgan lifted his eyes to the old man. "My strength *is* in the past, Kim Le," he snapped. "Trying to deny that won't change it!" It was, he realized, the first time he'd confronted the truth since the incident began over eight months before. "Without the *Starling*, without my friends, I'm–."

"The same man you have always been," Kim Le interrupted with remarkable gentleness. He silenced Morgan's impending protest with a squeeze of his hand on the other's arm. "Do not be afraid to admit to yourself, your own inner strength – *and* your inner wisdom. The experiences we accumulate during life are nothing more than memories to keep us company in our final years. What we *are* does not change."

Temporarily distracted from his own anger, grateful to change the subject, Morgan considered the old man's words. "Then what you're saying is that we *can't* change. We can't grow, or even learn from our mistakes."

Kim Le shook his head. "No," he replied emphatically. "The changes we endure, the growth we accumulate within ourselves, the knowledge we acquire... all these things are merely the *result* of our experiences. Change is *necessary* to growth, and growth is a result of change."

Morgan found his head reeling; ancient philosophies were best left to Alfarian mystics and ancient philosophers. He sighed heavily, glancing at his hands which were, surprisingly, clenched into tight fists.

"That is the anger you must learn to internalize," Kim Le said, indicating Morgan's hands. "Once it becomes a part of you, it can no longer destroy you as it now seeks to do."

Morgan frowned deeply. "I don't understand," he said wearily, wondering what, other than hunger and necessity, had motivated him to join a group of self-proclaimed mercenaries in the first place. "I'm sorry, but I just don't understand," he repeated, wondering if he *wanted* to.

Kim Le's features tightened to a compassionate smile. "Understanding will come, Morgan," he promised. "You must have patience."

Morgan laughed lightly, almost bitterly. "Not one of my better virtues."

"Now, your anger exists as a separate entity, Morgan," Kim Le replied, drawing the conversation back to its original point. "And as a separate entity, it can attack – perhaps even destroy you. If, however, you accept it into yourself as a natural part of your *chi*, it can no longer threaten you. Control it, yes! Use it, yes! But do not surrender to it! And do not resist it. It is an art of balance, you see."

Again a small, half-embarrassed laugh parted Morgan's lips. "If I *don't* resist it," he said, "I'm going to make hamburger out of the first Galaxy Corps bureaucrat I can get my hands on!"

Kim Le seemed to consider that. "Then... your anger is focused?"

Morgan shook his head, looking again at his clenched hands which rested in his lap. "You bet it is."

Kim Le was silent for a long moment, then ventured ahead cautiously. "It was my understanding that the Mizarian Empire was responsible for your exile," he said quietly. "Is it not your former captives who should be deserving of your anger?"

At that, Morgan looked up, his eyes narrowing as he met Kim Le's questioning gaze. "The Mizarians?" he mused, then shook his head. "They're just doing what they think is necessary to protect themselves." He'd had a while to think about it and, ultimately, that was the only possible explanation. "We're the ones who trespassed into their territory. And *I'm* the one who took the fall." He shrugged. Then, without false modesty, he added: "I suppose they figured that, by making an example of the so-called 'best' Galaxy Corps had to offer, others would think twice about repeating my mistake. What kills me is that I went in there, knowing in advance what could happen, and Galaxy Corps set me up to take their fall from the beginning." His anger matured once more, his short nails digging painfully into the palms of his hands. "I don't like being someone else's patsy."

Kim Le considered that. "What, hypothetically, could have been done differently?" he asked at last. "Could this experience have had another outcome?"

Morgan pondered the question for the thousandth time since the nightmare began. The answer was obvious. "There were at least a dozen different diplomatic solutions that could have been negotiated," he said at last, his frustration waning to resignation. "The Mizarians, in spite of their advanced technology and inherent desire for peace, are a relatively poor people." He dredged up memories of things he had picked up through the mind of the seer who had plundered his thoughts. "Their acquisition of the Delphorian System was a drop in the bucket to what they *could* have had – and our ambassadors would have agreed to other solutions."

"You were the human casualty of a desperate political bargain," Kim Le surmised.

Morgan's eyes lifted; his jaw tightened. "It seems that way," he agreed. "When I was debriefed in San Francisco, no one even *asked* me what the Mizarians looked like! No one seemed to care what might *buy* them, what negotiations should be considered in the future." He shook his head, gazing at the cold metal bulkhead. "It was all cut and dried from the beginning. Galaxy Corps tucked their tails between their legs and ran, and the Empire Council cheered them on from the sidelines. They've met their match and they know it. Right now," he concluded, "you can bet they're plotting counter-measures, designing a bigger, faster ship with more effective weapons. And sooner or later, they'll find another fool to stick one toe over the line. *We'll* start the war... not the Mizarians."

Again, Kim Le was silent, rubbing his chin with one hand. "What do the Mizarians possibly *want*, Morgan?"

Morgan frowned. "Want?" he repeated. "I'm not sure they want anything – other than to be left alone." He smiled wistfully. "It's not unlike the Native Americans finally standing up to the white man – telling us that they don't *want* our missionaries, they don't *want* our God, and they don't *want* our half-baked belief systems." He shook his head with a certain sadness reflected in his eyes. "Maybe that's the problem," he decided. "We never *offered* them anything. We just marched in there with our weapons and our technology and tried to take what we didn't rightfully own. The repeating history of

36

Man...."

Kim Le's graying brows lifted. "Yet you have been a member of the Galaxy Corps for many years. If you do not agree with their philosophies, why did you remain?"

It was a question which inevitably made Morgan squirm. Now was no different. "Commanding a star cruiser isn't something most men ever get an opportunity to do. Compromises were necessary."

"Then... you have been a mercenary before," Kim Le surmised inoffensively.

Morgan glanced up sharply. "Wh-what?" he stammered.

The old man inclined his head in the affirmative. "You sold your skills to an organization in order to gain what was important to *you* – as a man."

"Well, maybe, but–."

Kim Le shook his head with a gently admonishing smile. "It is all a part of the learning, a part of the changes, Morgan," he said very quietly. "There is no dishonor in selling one's skills. The dishonor comes when the terms of the agreement are knowingly broken for gain."

"What do you mean?"

"Galaxy Corps and, indeed, the Empire, have shown no honor to you, Morgan," Kim Le explained patiently. "You completed your part of the agreement by permitting them to utilize your skills to infiltrate the Mizarian Empire. It was their honorable duty to offer you the protection a parent would offer a child, yet they abandoned you to protect themselves. That is not honorable."

Morgan didn't argue. "Honor and espionage aren't a compatible mixture, Kim Le," he replied, realizing it internally for the first time in his career. "And besides, I couldn't expect anything else. Galaxy Corps couldn't protect *me* without endangering the lives of others." His chin lifted just a little, a spark of the old defiance returning. "I knew the dangers when I went in there; I guess I just never let myself believe it would turn out like this."

Kim Le smiled wistfully. "Your battle is not yet finished, Morgan," he revealed as if possessing the ability to foresee the future. "You still have value to those who betrayed you – your superiors, and the Mizarians as well."

Somehow, when Morgan looked back on the dramatic changes which had occurred in his life over the past seven months, he found himself doubting Kim Le's wisdom. "I don't see how," he said, as much to himself as to the old man.

But Kim Le only smiled. "Patience, Morgan," he instructed gently. "You are still a ram, my friend. Your strength is merely diminished in this brief winter, your horns dulled by battering them uselessly against the stones of self-recrimination." He stood then, offering a hand. "Come," he said once more. "When you have eaten and bathed, Myrddin will further your learning."

Morgan hesitated for only a moment, trying to digest Kim Le's peculiar brand of philosophy – *and* trying to comprehend why this strange little mercenary had taken such a personal interest in him. But for the moment, he held his questions in silence, his stomach growling as he followed the spry old man through the small ship and into the meager dining facilities.

Four tables, each with four bench-style chairs, lined the pale green walls. A mural depicting a lush garden completely covered the portside bulkhead, and pleasant music played softly in the recycled air. The melody was minor-keyed and haunting, and Morgan realized it wasn't the first time he had heard it. On the day he'd first met Lucien, that same Alfarian music had been playing in Lucien's suite. Almost a flute. Not quite a harp. Alien instruments. Keen and sharp and infinitely sad yet acutely beautiful. He wondered now how he hadn't seen it from the start. How could he have served for so many years next to Lucien and not noticed what was so obvious in hindsight.

Fate was an unparalleled bastard, hindsight the bastard's bitch bride.

Swallowing the sudden lump in his throat, he turned to ask Kim Le about the music, but the old man had vanished, leaving the room vacant except for the steaming plate of eggs, ham and hash browns which rivaled anything even his own mother had made for him when he was a boy back home in the California desert.

He ate hungrily, barely noticing that the hand resting in his lap was curled tightly into a fist of anger.

~

One of the things that surprised Morgan somewhat was the fact that, aside from Kim Le, he had seen no one on board the *Dreaming Bird* since he'd awakened that morning. The old man had spoken of Myrddin and Jones and, judging from the moderate size of the vessel and the number of sleeping bunks in the crew's compartment, Morgan was beginning to wonder where the others were, or if indeed they existed at all.

As he finished the breakfast which had been prepared for him, he glanced around the small dining hall, noting once more the differences between it and the facilities on board the *Starling*. The tables and chairs here were secured tightly to the bulkhead rather than dependent on the whims of artificial gravity; all available space was efficiently utilized without the luxury of "elbow room"; and other than the garden mural, the colors were all muted shades of gray and brown.

But before he could ponder it further, he turned toward the door at the sound of approaching footsteps.

Kim Le stood in the doorway, his slight stature clothed in the pale blue cotton-gauze shirt and draw-string pants once again. Under one arm, he carried what looked to be a stack of white linen which, upon entering the dining hall, he proffered to Morgan.

"During your training, you will wear this," the old man explained with his usual economy of words.

Rising from the table, Morgan tried to push the chair underneath, stopping when it remained bolted firmly to the floor. He reached out curiously, took the stack of neatly folded clothes and began examining them. But before he could discern just exactly what each piece consisted of, Kim Le spoke again.

"It is time now to begin your meditation, Morgan," he said. "Please, come with me and I will guide you to the Hall of Silences."

Morgan gazed at the old man for a protracted moment, wondering if they'd both made a mistake. For himself, he had at least a hundred reservations concerning the mental soundness of any mission that would take a small, unshielded vessel into the Nel-fen Neutral Zone. And additionally, he couldn't deny a certain bad attitude on his own part regarding some of the hocus-pocus philosophies that Kim Le subscribed to. Throughout his own life, he'd depended on sharp intellect, a quick fist and a well-charged laser to see him through any entanglements with undesirables. Now, if he understood Kim Le's reasoning, he was being asked to lay all that aside for a philosophy of pacifism and a few well-spoken parables.

It wasn't his style.

And yet, as he considered his alternatives, he found them few and far between. Still, the frustration mounted, causing him to sigh as he gathered the bundle of assigned clothes under one arm and followed the old man down the cramped corridor. They stopped at a flight of deck stairs, climbed down two levels, and eventually came to a closed door bearing a symbol which Morgan recognized only vaguely.

At the door, Kim Le turned to face him once more, his round, wrinkled face crinkling to a smile as he touched the painted symbol with a weathered hand. "The yin and the yang are in perfect harmony at all times, Morgan, in perfect balance. Without the darkness there can be no light. Without the masculine, the feminine becomes insignificant. Without the negative, the positive grows weak and eventually falters. Without evil, good has no meaning." He paused as if to let that sink in, his dark eyes intense as he studied his youthful protégé. "Do you understand?"

For the briefest of moments, Morgan felt his anger flare deep within, but he bit back the automatic response that sprang to his lips, tempering it with learned respect for other cultures. It occurred to him that, with a meal under his belt and a bed on which to sleep for a night, he'd managed to lose sight of the humbleness that had overwhelmed him when he'd first met this peculiar little man. But, recalling that he had little else to do with his life at the moment, he made an effort to be tolerant.

"I understand," he said, more stiffly than he might have preferred.

Kim Le seemed dubious. "Indeed?" he questioned, clearly dubious. "How is it that you can understand in a moment what has taken a lifetime of lifetimes to create?" he asked philosophically.

"And what part of you is it that understands, Morgan? Is it your mind, or is it your spirit?"

Both baffled and annoyed by the question, Morgan sighed heavily, his patience already wearing thin. "Kim Le," he said, steeling himself to courtesy, "I'm not sure what it is you want me to do here. It was my understanding when I came aboard that you were interested in my abilities, my space experience." He paused, wrestling with the unwanted edge in his voice. "I mean no disrespect, but I fail to see how meditation is going to help you regain the Dagger of Zilphoron. Shouldn't we be concentrating our energies in a different direction?"

The old man smiled faintly. "What direction would you suggest, Morgan?" he inquired with cool self-confidence. But he didn't wait for a reply. "As I have already mentioned, this is not the time to question; for as you have seen demonstrated many times in your life, things are seldom what they appear on the surface."

For a moment, Morgan almost accepted that response. Then, realizing that it was a no-answer-answer, he sighed quietly. "Why do I have the distinct impression that you're avoiding my questions?"

Kim Le shook his head with a genuine sadness reflected in his eyes. When he spoke again, his voice was low and deep. "There is much you do not understand yet, Morgan," he said quietly. "And if I *should* answer your questions with directness, you would not be able to accept what I would say to you." He paused briefly, reaching out to take Morgan's hand and cover it between both of his own. "I must ask, my young ram, that you simply trust me for the time being. I wish to be your friend as well as your employer; and if you will give me your trust, I will endeavor to prove to you that I, too, am a man of honor."

Morgan found himself feeling decidedly chagrinned, though he was hard-pressed to say exactly why. "I meant no disrespect," he repeated, realizing that part of his frustration and anger was only now beginning to awaken. The Mizarian incident had left him drained, depleted, broken and alone. It had stripped him of rank and pride, friends and even family. At first, the shock had protected him. But now that that shock was dissipating, he found himself not only alone, but alone with his anger, bitterness and regrets.

"Morgan?"

He looked up, only then realizing he'd been lost in thought for several seconds.

"Will you allow me to teach you new ways?" Kim Le asked expectantly. "Then, afterwards, if you wish to return to your former ideals, no harm has been done."

Morgan was struck with the sudden realization that *old* ways were no longer serving him very well and, haltingly, he nodded. "I'll try," he said.

"That is the most anyone can do," Kim Le replied quietly. Then, touching Morgan's elbow and urging him toward a small dressing stall just outside the door which bore the yin/yang symbol, he added: "You may change into your robes in there," he instructed. "Once you have done so, enter the Hall of Silences and allow your mind to take you on a journey of its own choosing."

Morgan frowned thoughtfully. "I thought you said meditation was the art of *focusing* the mind," he recalled.

"*That*," Kim Le replied, "will come later. First, you must see what it is that you thoughts wish to show you. Only then will you have a symbol upon which to focus."

For the moment, Morgan didn't argue. He slipped quickly into the dressing chamber, shed the nondescript jumpsuit Kim Le had earlier provided for his use, and began donning the gauzy white clothing. The pants were ankle-length, and tied at the waist to form a slightly ballooned effect at the hips and thighs. The shirt/jacket was light-weight and of a thinner material. Once pulled over the head, its sleeves fell to exactly the middle of his wrists, and the upstanding collar and loose fit allowed an ease of movement of arms, torso and shoulders. It was similar to a gi, but the fact that it was drawn over the head rather than cross-lapped in front gave it a sleeker, more subtle look.

Once dressed, he gathered the discarded jumpsuit under one arm, then returned to stand before the door bearing the yin/yang symbol. Depositing the bundle of unnecessary clothes and shoes outside the room, he closed his eyes, took a deep breath, and entered the room with an air of reverence.

His first thought was that the room had been aptly named. The silence was all-consuming.

He knelt as he'd been instructed to do, then found himself consumed by darkness when the unseen light-source dimmed as if sensing his presence.

Then, alone in the dark silences, he followed Kim Le's instructions, fully unexpecting of any results. He had nowhere left to go, he told himself, nothing left to learn that could change his wrecked life. But in accordance with the old man's wishes – perhaps even to prove him wrong – he opened himself nonetheless.

What surprised him was that *he* was the one to be proven wrong.

~

The stubborn oak stood tall but trembling, its long limbs heavy with the burden of winter's snow. The Earth had grown silent and cold, and as Morgan Diego stood in the white-frosted driveway, glancing back at the house which had been his childhood home, he felt a peculiar strangeness settle like a lump in the pit of his stomach.

Soon, he knew, the hired air-car would arrive to take him to Los Angeles; and, from there, he would board a commercial shuttle bound for the Galaxy Corps training facility at Marsport.

He stood for a very long time without moving, watching the fog of his breath create ghosts on the air, listening to the clatter of dinner dishes being put away in his mother's kitchen. The chimney billowed with smoke, and heat-demons distorted the air above the house until the roof seemed to shimmer with warmth and fond memories.

The family dog plodded through the heavy snow – rare for so much snow here in the desert. Then, eyeing its young master, it leaped through the whiteness, gathering crystals of glittering ice on its winter coat as it came up to lick Morgan's hand, questioning him with wide brown eyes.

"Hi there, Eagle, old friend," Morgan greeted. "How's it going?"

The dog made soft whining noises deep in its throat, nuzzling his hand with its elongated Shepherd nose, demanding further attention.

He rubbed and scratched fondly, though his eyes remained locked on the house and the stormy sky beyond. Distantly, he could hear the sound of an air-car's engines, growing louder as it approached.

His heart pounded. His stomach knotted painfully. His throat was tight.

"Mom!" he called, feeling suddenly as if he no longer belonged, yet wanting to make some last-minute attempt at reconciliation. "Mom! The taxi'll be here in a minute!"

The front door opened and, for a very long minute, Morgan Diego stood looking at his mother, wondering at what moment her hair had turned from brown to salt-and-pepper gray, wondering when she had lost her smile to have it replaced with an expression of perpetual, subliminal grief... wondering even more if he would ever see her again.

She came forward in slow motion, it seemed, and Morgan moved through the thick carpet of snow until they met, embracing awkwardly. Through the stiffness of her arms, Morgan could easily read the sense of loss his mother was experiencing again. He'd read it twice before – once when his father had been lost and declared dead in the Delclarion system, and again when his brother, Neil, had left for a research posting on Alcor – a posting which had lasted less than a year before some terraforming accident left him dead and buried on a far-flung alien world where not even his body could be safely recovered. Now, he thought, he was bringing that grief to her again, leaving her alone with the house and the dog and responsibilities too weighty for one elderly woman to handle alone.

"Don't have such worries, Morgie," the warm voice scolded fondly, almost as if reading his thoughts. "There comes a time in everybody's life when they have to leave the nest and fly on their own."

The air taxi's engines whined, retro-thrusters firing as it settled near the end of the driveway, kicking up a spray of melted snow and smoke in its wake.

Morgan's throat tightened again and when he spoke, his words were barely a whisper. "I'll be back soon. I promise."

A warm-but-weathered hand reached out, lifting his chin until their eyes met. Thin lips puckered to a smile. "Don't be makin' promises you may not be able to keep," she said gently. "Just go out there," she added, gesturing to the sky with her head, "and live your life the best way you can. That's good enough, isn't it?"

Morgan tried to smile, though it felt more like his face was cracking. Abruptly, he seized the aging woman into his arms, hugging her fiercely. "I love you, you know," he said, a single tear sliding down each cheek. *"I love you."*

Comforting hands rubbed his back affectionately, then gently took his shoulders and pushed him back to arms' length. "I know you do, Morgan," she said, calling him by his grownup name for the first time. She gestured toward the waiting taxi. "Go on now," she scolded, taking a step back until they no longer touched. "You don't want to be late for your first interview at the college, do you?"

Morgan shook his head, trying again to smile. But it faded as his mother turned away and began the slow, shuffling walk back toward the warmth of the home he was leaving.

He stood for a long minute gazing at her retreating back. Then, swallowing the pain in his throat and dragging his sleeve across his face, he picked up the two small suitcases and turned toward the waiting taxi.

Soundlessly, without tears, he wept throughout the flight to LA.

~

"What did you learn?" Kim Le's voice inquired, breaking the silence and penetrating the darkness that had surrounded him.

Morgan opened his eyes to discover himself standing just outside the Hall of Silences, and only in retrospect did he recall stumbling, disoriented and shaken, from the room. The curve of steel-gray bulkhead was disorienting, the scent of home still filling his head. For a moment, his voice didn't want to work properly; words seemed inadequate to relate the experience.

Finally, taking a deep breath to steady his rattled nerves, he managed to focus his gaze on Kim Le. "I... went home," he said haltingly, astounded as much by the fact that *anything* had happened as by *what* had happened. He swallowed with difficulty, trying to re-orientate himself to the environment of the ship. He felt remarkably cold and, rubbing his hands briskly up and down his arms, he was amazed to find his clothing inexplicably chilled.

Kim Le only smiled, but made no comment. "Come," he said quietly. "It is time for your first lesson."

Morgan blinked, staring at the yin/yang symbol on the closed door of the Hall of Silences. "Wait!" he protested, reaching out to grip the old man's elbow in an effort to halt his retreat. "I – I feel as if I was really there," he explained to Kim Le's expression of curiosity. He glanced again at the door. "What... what's *in* there? I mean... is there some sort of hypno-regression device in that room? Something that allows a person to re-live past experiences?"

The old man's brows lifted high as the corners of his lips curved upward. "It is only an empty room, Morgan," he replied. "The only thing in there is what you carry with you."

Unconvinced and still shaken, Morgan released Kim Le's arm and returned to the closed door. He stood gazing at the black and white symbol painted there for a long moment, then gently pushed until the door opened.

The lights were once again at full intensity, revealing a square room with no modern furnishings. The carpeting was a nondescript beige, worn thin in the center where hundreds had obviously knelt. There was no hum of technology, no openings in the walls, ceiling or floor which would allow even a hidden hypno-regression device to focus on its subject. Even the air vents were situated in such a fashion that no device could have been concealed behind them.

Morgan stared into the thick, beckoning silence for a long moment, feeling like a paranoid fool as he cautiously kept one foot securely anchored outside the room, planted firmly on the metal bulkhead of the corridor.

It was only an empty room.

A hundred new questions swam in his mind, but when he turned to the other man to ask them, all he saw was Kim Le's back retreating soundlessly down the corridor.

Not knowing what else in all the worlds to do, he followed, trotting to catch up to the seemingly omniscient little old man.

CHAPTER FOUR

The dream was disturbing, and Lucien awoke with a start to discover an unprecedented sheen of perspiration clinging to the long, lean lines of his body. His skin was cold and clammy, but upon running a system-check of all bodily functions, he concluded within moments that no physical anomaly was to blame for the condition.

He sat up in his bed, glancing at the clock. It had been precisely four hours, ten minutes and nineteen seconds since Vanya had left him; and after a fruitless attempt at meditation which terminated in a kneeling sleep, he'd finally fallen, exhausted, into his bed.

With an effort, he calmed his breathing, concentrating on slowing the pattering rhythm of his heart as it beat more rapidly than normal. Within a few minutes – longer than usually required, he noted – his body once again obeyed his commands, though it was easy to discern that the months of stress had taken their toll on him. It was, he thought ruefully, a fact he did not care to mention to the *Starling's* shrink.

As he regained control of his physical form, he realized with a sense of dismay that his thoughts were as rampant as his dreams had been. Without reason, his mind tumbled backward and forward, lost in a chaos of images which failed to register within the conscious realms of the brain.

With no provocation, he had dreamed, irrationally, of the day he had departed Homeworld Alfar to join the Galaxy Corps. His mother had stood silently supportive of his decision, perhaps understanding in her fashion that he had chosen a path which would serve two purposes – it would give him the opportunity for personal expansion which the Alfarian University could not; and it would lead him away from the silent, unbending scrutiny of his father.

What Lucien recalled most of that day was the intensity of his father's eyes – the unspoken lectures, the unvoiced disagreements, the final parting of parent and child, left unresolved like an open wound.

In Lucien's dreams, his father's eyes still bored deep into his soul, condemning him for abandoning the family's chosen path, for breaking tradition and allying himself with Galaxy Corps instead of remaining on Homeworld to become a healer and shaman as his Life Reading taken upon his birth had said he would be destined to do. To turn one's back on such a calling was no less than betrayal of one's race – or so the legends said and so Lucien's father liked to remind him – but what Lucien had never told any of them was that the only crime worse than betraying one's race would be to betray *oneself*.

There was something out there, Lucien knew. There was something he had to do, something he needed to find. There was someone he needed to *be* other than the sole son of Xander and Katrice.

On the day Lucien left , Xander had stood in the doorway of the family's ancestral home while his son walked the long path away from the house to board the shuttle. Lucien still recalled the humid heat of the forest, the brush of the Bel-gannador leaves against his face, his arms. He still recalled the weeping of the Nettle dwellers who lived high up in the tallest branches of the trees, but who had befriended Lucien since he was a boy, often flying down from their secret lairs to alight on his shoulder when he journeyed alone into the Wood. He would miss the forest, he knew, but even the Nettles had told him he couldn't stay when there were dreams to be chased and stars to be followed and mysteries to be lived.

Time to grow up.

And he still remembered Xander standing under the shade of the marble arches, his face stern and unforgiving.

At the last minute, Lucien had turned, lifting his hand in a gesture of parting. "May the elements of creation bring you joy, Father," he had said, nonetheless sensing Xander's disapproval through the parental link which had grown more and more strained in the months since Lucien had announced his decision.

But Xander had turned away, and in that moment, Lucien felt all ties with his past severed as if by an executioner's blade. The familial link which had nurtured him to adulthood was abruptly terminated, leaving him alone and without emotional support.

He had boarded the shuttle without looking back, though he

could still sense the tears streaming silently down Katrice's face.

He did not allow that anguish to reflect in his own eyes and, steeling his mind against it, he had made the flight to Alfar's largest city in silence, knowing that, now and forever, he was alone.

Feeling himself slipping once more into the dangerous realms of sleep, Lucien commanded himself back to full awareness, gazing around his cabin until his eyes met those of the Keeper of the Cauldron – a stone face reminiscent of Earth's greenman. There, he found a focal point upon which to concentrate and, with a supreme effort, managed to consign the painful memories back to their tomb, sealing them away from conscious thought.

As he sat in the middle of the small bed, however, it occurred to him that the parting from his family was not the sole subject of his disturbing dreams. As he concentrated, schooling his mind to some semblance of discipline, he also recalled images which made no sense, and which followed no pattern. In his dreams, he had visited a peculiar room peopled only by silence and throbbing darkness. In that room, he knew, Morgan Diego lived.

For a moment, he believed himself mad, mentally reciting the fact that dreams were nothing more than projections of fantasies which could not be lived in reality. It stood to reason that he would dream of his friend's well-being, for it was what he hoped Morgan would find. It even made sense that his subconscious mind would seek to alleviate his guilt of the fact that *he* had been impotent to act when Diego had been placed in the hands of the Mizarians and had later become victim to their Law.

His mind reeled and dizziness gnawed hungrily at his control, threatening to topple him over the edge of some treacherous cliff. He *should* have acted, he told himself. He *should* have found a way to keep Morgan safe on the *Starling*. He should have offered himself, or perhaps he should have given the order which would self-destruct the ship entirely. At least in that manner, he knew, these dreams would not now be occurring. And, one way or another, Morgan would be spared the lonely existence of an exile.

In light of his own dream, Lucien now realized *he* had been an exile most of his life. Even on Homeworld, he had never fit in with the other children. While they spoke of their betrothals and marriage and the bright prospect of raising their own families in the nurturing greenery of Mother Forest, Lucien had secretly dreamt of star cruisers and far-flung worlds and something – *anything!* – other than the drudgery of settling into a Life Path with Shalice, the beautiful but frighteningly mundane and traditional daughter of the shaman-healer from whom Lucien had been slated to learn his trade in order to answer his calling.

When they had both come The Age of Breath, the old shaman had sealed their palms with wild honey and tied their wrists together in a symbolic betrothal which would draw them together when the forest deemed it was time to create children of their own. And though Lucien had pretended to go along with the ritual – for there was little else he could do – he had been horrified at the prospect of giving himself to Shalice or any other Alfarian female. Put simply, he wanted neither the responsibilities of a family nor the obligations of a wife.

No doubt Shalice had felt that reticence when they were betrothed, and no doubt she had mentioned it to her powerful father. And yet, even when Lucien had requested an audience with Dunwillow to explain his position in the matter, the old shaman had steadfastly refused to nullify the link, leaving Lucien betrothed to a woman he neither loved nor even particularly liked. Dunwillow had assured him he would change his mind. Come to his senses. Wake up to his calling. The usual rhetoric adults spoon-fed to their children to make them agreeable members of society.

But even if not, he *would* return to Homeworld to wed Shalice when the forest called them both to the Clearing.

With supreme effort, Lucien pushed those thoughts from his mind, not wanting to remember at that moment just how much his decision *not* to heed that call had cost him.

Yes, he knew what it was to be an exile, even among his own people.

Recognizing the pointlessness of his mental masturbations, he drew himself once again from his reverie, contemplating the feelings of impotence which continued to haunt him like restless spirits. Then, on the heels of that familiar pattern came a new realization.

Alfarians did not normally dream. And while his unusually high stress levels could account for some of the distressing events, he was presented with a remarkably simple explanation. He and Morgan had essentially sworn a pact to one another when they had shared the Embrace before the human's departure for Mizar.

It would explain much.

It was conceivable, he thought, that following Morgan's release from the Mizarians, the human had mastered the art of meditation. If such were the case, and if they happened to enter the heightened state of awareness at the same moment, it was additionally conceivable that their minds would be drawn together in some inexplicable fashion.

Closing his eyes and sighing heavily, Lucien dropped his head into his hands, listening to the alien hum of the star cruiser's engines. He did not belong in the commander's chair, he knew, and only on Bryse's insistence that Morgan had requested it had he agreed to accept command.

But as he thought again of Bryse and of the old admiral's emotional recounting of his brief visit with Morgan, Lucien found his mind filled with multiple possibilities.

He sat bolt upright as understanding overwhelmed him.

It was in that moment that he began to fully suspect the truth. And with his suspicions to guide him, he stumbled wearily from his bed, punched the intercom and waited until the junior communications officer responded.

"Lieutenant," he ordered, "I wish to speak with Admiral Bryse at Galaxy Corps Central. Contact his office immediately, and relay the communication to my suite once established."

The young woman's hands traveled instantly to her board, though Lucien noted that she moved with more apprehension at *his* commands than if Morgan had been the one to issue the same order. He switched the two-way visual contact off, then sank into the chair at his desk

He wondered briefly what he planned to say to the admiral, or if indeed he should say anything at all. And yet, he knew Vanya was right about one thing.

He had to do something.

~

"I'm sure you're aware, Captain Lucien, that the accusations you have made are grave," Bryse said, his voice bland, his eyes wary.

Lucien's brows lifted. "I have made no accusations, Admiral," he corrected. "I have merely inquired as to the whereabouts of Commander Diego."

Bryse sighed loudly. "You're aware of the contents of the Mizarian Treaty, Commander. And you're also aware that this is an unsecured channel," he warned. "The matter isn't open for discussion."

For a moment, Lucien remained silent, studying Bryse's image on the screen. The admiral appeared wary, overly-cautious; though something in his tone caused Lucien to wonder precisely what was being left unsaid. He knew that Morgan and the admiral had been fast friends for many years, and he suspected that Galaxy Corps would hardly lose track of a former commander despite his technical state of exile. They knew exactly where he was, and if Lucien's suspicions were correct, they were undoubtedly calling the shots, even if through a long series of relays, false fronts and intentional illusions.

Considering those facts, Lucien made his move. "I was not aware that the Mizarian Treaty could not be discussed openly, Admiral," he said quietly. "However, if such is the case, I request permission to speak with you in private."

Bryse's eyes widened almost imperceptibly, though Lucien noted the reaction with interest. "Scrambler channels have been proven ineffective against the Mizarians, Captain Lucien," the admiral returned evasively. "I'm sure you're aware of that."

Lucien inclined his head in agreement. "I am, Admiral – which is why I additionally request permission to avail myself of my accumulated leave time immediately. The *Starling* is not currently involved in any missions of great importance, thus it should be possible to–."

"Permission granted," Bryse interrupted quietly.

"Sir?" He'd expected to argue just a little.

The admiral glanced away from the screen, then thumbed a switch just out of range of Lucien's vision. When he spoke again, his tone was hushed, his words clipped and short. "Look, Captain Lucien," he said quickly, "I'm way out of line in agreeing to even talk to you. But for the sake of everyone involved, I'm going out on a limb on this one. I don't know if what I'll have to say to you will make a bit of difference in the long run, but if you want to hear it, be in my office at 0800 hours in three days. The *Starling* is scheduled for a computer overhaul, so put in your request for docking at Earthbase One. Understood?"

Lucien wondered absently if the shock he felt inside were reflected on his face. "Understood, Admiral," he said. "*Starling* out."

But before he could switch the device off, Bryse spoke again, his tone still cautious as he glanced suspiciously out of the vid-cam's range. "Oh, Captain Lucien?"

"Yes, Admiral?"

"Have Doctor Vanya accompany you to my office. What I have to say involves both of you."

"Very well, Admiral," Lucien confirmed, though he wasn't particularly thrilled at the idea of yet one more encounter with Vanya. The overly emotional human reminded him all too much of an Alfarian Skidderlip – a small but annoyingly hyperactive pet which tended to hop up and down, chatter incessantly, and generally demand attention on a constant basis. He said nothing of that to the admiral, just noted it for his own perverse musement.

Bryse seemed to visibly relax, and a faint hint of what might have been a smile pressed at the corners of his lips. His hand moved once again, and Lucien assumed it was to re-activate whatever dampening control he had utilized previously. "If there's nothing else, we'll look forward to seeing the *Starling* within the week. Sorry to hear about the trouble you've been having with the turbo-drive system on the computers."

Lucien inclined his head in acknowledgement. "I am certain it is a matter which can be easily corrected with proper facilities, Admiral," he returned, content to play Bryse's game if it would advance his own knowledge of Morgan's whereabouts. Perhaps his greatest surprise was that Bryse had agreed to meet with him at all.

Long after the screen had gone blank, Lucien continued to stare at it, trying to avoid the inevitable questions which tumbled head-over-heels through his mind.

One thing was certain. Bryse knew something – something which, if Lucien's suspicions were correct, was a secret even from the rest of Galaxy Corps.

He sat in silence for a few minutes longer. Then, mentally preparing himself for the barrage of questions he knew would come, he opened the intercom channel to Vanya's cabin.

CHAPTER FIVE

Morgan's journey ended at another closed door on a deck in the bottom-most sector of the *Dreaming Bird*. After following Kim Le through a maze of tightly-cramped corridors and down several flights of deck stairs, the old man came to an abrupt halt in front of a door which bore two symbols.

As he studied the markings, his heart beat a little faster, threatening to awaken too many old memories. The upper-most painting was of two hands pressed together, with the closed fist of the right being planted in the open palm of the left. The flesh was an Earthy rose/sand tone – the human symbol of the mental and physical discipline of The Art. The second symbol, however, was the main focus of Morgan's concentration. Two hands were also pressed together, yet the fingers of both were laced together, with the index fingers raised to form a "steeple" effect. The flesh tones were olive and, as he stood spellbound gazing at the two paintings symbolically intertwined with the rays of a brightly-colored red and yellow sun, he began to wonder if indeed his meeting with Kim Le had been an accident. The second symbol, Morgan knew, was Alfarian – the symbol of Knowledge, with the interlaced fingers pointing upward, toward the higher realms, the higher self, the secret self which waited to be discovered.

For the briefest of moments, Diego battled the heartfelt urge to run, to seclude himself in some dark corner of the *Dreaming Bird* and convince himself it was nothing more than another Mizarian-induced nightmare. And yet, as he turned to face Kim Le, an odd combination of serenity and intense curiosity caused him to remain.

The old man smiled faintly. "This has meaning to you, Morgan?"

Morgan glanced again at the door, then back to his odd little mentor. Things were happening too quickly. Less than an hour before, he had 'gone home', as he'd told Kim Le. His mind had transported him on some bizarre journey, and upon 'returning', the clothes he wore in the warm meditation chamber had been as chilled as if buried in snow. Now, on a Terran mercenary ship hurtling itself toward the Nel-fen Neutral Zone – or *through* it for all

56

he *really* knew – he encountered a little-known Alfarian symbol painted on the door of what he presumed to be a dojo.

"This symbol," he said, indicating the painting, "it's... Alfarian." His voice was low, almost a whisper, foretelling the awe which rose from deep within him.

Kim Le inclined his head graciously. "And Terran," he added. "One cannot gain too much knowledge, Morgan. The Alfarians have long been masters in the arts of discipline and self-defense. And certain Terran cultures have long sought to perfect those arts. Does it not stand to reason that the two cultures should combine to share the accumulated knowledge of both?"

Morgan blinked, only barely listening as he continued to stare at the intricately painted symbol. With one hand, he reached out, his index finger tracing the slightly raised area where the artist's brush had stroked.

"Morgan?"

Kim Le's voice broke his reverie and, still astounded, he turned to face the old man, trying to ignore the swell of pain which rose in his chest. "It reminds me of someone I used to know," he said quietly, realizing it was the first time he had allowed himself to speak of Lucien even vaguely since his exile. "Someone I cared about very much."

Kim Le once again acknowledged him with a slight bowing of his silver-flecked head. "You will meet again," he said omnisciently.

Morgan's heart wrenched and he turned abruptly away from the painting and all that it seemed to represent. "Not in *this* lifetime," he said with unanticipated sarcasm.

Kim Le's brows lifted. "I was not aware that you were a believer in reincarnation," he noted.

Morgan scoffed. "I'm not," he said, clipped, then waved his words aside as the old anger and bitterness tried to surface once more. With an effort which required total concentration, he pushed those feelings aside, reminding himself that *this* was his life *now*. He looked up, meeting the old man's sparkling dark eyes. "It's not important, Kim Le," he said, tasting the ultimate lie on his tongue. "Let's just get on with it."

Kim Le continued to look at him for a long moment, sadness

reflecting in his gaze. He seemed about to speak, then drew a deep breath which was released as a sigh. Then, reaching out, he placed one weathered hand on Diego's arm, squeezing with gentle reassurance. "You must learn to trust in what you *know*, Morgan," he instructed quietly, "rather than in what you *believe* to be true."

"Isn't 'belief' just another word for 'faith'?" Morgan countered. "Isn't what we *'know'* just a matter of subjective opinion?" His anger was dangerously close to the surface, though he was no longer certain at whom or what that anger was directed. He shook his head, battling the heartfelt urge to slam his fist against the nearest wall. "In the end, none of it matters anyway."

Kim Le was silent and contemplative, his hand still resting on Diego's arm. "The destiny of a ram is never an easy one, Morgan," he said. "But be assured that what you *know* to be true will always lead you down the correct path." He waved the other's impending argument aside with a quick gesture. "'Belief' is nothing more than faith, that much is true. But the *knowing* is something else entirely. When you *know* something to be true – when it *exists* within your own mind as a fact, it also exists within the molecular structure of the universe."

Morgan didn't bother to argue. He just stood, closed and hurting, staring at the wall behind Kim Le's back. "Are you trying to tell me that if I *know* none of this is really happening, it'll all just disappear? Poof? Into thin air?" He hated himself for his unwarranted sarcasm, but it came nonetheless.

But Kim Le's patience remained intact, his demeanor calm and gentle. "You know that it *is* happening, Morgan," he countered. "And even if you did *not* know, then the knowledge of others would over-ride your doubts. Reality remains constant. It can be molded and shaped, yes, but its basic structure is as it has been for millions of centuries." He watched Morgan's face for a reaction and, seeing no concession, chose a different angle. "If I should allow myself to believe, for example, or even to *know* that you are not really here, it would not alter the fact that you *are*."

"Then what you're saying doesn't make any sense," Morgan concluded.

Kim Le shook his head, his grip on the muscular arm tightening gently. "*Your* knowledge is a factor, too, Morgan," he explained. "*You* know that you *are* here, thus my beliefs or knowledge cannot undermine your reality."

Shaking his head, Morgan battled the tension ache which was crawling up the back of his neck. "It sounds like circular logic to me," he said, not the least bit sure what any of it mattered. Quantum philosophy had never been his strong point.

"Precisely," Kim Le agreed, then smiled faintly. "For now, that level of understanding is sufficient. But as you learn from Myrddin, you will come to know that the circle is the basis of all things. All things begin or end at the proper time and place. All thoughts eventually lead themselves back to their own beginnings, back to their roots."

"Then what's the point?" Morgan asked, more for the sake of asking than expecting an answer.

Kim Le's gray brows lifted as his lips curved to a smile. "The 'point' is to learn that you are not a prisoner of any circle. You may be held within it, or you may learn to escape it."

But again, Morgan shook his head. "I thought you just got through saying a minute ago that we can't escape reality," he pointed out.

Kim Le held his gaze for a long moment, then inclined his head toward the door. "Come," he urged. "Myrddin can better answer your questions. And if you will permit it, he can teach you to step outside the circles which bind you."

Morgan wanted to argue that he wasn't bound by anything or anyone. And yet, as he recalled how he had come to be in Kim Le's company, and the Mizarian Law which made him an exile from his own past, he held his tongue. But still, his anger and frustration continued to boil, steaming like a deadly cauldron deep within his spirit.

~

He wasn't certain what he'd expected of Myrddin, but it wasn't what awaited him as he was ushered through the door by Kim Le, then left alone with what the old man had called 'his new teacher'.

For an instant, his heart leapt wildly as recognition struck him. *Lucien!* his mind shouted, his feet starting automatically forward. But as the obviously-Alfarian man turned toward him, Morgan stopped cold, his hopes and impossible expectations shattered when he realized that this man bore only a faint resemblance to his friend.

Myrddin stood approximately two inches shorter than Lucien, and though he was of roughly the same build, Morgan observed that he was considerably heavier than Lucien through the shoulders, and that his legs were thicker. Powerful muscles rippled beneath the skin-tight black jumpsuit which completely covered his body save for his neck and head, bare feet and long-boned hands. Though it was the same intense black in color, Myrddin's hair was longer than Lucien's, parted in the middle and cut in such a manner than it was of graduated lengths on the side, then tapered to a precise "v" at shoulder-height in the back. It shone a glistening almost-purple under the muted lighting in the room, yet upon closer inspection, Morgan would discover that it was streaked with varying shades of deep walnut-brown. Myrddin bore the same angular features that Morgan had come to know so well, yet his eyes were more closely-set, his cheekbones slightly more prominent.

As Morgan perused the other, his attention was captured at once by the hands. – the long, lean fingers which tapered delicately at the tip, the fingernails which were naturally a pale shade of not-quite-blue. If he looked only at that focal point, if he allowed his mind to imagine, it would be easy to believe that this unknown Alfarian was indeed his friend – a friend with whom Morgan had fallen irrevocably in love and might now never see again. The gods – if ever there had been any – had a fucked-up sense of humor.

But his imaginings were cut short as Myrddin inclined his head graciously in the customary Alfarian greeting, then spoke in a voice which was slightly more bass than Lucien's melodic tones.

"I am Myrddin," the Alfarian said quietly. "Kim Le has told me that you are called Morgan, and that you wish to learn the disciplines which will bring you your freedom."

When the Alfarian continued to look at him, curiosity in the wide dark eyes, Morgan realized he'd been holding his breath for no reason he could pinpoint. He blinked, feeling uncharacteristically dense when no answer came to his lips. He fumbled.

"Uh... yes," he stammered, still taken aback by the fact that he'd so easily mistaken Myrddin for Lucien. He wondered wistfully if eight months were so long a time that he would make such an error. But when he recalled his final parting from Lucien that fateful day when he'd been unceremoniously handed over to the Mizarians, the answer was plain. He hadn't known until that moment how much Lucien meant to him, or even how much the *Starling* had meant. Both were integral parts of his life, as essential as breathing. And once separated from both, he was left as less than half a man. Obviously the Mizarians had known that; the seer certainly could have deduced it from his thoughts. And in accordance with their clever traditions, his punishment was a double-edged sword.

"Your mind is troubled," Myrddin observed, interrupting Morgan's distressing train of thought. He walked the two steps which separated them, and came to stand at his shoulder. "Was your meditation unsuccessful?"

For an instant, Morgan felt his face flush and, abruptly, he understood what Lucien had meant when he said meditation was an intensely private affair. Myrddin's question penetrated his defenses, leaving him uncomfortable and surprisingly irritable. But with an effort, he controlled that automatic response, reminding himself for the tenth time that day that at least he could now depend on regular meals and a bed. He could possibly even depend on the friendship of Kim Le – a man who had befriended him despite the invisible brand on his forehead. His jaw tightened almost imperceptibly.

"I guess everything's still a little new," he offered lamely, unable at that moment to look the other man in the eye. He stared instead at the bareness of the room, the corded gray carpet, the floor-to-ceiling mirrors which covered three entire walls. There were several work-out areas in the room, hydraulic weights, and an assortment of other items he couldn't immediately identify. In one corner, what appeared to be a small tree limb was suspended on two ropes which hung from the ceiling. An unmeasured amount of time passed. Then, taking a deep breath to steady touchy nerves, he met the other's unwavering gaze, determined not to make a fool of himself again within the next ten seconds.

"Where do we start?" he asked, trying to project an air of confidence he didn't even begin to feel.

"It is normally wise to begin at the beginning, Morgan," Myrddin said, the gentleness of his tone robbing the words of any possible tone of condescension. "The art I will teach you is a combination of the ancient and the modern, of physical and spiritual. It is also an art which will utilize strengths of which you may be unaware, and an art which will reveal weaknesses buried deep within." He paused as if to allow Morgan to absorb that, then added: "It is also an art that, once learned, can never be unlearned or abandoned. It is a commitment which will last a lifetime and possibly beyond."

Morgan considered the implications of his words. He'd studied the basic martial arts in the course of his command training, and while his instructors had been adequate teachers, none had possessed the quiet, controlled fire which burned in Myrddin's eyes. It alleviated just a little of his irritability and nervousness and, feeling slightly more at ease, he nodded his agreement.

"I understand," he said.

Myrddin inclined his head in acknowledgement. "In the training arena, you will refer to me as Master."

Morgan wasn't certain, though he thought he almost saw the thin lips curve upward slightly – a covert and alluring smile.

"When we are in training, Morgan, I am your teacher only," Myrddin stressed. "However, once we depart this room, I would also choose to be your friend if you will permit it. Many times, students hesitate to talk openly with their teachers; I have found, when working with humans, that it is often helpful to clarify such misconceptions in advance."

Despite the fact that they'd only just met, Morgan found himself hopelessly touched by the unrequired gesture. He smiled gently. "I could use a friend right about now... Master," he said, surprised that his subservient position didn't make him

62

uncomfortable as he'd half-way expected it would. He held the dark gaze for a moment longer than necessary, then took a deep breath and let it out slowly. "Thank you."

Once more, Myrddin's head bowed very slightly. Then, stepping back, he motioned Morgan to follow as he went to the far corner of the room, stopping in front of the tree limb which hung suspended between two sturdy ropes.

"The wood," Myrddin explained, indicating the branch which was roughly four inches thick, "comes from the heart of the Banalai Tree of Rigel. Of the students I have trained, none have been able to break it upon entering this discipline; all have succeeded when the training is complete." He paused, then gestured again toward the thick branch with one hand. "Break the tree, Morgan," he said then, and stood aside with his hands clasped neatly behind his back.

Morgan looked first at his new master, then at the branch. Upon closer inspection, he noted that the 'rope' was actually braided thongs of leather which were tied at the ends to form a loop in which the heart-wood rested. It was suspended at a height level with his hips, and it occurred to the silly part of his mind that it would have made an excellent swing. The Banalai Tree was noted for its strength; it would hold his weight and more, and he suspected that an attempt to crack it with his hand would result in more fractures to the bones than to the wood. He turned back to Myrddin, shaking his head with a knowing laugh.

"I assume this is a test to see whether or not I'm crazy enough to try it, right?" he asked.

But Myrddin remained unyielding, unfazed by his attempt at humor. He gestured toward the limb once again. "Break the wood," he instructed.

Morgan blinked. Obviously, he thought, the Alfarian didn't expect him to crack the Banalai Tree with one hand. He doubted that even the superior Alfarian strength could do it. And yet, it was clear by his teacher's attitude that he was expected to try.

He looked once more to Myrddin, then back to the hanging limb. It occurred to him that the Alfarian hadn't said *how* he wanted the wood broken and, relying on some inner intuition, he moved closer to the problem, toying for a moment with the leather thongs until they released the branch into his hands. Holding it, he tested its weight against his hands, and discovered that the wood was quite old, brittle; and though he probably couldn't have snapped it with a single-handed thrust, he noted that Myrddin hadn't moved to correct him from removing the branch from its resting place.

He glanced a final time at the Alfarian, found no encouragement or discouragement in the shielded elven features, nothing to indicate whether his intentions were right or wrong.

Then, taking a firm grip on each end of the three-foot-long limb, he closed his eyes, concentrating his full power on a single downward motion which brought the branch hard against his knee. To his surprise, a loud snap sounded in the room, overshadowed only by his own grunt as the force rattled him in and out of reality.

It happened in slow motion and, as he realized what he'd done, he also realized that his eyes were clenched tightly shut. Opening them, he glanced expectantly toward Myrddin, only to find an unreadable expression which might have been surprise on the other man's angular features. But as he watched, the thin lips began a slow upward climb, ending at last in a definite smile.

"Next time," the Alfarian said, "remember to keep your eyes open, Morgan. Had your opponent been a man rather than a tree, you could have found yourself in considerable distress, particularly if the appendage you sought to break had survived the attack."

Morgan blinked, the grin of achievement dimming from his face. His jaw went slightly slack, but he recovered his composure quickly, realizing that he *had* broken the branch, understanding that Myrddin was quite obviously pleased with him despite his Alfarian nit-picking.

"Yes, Master," he said, dropping each end of the branch to the floor with a sense of inner satisfaction motivating him. "I'll remember that." His shoulders lifted; his posture squared. He felt unaccountably whole.

Inside, for the first time in over eight months, he was laughing.

~

By the end of the fourth training session, it occurred to Morgan that he had seen no other students or even teachers on the *Dreaming Bird*. Save for Kim Le, Myrddin, and Jones, the ship's resident cook, there appeared to be no other living beings on board. The ship, it seemed, was run quite efficiently by computers and robotics, and though he had expressed his dismay of such a fact to Kim Le, the old man's sole answer had been a quirked smile and a response having little to do with the question put to him.

Now, standing in the meditation room as he mentally prepared himself for the fifth training session, he took a deep breath, attempting to calm the questions which tumbled at light speed through his mind. Despite the absurdity of the possibility, it "seemed" to him that the *Dreaming Bird* was moving in the wrong direction to be proceeding toward even the farthest corner of the Nel-fen Empire. There were, however, no view-ports as there had been on the *Starling*, and attempting to navigate the stars simply by numbers on a computer's holo-screen was a task at which he'd never excelled. He settled for the fact that, with increasing awareness, the ship's course simply *felt* wrong. It also seemed that a vessel with a mercenary mission should, logically, have been carrying more mercenaries. Additionally, the fact that Kim Le seldom if ever answered his questions left him feeling disoriented and more alone than he'd felt since the initial days of his exile. The questions mounted, and answers seemed as elusive as his own past.

He sighed heavily, and knelt in the proper place to begin the required meditations. Kim Le had instructed that, this time, he was to focus his concentration "old friends". The old man would say no more, steadfastly refusing to listen to his protests, his argument that such thoughts only reawakened temporarily numbed pain.

'Think on old friends today, Morgan', Kim Le had said. 'Such thoughts will bring strength in times of weakness, comfort in times of need'.

Now, kneeling, he listened to the protesting patter of his heart as it beat somewhat too fast. *What am I supposed to think about?* he wondered, hurting deep inside. *The good times we shared that we'll never share again? The rum we drank in Vanya's office on quiet afternoons? The silly card games that lasted long into the night when Lucien—?*

He stopped himself there, clenching his eyes tightly shut to close out the unwanted memories. And yet, as the light in the room mysteriously dimmed to total darkness, the memories claimed him regardless of his personal wishes.

His heart wept, though his eyes remained dry, unseeing.

~

The Alfarian forest pressed close, its presence like a heavy green weight on Morgan Diego's chest as he found himself pinned beneath the wicked gravity of his second-in-command when he was toppled to the ground by an unexpected tackle that left him breathless.

At first, Morgan had no idea what the hell had just happened. Last thing he'd been aware of was standing at the edge of the Clearing, an invited guest at the equivalent of an Alfarian wedding. It wasn't lost on him that several high-ranking Alfarian dignitaries were in attendance – including but not limited to Xander and Katrice, both vital members of the Alfarian Council, direct advisors to the king and queen of Alfar, and as such, two of perhaps only a dozen Alfarians who even knew the identity of the ruling royal family. Legend had it that the king and queen lived deep within the forest, perhaps even in an underground palace guarded by unseen forces which no human could even begin to perceive, let alone comprehend.

Morgan had known Lucien came from an influential family, though he had never known *how* influential until now – when his best friend tackled him and dragged him to the leaf-scattered ground while all those important dignitaries, ambassadors and liaisons of royalty looked on as if this were nothing at all out of the ordinary.

Stunned, Morgan rolled with the momentum of the attack until he was able to wrench free of Lucien's superior elven strength. Clamoring to his feet, he brushed the dirt and debris from his eyes, staring at his friend who now bore little resemblance to the man Morgan had known and served with for the past three years.

Put simply, Lucien looked more like a madman than any

madman Morgan had ever met – and he'd met a few. With the long black hair disheveled and falling forward to half-cover his face, the black eyes blazed with a combination of rage and what might have been abject disbelief – a feeling Morgan himself shared utterly.

"Lucien?" he said, though the word came out as barely a whisper.

Lucien looked at him, seemingly without even recognizing him. And then he lunged again.

Morgan managed to evade the full force of the second attack, though in his haste to side-step the onslaught, the heel of his boot caught on a rock and caused him to stagger backward and land with a painful thud on his ass. He was smaller than Lucien, and faster – or so he thought. Under normal circumstances, perhaps that would have been the case. But what Morgan didn't know was that the same force which had compelled Lucien to return to the Clearing to formally acknowledge Shalice as his lifemate was also responsible for his friend's inexplicable and unrelenting assaults. They were both pawns of the same woman, though neither could have known it at the time.

By Alfarian tradition, it was the right of the betrothed female on her wedding day to make a wish which her husband was honor-bound to grant. Well, more like psychically-*compelled*, but that was a whole other can of worms. Most times, of course, it was some silly sentiment. *Bring me that purple flower growing at the base of the fertility tree.* Or… *Tell me a secret you have never shared with another living soul.* Sentimental stuff. The kind of things men and women have been doing since the dawn of time, no matter their homeworld.

But Shalice was no ordinary female. And clearly she had known Lucien was no ordinary man. For as long as the stars remained at his fingertips, he would be *their* lover and never hers. The only way to force him to remain on Homeworld and in her bed would be to ruthlessly sever all ties he held to Galaxy Corps, to the *Starling*, and especially to Morgan Diego. Translated: if she could use the telepathic power of the betrothal link to force Lucien to kill Morgan, he would be compelled to leave the service and surrender himself to the laws of his own people.

Of course, there were no laws regarding what a woman could

or could not ask for on her wedding day. Lucien would be pardoned and, having nowhere else to go, he would have no alternative but to turn to her family and, in particular, her father, Dunwillow. He would see the kindness she had done him, he would submit himself to the traditions of the Alfarian people by becoming a healer and shaman, and that would simply be that. All in the day's work of a madwoman.

Of course, Morgan knew none of that when he felt himself crash to the ground and Lucien's powerful body wrestled him into the colorful carpet of fallen leaves and fresh black soil. He was peripherally aware of Vanya shouting something from a distance, but as he rolled and squirmed with Lucien on top of him, he caught only a glimpse of the *Starling's* resident shrink being held in check by two powerful Alfarian guards. Other voices were shouting, or maybe it was singing. With Alfarians, it was sometimes difficult to know the difference.

All Morgan knew in that moment was Lucien's lean and unrelenting hands around his neck, strangling the life out of him as if they were long-time enemies instead of confidants and friends. His senses dimmed. And suddenly the world was going dark, the arms of Mother Forest reaching out to welcome him even though he was a stranger there. In death, he would exist forever within the Spirit of the trees, the rain, the earth… all the things which comprised the totality of the forest itself.

It was almost a comfort.

But just as his eyes were about to close, something he could not explain gave him one final burst of strength with which to fight. And yet, as he looked up into the mad whirlpools of Lucien's black eyes, he knew he didn't want to fight this man. He certainly didn't want to harm him, even to save his own life. And so Morgan did the only thing that felt right in that moment – though it was quite probably the most insane and unpredictable thing he had ever done in the course of his career. Indeed, in the course of his entire life.

With the last shred of strength, he simply commanded his body to go slack, unresisting, in total surrender. The immediate result was not unlike what happens when one man lets go of his end of the rope in a tug-of-war. Lucien fell forward on top of him, their bodies chest to chest, abdomen to abdomen, cheek to cheek… man to man.

The fight went out of him.

And that was when, without any predetermination, Morgan took the tormented face between his hands and pressed his lips to the trembling mouth in a kiss as intimate as any he had ever shared with a lover.

Time stopped. The forest itself did not move or breathe.

It was a kiss to break a spell, Morgan heard some distant voice within himself explain. It was the kiss of the prince to cast off the dark magick of the evil princess who had bewitched Lucien.

And he felt no shame in that kiss despite the even more distant sounds of gasps, a little shriek which might have been a sound of delight coming from Lucien's mother, and finally a heartfelt burst of cheers and applause from the primarily Alfarian audience of onlookers. Maybe it even made sense. The Alfarians loved their traditions and their myths and their mysticism, so maybe it stood to reason that they would approve of a strange foreigner who had the power to break such an evil spell with such a profound and forbidden kiss.

All Morgan knew was that he literally *felt* Lucien surrender to him just as he had surrendered to Lucien moments before. They could no more fight one another than they could sprout wings and fly – though there were times when Morgan did wonder about that where Lucien was concerned.

Because time *had* stopped, Morgan didn't move or even dare to breathe for quite some time. He merely lay there in the welcoming soil of Mother Forest, feeling the weight of Lucien against him, the cool elven lips pressed tight to his own until reality seemed to knock on the door of rationality, and returned them both to their senses.

When they pulled back and met one another's eyes, Morgan winked conspiratorially. "You okay?"

Lucien smiled. At least that's how Morgan interpreted the other man's expression. Maybe it was a wince of embarrassment. He chose to believe it was an unspoken expression of gratitude.

The next thing either of them knew, Lucien was being helped to his feet by members of his clan, and Morgan found Vanya climbing all over him with a field medical kit. He met Lucien's eyes one last time just before they were led away in opposite directions – Lucien back to his clan's gathering place where it would be decided what was to be done about Shalice; and Morgan back to the landing shuttle where he found himself being further poked and prodded until he smacked Vanya's hand away and muttered something vulgar under his breath.

His heart was still racing, so much so that he barely heard Vanya's ongoing prattle.

"Jesus Christ in a solid gold limo, Morgan! Damned if I haven't see it all now!" the shrink said as much to himself as to anyone else. "Never thought I'd see the day when you'd actually kiss our resident alien princeling! Yee hah!"

Morgan glared at the other man. "Enjoying yourself, Liam?"

The shrink slapped one hand on the other knee. "Damn right! That was something!" He paused, eyeing Morgan critically. "Well...?"

Morgan frowned. "Well... what?"

Vanya fidgeted. Looked away. "Is it true what they say?"

"You lost me," Morgan confessed, his own thoughts still drifting back to the floor of the forest, the feel of Lucien's weight on him, the brush of lips, light as a feather at first, then more demanding. He wondered fleetingly where it *might* have gone.

"Legend says if an Alfarian kisses you, you're under his spell for life," Vanya ventured cautiously. "So... is it true?"

Morgan didn't feel like playing games. So he played one of his own. "First, Lucien didn't kiss me. *I* kissed *him*." He paused to let that sink in, then added, "And if it's any consolation, legend *also* says that if a star commander kisses you, you're *his* slave forever. So go ask Lucien."

Vanya just stood there, the wind taken from his sails.

They were back on board the *Starling* within the hour. And he and Lucien had never spoken of the kiss again. It was, in the end, all in a day's work – the trick *du jour* they had employed to keep the reaper away and return to their shared mistress, the *Starling*.

At least that's what Morgan had tried to convince himself,

70

though memory of that kiss had haunted him from that day forward…

What might have been never was.

And though he had never admitted it even to himself, the emptiness Morgan felt inside had driven him from bed to bed, woman to woman until the day of his capture by the Mizarian Empire. There were, on occasion, vague dreams of powerful alien arms enfolding him, thin lips caressing him intimately, long-boned hands cupping his face.

Maybe the legends were true after all. Maybe Lucien really had cast a spell upon him forever.

What might have been…

But in the Mizarian prison, Morgan's dreams became less frequent. The memories started to fade. The past abandoned him, leaving him once more alone.

Now, mercifully, he no longer remembered his dreams.

~

Morgan stumbled blindly from the room, his breath catching in his throat as he burst through the doors and staggered, trembling and shaken, to lean heavily against the corridor wall. For a moment, he could actually smell the cool scent of Mother Forest, could taste the spicy flavor of death as Lucien's hands strangled life from his body. But worse, he could still *see* the aftermath laid out on the table of his mind like pieces of a puzzle waiting to be worked.

Reality and illusion overlapped in his thoughts, tearing down the fabric of what had been and re-forming into the dangerous tapestry of fantasies never lived out. His stomach heaved, clenching violently as his mind replayed a scene from the nightmare the meditation had revealed.

He saw himself on his own bed, asleep in his quarters on board the *Starling*. Like a distant lullaby, the ship's engines sang to him, calling him into a peaceful slumber, making him secure in the knowledge that, once again, he and Lucien had beaten the odds. They had taken on all of Alfar, Xander and Katrice, Dunwillow and Shalice, tradition and alien biology... and they'd come out on top.

And as an added bonus, he had the distinct impression that, given time, their friendship would blossom into something... more. Their minds had touched – in the chaos of combat, true, but they *had* touched. Secrets long denied had been there for the viewing. In the throes of his own death, Morgan had revealed himself – heart, body and soul. And he'd seen Lucien's fantasies played out as well.

And yet, as he lay in a state half-way between sleep and wakefulness, he was only peripherally aware of the door to his suite opening. A tall, elegant silhouette seemed to float across the misted space of dreams; and in another moment, a comforting weight settled on the bed.

Lucien?

A cooler than human hand touched his face, fingers skimming through his disheveled hair. And without even considering the possible consequences Morgan had opened himself, his mind screaming "*Yes!*" as he realized time had finally stopped for them. In a split-second fantasy, he saw himself in Lucien's arms, felt their mouths come together in a phantom kiss that rivaled even the one they had shared in the arms of Mother Forest, experienced the anticipation of knowing that, in another moment, they would make love.

It was then that the position of the hand had shifted, alien index finger pressing softly against the human 'third eye', and the overwhelming totality of Alfarian telepathy flared open between them. Love had been there. Lucien's alien love. Morgan's human love. And the fear spawned in the darkest space between both worlds.

And yet, in another moment, the memories were gone, and Morgan was left with only what Lucien allowed him to recall, and that through a vague and distant haze, like a half-remembered dream. They had fought together as a result of Shalice's command on Lucien. They had re-affirmed their friendship back on board the *Starling*. And they had, with honor and respect, returned to the lives they had led before. Indeed, with the memories discreetly removed, the "before" and the "after" were precisely the same.

That, Morgan now knew, was the ultimate lie.

And yet, leaning against the cold metal bulkhead of the

Dreaming Bird, he was no longer certain what had *really* happened, and what his mind had only conjured. He gasped again as the memory stabbed at him like a merciless knife, then slapped his fist hard against the wall, barely flinching as his knuckles came away bloody.

"Ta ta ta!" a now-familiar voice scolded. "The ship is old. Does not take well to unwarranted punishments from angry students!"

Barely realizing where he was at that moment, Morgan glanced up sharply to find Kim Le standing less than a foot away, his face twisted into something bordering on a frown. For a moment, he wanted to vent his frustrations on the strange little old man, wanted to shout and scream and pound his fists against the other's weathered flesh. And yet, as he recognized the frailness of age, he held his physical violence inside, his hands clenching and unclenching as he wrestled with the heat of his rage.

"I can't *do* this!" he snapped emphatically.

"Can't do what?" the other inquired with utter calmness guiding his words.

Morgan sighed heavily, gnawing his lower lip to keep from screaming. "I don't know what's *real* anymore!" he returned harshly. "I go into that room for what's supposed to be a serene period of meditation, and I come *out* feeling like I've been beaten to death by my own mind!"

Kim Le's grayed brows lifted slightly. "The man who perpetrated the idea that meditation is only for relaxation was indeed a fool, Morgan," he said, his answer more direct than normal. Then, taking a step forward, he reached out to rest one hand reassuringly on Morgan's arm. "The mind is like a small stream flowing into a much vaster sea. So long as one remains in the shallow waters or sits on the shore, the dangers do not exist. But," he added with a gentle squeeze to Morgan's elbow, "when one begins to explore the *sea... that* is where the waters can become rough, and where the explorer can drown without proper precautions."

For the moment, Morgan wasn't interested in analogous philosophy. His arms and legs were trembling violently, and his stomach remained tied in knots which sent pain shooting through every molecule of his existence. He jerked his head toward the door which bore the suddenly-ominous yin/yang symbol.

"Don't you understand?" he pressed angrily. "I can't even tell the difference between what *is* real and what I *want* to be real?" His face reddened and, putting a tighter leash on his rampaging emotions, he closed his eyes and drew a deep breath through his nostrils. Then, with desperation in his heart, he looked up until he met Kim Le's gaze. "Look, I don't expect an answer. I don't expect you to even understand."

"Answers change as your questions become more complex, Morgan," Kim Le said quietly. "And as for understanding, that is something which must come from within yourself. Reality is as you perceive it. It is not necessary that your reality and mine be compatible. It is only necessary for you to accept *your* reality and mold it according to your own wishes."

Sighing again, Morgan leaned more heavily against the wall, grateful for its solidity to hold him upright. He said nothing, weary of trying to reason with wisdom. In a flash of self-doubt and fury, he wondered what had become of the starship commander he had once been, the legendary Cap'n Morgan Diego who ate bureaucrats for breakfast and washed them down with Sirian Rum. That man had endured the tortures of space, the rejection of kings and lords, the scorn of the brass, the notorious labels of pirate, scoundrel and worse... only to be ground up and spit out by this dastardly state of love.

If it weren't so pathetic, it would have been... well... pathetic.

And as if sensing his very thoughts, Kim Le sighed, too. Then, folding his legs neatly, he lowered himself to the uncarpeted floor of the narrow corridor, looking up to Morgan's fearful, determined stare.

"Sit with me," he encouraged.

Morgan blinked. Somehow, the corridor seemed an unlikely place for an extended conversation; and he wasn't at all interested in psychoanalyzing his mind's fantasies for an audience. He waved the old man's words aside with a gesture.

"Maybe later," he evaded, and started to turn away, stopping only when he felt a surprisingly firm grip on his ankle.

"Sit," Kim Le instructed, his tone becoming more authoritative. "Until you find your peace, you are of no use to me."

For a reason Morgan couldn't pinpoint, that insinuation penetrated his anger, causing him to stop in his retreat. It would have been easy to allow his fury full reign, even easier to strut off to his assigned bunk and tell the crazy little old man to throw him out at the next habitable planet. And yet, he realized with a pang of humbleness that he had no desire to sleep again in the streets, no wish to fight with rats for his food or trifle with beggars and misfits for passage on another rocket bound for Nowhere.

It wasn't a simple matter, however, to bend, to admit that, for once, he was completely dependent on the kindness of others. He looked down at Kim Le, not terribly surprised to find an encouraging smile on the little man's face. It softened him just enough and, reluctantly, he leaned against the bulkhead and slid wearily to the cold deck.

For a few long minutes, silence passed between them; and though he couldn't be certain, he had the distinct impression that the old man was attempting to project some vibration of calmness into the space which separated them. He waited, listening to the drone of the small ship's engines, counting the seconds as they lengthened and grew. An unlikely scent of pumpkin pie and cinnamon wafted on the recycled air... portends of dinner sneaking out from the small galley at the end of the corridor.

Finally, Kim Le spoke, his voice soft and filled with compassion. "Your past haunts you," he murmured. "It will continue to do so until you are at rest with it."

It wasn't what Morgan wanted to hear, but he made an honest effort to be civil. His mind was still raw with the meditation-awakened memories and, closing his eyes for just a moment, he tried to gain some perspective which refused to manifest. "The only way I'll ever be at peace with the past is to go back to the *Starling*," he said quietly, "to go back to my... friends." Somehow, the word seemed strangely inappropriate now as he thought of Lucien. It was more than that, he knew... yet somehow far less. But he didn't permit himself time to dwell on it at that particular second. Instead, he looked up, facing the truth which lingered like a demon in his mind. "The hard part is accepting that I *can't* go back."

Once more, Kim Le was silent as he contemplated that statement. "As you are now, Morgan, you are correct. You cannot return. For if you did, your Mizarian tormentors would undoubtedly carry out their threat and many innocent lives would be lost to their treachery." He shook his head. "There would be no honor in that – not for you, not for your friends, not even for the Mizarians." He paused as if to let that settle. "But if you will trust me, if you will try to stop fighting *yourself*, it is possible that what you now *believe* to be true will turn out to be nothing more than an illusion."

Morgan's brows narrowed. "I don't understand," he confessed, frustration growing.

Kim Le smiled faintly. "Knowledge is the greatest bargaining tool of all, Morgan," he replied evasively. "When your training is complete, you will have acquired great knowledge, even greater awareness. It is a marketable commodity."

But Morgan only scoffed. "But it won't change anything, Kim Le," he said quietly, fervently. "No matter what I learn now or in the future will change the *past*." He shook his head, fighting the urge to pound the walls again.

"Are you so certain?" Kim Le asked, interrupting his misery and self-pity.

He glanced up sharply. "What are you trying to tell me?"

Kim Le looked away for a moment, his eyes closing as he drew a deep breath, seemingly lost in some private thought. When he met Morgan's gaze again, his expression was more open, his words more direct. "Past, present and future all co-exist simultaneously, Morgan," he said. "All are connected, therefore all can be affected by one's actions at any moment. What was true yesterday is not necessarily true today... nor will it be true tomorrow."

Morgan considered that in silence for a moment. He realized abruptly that Kim Le *was* trying to tell him something. He also realized that the old man was quite deliberately couching his every word in riddles. And yet, relying on intuition which had seen him through a lifetime of decisions, he understood that his trust in the other wasn't misplaced. Still, *giving* that trust didn't come easily.

He started to pursue it with another barrage of questions, then abruptly changed his mind as the meditation-awakened memories whispered uninvited through his thoughts. His stomach clenched involuntarily, his hands tightening to fists, then relaxing as he noted the reaction.

Looking up, he held the old man's gaze steadily. "If you'll answer just *one* question for me – in terms I can understand," he clarified, "I'll try to go on with all of this."

Kim Le's brows lifted in conjunction with the corners of his mouth. "A bargain?"

Despite himself, Morgan smiled, shrugging one shoulder. "I guess you could call it that."

Kim Le bowed his head in acknowledgement. "What is your question?"

Morgan took a moment to phrase it correctly, choosing words which would leave no room for philosophical interpretation. Then, haltingly, he laid it in the air. "In my meditation, I experienced something that may or may not have really happened. It involved an old friend," he added, the word wringing his heart, causing his voice to drop lower. "If it *did* happen... then I have no choice but to try to somehow get back the life I had before."

"And if it didn't?" Kim Le inquired.

Morgan took a deep, trembling breath. He hadn't had time to think about *that* possibility, hadn't even had time to analyze the plethora of emotions tumbling head over heels through his mind. But his answer came quickly.

"If it didn't... then I want to know that, too," he decided.

Kim Le studied him for an extended period of time. "Why is it important for you to know?"

Holding his breath, Morgan realized he had no immediate response. He settled for the feelings which far outweighed reason. "He was someone I cared about a great deal," he said evasively.

Kim Le smiled faintly. "A lover?"

Despite himself, Morgan felt heat rise in his cheeks. "No!" he protested automatically. "We were friends. We served together for many years."

But the smile didn't recede from the old man's colorless lips.

"Lovers are not only those who share bed and wine, Morgan," he said gently. "A lover is anyone deserving of your love... anyone who loves you in return. In the night, when we sleep, all compatible souls sleep together; what we do with our physical selves is of secondary consideration."

Feeling the uselessness of denial, Morgan lowered his eyes, staring at the nondescript gray floor. "I... I have to know if what I saw in my meditation... really happened," he repeated.

Silence answered him, then Kim Le. "Do you believe it did?"

But Morgan waved that response aside with a gesture of his hand. "It doesn't matter what I *believe* anymore," he said, sounding like a looped tape message even to his own ears. "I have to *know*."

"The knowing, as we have discussed previously, must come from within." Kim Le paused, then reached out once more to rest his hand on Morgan's arm. "Within yourself, you can access all truths – whether personal or higher truths." He squeezed gently, reassuringly. "Through meditation, things of the past are often awakened – things the conscious mind may have forgotten–."

"Or been *made* to forget," Morgan interjected quietly.

Kim Le inclined his head. "Nothing is ever truly forgotten, Morgan. It can only be temporarily misplaced. Perhaps what you experienced in your meditation was the reunion of a temporarily misplaced thought with your contemporary reality."

Morgan scoffed despite himself. "Or maybe it was nothing more than wishful thinking," he countered, not knowing whether that conclusion was a comforting hope or a miserable truth. He sighed again, shaking his head. "In the end, it doesn't matter anyway."

For a long time, Kim Le didn't reply. Then, squeezing Morgan's arm fervently, he released the breath he'd been holding. "What you experienced was real," he said very quietly.

Morgan didn't look up, didn't even move. "How can you be so sure? You don't even know what I experienced."

Kim Le smiled faintly, almost to himself. "If the pain is this great, the need to know so strong, then your experience is based in truth. Illusions are fleeting, quickly set aside. Only the truth holds the power to nurture such pain... or the ecstasy which is its opposite."

Somehow, that explanation seemed entirely too simple to be correct. And yet, when Morgan mentally relived the experience in a second's fraction, his stomach clenched, driving the pain a little deeper. It was the same pain, he realized, that he'd felt the day he'd been taken by the Mizarians, the same pain of separation he'd felt when he and Lucien had embraced... and ultimately parted.

What troubled him most was the fact that he'd been somehow blinded to the truth for such a terribly long time. When he'd gone into the Mizarian Empire, the incident with Shalice had been two years in the past. Now, re-awakened, it seemed to be happening all over again. Perhaps, he conceded, Kim Le was right. Perhaps the past, present and future *were* all interconnected. Memories of the past awakened impossible dreams of the future, all of which culminated in his present confusion, anger and depression.

Emotions tumbled like destructive rock-slides through his spirit, leaving him drained and uncertain. A part of him rebelled against the idea that he'd been unconsciously in love with his second-in-command without even knowing it. It rebelled even more at the thought that he'd been in love with Lucien *at all*. Not in the rule books. No fraternization among crew members. The usual yada. The bureaucratic rhetoric. And Morgan liked to think he played by the rules, though both Vanya and Lucien had pointed out to him numerous times that – regardless of the braid on his shoulder – he was a pirate at heart and a rebel in spirit. And though he would have been hard-pressed to admit it just then, he came to see that without the power sparking from his fingertips as a star commander, it was just a little easier to visualize loving someone more powerful than himself.

His face darkened, shame filling him at the thought. He wondered absently how he'd survived his arrogant youth. He'd gone from bed to bed, planet to planet, lover to lover, with his cock pointing the way to the next encounter. Mostly women. One or two exceptional men. Even an androgynous alien or two. But he'd never been in love.

Never, that is, until *now*.

Now, humbled by the sacrifice Lucien had apparently made –

for there was no denying that the love *he* had felt in that telepathic whirlpool had been vital and alive - Morgan dropped his face into his hands, rubbing his eyes with the heels of his hands. Lucien had sacrificed *love* in order to give him back his command, his sense of equilibrium, to insure that the rules and the regulations were safe, and that the two of them would go on rescuing damsels in distress and notching their bedposts with the spoils of their shore leave seductions (all meaningless, he reminded himself)… and somewhere in the background of telepathically-erased ex-memories lay the only *real* love Morgan had ever known.

Forgotten.

Lost.

Taken.

What bothered him most of all was the fact that Lucien had made that sacrifice for *him*, never asking him what in all the worlds *he* might want. He wondered fleetingly if Lucien had *wanted* to forget… if indeed Lucien *had* forgotten the outlandish incident just as he forced Morgan to forget.

In that moment, he was too shaken to mentally ask *why* the sacrifice was even necessary.

CHAPTER SIX

Lucien jerked awake, confused and disoriented as he peered through the oppressive darkness. Even without sufficient lighting, he perceived that the colors were wrong, the scent of the room different, the oxygen-mixture too rich in the air.

Fragments of a dream taunted him to full awareness, causing him to realize with a very uncharacteristic sigh of dismay that he was still at Earthbase One, in a room reserved for visiting dignitaries and star cruiser commanders.

Somehow, the title seemed inappropriate when he overlaid it onto himself. It occurred to him that, in all probability, Morgan Diego had slept in the same bed *he* now inhabited; and though that thought should have brought some sense of comfort, it only served to awaken the sharp pain which had been his constant companion for more than eight months.

Frustrated with his inability to meditate properly or even to sleep, he sat up in the strange, too-soft bed, folding his legs underneath him and drawing the covers up over his shoulders to ward off the cold draft from the air conditioning vents. He realized with some sense of distress that the dreams were becoming more pronounced, more disturbing; and the fact that no physical cause was to blame left him feeling decidedly undisciplined. His father certainly would not have approved, and though that thought *should* have renewed his commitment to discipline, it brought a nasty sense of satisfaction to his heart instead.

And yet…

Now, the dreams had even dared to trespass into forbidden territory – territory clearly marked as untouchable, memories labeled in blood and tears as impossibilities.

For a moment, as he'd awakened, some once-known truth had been there. And yet, as awareness returned, the fragments of the past slipped away, burying themselves in the blanketing forest of his own distant planet. For an instant, he had been back on Alfar, his mind befuddled by Shalice's sorcery as he fought the one man he had ever dared call 'friend'. For a second, he had brushed the human's thoughts, had felt his own blood surge as their minds locked accidentally together. The fire of the Need had filled him as certainly as if he'd imbibed it in an aphrodisiac potion. And, in his delusional state, he had imagined throwing Morgan to the floor of Mother Forest, avowing himself to the alluring human for all of eternity, and burying himself body and spirit into the other's pliant flesh.

Then, abruptly, he was back on the *Starling*. Morgan was whole. And something in the human's eyes had terrified him to the core of his soul. That alien something, Lucien knew, was human love.

And fear had motivated the only possible choice. He'd torn the love from Morgan's heart as he slept – taking the memories and wrapping them in a sterile bandage, then burying them in a crypt far beneath the surface of Alfar's golden moon. He'd buried his own feelings in the same tomb – so deep that even the memories themselves had been lost in the frantic shuffle.

But now, sitting alone in a strange bed, he realized with a sense of horror that the burial vault had cracked open, spilling its fermented contents on the ground before him. He backed away, yet the images followed him, accusing him of a thousand dreadful atrocities as he retreated from the onslaught.

What surprised him was that, in reality, he never flinched. Instead, he remained mute and still in the center of the bed. His body trembled against the cold of the room, perhaps even against the coldness that had once resided in his heart. He didn't move, didn't breathe, and eventually he even ceased resisting the truth.

The truth stated, in elegant and simple terms, that his mind was already inexorably linked with Morgan's. It also informed him with remarkable simplicity that the link hadn't been broken in his desperate attempt to remove shameful fantasies from his own memories and from the human's mind as well.

The truth also told him something else. Somewhere, in whatever life he was consigned to live now, Morgan knew the same truth. It didn't matter that they had never had an opportunity to carry out the thoughts which had trampled uninvited through their minds. It didn't even matter that he, in his own admitted terror, had stolen those thoughts and drowned them like helpless animals in some rushing river.

What mattered was that, somewhere, Morgan *knew*.

Lucien sat for a very long time contemplating that thought, unable to drive it from his mind, unable to convince himself that he was alone in his re-awakened knowledge. He glanced at the clock, watching its red digital numbers count off the minutes and seconds until morning.

When the dawn came, he would meet with Bryse.

But his eyes grew heavy and, exhausted, he fell into a restless sleep, clutching the blanket desperately to his chest as he sat crumpled in a cold and lonely bed.

~

"I'm sure you can understand, Captain Lucien, Doctor Vanya, that anything I say to you today is completely off the record."

The 'meeting' was anything other than what Lucien was accustomed to. Instead of the sterile atmosphere of the admiral's office at Galaxy Corps Headquarters, Bryse had insisted they meet at a secluded end of a public beach on Coronado Island. Now, walking through the hard-packed wet sand near the water's edge, Lucien recognized the symptoms of nervousness in Galaxy Corps' most controversial figurehead.

Bryse moved cautiously, looking over his shoulder from time to time, continuously adjusting an electronic device attached to his belt – a device which Lucien recognized as a sophisticated voice scrambler, capable of garbling their conversation in the event anyone was bothering to listen. He took those facts in quietly, glancing to Bryse's other side to see Vanya fidgeting unnecessarily with the tie belt on his civilian clothing. As was usual when dealing with the Galaxy Corps bureaucracy, Vanya had said nothing other than customary small-talk since their arrival at Bryse's specified meeting place.

The morning was cold, Lucien thought, walking slowly at Bryse's side as he waited for the old admiral to reveal whatever secrets he saw fit. The fog was thick along the shoreline, and low gray clouds misted the ground – and the only three figures on the beach – with an almost invisible spray. Concealed in the fog, distant and somehow eerie, a lone seagull whistled a repeating cry, calling to a lost mate.

Lucien straightened his jacket, pulling the collar more tightly about his neck to ward off the brisk San Diego wind as he shivered involuntarily.

At last, Bryse stopped walking, adjusted the device on his belt once more, then sighed heavily as he turned abruptly to face the other two. "I realize this may seem a little bit too much like cloak-and-dagger, Captain Lucien," he began with a wistful smile, the wind teasing through the straight black hair. "But as I'm sure you're aware, this whole Mizarian Treaty has caused somewhat of a stir throughout the Empire."

Lucien considered that; Bryse had always been noted for his achievements in the art of understatement. For himself, he was weary and tired, and a quick glance at Vanya confirmed the doctor's impatience as well.

"Just exactly what's being done to locate Commander Diego?" Vanya inquired, shivering just a little as the winds whipped over the shoreline.

Bryse was silent for a moment as he looked back and forth between Vanya and Lucien. When he did reply, his voice was low, strained and weary. "Locating Morgan isn't the problem. We've known exactly where he's been ever since his exile." He paused, seemed to wrestle with some inner turmoil, then took a step closer as if fearful of the conversation being overheard by invisible phantoms. "The problem is simply that there's a wide difference of opinion in Galaxy Corps and the Empire Council as well at this time, gentlemen."

"Meaning?" Vanya inquired.

"Meaning," Bryse repeated, "that there are more than a few people who are for maintaining the status quo exactly as it is." He paused, glancing at the ground. "In simple language, gentlemen, the majority of those in power don't want to do *anything* that might provoke a war with the Mizarians." Then, turning his gaze on Lucien, he added: "We've had ample time to view the holo-tapes

84

provided by the *Starling*; and if the reports filed by yourself and Commander Diego weren't sufficient, those tapes were more than enough to convince everybody that we can't possibly come out on top of any confrontation with the Mizarians."

Lucien felt his patience stretching thinner as he listened to Bryse reciting facts and figures, stating the obvious and, in words Morgan might have chosen, 'doing a song and dance' around the main issue. When the admiral finished his lengthy speech concerning protocol and proper Galaxy Corps/Empire diplomacy, Lucien found himself barely listening.

"Admiral," he began, coming directly to the point, "certainly Galaxy Corps must realize that the Mizarian ultimatum could possibly be only the first step in a series of demands. It was my understanding that the Empire was intolerant of such insinuations of aggression, whether immediate or implied."

Bryse smiled knowingly. "We *don't* tolerate it under normal circumstances. But I'm sure you'll agree that the circumstances here are anything but normal. From what we've seen, a single Mizarian ship has more fire-power than the combined forces of the Galaxy Corps and private military vessels in Empire territory. We can't even *begin* to fight them."

"Agreed," Lucien conceded. "However, the Mizarians most certainly understand that. Were they a conquering race such as the Prelians or even the Nel-fens, they would have attacked some time ago." He wondered why *he*, too, seemed compelled to rattle off the obvious. Passing it off to lack of sleep and mental exhaustion, he forged ahead. "I assume that normal channels of diplomacy have proven ineffective."

Bryse shrugged in an uncharacteristic fashion. "The Mizarians are a reasonable people – at least some of them are," he added hastily. "We're hopeful that some sort of compromise can eventually be reached."

"And is Commander Diego to be considered a part of such a compromise?" Lucien inquired.

Bryse was noticeably uncomfortable with the question. "Unfortunately, from what little feedback we've been getting through diplomatic, the Mizarian High Council is immovable so far as any possible reversal of their decision concerning Morgan." His jaw twitched almost imperceptibly. "As I understand it, it's a matter of honor with them; they *know* that Morgan was acting under covert orders, and they want to make an example of him for anyone else who might be foolish enough to accept similar orders in the future. They don't even want to discuss it."

"Then what do they want?" Vanya demanded, blue eyes intense as they met Bryse's brown stare. "And for that matter, if they wanted *anything*, they could just walk in and take it. Why don't they?"

"It's not that simple," Bryse said. "They don't want a war anymore than we do. If they did, the incident nine months ago would have been sufficient to provoke one." He was silent for a moment, seemingly lost in thought. Then, looking up to Lucien, he continued. "From what we can understand, they communicate primarily with telepathy. They've even fought wars with it in their ancient past."

Lucien's brows lifted. It was a fact of which he'd been previously unaware. "Wars?"

Bryse nodded. "They're very formidable telepaths," he explained quietly.

Lucien had no immediate comment as he contemplated that information in silence. The clouds had parted just enough to allow a single ray of sunlight to penetrate and, looking out toward the ocean, he watched the warmth glisten on cold waters. Then, drawing his attention back to Bryse, he tried to drive away the sense of hopeless frustration and melancholy which had followed him to the shoreline.

"Admiral," he began with as much diplomacy as he could muster, "while I am intensely interested in the Mizarian matter, I am certain you are aware that my primary concern is for Commander Diego." His sudden forthright attitude surprised him less than the weariness which prompted it. "I have formulated a plan whereby it may be possible for me to contact the commander without his direct knowledge of who I am."

At that, Bryse's thick brows shot high, and Lucien saw him fidget uncomfortably, his eyes glancing quickly away. He also saw

86

Vanya execute a classic double-take, but ignored the shrink's unspoken barrage of questions.

"Galaxy Corps won't authorize any contact with Commander Diego," Bryse stated firmly.

"I am aware of that," Lucien said, knowing he did not need to voice the rest.

Again Bryse shifted weight uncomfortably, then reached to the device on his belt, checking its settings, adjusting it slightly, then finally looking up. "For what it's worth, Captain Lucien," he replied evasively, "there are a number of us within the hierarchy of Galaxy Corps – and the Empire Council, I might add – who *don't* agree with the public stand."

Lucien considered the double-talk carefully. "And?"

"Unofficially, there are a lot of people in high places who feel that Morgan got the short end of the stick – he ended up taking the blame for what was, essentially, an Empire screw-up."

"So what's your point?" Vanya asked, becoming more obviously perturbed as the conversation progressed. "If everybody's so damn worried about starting a war, and if this Mizarian mind-whatever-it-is-link is as powerful as everyone seems to think it is, then there's only two possibilities." He paused grimly, glancing to Lucien, then back to Bryse. "We either accept the Mizarian Law – and the best commander in the Fleet is sent up the creek without a paddle. Or we ignore the Mizarian Directive and start a war we have no chance of winning."

Bryse perused Vanya silently. "What would *you* do, Liam?"

Vanya blinked, seemingly taken aback by the question. "I'm not a politician," he snapped. "If it were up to *me*, I'd probably give some serious thought to eradicating the entire Mizarian race!"

"Which is precisely why you are *not* a politician," Lucien commented, realizing the human's renowned temper was close to flaring. "At any rate," he added, turning back to Bryse, "since you profess to know the whereabouts of Commander Diego, I presume you have some plan."

Bryse glanced back and forth between the two of them, seemed to have some lengthy mental argument with himself, then finally replied. "As I understand it, the Mizarians have established a permanent directional link with Commander Diego. If that link is broken by another telepath, such as an Alfarian healer, for example, war is the result. On the other hand, if Morgan could learn to *block* the link without breaking it...." His voice trailed off, leaving volumes unspoken.

Lucien traded glances with a seemingly confused Vanya, then returned his attention to Bryse. "If the commander could learn to block the link, it's conceivable that the Mizarians would regard such an occurrence as a natural weakening."

Bryse shrugged. "Maybe," he agreed. "Or maybe that's the *one* thing the little bastards would consider trading for Morgan's freedom."

Lucien's brows narrowed. "I do not understand."

Bryse smiled deviously. "From what we understand, their telepathic wars almost destroyed their entire civilization – because of their *inability* to shield. Now I'm no telepath myself, but isn't it true that a telepathic attack could just as easily work against the *attacker* as against the person or persons under attack?"

Lucien considered that. "It is a possibility," he conceded, though he saw it as a slim hope. "Any form of telepathy, no matter how advanced, is still relatively imprecise. Without the ability to shield against such attacks, it is certainly conceivable that both sides would be equally at risk regardless of which 'side' perpetrated the initial assault."

Bryse nodded. "Exactly."

Lucien frowned. "I don't see what that has to do with Commander Diego."

"I'm sure you're aware of the legend of Achilles, Captain Lucien?"

Lucien nodded, not quite sure what ancient myths had to do with his commander either.

"It's a long shot," Bryse admitted, "but we're *hoping* that the Mizarians' inability to shield against their own telepathy is *their* Achilles' heel."

Lucien wondered fleetingly if his powers of comprehension had evaded him. "I *still* fail to see how that has anything to do with Commander Diego's current situation."

"If he can learn to block against their link," Bryse explained, "then *maybe* the Mizarians will see us as more of a threat than they do at the present time. They've had essentially no contact with the Empire other than what the *Starling* and Morgan has brought them. Now if he *can* learn to shield, to block their link, it's possible that they'll start to worry about the possibility of our attacking *them* telepathically."

"Now *that's* a long shot if ever I've heard one!" Vanya interjected, frowning. "Do you honestly believe that a race with that much firepower is going to give a damn if one insignificant human learns to block some hocus-pocus mind link?"

But Bryse only smiled. "Have you ever heard the saying, Doctor, that the man with the club must fight twice as hard to defend himself against the man with the sword?" But he didn't allow Vanya to reply, turning instead to Lucien. "I f we want to regain some sort of balance of power with the Mizarians, we're going to have to take a few unconventional risks. Which," he emphasized, "is where Morgan comes in."

Lucien's brows lifted. He was beginning – slowly – to follow Bryse's convoluted thought patterns. "Precisely where *is* the commander?"

The old admiral smiled confidently. "Within another two days, he'll be right here on Earth."

"I see." Lucien ignored the fact that his heart beat a little faster at that revelation.

Bryse nodded, his brows furrowing to a thoughtful frown. "To be perfectly honest, Captain Lucien, I hadn't planned on telling you as much as I have. There are a lot of people involved in this; a lot of careers and a lot of lives are at stake."

Lucien inclined his head, ignoring the confused expression on Vanya's features. "I understand, Admiral," he said quietly. "However, I am certain you are aware of the fact that Commander Diego and myself served together for many years."

Bryse smiled faintly. "I'm well aware of Alfarian loyalty," he agreed. "That's why I'd rather have you in on this – where I can keep an eye on you – than off doing god knows what behind my back."

Bryse seemed to know him well.

"You said you had a plan," the admiral recalled, starting once more to walk down the jagged California shoreline. "I'd like to hear it."

"You're not the only one," Vanya agreed, mumbling as if to himself, but nonetheless falling into step as they moved on through fog and misting drizzle.

Lucien ignored the doctor for the moment, focusing instead on Bryse. But before outlining his plan, one question had to be answered – for his own peace of mind if nothing else. "Precisely where is Commander Diego at this time, Admiral?" he asked again.

The other man shook his head with a light laugh. "A long time ago – when I was a Cadet at the Academy," he clarified, "I met this old man at a bar in Chinatown. He was one of those people who was *born* old, if you take my meaning. Anyway, to make a long story short, he has more wisdom in his little finger than most of us store in our brains in a lifetime. Right about now, if I know Morgan Diego, Kim Le is probably tearing out his hair – if he has any left to tear out after all these years."

Lucien didn't pursue the string of confusing statements, but honed in directly on the point. "Then... you have hired this Kim Le to guard Commander Diego."

"Guard?" Bryse repeated. "Not really. We hired Kim Le to get Morgan and bring him back to Earth – at space-standard speed. Morgan has a lot to learn," he added. "And Kim Le was the only person on this planet or any other that I could imagine trying to *teach* him anything." He laughed again, more relaxed and with genuine amusement. "Kim Le is also the only person I know that probably can't be hood-winked by Morgan's bullshit – *or* his charisma."

That was something Lucien easily comprehended. Entire empires had fallen in the wake of the infamous Morgan Diego. Sorcerers and self-proclaimed gods had been driven to ruination by his cunning. But, with a supreme effort, he tore his mind from that dangerous train of thought and concentrated on the problem at hand. Then, with slow and deliberate words, he detailed his plan to Bryse, stopping occasionally to silence Vanya's incredulous protests.

By the time he'd finished, the clouds had burned off just enough for the sun to cast dim shadows on the wet-packed sand. And, for a single instant as he looked at his own shadow on the ground, it almost seemed as if another, shorter and thicker, stood at his side.

At the very least, with Bryse mentally digesting the details he'd laid forth, Lucien began to hope once more. He knew that, realistically, the admiral would be hard-pressed to deny the possibilities inherent in his well-planned scheme.

For the first time, he felt remarkably like a star commander, though he couldn't help wondering if that sensation was merely a bleed-over from the invisible shadow lingering at his side.

CHAPTER SEVEN

Exhausted and bone-weary, Morgan held his fighting stance until his arms and legs trembled. Myrddin, not even winded from the extended work-out, stood before him, the long legs neatly bent into a horse stance powerful arms performing the intricate sets and forms which were the basis for the entire training.

As they simultaneously performed the final move of the Leopard Set, Morgan took a deep but slowly controlled breath, feeling an odd combination of tiredness and exhilaration. He had been training with Myrddin for less than two weeks, and already he'd advanced through two ranks – perhaps not with as much grace and style as his experienced teacher, but certainly with sufficient knowledge and prowess to perform the techniques recognizably.

Completing the formal salutation which marked the end of the Set, he stepped at once to a natural stance, catching his breath as Myrddin perused him. It occurred to him that he had taken an intense liking to the Alfarian, that he wanted to perform well to please his teacher as well as to please himself. And, judging by the look in the normally impassive dark eyes, Morgan had the feeling he'd succeeded in both departments.

But, as usual, Myrddin gave no outward praise or encouragement. His lack of criticism, Morgan had figured out, was more than adequate approval.

The thin brows narrowed very slightly as Myrddin stood with his hands clasped neatly behind his back. "What do you think of as you perform the Set, Morgan?"

Morgan frowned at the unexpected question. "I *don't* think," he replied, only then realizing it. He grinned slightly. "It's hard enough to keep all the moves in the proper sequence."

Myrddin inclined his head in acknowledgement. "It is good you understand that, Morgan," he said in his normal quiet tone. "And as you perfect this art, you will achieve even greater awareness."

Morgan considered that, feeling decidedly more relaxed with Myrddin now than he had a week before. "Awareness?" he questioned. "Of?"

The thin Alfarian lips curved upward just a little and, with a momentary pang, Morgan realized that Myrddin smiled far more easily than Lucien had ever done. It was both comforting and reassuring.

"As you perfect this physical art, Morgan," Myrddin revealed, "your mind will begin to flow naturally in a balanced rhythm. Focus becomes a part of your nature rather than something requiring concentration." He paused briefly, then took a step forward, indicating with his body language that the day's work-out was completed. "By practicing the physical art, you are training your mind to ignore those things which are of no consequence."

Morgan wondered what he was driving at, and frowned as he considered the other's words. "You mean I'm gaining one kind of awareness by sacrificing another?"

Myrddin turned his head slightly to one side. "In a manner of speaking, yes," he agreed. "What you are gaining is the awareness of your Self and your surroundings. What you are dismissing is the petty awareness of trivialities."

Not certain he understood, Morgan pondered that idea further, and found that it didn't entirely set right with him. "Intuition has been something that I've always depended on, Master," he said humbly. "Will the training diminish it?"

Myrddin's thin black brows furrowed slightly, as if in private contemplation. "In the beginning, it is possible that your intuition will be diminished," he confirmed. "But remember, Morgan, you are still at the initiate level in your training. A man must learn to kill before perfecting the finer skills of knowing how *not* to kill. Later, when you are an adept, your intuition will be more finely-tuned than ever before. But you must learn to focus on a single goal at each given moment."

"I'm not sure I understand," Morgan confessed honestly. On the one hand, Myrddin was telling him to shut down his intuition. On another level entirely, the Alfarian seemed to be saying that *gaining* intuition was the long-term goal. What puzzled him was why he needed to *gain* what had always been a natural part of his existence.

Myrddin was silent for a long moment, in unspoken thought. Finally, looking up, took a step back and moved into the typical training horse stance. "Ready position, Morgan," he instructed.

Morgan blinked, wondering if he'd missed something along the way, but moved nonetheless into the requested stance.

"Now," Myrddin said in a quiet but firm tone, "ready yourself for attack."

Doing as he was told, Morgan shifted into a right fighting stance, relying as he'd been instructed to do on the strength of his natural right-handedness. Normally in such exercises, Myrddin would spring some unannounced attack, expecting him to defend himself accordingly.

But as Morgan waited for what seemed like several minutes, staring fixedly into his instructor's penetrating dark gaze, the Alfarian never moved until, finally, he returned to a relaxed natural stance.

Morgan was admittedly perplexed, but didn't move from his defending position, well aware that the Alfarian could easily swing around behind him, catching him unprepared the moment he dropped his guard. It wouldn't be the first time and, having learned from that particular mistake, he held his ground.

"The attack is done, Morgan," Myrddin said. "Face me."

Blinking the confusion from his eyes, Morgan straightened, waiting for some explanation. "I don't understand," he repeated. It seemed to be his favorite phrase while in the training area.

Myrddin's lips pressed together, a faint smile. "An attack need not be perpetrated on a physical level, Morgan," he revealed. "In learning to protect your body, you are also learning to protect your mind."

At that, Morgan felt a keen sense of surprise. It occurred to him that he hadn't sensed the presence of the Mizarian mind link in several days. And yet, there could have been a completely logical explanation for that fact. It was, he conceded, entirely possible that the seer simply hadn't bothered to probe.

He considered his response carefully. "I mean no disrespect, Master, but I have to be more certain than that. Kim Le has obviously told you who I am, and why I'm here."

Myrddin nodded agreeably. "I am aware of your past, Morgan."

"Then you know that I can never go back to the life I led

before," Morgan replied, still tasting the bitterness of that statement on his tongue. He also considered another fact. "No matter how proficient I might ever become at the art, I could never risk starting a war between the Empire and the Mizarians. And no matter how much I may *want* to go back – and believe me, I *do* want to go back – I couldn't put my own wishes above the safety and well-being of so many others."

Myrddin nodded once more. "You are wise to think in such terms, and honorable as well. However, for as long as you are a slave to the Mizarian Empire, your life no longer belongs to you."

Morgan started to protest that he was nobody's slave, but Myrddin waved him to a respectful silence.

"As Kim Le has noted before, you are indeed a ram, a leader. And as you are undoubtedly aware, your own nature is your worst possible enemy."

Morgan frowned. "What do you mean?"

"Simply that, for this moment, you have accepted your exile; perhaps you have even resigned yourself to it as a consequence of the foolishness of the actions which created it," Myrddin said. "But as time progresses, the mind rebels against restrictions of any type. Eventually, you *will* go back, for it is as much a part of your nature to defy and to test your restrictions as it is for you to breathe."

For a very long moment, Morgan stood stunned to silence, mentally digesting Myrddin's conclusions. In the end, he shook his head with a heavy sigh. "I'm not that selfish, Master," he argued. "I know what's at stake if I should ever try to go back to my old life."

"Perhaps that is indeed true now," Myrddin agreed, "but will it be true tomorrow – or in a thousand tomorrows?" He didn't wait for a response. "By the nature of all sentient creatures, the mind forgets what it does not wish to remember. And even if it does not forget, it begins to test its limitations. Now, you have accepted your exile, and your mind is perhaps testing how far and how long it *can* accept. But tomorrow?" he repeated with a wistful shake of his head. "No man can guarantee his actions for the next day, Morgan."

Feeling impossibly confused and even slightly rebellious, Morgan launched a reasonable protest. "But isn't there a point when intellect has to rule over emotions?" he asked hypothetically. "A

95

man *can* guarantee his actions if he understands what's at stake, and if he believes strongly enough in his own principles."

Myrddin's brows lifted skeptically. "A man, perhaps," he conceded. "But never a ram."

Morgan sighed, realizing he had no immediate counter. He wanted very much to protest his innocence and proclaim his honor, yet he realized that neither were in question. And, recalling his own past, he also understood that Myrddin was quite probably correct. In another ten years, or perhaps less, he *would* test his limits in one way or another. Grief could drive him to it. Or anger. Or even arrogance. Sooner or later, the memories of the seer, the recollection of the probe's feel would be softened by time. He'd put one toe over the line, and then a foot. And, if he turned out to be wrong, it wouldn't make much difference. He'd start a war trying to establish his own limitations, much like a child throwing a tantrum to find out exactly how far its luck could be pushed.

Realizing that about himself – about his *species* – did little for his self-confidence and, wearily, he drew a deep breath.

"As I see it," he said with a definite measure of bitterness, "the only solution is to throw myself out an airlock right now. Because if you're right, then it's inevitable that I'm going to do something that'll throw off the entire balance of power between the Empire and the Mizarians." He shook his head, suddenly angry all over again. "Is this just another test?" he asked, not expecting a response. "To see if I'm decent enough to do myself in for the good of the goddamned galaxy?"

Surprisingly, Myrddin had an answer. Even more surprisingly, it came at once, without the normal hesitation. "I will never test you, Morgan, except as a student of the art. As a man, you have already proven your worth."

But Morgan wasn't interested in hearing any of it. He turned abruptly, and started for the door, his awakened anger forcing a heaviness into his steps. He wasn't even certain what *caused* the anger. Perhaps, he conceded, it was the fact that Myrddin was correct: sooner or later, his pride would demand that he defy the Mizarians. No amount of training and discipline would alter what he was inside. He would be as he had always been: a ram among a galaxy of sheep, a pirate soul in the heart of a civilized galaxy.

He wasn't even aware that Myrddin moved until, a moment later, he felt a powerful hand constrict around his upper arm, using his own momentum against him until he turned, stumbling, to face his teacher. Old instincts warred with new training, and he faltered for a fraction of a second. By the time he thought to raise his hand in defense, it occurred to him that Myrddin had no intention of attacking. Instead, the Alfarian stood gazing down at him with an expression which might have been a smile.

"You learn quickly, Morgan," the deep voice intoned.

Morgan experienced a flurry of inconsistent emotions – anger, frustration, confusion, depression, anger again. His jaw tightened. "What do you want from me?" he demanded. "We've spent hours in this room sparring with punches and words, and no matter what I do, you can point out a dozen reasons why it's wrong! You tell me one minute to guard my mind against the Mizarians, and the next minute you're standing there speculating – no *predicting* – that it isn't going to make any difference. No matter what I do, I'm *destined* – according to you – to fuck it all up in the end! What's the point?" he snapped harshly, almost despising the serenity which emanated from Myrddin's subdued aura. "What's the goddamned *point*?" His emotions were dangerously alive, causing his throat to constrict as he spoke, and he realized with an odd sense of horror that he was near the breaking point.

"Your anger serves you well," Myrddin said, releasing his hold on Morgan's arm as his hand dropped back to his side. "By internalizing it, you have already learned to shield against unwanted invasion."

Not hearing the other's words, Morgan turned abruptly and slammed a closed fist hard into the training bag suspended from the ceiling. It jarred with the impact, shuddering like a string stretched taut. "I don't give a damn about shielding!" he exploded, spinning back around to face his teacher, fire igniting in his eyes. "I'm not like you! I can't walk around for the rest of my life trying to block out something that I don't even understand! It's *normal* for me to *feel*!"

"It is also normal for you, as a human, to grieve for what you have lost, to desire to have it again," Myrddin pointed out with utter calmness. "By balancing your desires with your controls, all things become possible. Please," he entreated. "Put your spirit in balance for just a moment, Morgan. Only then will understanding become possible."

Morgan caught himself holding his breath as the anger burned and raged deep within him. He wanted very much to smash the training bag until its guts littered the floor. And yet, as some shred of sanity penetrated his bitterness, he felt his face heat with unbidden shame. In slow-motion thoughts, he saw himself acting very much like a small child rebelling against a wiser parent, his emotions swelling and dancing as if he were a pre-pubescent teenager at the mercy of his hormones. And the image he saw of himself became an ugly, self-serving monster.

Morgan Diego was not accustomed to feeling impotent. It simply did not exist in his repertoire.

In a fraction of a second, he re-lived the eight months and some odd days which had passed since his journey into the Mizarian Empire. He saw on the canvas of his mind the friends he had once known, the ship that had been his mistress, the streets and alleyways in which he'd slept after his exile, the dirty spaceport on Calipri where he'd first encountered Kim Le. But most of all, his mind returned again to Lucien – to the expression the Alfarian had worn when they'd parted for the final time, to the sparring matches in the gym and unended conversations, the philosophical confrontations and the unvoiced friendship now forever lost.

And suddenly, with a pain that was more profound than any torture he had ever endured, he doubled over, fully realizing for the first time that he *couldn't* go back. Before, it had been words suspended in the air – the right words said for the politically correct reasons. But now, with Lucien's image burned to his inner eye, those words fled like leaves from the wind, leaving him as a barren, brittle tree at the mercy of an inner storm. He could not help but remember the kiss on the floor of Mother Forest – *a kiss to break a spell*, he had mused at the time. But it had also been a kiss to *cast* a spell which now, it seemed, could *never* be broken.

Lucien was part of him, a piece of his soul that had broken away and resided in a different body – a magnificent elven body,

Morgan amended – yet now, as the full force of what he had lost overwhelmed him, all he could do was sob wordlessly, soundlessly, without even the luxury of actual tears. Just the heaving of his body, the wrenching of his spirit, the tearing of his sanity like some fragile bit of parchment tossed about and shredded by the relentless tempest

He did not know how long he remained that way, but when some semblance of coherency returned, he discovered himself kneeling on the floor with his face buried in his own trembling hands. Opening his eyes slowly, he caught his breath, only then realizing that a powerful arm was resting on his shoulder, and that he was leaning like a lost child against a cooler-than-human support.

For a reason he didn't understand, he closed his eyes once more, and turned his face into Myrddin's shoulder as his arms convulsed helplessly around the other's back. He heard his own voice speaking, though the words held no meaning. He listened from a distance to the pathetic cries which were torn from his throat. And somewhere, far away and terrified, he watched himself weeping bitterly – with little provocation, he thought – in the arms of a man he'd known for barely two weeks.

Myrddin's arms were strong as they held him, the Alfarian's scent a soft mixture of myrrh and the healing herbs used by all students of the art. And with his eyes closed, Morgan realized with a sense of impending horror that he *could* imagine his teacher to be Lucien. By holding his breath and refusing to think, by relying strictly on four of the five physical senses, he could trick his own mind into accepting that fallacy as fact. He could love Myrddin as he had loved Lucien – unspoken, safely, without repercussions. And yet, some part of his mind sworn to the art of purism reminded him that, regardless of what he and Myrddin might eventually share, Myrddin was *not* Lucien... and never could be. It also occurred to Morgan that he didn't *want* him to be. Still, the temptation to pretend, even if only for a moment, remained strong.

Suddenly terrified that he would fall forever into that fantasy, he pushed hard against the other's chest, attempting to extricate himself from the comforting embrace, seeking the safety of distance.

But somehow, it didn't surprise him when his teacher's arms tightened, holding him immobile as a parent might hold a small, unruly child.

"All of your life, Morgan," Myrddin said quietly, soothingly, "you have been concerned about the needs of others. Perhaps now it is time to focus solely on yourself, on the things you have denied to yourself for the good of all those others."

For a few long minutes, there was silence in the room and, gradually, Myrddin's words worked their way through his unbidden despair. He took a deep, shuddering breath and, opening his eyes, he had the peculiar impression that he was being reborn. Sounds were clearer. Colors appeared more vivid. A variety of new scents and sensations tested him.

Reality wavered, re-forming itself until he was able to breathe normally. He wasn't certain *what* had changed, yet he was filled with the knowing that, somewhere deep within himself, something was different.

"You have balanced your grief with your courage," Myrddin explained as if reading his every thought, "your anger with your gentler passions. Now," he added, his arm tightening reassuringly around Morgan's back, "you are ready to enter the next phase of your training."

Morgan didn't move, *couldn't* move. He blinked, trying to clear his vision. As he looked around the room, he saw his own reflection in the mirrors, saw himself being held like some infant in the protective arms of a strange Alfarian who bore faint resemblance to a former friend.

"What... I mean... what *happened*?" he asked, his voice seeming too loud in the air. He didn't feel out of place in Myrddin's arms, and made no attempt to move away, realizing that he *did* need the other's strength in that inexplicable moment.

"What happened," a familiar voice intoned from the direction of the door, "was that the ram butted its head too hard against a stone wall. Now the ram's head aches and it is angry at the wall – which had nothing to do with provoking the attack."

Startled by the sudden intrusion, Morgan jerked abruptly around, wincing slightly as the abused muscles in his back protested. His face darkened as he saw Kim Le standing in the doorway, a smile playing on the weathered features. He tried to extricate himself from Myrddin's embrace, but succeeded only in putting too much weight on a foot which had been tucked under his own leg. It prickled with needles and knives, numbed by lack of circulation, and buckled beneath him, dumping him awkwardly in Myrddin's lap. So much for dignity.

"Ta ta ta!" Kim Le scolded, coming further into the room and standing less than a meter away. "Sit."

Morgan blinked, swallowing hard as he grew decidedly uncomfortable. He tried again to squirm away from Myrddin, easily imagining how embarrassed Lucien would have been in a similar situation. But in the end, he only managed to sit – too close, he thought – to Myrddin's side as Kim Le motioned him to be still.

"Sit," the old man repeated, then knelt gracefully in front of him. "It is time for the student's evaluation."

Morgan's jaw slackened, his mouth opening to speak, to inquire what in all collective worlds was going on; but once more, Kim Le waved him to silence with a quick, effective gesture. When he spoke, his voice was low and quiet.

"You must forgive our methods, Morgan," he said softly, apologetically, "but there has been no time for explanations. In order to teach, it is often necessary to alter previously-established ideas. The student must learn by experiences rather than words."

Once more, Morgan wondered if he'd missed some important transitional phrase somewhere along the line. He frowned deeply, intensely aware of Myrddin pressed against his right side. He glanced side-long at the Alfarian, then back to Kim Le, the weariness catching up with him.

"Sometimes," he ventured, "words are necessary. It's easier to do something if there's some understanding of what you're doing."

Kim Le smiled faintly. "Perhaps," he conceded. "But is it not also true that you must *do* something before you can fully understand it?"

Morgan tried not to get frustrated with the circular reasoning. It occurred to him that his eyes were red-rimmed and swollen, yet he felt no shame for his recent outburst as he lifted his gaze to the old man. "What is it that you want me to do, Kim Le?"

The old man curled his legs into a full-lotus position, his brows tightening to form a line across his forehead as he gazed intently at him. "I want to see your pain ended, Morgan," he said quietly. "Only when your bitterness is gone will you be able to fully embrace the art."

Morgan considered that in conjunction with the events which had just transpired in the room – and within himself. He glanced to Myrddin. "Is that what you meant when you said I'd balanced my anger?" he wondered, feeling it to be true.

Myrddin inclined his head in agreement. "That is the first step," he said quietly. "When all facets of the man are in harmony, he becomes instantly aware of discord."

Morgan's brows tightened. "I'm not sure I see what you're getting at."

"No warrior can breach an impenetrable wall, Morgan," Kim Le explained. "When your wall has been built strong enough and high enough, the Mizarians will be nothing more than a memory, a part of your past experience. Your life will belong again to *you*."

Drawing a deep breath, Morgan pondered that in silence for a long moment. Then, holding Kim Le's penetrating stare, he spoke. "I mean no disrespect," he began, "but I don't see why this thing with the Mizarians is a concern to you."

Kim Le traded glances with Myrddin and as Morgan looked at his teacher, he saw the dark head bow as if in acknowledgement of some unspoken communication between them.

"Morgan," Kim Le said, "have you not wondered where this ship is bound?"

Morgan glanced up sharply, recalling his thoughts concerning the course of the *Dreaming Bird*. He wondered if his intuition had been even more accurate than he'd realized. "The ship's course doesn't... *feel* right," he offered, then smiled softly. "Of course, I've never been an expert on the 'feel' of anything."

"Do not deny your gifts, Morgan," Kim Le said, then paused thoughtfully for a moment. "You are correct in your assumptions. The *Dreaming Bird* is not bound for the Nel-fen Empire."

For a split second, Morgan experienced a wave of panic as it

102

tightened the muscles in his stomach. And yet, he knew instinctively that Kim Le had no elaborate plans to sell him into slavery or place him in mortal danger. He waited in silence.

"We are bound for Earth, Morgan," the old man said at last. "There, in the Temple of Ho Ling, your studies will continue."

Morgan's eyes widened. His heart beat faster. "Earth?" he repeated incredulously. Even though he'd somehow known the *Dreaming Bird* wasn't bound for Nel-Fin Homeworld, he'd had no insight as to the true course. "Why?"

"There are many masters in the Temple," Kim Le explained. "You will work with them as you have worked with Myrddin. They can teach you more."

Somehow, that idea didn't set well with Morgan. He had the distinct impression that this was some convoluted form of 'farewell'. "But... *why*?" he asked quietly, almost desperately. "I was under the impression that this 'training' was so that I could serve on this ship."

Kim Le smiled gently. "That was a necessary illusion on which you needed to focus temporarily. But the knowledge you will acquire at the temple will increase your worth a thousand-fold."

It wasn't what Morgan wanted to hear, but he made an effort to accept it, realizing the futility of arguing with the old man. Still, a deep sense of sadness and regret overwhelmed him, causing him to ask, "What about you? Both of you?" he added, glancing back and forth between Kim Le and Myrddin.

"The temple is my home of youth, Morgan," Kim Le replied, then smiled as his head tilted slightly to one side. "It is not our way to begin a student's training only to abandon him. We will stand at your side throughout your mastery of the art. But at the temple, you will perfect the skills you have learned here – with the benefit of more learned teachers and a more varied environment."

"There," Myrddin added, "you will learn not only to shield your thoughts, but you will learn to discriminate *when* to shield. Your mind will become as disciplined as your body, your spirit as strong as your flesh."

Too many questions raged through Morgan's mind and, once more, he settled for the first in line. "But... *why*?" he pressed. "Why is it so important to *you* that I do this?"

"If one man is oppressed, then all are slaves," Kim Le stated. "Only when *you* are free of the Mizarians will your Empire be able to exist in peace with them."

Morgan started to protest that he was only one person in a galaxy of trillions of sentient lifeforms. And yet, as he contemplated Kim Le's words, he began to realize the truth inherent in them. As long as the Mizarians controlled his life and his future – even if not his personal actions – he was a symbol of their rule. No weapons ever needed to be fired, no wars would ever be fought.

And yet, in a distant corner of the vast galaxy, the Mizarians had effectively begun their invasion. As with any invasion, it started with a thought. If the Mizarians knew their authority to be absolute, it would eventually become just that. No physical take-over would ever be necessary; for the rest of the galaxy would learn to live with the implied subjugation.

Feeling suddenly and perhaps even arrogantly critical to all those trillions of other sentient lifeforms, Morgan lifted his shoulders and took a deep breath, considering his new perspective. And, almost at once, he felt himself applying the techniques Myrddin had taught – the subconscious shielding which now held far more meaning than it had in the past.

If the Mizarians couldn't read him, it would give them something to think about, some new twist to consider. He realized abstractly that Myrddin had been right: he would be temporarily sacrificing his in-born intuition by shielding against all potential mental invasion; yet he was confident that the masters at Ho Ling would teach him to balance even that. Sooner or later, he told himself, he would have both: his shields *and* his instincts.

But temporarily at least, it was a sacrifice he could live with.

~

Alone in the sanctuary of his assigned bunk several hours later, Morgan stared at the walls which surrounded him, his mind replaying the events of the day as sleep eluded him. A strange, unprecedented loneliness had settled in the deepest part of himself – a loneliness he hadn't felt since early childhood when he would

104

find himself alone in the desert, walking bare-foot through the sandy-bottomed dry creek. Now, that same feeling arose again, bringing with it a longing he couldn't immediately identify.

He thought briefly of Myrddin, of how the Alfarian had held him as he wept. And he considered that he *had* wept bitterly. What continued to evade him was the precise reason for that emotional overload. He couldn't help wondering if, in accordance with his training, Myrddin had attempted to probe his mind, to test his shields and his ability to block all intrusions. And he also began to wonder if he had passed that test or failed it miserably. He *had* felt something – some deep, awful, aching longing and loneliness which had been temporarily soothed by his teacher's embrace.

What troubled him was the intensity of his own reaction as he studied it in retrospect. For an instant, he had wanted nothing more than to bury himself in the other's strength, to give up his struggle and allow mysterious Alfarian power to protect him, to shield him from his past, from the Mizarians, perhaps even from himself. He had wanted, he suddenly realized, to be taken into Myrddin's arms and perhaps even into his bed. And *that* realization shocked him as much as anything ever had.

Despite the fact that he was alone, Morgan's face darkened, his jaw going slack as he considered the implications of that revelation. Realistically, he understood that he was reacting to *Lucien* – to the *memory* of Lucien, and to the unfulfilled promises left hanging when the Mizarians had intervened. It wasn't Myrddin he wanted. And yet, knowing that he may never see Lucien again, Myrddin's strength and companionship became an oddly enticing allure.

Closing his eyes, he tried to drive those thoughts from his mind, yet the fantasies grew more powerful, more intriguing. It occurred to him that he was behaving in a classic schoolboy fashion – falling in love with a teacher who had shown him a moment of kindness, a few minutes of physical support when he'd been broken. Pathetic. For after all, he was Morgan Diego – commander of the finest ship in Galaxy Corps, seducer of the fairer sex from one end of the Empire to the other, breaker of hearts both human and alien…

Pathetic. Even his own usual rhetoric did nothing to convince him to accept the lie he had been living for so long. That he had *believed* it was neither here nor there. Man had once believed the earth was flat, but Man was just another pathetic, deluded fool, too, he concluded. Now that he knew the lie *was* a lie, it fell at his feet in a tangled mess of broken programs and false belief systems.

Morgan Diego did not exist. At least not as he had perceived himself to be.

Images of Lucien continued to haunt his memory. In his mind's eye, he saw the two of them wrestling on the lush floor of Mother Forest, playing poker long into the night, taking leisurely walks together on the shores of far-flung worlds on shared leaves. And then there was the kiss. *That* kiss. At the time, Morgan had patted himself on the back as a reward for his own cleverness. All in a day's work. Just a quirky aspect of command training. When all else fails, do the last thing anybody anywhere would expect. Only *this* time, he realized *he* was the one caught with his pants down. *He* was the one who had fallen under the spell. Not some bit of Alfarian magick, but a very human kind of spell.

A love spell that burst open like some nasty nova the moment he touched his lips to Lucien's in the presence of so many self-important witnesses. And now there was no going back. Not just metaphorically but literally. No going home. No picking up where things left off. No asking Lucien why he had seen fit to excise that memory when Morgan now wholly *knew* it was what they had both wanted for longer than he could conceive, maybe even from the moment Morgan first laid eyes on the elven prince three years and an odd number of months in the past.

So much was left unfinished, Morgan thought morosely. And now, unless he could learn to shield against the Mizarians every second of every hour of every day, those unfinished things would remain forever a mystery.

Weary and tired, he turned onto his side, burying his face into the hard pillow and trying to ignore the ache which had settled in the vicinity of his heart. *Who am I?* he wondered.

There was no answer, for whoever he had been *pretending* to be had died that very afternoon in the training arena. What was left, he realized, was the raw matter of whatever he *might* be tomorrow.

And even as he reached toward sleep, Lucien's face haunted him, and half-forgotten phrases and never-spoken words of love were shared. Promises were sworn, allegiances formed. The word 'forever' was mentioned more than once.

And yet, Morgan knew, forever was little more than a dream. He wanted to *believe* it would happen; yet some dark, undisciplined, unfaithful corner of his mind *knew* it wouldn't. And there he was again, face to face with the stark, cold, relentless difference between belief and knowledge. For another thing was also painfully clear: for as long as he *believed* he could never go back, *that* was the dominant reality, the quantum manifestation of every thought he would think, every action he would take. Another thing he had learned and learned well from Myrddin: *"Each of us creates our own reality, which we either inhabit or abandon, depending entirely on our intent."*

Intent. He tumbled the word through his mind, trying to define it in relation to himself. Intent. What was it? *Where* was it located in the confines of the mind, body or spirit?

Frustrated at the lack of sleep, he drew a deep, trembling breath, feeling terribly, awfully, eternally alone. In the corridor, he heard footsteps moving with quiet purpose, but passed it off to nothing more than Kim Le's late-night prowling of the ship.

Sleep moved a step closer, and he longed for the dark forgetfulness which would accompany his rest. He was peripherally aware of a weight settling on the edge of his bunk, but explained it away as the preamble to a now-common dream wherein he shared bed and body with a friend he would never see again.

But this time, the dream continued with surprising realism. Morgan felt himself turned, taken into powerful arms, felt powerful Alfarian fingers caressing his cheeks, running lightly through his hair. He was cradled in a protective embrace, his head resting on a cooler-than-human shoulder, his face buried in the other's neck.

Throughout the long void-night, he was held. He was loved – gently, carefully, reverently. His mind seemed to have flown away, scattered in a thousand different directions and, abandoning pride and male attitudes he'd clung to fiercely in the past, he accepted the fact that he *wanted* the anonymity which came with this peculiar incubus' loving. He wanted to be sheltered and protected, caressed and worshipped. He even wanted to be taken – to have the burden of conscious choice removed by one more physically powerful than himself.

And understanding those things to be true, he opened his body to the dream, his mind shielding him from whatever truth he didn't care to face. In his dream, Lucien came to him, caressed him to arousal, then took him with a force which left his heart trembling. He felt himself opened by a sleek, powerful shaft, his body explored for his own pleasure as well as the other's. His flesh was plundered – though tenderly, reverently – and he was manipulated to a climax which blotted consciousness from his reality, the cries of his release smothered in the dark one's neck.

But his mind remained shielded – safe within its fantasy, secure with the knowledge that this dream-Lucien would be at his side forever. It would never be enough, Morgan knew, but it would help to alleviate the aloneness which had moved in to the spot where Lucien once dwelled.

When his passions subsided, he kept his eyes tightly closed, clinging desperately to the phantom-incubus-Lucien conjured from his dreams. Here, in this reality, he could whisper his love to the Alfarian.. Here, they were no longer human and alien, ram and shepherd. Here, they were only the soft, ethereal matter of dreams.

Satisfied and secure, Morgan began to drift further into the compelling territory of his own fantasies, floating gently into the deeper levels of sleep.

He awoke in the morning with a lingering smile on his face and his arms wrapped tight around the pillow... and Myrddin's unique scent clinging to his body.

~

Bolting upright in the small bunk, he barely managed to avoid smacking his head on the bed directly above him. His heart pounded furiously as he grabbed a robe, tying it about his waist as he stumbled from the bed and took off at a run toward the training area.

But as he ran through the narrow corridors, bare feet slapping the bulkhead, the emotions coursing through him grew more intense, his own certainty diminishing as he put more distance between himself and the bed. It was entirely possible, he told himself, that it had been nothing more than an elaborate wet dream. It was equally as possible, he conceded, that he was losing his mind right along with his intuition. Normally, he would have *known* whether he'd been laid in the middle of the night, or whether his errant and legendary cock had merely tricked him into believing it.

And yet, he couldn't deny the evidence. Myrddin's scent was a part of him – a blend of myrrh and healing herbs used only by those studying the art. And then there was the matter of the pleasant ache where he had obviously been opened, stretched, loved with a blunt force that could not be denied. Though not entirely a virgin with men, it had been awhile – but not so long that he had forgotten the sensations which were remarkably erotic despite the lingering sense of discomfort.

There was no denying it. He had been nicely fucked.

At last, he reached the training area and, without the formality of bowing or even announcing his presence, he burst through the door to find his teacher kneeling in meditation in the center of the room.

Myrddin looked up, long brows lifting questioningly. "Morgan," he intoned as if everything were completely normal. "Your lesson is not until the afternoon. Are you well?"

Morgan stood there for a very long second with his heart pounding and his jaw slightly slack. "*Well*?" he repeated, flustered and confused. "After that little episode last night, I find it funny that you can sit there and ask me that!"

Myrddin rose from the floor, gathering himself into an utterly graceful pose with his hands clasped neatly behind his back. His eyes were darker than normal, Morgan noted, and his posture denoted a relaxed and confident aura. He said nothing.

And the silence was just enough to rattle his certainty all the more. Time stretched out in front of him, behind him. He couldn't hold the other's gaze for more than a moment. And yet, as he started to breathe again, the scent of myrrh and herbs brought back his certainty.

"Was that supposed to be another part of my 'training'?" he asked, hard-pressed to keep the sarcasm from his voice.

Myrddin continued to look at him for an extended moment, then released his breath as a gentle sigh as he took a step forward. "Even the ram cannot live in solitude indefinitely, Morgan," he said quietly. "The mind and the body cannot live in harmony until each exists in harmony with itself."

Morgan blinked, staring incredulously as he translated the seeming double-talk into plain English. "I'm not into mercy-fucks!" he snapped, though he noticed that his stomach knotted almost pleasantly at the memories of the night before. "You violated a trust, goddammit!"

But Myrddin remained unfazed even by his anger. "I took only your loneliness, Morgan," he said, "and replaced it with belonging."

At that, Morgan's anger flared once again. "Belonging!" he repeated. "I don't *belong* to you!"

"I am aware of that," Myrddin replied quietly. "And what occurred last night was not between the two of us." He paused as if to let that sink in, then added, "Your heart cries out for one you have lost, for Lucien. And in your dreams, in your mind, you required fulfillment from *him*."

"Not in the form of an illusion," Morgan argued bitterly. "I've had enough illusions and delusions to last ten lifetimes!" He felt himself starting to squirm uncomfortably, however, as he realized with an odd sense of detachment that he *had* been fulfilled. But, for the moment, he ignored that nagging little fact. "I can't live with only fantasies for company, Myrddin!"

"Precisely," the other man agreed.

Morgan stared at him, but no words came out. He stammered helplessly, yet as reality settled around him with a sudden heaviness, he realized with a horrible sense of truth that his anger was nothing more than a meaningless protest. He *had* wanted Lucien. But in some lonely corner of himself, he'd also wanted Myrddin, had consciously acknowledged that nasty little fact to himself in his mental masturbations prior to sleep. And through a peculiar transmutation of fantasy and reality, he'd had both.

110

Now, standing in the middle of the training area wearing only a thin robe and his arrogant male pride, he realized he sounded like a virgin bride protesting the loss of innocence while at the same time craving the luxury of having the decision taken from him and placed into the hands of another. For once in his life, *he* hadn't had to be the one to decide, the one to make the life or death command decision. For once in his life, he had placed his fate in the capable hands of another… and whether he liked it or not… he *liked* it.

Of course, that only pissed him off. *He* was the commander! *He* was the infamous Cap'n Morgan, notorious breaker of rules, legend from one side of the galaxy to the other, destroyer of the pious virtue of men and women alike. *He* was the one in charge!

Not anymore, Asshole, one of the little voices reminded him with a nasty poke. His bravado fizzled at that realization, like the air leaving a balloon.

Heat tinged his cheeks and, breathing raggedly, he tried to regain some grip on his rampaging emotions.

"It is important, Morgan," Myrddin said at last, "that you internalize your feelings, *and* that you understand them. What you feel for Lucien remains the same, regardless of what you feel for another, regardless of how your body responds to another's touch."

Somehow, it didn't matter that Myrddin was right. Morgan *wanted* to protest by accusing the Alfarian of using him; yet he realized that the reverse application was much closer to the truth. And yet, admitting that – even to himself – was a difficult task. He stared at his teacher for a very long time, trying to make some sense of what had happened between them.

In the end, he was left only with the truth. "I... love is important to me," he said at last, not entirely certain where that statement would lead. "I *loved* Lucien." His voice sounded weak, lame; but the statement was nonetheless valid. In the absence of logic, invoke love.

Myrddin inclined his head in acknowledgement. "You always will, Morgan," he said knowingly. "I envy him that devotion from one such as yourself."

For a long minute, Morgan remained speechless. It was the closest thing to an outright compliment or any form of praise

Myrddin had ever voiced and, despite the circumstances, it penetrated his stubborn resistance and soothed the anger away. And yet, as he contemplated the other man's words, a question formed in his mind, parting his lips before he could stop it.

"I thought you were a priest," he said, almost to himself.

Myrddin responded with a warm, gentle chuckle. "A priest?" he commented, then shook his head gently. "No. I am a teacher, Morgan. And I am also a man."

Morgan flushed deeply, realizing that Myrddin was paying him a deep compliment. "But... you're also an Alfarian," he pointed out.

The other smiled faintly. "To be Alfarian is not to follow a religion," he explained. "It is true that we are devoted to peace, to the mystical arts, and to a code of ethics. But most of all, we are devoted to the miraculous power within every living being – and as a teacher, I am dedicated to bringing my students into alignment with their highest potential."

Morgan studied the other man for a moment "No matter what?" he replied, not quite sure if it was a legitimate question or an indirect accusation.

Myrddin smiled reassuringly. "It is true my methods are unorthodox, even for an Alfarian. It's one reason I left homeworld," he confessed, then waved his own words aside with a graceful gesture of one hand. "But please do not concern yourself unduly. The love I feel for you is as a teacher for his student: I wish very much for you to learn. And I also wish for your learning to be a pleasant experience." He paused, then continued very gently. "I would not attempt to bind you with feeling – for I am well aware that the devotion you feel is for Lucien."

Morgan couldn't speak for a very long time. Instead, he stood there holding his breath and feeling alternately honored and embarrassed. But he *did* understand now. Myrddin was a compassionate, caring man – a man undoubtedly lonely in his chosen profession. They had come together under extreme circumstances – circumstances which, Morgan realized, may never happen again. For one night, each had taken refuge and solace in the other. It seemed a fair, even honorable trade and, realizing that,

112

he nodded slightly.

"Thank you," he said quietly, meaning it. But for reasons he couldn't fathom, it sounded lame, even to his own ears, so he shut up and just made the decision to be okay with it. Once he made up his mind to simply accept what had happened, to swallow his arrogance and fierce male pride, the taste in his mouth was no longer bitter. It was the decision to *do* it that hurt the most; but once done, the pain quickly subsided.

Myrddin's eyes continued to smile knowingly. "I would say that the pleasure was mine, Morgan," he replied, "but I fear that such a comment would only serve to re-awaken your anger."

Despite himself, Morgan grinned broadly. It was the first time he'd seen Myrddin display any sense of humor whatsoever and it set him more at ease. "No... it wouldn't make me angry," he said, "but it wouldn't be entirely true either." When he recalled his own reaction of the night before, he had to admit that the 'pleasure' had probably been very equally divided.

Feeling confident and composed once again, he inclined his head in the customary fashion to excuse himself and started for the door.

"Morgan?" Myrddin's voice called behind him.

He turned, meeting his teacher's eyes, found them glistening with an odd sense of mischievousness.

"In the future, the student should remember the courtesy of announcing his presence before entering the training arena," Myrddin stated coolly.

Morgan laughed out loud, incredulous. "I'll keep that in mind," he said. Then, on second thought, he added: "In the future, the master should remember the courtesy of announcing his presence before entering the bed."

Myrddin's eyes widened with genuine surprise, his expression painfully reminiscent of Lucien at times when Vanya would jab him with some unexpected barb.

"I shall remember that, Morgan," he said, then bowed with formal etiquette. "I trust you will not be late for today's lesson?"

Morgan shrugged, then stopped with one hand resting on the swinging door. "What's the topic of today's lesson?"

"Trust," Myrddin replied. "An area in which student and teacher can never know too much."

Morgan didn't argue.

CHAPTER EIGHT

"This is the single most insane scheme I've ever heard of, Lucien!" Vanya protested, standing back from the diagnostic console at Galaxy Corps Headquarters. "I'm surprised you'd think you could get away with it – and I'm even *more* surprised that Bryse sanctioned it - under the table or not!"

Lucien paid little attention to the other man's rantings as he swung his legs over the edge of the bed and moved quietly to the mirrored wall in the base doctor's office. There, leaning close to the reflective surface, he inspected his face carefully, not surprised that the man in the mirror bore only marginal resemblance to his former self.

His eyes were a glistening golden-brown, the perma-plant lenses completely unnoticeable even under the intense surgical lights. Through the use of surgical implants, his cheekbones were slightly more prominent, and the deep black goatee-beard gave his face the illusion of being slimmer than that to which he'd grown accustomed. Injections of hair-growth stimulants left him with a cascading glimmer of black which tapered down his back, cut shorter on the sides. A single streak of bronze-gold approximately one-quarter inch wide began at the crown of his head and fell forward into the long bangs which were now slightly parted down the center. Around his neck, he wore a black choker-style collar with a hematite cabachon in the center. For the moment, it was inactive; but once activated, the electronics imbedded in the stone would effectively alter the pitch of his voice, lowering it to a slightly deeper bass with sufficient changes to make it unrecognizable even to those who knew him well.

He studied himself for only a moment longer, then nodded an unspoken approval to his reflection before turning once more to face Vanya.

"–and another thing," the psychiatrist was saying, leaving Lucien to realize he'd been talking the entire time, "Morgan'll never fall for it! Surgery and long hair or not, he's going to take one look at you and know damn well who you are! And then, my dear *Captain* Lucien, the cat will be out of the bag! The cap will be off the bottle! The fat will be in the fire–."

"Please, Vanya," Lucien interrupted wearily, "you don't need to lengthen the list of clichés to make your point." Vanya had done nothing but argue for three days – since the time that Bryse had agreed to the plan. "If it were yourself going to the Temple of Ho Ling, I don't believe you would protest as often – nor as loudly."

Vanya blinked, stretching up on his toes then lowering his weight to the floor. "You mule-headed elf!" he snapped. "It doesn't matter who goes. The point is that, if Morgan *does* recognize you, and if the Mizarians *do* catch on to this little charade of yours, the entire Empire is going to be up Shit's Creek without a paddle!"

"And what would you suggest as an alternative?" Lucien questioned, growing weary of the other's constant complaining. When Morgan had been there, he'd created a buffer between them; and though they had learned to work together over the eight months of the commander's absence, Lucien acknowledged that his patience was worn thin. He met the other's eyes, holding them steadily. "I believe it was you who initially suggested that someone attempt to covertly contact Commander Diego. Now that it is being done, you appear to have changed your mind. *Again.* If we wish to contact the commander, I see no other alternative. The dangers are minimal."

But Vanya didn't back down. "Minimal?" he repeated incredulously. "You've got to be joking. Since when is every living thing in Empire territory considered 'minimal', Lucien? And for that matter, what makes you so certain that you can even get *in* to the temple? From what I've heard, you practically have to been born there to even be considered for an initiate's position. But *you* – oh, no, not you! *You* plan on just walking through the doors, announcing your holy presence, and having yourself set up as a master without so much as a how-do-you-do!"

Lucien stared at the other man for a moment, mentally retreating from the onslaught of powerful emotions. It occurred to him that the behavior was peculiar even for Vanya and, with an effort, he curbed the remark which sprang to his lips.

"Liam," he began quietly, "the arrangements have already been made in my behalf. Since Kim Le is the current head of the temple,

116

and since Admiral Bryse was able to speak with him directly, I am expected within forty-eight hours." He paused to allow Vanya's thick head to absorb that, then continued. "Indeed," he added, more as an admitted jab than any informational tidbit, "I was informed by the admiral that I am most welcome by the masters currently teaching at the temple."

Vanya only glared back at him. "Why? What makes you so special?"

Lucien wondered fleetingly if the other man were dense or merely pretending to be. "Alfarian mental disciplines and the Terran disciplines involved in martial arts training and philosophies are not drastically different," he explained for what seemed like the tenth time that week. "When both can be combined, students gain the advantage of superior training."

But Vanya shook his head with a sarcastic laugh. "Somehow, I just can't see you sitting lotus-position in the middle of a stone floor trying to levitate yourself." But he waved his own words aside with a quick gesture, his mood shifting from one of anger to one of disbelief. "I dunno," he said, almost to himself, "I guess this is just the first thing we've come up against that scares me as much as it does. It's easy enough to do battle with the Nel-fens – we know what they're capable of, and we know what *we're* capable of. But this Mizarian thing...."

"If our principles were based solely on following a safe path, you and I would never have met." Lucien wondered why that thought sounded particularly appealing just then, yet quickly dismissed the unbidden sarcasm from his thoughts. "At any rate, Admiral Bryse is correct in his assumptions that the Mizarian Directive regarding Commander Diego is possibly the first in a series of additional demands. If we do not do something to attempt to dissuade them, it is almost a certainty that additional confrontations will follow. Eventually," he concluded, "there will be no freedom within the galaxy."

"Aren't you being just a little pessimistic, Lucien?" Vanya persisted. "Morgan spent several months with the little bastards, and from what the base doctors have told me, he didn't even have a scratch. The Mizarians don't want a war."

"Perhaps not," Lucien agreed. "However, one of your Terran proverbs is somewhat applicable in this instance."

"What proverb?"

"Absolute power corrupts absolutely," Lucien recited. "It is not necessary to review the possibilities; you are as aware of them as I. We must endeavor to solve the problem at its source – and in this moment, the source is Commander Diego."

Vanya perused the Alfarian for a long moment. "He'll never fall for it," he repeated skeptically.

"Fortunately, I do not share your pessimism," Lucien returned. "I am told that the commander has been studying the art for several weeks; his instructors would have taught him the basic knowledge of how to shield his thoughts from unwanted invasion."

Vanya frowned. "What does that have to do with anything?"

"Much of human recognition is based not only on sight, Doctor, but on sub-psychic vibrations," Lucien explained. "Since my physical appearance is now somewhat altered, and since the commander will undoubtedly be shielding against all potential mental invasion, he will be essentially 'blinded' in two critical areas." He paused briefly, then added: "Additionally, I will be somewhat shielded mentally as well; the risks of the commander identifying me are slim."

Vanya seemed unconvinced. "And just what do you plan on calling yourself at the Temple?" he asked. "Somehow I have trouble with the title of 'Master Lucien'."

Lucien's brows lifted. "That is precisely how I shall be known."

Vanya blinked. "You've got to be joking. If your own good looks and your inherent Alfarian scent don't give you away to Morgan, why not hit him over the head with the obvious." He shrugged elaborately. "Seems *perfectly* reasonable to me."

"It is," Lucien countered seriously. "The name is common among my people, much like Morgan or even Liam is common among Terrans."

Vanya didn't bother to argue. Instead, he glanced at the clock, sighing heavily. "Well, if you're crazy enough to go through with this, your transport leaves in an hour."

Lucien nodded curtly, then started for the door.

But the psychiatrist stopped him with one arm on his elbow, causing him to turn to meet the intense blue eyes which seemed moister than usual.

"Lucien," he began, "I... I don't want you to get the impression that I don't want you to do this."

Lucien's brows lifted. Vanya had spent the past two days trying to convince him of just that.

Vanya smiled wistfully. "It's just that... well... I wish I could come along."

Softening just a little, Lucien made an effort to take the other man's feeling into account. "Unfortunately," he said, "your presence would be more difficult to disguise than my own."

"There's another reason, too, you know."

Lucien waited.

And Vanya fidgeted, glancing away as he spoke. "Morgan's been gone for over eight months," he said quietly, almost as if attempting to accept that fact. "And now you're running off to some ancient temple in the badlands of China." He shrugged again. "I know it's silly, but I can't help having this thought that I'll never see either one of you again."

Despite the tension which had lingered between them for months, Lucien softened inside at the other's gesture. And, almost without thinking, he lifted his arm, covering the hand which still rested on his elbow with his own. He didn't speak, realizing that, for once, words weren't necessary.

Then, taking a deep breath, he released Vanya's hand and strode purposefully through the door. Stopping briefly by his assigned quarters at the base, he retrieved a few personal belongings, packed them neatly into a standard shipping case, then headed at once for the civilian transport already hired for the trip to China. Along the way, he slipped one finger into the collar-band of the voice crystal, activating it almost symbolically as he began what he knew would be a long and possibly dangerous journey.

He tried, very hard, to ignore the fast beating of his own heart, even harder to ignore the sense of regret which, inexplicably, had been with him since morning. It was, he conceded, almost as if someone somewhere were filled with a profound sense of loss.

He didn't need to confirm precisely who that someone was. He did, however, wonder why it manifested so abruptly as he'd awakened that morning.

CHAPTER NINE

With the *Dreaming Bird* in her assigned parking orbit over Luna, Morgan, Kim Le and Myrddin boarded the small shuttle, leaving Jones on the mother vessel to tend to the normal maintenance and re-provisioning. Kim Le sat at the controls of the shuttle, and Morgan noticed that he and Myrddin were almost deliberately left alone in the rear passenger compartment.

The incident which had occurred between them two nights before had not been repeated, and though Morgan was grateful for that, he was also somewhat saddened by it.

He glanced briefly toward Myrddin, and found his teacher gazing contentedly out one of the six small ports, watching Luna's retreat as they left Earth's moon behind. For a moment, his spirit panged; the Alfarian *was* beautiful both mentally and physically, and he couldn't help wondering what kind of life they might have been able to make together under other circumstances. And yet, he realized that it wasn't meant to be. Whether he liked it or not, he would always compare Myrddin to Lucien – a comparison which was fair to neither, a comparison which would ultimately condemn any relationship which might develop between himself and his teacher.

But his consolation came with the knowledge that Myrddin had the wherewithal to understand those facts as well. And, given time, he thought almost hopefully, it was possible that they would learn to share companionship, perhaps even on a physical level. It seemed a fair exchange to both parties, a way to alleviate the loneliness of the teacher and calm the fiery blood of the student.

At the very least, Myrddin was a trusted friend, one who understood him well. Morgan smiled to himself at that knowledge, unconsciously lifting his head a little higher as the shuttle rolled and began its inevitable descent into the high mountains of China.

When did you become such an introspective little bastard? The Little Voice wanted to know. *Calico Jack swinging from a rope, what the hell is the matter with you? He fucked you. You liked it. Get over it. Nothing men haven't been doing since the dawn of time. And nothing wrong with it, just FYI.*

121

Maybe the little voice had a point, he conceded, his head beginning to ache.

In the peculiar null-gravity, Myrddin turned toward him, their eyes locking for just a moment.

Morgan smiled, trying to disguise his nervousness – not only with what had happened, but with what was happening at that moment. Soon, he knew, they would enter a sacred temple dedicated to the study of the art. Soon, he would be only one student, and his teacher would divide his attentions among many.

But Myrddin's brows lifted as his lips curved upward. "Unique students require individual attention, Morgan," he said quietly, causing Morgan to tremble within as he realized how very transparent his thoughts had become. "I will be instructing you in the disciplines of spiritual balance and physical stamina. Master Lucien will be your instructor in the finer techniques required for self defense, and in the art of wholistic awareness."

Morgan felt the color drain completely from his face, his jaw going slack. "Master... *Lucien*?"

But Myrddin only inclined his head in agreement, his lips curving to a gentle reflection of a smile. "He has been at the temple for quite some time," he replied. "You will find him an excellent teacher, and I am confident you will like him very much. You will spend your mornings with myself or with Kim Le, your afternoons with Master Lucien."

Morgan's heart sank as he realized Myrddin was referring to another man, another Alfarian, another master. Somehow, he'd irrationally thought that Lucien – *his* Lucien – held a copyright on the name. But he nodded his understanding nonetheless, trying not to let his disappointment register on his face.

"Morgan?"

He looked up, aware of the shuttle's sharp descent, knowing they would land in another minute.

"You must not trouble yourself with grief and guilt at the temple," Myrddin said gently. "Accept your feelings as a part of yourself and deal with them accordingly. They are nothing to fear."

Morgan wasn't even certain what he was feeling. He only knew that, in some hidden part of himself, he was suddenly lonely. He

122

also knew that Myrddin was completely agreeable to alleviating that loneliness, to holding him as he slept, or joining with him when he hungered for another's touch.

He sighed softly and turned to gaze out the window as the shuttle continued its descent, its retro-thrusters tossing up a cloud of dust as it settled like thunder to the ground.

In the dust-storm, he saw Lucien's face – tender and young and beautiful. But it was Myrddin's hand that touched him lightly on the arm, drawing him from his reverie and encouraging him to stand as the ramp descended, pointing the way to still another new life.

Are you going to carry on like this for the rest of eternity? The Little Voice inquired with no small amount of sarcasm. *Because if you are, please do me the courtesy of throwing me out the airlock right now.*

Had there been an accessible airlock on the tiny shuttle, Morgan might have obliged. As it was, he could only concede that at least one old cliché was altogether too true. He had become his own worst enemy.

The Little Voice rolled its third eye, then fell silent for the remainder of the trip.

CHAPTER TEN

It was early afternoon by the time Morgan was settled into his assigned room. The temple was built on a round, almost donut-shaped floor-plan, the main building alone covering an expanse equivalent to more than two city blocks. The central garden area, he was told, was reserved for the privacy of the masters, or for meditation and consultation. Several large training arenas were located throughout the round structure, as well as students' living quarters, private meditation chambers, two group dining rooms, the Room of Eternal Flame which bore a candle for every student and master ever to serve at the temple, and an assortment of small storage rooms for traditional and modern weapons.

As Morgan stood in the center of his own assigned living quarters, he was somewhat surprised to discover that the room was not purposefully uncomfortable as he'd imagined it might be. Located on the outer wall of the central facility, the single cut-away window afforded a serene view of the outer garden area and, further distant on the grounds, the small stream which cut through the temple's property and the ornate plants and trees. The window itself, Morgan noted, was more of a cut-out in the stone walls rather than a traditional paned structure. It had no screen and no glass, yet the precise slant of walls and roof would effectively prevent the frequent rains from intruding.

He stood for a very long time simply gazing out into the garden and to the high stone wall far in the distance which completely surrounded the temple grounds. A scent of lotus and jasmine drifted in on the light spring breeze, and a hundred unseen birds twittered and sang from high among the stately trees in the outer garden. The afternoon sun filtered through leaves and blossoms, creating a patchwork of light and dark on the thick green grass and inlaid stone paths which covered the grounds.

It was hard to believe that cities teeming with life were less than 25 miles away, harder still to imagine that Earthbase One with all its pomp and circumstance was undoubtedly bristling with action on the outskirts of San Diego. In New New York, dozens of Broadway plays would be performed in as many different languages, both Terran and alien. Tokyo would be hosting the Galactic Games right about now, he recalled. And in his hometown in the desert, the Joshua Trees would be starting to bud. Earth was a mecca of civilization, hub of Galaxy Corps, and home to many ambassadors and dignitaries serving the Empire.

And yet…

Leaning on the window-sill, he sighed softly to himself, realizing with an odd pang that he was home on Earth once more, yet he had never seen the Earth look so alien. Though he had visited China before, his journey had taken him primarily to the cities – which were, he conceded, not dissimilar to cities anywhere. But here, the very air itself was different, somehow ancient and sacred, yet new and filled with mystery.

After awhile, he turned from the window and went to sit on the edge of his small bed. Save for a small dressing table and a single straight-backed chair, it was the only furniture in the room. A small private bath and toilet area were located through a door on the wall opposite the bed, and upon exploring it, he had discovered the cabinets well-stocked with fresh linen, an assortment of toiletries, and the customary bottles of healing herb solutions used for bruises and sprains.

For awhile, he remained sitting on the edge of the bed, his fingers absently toying with the white cotton blanket which was neatly folded at the end. It occurred to him that, after Myrddin had seen to his being assigned a room, he had been left alone. And the solitude was somehow comforting, giving him time to mentally prepare for the meeting with the masters – which, Kim Le had informed him, would transpire promptly after the evening meal.

But as he contemplated that future meeting, he felt a sense of futile melancholy and wondered briefly how he had come to be in such a strangely alien place in the high mountains of China.

But before that melancholy could become profound, his reverie was interrupted by a soft knock at his door. He rose at once, half-way expecting to find Myrddin or Kim Le on the other side, but as he opened the door, he was confronted with a very small boy who could have been no more than five years of age.

Morgan smiled warmly, thinking the boy to be the son of a

fellow student, or perhaps the child of a poor family who sometimes worked at the temple for wages. "Hello," he said, automatically dropping to one knee to bring himself to eye-level with the other.

The youth bowed gracefully from the waist, his blue-black hair shining as the sunlight streamed in through Morgan's window. It was then that he noted the elegantly elven features, the sloping brows, the slightly blue flush of the pale skin. Morgan blinked as his illusions were abruptly shattered. Obviously, the boy was another initiate; though a closer look revealed that his uniform was a pale yellow – denoting his status as having mastered the accomplishments of two years' of difficult training.

"I am Jahan," the boy said, his voice remarkably defined for his age. "I am told that you are called Diego."

Quickly concealing his astonishment, wondering why it should have surprised him to find children as students in the first place, he nodded. "Actually, I'm Morgan," he clarified with a grin.

Once more, the youth inclined his head agreeably. "As you wish," he said. "I shall inform Master Myrddin of the error."

Morgan chuckled to himself. He could just imagine this straightforward little boy telling Myrddin he'd made a mistake. "What can I do for you, Jahan?" he asked, taking an instant liking to the boy.

Holding his gaze steadily with a brown-eyed stare, Jahan replied succinctly. "I require nothing, Morgan. You, however, are requested to accompany me to dinner. I am to answer your questions, and to show you the temple and its grounds, as well as provide you with a brief history."

Morgan liked the youth's stern, forthright attitude. The child warmed him, reminding him of his own humanity after so long away from Earth. It didn't matter that the boy was Alfarian. It mattered only that he was a child – alive, vibrant, and wise beyond his years.

"Okay," Morgan agreed, rising to his full height and gesturing toward the open door. "Where to first?"

Jahan frowned slightly. "Master Myrddin has instructed that I am to show you the grounds first," he intoned. "Any questions you

126

may have, I will attempt to answer. If I cannot answer them, we are to seek the counsel of an adept."

Morgan continued to smile to himself as they stepped into the dimly lit inner corridor and began their trek through the massive stone structure. It occurred to him that he *might* have felt silly under other circumstances, being led around by a five-year-old boy. And yet, as he gazed at Jahan, noting the inner strength and quiet confidence, he allowed himself to relax.

As they began the tour, Morgan made a concentrated effort to absorb Jahan's intricately told history of the Temple of Ho Ling, listening intently to the line of masters from Earth's ancient past, even more intently as the boy described how Alfarians had come to Ho Ling shortly after the inclusion of Earth into the Empire in the year 2075. Morgan noted that he referred often to Myrddin, and as they stopped for a moment before entering one of the training arenas, he took advantage of Jahan's offer to answer his questions.

"You must have been here for a long time, Jahan," he observed.

The youth bowed his head in agreement. "I have studied here with the masters since the second year of my life," he replied formally.

Morgan frowned, a dozen more questions popping up as the result of a single answer. "What about your parents?" he wondered. "Do you live here all alone?"

Jahan seemed perplexed. Then, seeming to translate the question in his own mind, the confident expression returned. "She who bore me was of little consequence," he intoned as if speaking of an animal rather than his own mother. "I am told she was a worker in the brothels, hired to serve my father at the time of his Calling. As he was unbetrothed, there would have been little point in returning to Homeworld, and so a suitable female was selected in Hong Kong. I am told she was human, and that I am therefore a product of two diverse cultures." He paused, shy for the first time. "Master Myrddin tells me this makes me special, though I do not know what special should feel like."

That did surprise Morgan – not only that Jahan spoke so casually of it at his tender age, but that he seemed to fully understand the intimate details of the Alfarian mating cycle – the same cycle which had once brought Morgan and Lucien into a tangle on the floor of Mother Forest as the result of Shalice's unparalleled treachery.

He had no immediate answer and, much to his surprise, he faltered.

But the boy seemed unconcerned and as Morgan held the dark eyes, Jahan's lips curved upward just a little. "Come," he said. "The temple is large, and we have much ground to cover before supper."

Morgan blinked again. "But... what about your father?" he asked, his heart wrenching at the thought that this child had been orphaned by Alfarian parents and sent to Earth alone.

Jahan's brows lifted. "Master Myrddin *is* my father," he stated as if Morgan should have already known it.

The human's eyes widened. His mouth opened, then closed again. But as he looked at the child, it was easy to see the resemblance. Jahan had the same fine-boned features, the same broad-shouldered build, the same powerful arms and legs. The major difference, Morgan noted, was that one was considerably shorter and younger than the other. For all intents and purposes, Jahan appeared to be completely Alfarian, no doubt the result of the dominant elven genetics.

And Jahan's explanation also answered several other questions. Obviously, Myrddin *could* easily have secured a permanent life-mate. The fact that he hadn't done so could only mean one thing: he was wed already to his profession, to the students he instructed, to the art itself. It was a marriage Morgan could fully comprehend.

They were, he conceded, very much alike.

~

Lucien sat alone in his private quarters at the temple, contemplating the serenity of the sun as it slipped beneath the horizon, creating a spray of purple, pink and orange clouds. As he gazed out the cut-away window, the smell of tea roses brought all the scents of Earth to his nostrils: the rich, fertile ground of the garden, the slight dampness of the pre-evening air, the wild flowers and cultivated hybrids blooming in the meditation garden. For a

128

moment, he could almost believe he was back on Homeworld, back in the arms of the forest that had nurtured him as a boy.

And yet, he scarcely noticed those things which his five physical senses could confirm. Rather, he focused his concentration inward, consciously shutting down his normal sub-psychic vibrations as he would during meditation. His world grew silent and still, and though the Earth's early spring surrounded him, his mind returned to Alfar, reviewing the training he had undergone as a youth, preparing him to accept his new role as a master of Ho Ling. At the same, he gained a firm control of his normal emotional and spiritual emanations, disciplining his mind until no vibration of Self escaped. It was imperative that Morgan not recognize him; and the deliberate shut-down would at least make that task easier to accomplish.

Then, returning slowly to the reality of his surroundings, he turned his attention to the plate of food which had been brought to his door by one of the junior students. As was customary during the first day of his residence, he ate alone. Later, when he had been allowed his Time of Solitude, he would take his meals with student and masters alike; he would live the humble life of a teacher. That life, he acknowledged as he slowly ate the rice and snow peas, would at times be trying, even lonelier than the life he'd known on the *Starling*.

He wondered fleetingly why he had come to Ho Ling, wondered even more why Bryse had permitted it. Obviously, Kim Le and Myrddin were capable instructors, far more skilled in the fine details of the art than Lucien himself. And yet, risking everything, he had come here nonetheless.

He finished the meal quickly, then set the tray outside the door as he relied on his inner time sense to determine the hour. There were no clocks at the temple; only the sun's position in the sky and one's own personal awareness kept track of the passage of time.

His instincts informed him with complete precision that the students' supper would be concluded within minutes. After that, he was to meet with Morgan in the privacy of the central garden. His heart beat somewhat quicker with that knowledge, and he couldn't help wondering how he could pretend not to know the human, not to recognize the fire in the green-gold eyes, not to know the illustrious history of his former commander and his friend.

And yet, fully understanding what was at stake, he drew a deep breath for control, then slipped out of the cumbersome traveling garments. Picking up the black clothing which would distinguish him as a master, he began to dress, pulling on the soft cotton pants and tying them with the traditional knot in front. The thinner pull-over tunic followed, and his attire was completed by a purple sash which crossed twice around the body, and was tied with a flat reef knot on the left. It occurred to him that there were no mirrors in the living quarters, and only by instinct did he manage to comb the shiny black hair into the v-cut style.

He stood for a long moment at the door, further gathering his composure around him, making a conscious effort to still the hammering in his chest. With one hand, he smoothed the thin black beard into place, still unaccustomed to its feel against his skin.

Then, realizing he could procrastinate no longer, he opened the door and proceeded to the garden to wait. The air was cool and crisp, though he barely noticed the physical discomfort as the twilight thickened. The garden itself was immense, with stone blocks forming a maze of paths throughout the grounds. At various points, trees and plants had been cultivated to form circles of greenery and, within each circle, a woven grass mat the size of a small blanket had been provided. Approximately one meter from the ground within each of the circles, a torch burned, providing a flickering focal point for meditation, or a source of light for consultation between master and student.

Choosing the circle which summoned him at the level of spirit, Lucien entered reverently, closed his eyes for a moment as he called forth the *chi*[*1] from deep within his inner reserves. Then, kneeling before the flame of the torch, he closed his eyes and began a light meditation, awaiting the arrival of his new student.

~

---

[1]. Chi: The inner strength and essence of the being; a source of power.

"Master Lucien?"

With an effort, Lucien managed not to start at the abrupt intrusion into his meditation. In a fraction of a second, his heart leaped, then quieted as he realized full well that the voice was not that of Morgan Diego. He opened his eyes, lifting his head slowly to encounter another Alfarian – a man whose face was known to him through holos Bryse had provided.

"I am Myrddin," the other said softly, taking but one step into the meditation circle. "Your presence does honor to the Temple, Lucien."

Lucien inclined his head graciously, then gestured to the mat with one hand. "I am honored to serve, Myrddin," he replied correctly. "Please, sit with me." It wasn't at all what he wanted, yet protocol demanded his courtesy. And he had to admit that this man knew far more of the current situation than he did himself. With an effort, he curbed his own impatience.

Myrddin bowed, entering the circle, then knelt on the grass mat facing him. "Since there will be little time for us to speak freely tonight," he began, "I will dispense with formal amenities for the sake of expediency."

Lucien indicated agreement, waiting.

"Morgan is an exceptional student of the art," Myrddin said quietly. "But there is also great anger within him." He paused, and Lucien noticed a faint, easy smile on the edges of his lips. "As the two of you have known one another previously, and as you have been separated, I think it only right that you be aware of current circumstances."

Once more, Lucien inclined his head in acknowledgement.

Myrddin was silent for a moment as if in contemplation, then continued slowly. "Morgan has learned to shield almost totally against undesired invasion. However, it is clear to me that his efforts at control are occasionally subverted by his own anger, his powerful emotions."

"He has always been so," Lucien commented, nonetheless grateful for the confirmation of what he'd already suspected.

"Additionally," Myrddin continued, his face seemed to glimmer in the torch's flickering glow, "he has become aware of certain incidents which were removed from his memory."

Lucien's brows lifted. He hadn't expected such a direct accusation so abruptly. And yet, as he studied Myrddin in the dim light, he realized that no disrespect was intended. Rather, Myrddin was morally bound to reveal full truth to another recognized master. Still, the additional confirmation of another of Lucien's suspicions left him momentarily unnerved.

"It was necessary," he stated, his tone far more clipped than he would have preferred.

"I do not question your motives, Lucien," Myrddin replied without defensiveness. "I merely seek to inform you of the obstacles you will face in Morgan's continued training." He paused as if to let that settle, then continued. "At any rate, he holds no anger against you for the incident which occurred during your time of Calling. However, it is clear to me that his feelings for you are intense, and are also a great source of turmoil."

Lucien found himself fidgeting uncomfortably as Myrddin's eyes penetrated his defenses. He realized fleetingly that, in many ways, he was out of his league here. Myrddin *was* a master; and though Lucien had studied the art faithfully for many years on Alfar and had achieved the status of an accomplished adept, he had not completed the disciplines required for mastery of the art. But with an effort, he curbed his defensive impatience and merely waited for the other to go on.

Myrddin was once again silent for a time, then spoke very softly. "Please understand, Lucien, that I do not tell you these things to awaken any rivalry between us, nor to place you ill-at-ease in my presence. It is for Morgan's sake that I must speak the full truth with you at this time."

Lucien realized absently that he was holding his breath and, releasing it, he sighed softly. "I do not understand. If Morgan is capable of shielding against the Mizarian probe–."

But Myrddin waved him to silence. "It is not his ability to shield which troubles me, Lucien," he said. "It is the fact that his feelings for you weaken his concentration." He paused, meeting and holding Lucien's gaze, then saying exactly what had to be said. "He will not be at peace until both body and spirit are fulfilled – and that fulfillment shall not come until he shares your thoughts... and your bed."

Lucien blinked, grateful that the dim lighting effectively concealed his deep flush. It surprised him to hear another speak so openly and casually of a kinsman's private affairs. And yet, once again, he reminded himself of the reasons. But his greater shock came with the sudden, unannounced and unexpected revelation that Morgan wanted him as he had wanted Morgan for over two years. He took a deep, trembling breath, attempting to summon the same degree of honesty and openness which Myrddin had already displayed. But it wasn't a simple task.

"My... feelings for… Morgan," he corrected, surprised he could be so rattled in such a short period of time, "are a matter of private concern, Myrddin. I mean no disrespect by that statement, yet–."

"It is not *your* feelings which are a matter for concern, Lucien," Myrddin said when Lucien's voice trailed off. "If Morgan fails to shield from the Mizarians because of his feelings for you, not only will your identity be revealed to him as a result, but it is conceivable that the Mizarians will also be able to distinguish the ruse. Should that happen, the consequences are grim."

Lucien wanted very much to flee to the sanctuary of his room, to bury his face in the pillow and make some attempt to control his suddenly rampant and conflicting emotions. And yet, he realized with an odd sense of detachment that, once again, Myrddin was correct. He was within his rights as an Alfarian and as a master of the art to reveal the truth – *and* to demand it.

Forcing a calmness onto himself, Lucien looked up at last, meeting the other's penetrating dark gaze. "What would you have me do, Master?" he asked, indicating his acquiescence to the other by use of the title.

Myrddin bowed his head in acknowledgement of the position of authority. "For the sake of all concerned, Lucien, you must endeavor to fill the emptiness within him – and soon."

Lucien's brows furrowed. "I do not understand."

Myrddin was thoughtfully silent for a moment, then took a deep breath of the cool evening air. "He has the needs of a human,

Lucien," he explained. "Currently, he can think only of you. For as long as he is unfulfilled, he will continue to long for the relationship you never shared; he will continue to be distracted by thoughts of yesterday rather than focused on thoughts of tomorrow. Eventually," he concluded, "his shields will buckle – and we shall all be at the mercy of the Mizarians."

Lucien wondered fleetingly if Myrddin were attempting to tell him he shouldn't have come to the Temple of Ho Ling in the first place. And yet, considering all else his kinsman had said, he had no doubt that Myrddin would have stated it straightforward if that were his insinuation. He waited, then spoke haltingly.

"If I understand you correctly," he said, "you are encouraging me to... establish a...."

"I am encouraging nothing, Lucien," Myrddin said firmly. "I am telling you that, if Morgan's survival – or even your own – is important to you, you have no alternative but to fill his mind and his heart with thoughts of something other than his past." He paused, his tone softening just a little. "It is *you* he desires," he stressed. "But if you cannot bring yourself to do what must be done, then I shall have no choice but to act in your stead."

At that, Lucien's eyes widened. He stared at the other man almost without seeing as that statement penetrated his thick layer of resistance. "I would recommend, Master Myrddin, that you do not threaten me."

But instead of anger or even disapproval, Myrddin only smiled very gently. "Please, Lucien," he said. "Morgan is not a morsel of bread over which we should quibble. If you will internalize that knowledge, it will be much easier for the two of us to work together."

Lucien fought the heart-felt urge to snap the other's neck then and there. But as he allowed Myrddin's words to register, he realized with a sense of profound embarrassment that his kinsman was only doing what he would have done had their positions been reversed. And he reminded himself once more that Myrddin was a master – a man devoted to accomplishment of the art, incapable of lies or ulterior motives.

With a supreme effort, Lucien checked his emotions,

summoning up the discipline of reason. "If Morgan's feelings are as you say, it will be difficult to establish a relationship with him in my current guise."

But Myrddin's brows lifted. "Do not sell yourself short, Lucien," he said quietly. "Only your physical appearance has changed – and not so much, judging by holos I have seen. What you are inside remains unaltered. The part of you that has captured Morgan's heart and mind will do so again."

"In which case," Lucien pointed out, "recognition of my identity is inevitable."

But Myrddin shook his head. "Morgan will recognize the spirit, perhaps; but he will remain uncertain of other attributes. That uncertainty is what will shield him from the Mizarians. And eventually, his shields will become so powerful that no unwanted mental contact will be possible."

Somehow, that thought disturbed Lucien deeply. "In which case," he stated, "he will be giving up any possibility of regaining his intuition." It also occurred to him that, without the mental contact, a lifelink would be impossible. But he quickly set that thought aside, surprised that it surfaced without warning; he wondered if he were moving too fast.

"You are forgetting one key thing, Lucien," Myrddin said quietly, drawing him from his reverie.

"Which is?"

"*'Unwanted'*," Myrddin explained. "As Morgan progresses in his studies, as he becomes an adept, he will learn to selectively choose what to allow within his spirit, and what to decline." His eyes softened, his tone lowering when he spoke again. "In time, even if it is not possible to reverse the Mizarian Directive, the two of you *can* share what you have both been seeking for many years."

Lucien wondered fleetingly if Myrddin were capable of reading his thoughts, or if he had simply become proficient at guessing. "You assume much," he commented, though without anger.

Myrddin's lips pressed to a soft half-smile. "It is not necessary to assume, Lucien, when truth is so clearly visible in both parties." But he didn't wait for an answer as he rose gracefully to his feet. "I must leave you now. Your student will arrive momentarily."

In accordance with courtesy and tradition, Lucien likewise rose, bowing from the waist as was customary among the masters. But his surprise came when the other Alfarian took a step forward and placed both arms firmly around his back, pulling him into an ancient embrace reserved for Warriors of the Clan.

Stunned, but realizing that to refuse such an embrace would be a mark of dishonor, Lucien allowed his arms to raise until his hands clasped palm-to-palm behind Myrddin's back. Then, lifting his head, he tried not to flinch as his distant kinsman completed the ritualistic gesture which had been common practice on Alfar thousands of years in the past.

The master leaned forward, placing his lips softly against Lucien's bearded cheek. "That is for honor," he murmured. Then, turning to the other cheek and placing another kiss there, he intoned, "That is for *chi*." And finally, placing one hand on each side of Lucien's face, Myrddin pressed his lips lightly to his mouth. "And this is for you."

Too stunned to protest or even to react, Lucien merely held his breath, relieved when Myrddin at last took the customary step of parting, disappearing from the meditation circle and padding silently into the darkness beyond. For a very long time, Lucien simply stood there, his lips still tingling from the other's uninvited kiss.

The meaning of the gesture was plain – a gesture among warriors. In times of need, it was an invitation. In times of solitude, it was an offer of comfort. In times of war, it was the offer of a brother's blade to end a life of pain.

Between masters, it was all of those things and more. It was a statement of brotherhood, a declaration of union. Morgan Diego, it seemed, was their common bond.

CHAPTER ELEVEN

Morgan stood at the head of the garden path, gazing out over the serenity before him. The stones wound through the grounds in a maze, illuminated slightly by the pale iridescence of the almost-full moon. In the cool night air, the scent of jasmine was delicate, and as he mentally gathered his bearings, he set his sights on the spot where Jahan said he was to meet with his new master for the first time.

Despite the fact that he'd resigned himself to this peculiar new life, to the responsibility which had settled squarely on his shoulders even in the midst of social exile, he felt an odd sense of rebellion threatening to surface. For a moment, as he stood gazing up at the night sky, the moon and the stars, his heart wrenched, reawakening memories he had thought put to sleep. In that instant, he could easily understand the frustration ancient man must have experienced – the primal need to jump toward the lights in the sky, or to toss stones at the face of the moon.

The stars are in your heart like grains of sand. Words some psychic gypsy lady had spoken to him when he was barely nine years old, yet words he had never forgotten.

And yet… now the stars were only fool's gold, glittering and out of reach.

He stopped himself before he could become maudlin, focusing on the Now instead of the distant past or the unreachable future.

Myrddin had said only that his new master – Master Lucien – would instruct him in the arts of defense and wholistic awareness. Myrddin had also insinuated that this new teacher would in some manner help him to find the inner peace which seemed elusive and every bit as distant as the farthest speck of light glimmering in the void.

And yet, it was difficult to trust; and he wasn't at all certain that he truly wanted that kind of peace. If it meant losing the ability to dream, the drive to excel, then it seemed counter-productive. But as he recalled Kim Le, the harmony the old man had achieved while still maintaining the fire in his eyes, he couldn't help envying his peculiar little mentor. Kim Le had found his peace, yet he still had the drive to free the oppressed, to speak of slavery and freedom in realistic terms, and to instill within at least one human student the importance of every single sentient entity.

Sighing heavily, Morgan tried to reconcile the clashing philosophies in his mind, tried even harder to expel the nervousness which crept into his stomach as he began the short walk along the stone path. He did not know what this new master would expect from him, if he would speak in philosophies and riddles as Kim Le was fond of doing, or if he would pick away at truth and perform elaborate tests to expose inner weaknesses as Myrddin had done.

But the thing he knew would be the hardest would be to call his new master by the one name which haunted his mind like an eternally restless spirit.

It occurred to him that he was walking much slower than necessary. It also occurred to him that his new master was undoubtedly as sworn to punctuality as Myrddin or Kim Le. And with that in mind, he quickened his stride, lifting his chin just a little as he walked the last few steps, then stopped respectfully just outside the meditation circle.

Whatever awaited him would simply have to be viewed as another challenge, the next step along a path of knowledge which Myrddin had promised would be a difficult road.

With his head bowed, his eyes closed to show trust and respect, he stepped into the cleared circle, kneeling on the grass mat as he presented himself to his new master. He was aware only of another presence, and a single silly thought caused him to hope he'd come to the right place.

After another moment, he opened his eyes, lifting his head as he continued to kneel. He took a few seconds to study the man before him, his stomach knotting as he realized this new master was not what he had been expecting. Somehow, he'd been prepared for a much less imposing figure than the black-clad Alfarian who knelt before him. Somehow, he'd expected a smaller stature and more weathered features. Somehow, he hadn't been prepared for *this* Lucien to bear a striking resemblance to *his* Lucien.

But with the training Myrddin had given him, he contained his

138

reaction well, and began studying the other more dispassionately. The other man's features were angular, with prominent cheekbones and a defined jaw-line. His eyes, Morgan immediately noted, were lighter than he might have expected; and the long black hair with its glimmering gold-bronze streak, and the short-clipped beard gave him an appearance which might have been mistaken for sinister had it not been for the kind and compassionate expression. He wore the black robes of a master, as well as a single piece of ornamental jewelry – a black collar with an ebony-stone imbedded in the center. An uninvited thought caused Morgan to contemplate the idea that the man in front of him would have made a good pirate.

For a noticeable interval neither spoke and Morgan began to wonder if he had made some breach of etiquette and had succeeded in displeasing his new teacher already. It almost seemed as if the Alfarian were studying him every bit as intently as he had done in reverse.

"Morgan," the deep voice said at last, stating his name as a fact rather than a question.

Morgan inclined his head in the proper acknowledgement, though his eyes remained lifted and locked with those of his master. There was something in the Alfarian's demeanor which instantly put him at ease, and he couldn't help wondering if he were a hopeless sap for anyone bearing even a faint resemblance to his former friend.

Hopeless, The Little Voice agreed. *Hopelessly introspective. Hopelessly indecisive. Hopelessly in love with every Alfarian male who crosses your path. Hopeless.*

He shot The Little Voice a nasty comment which silenced it, at least temporarily.

In a fraction of a second, the incident with Myrddin replayed itself in his thoughts, leaving him with alternating feelings of emotional frustration and spiritual exhilaration. But as he tore those over-analyzed images from his mind and focused his attention once more on his newly assigned teacher, he swore a silent vow of loyalty. To what or to whom, he was no longer certain. Perhaps, he conceded, it was even an oath of celibacy.

Yeah... right.

But his annoying reverie was cut short as the Alfarian spoke again.

"I am told, Morgan," he said quietly, "that your recent path has been a difficult one, and that you seek to master the art in order to regain your own past."

Morgan considered the words, not certain if an answer were expected or not. As the silence, grew, however, he was almost compelled to respond. "Yes," he confirmed, his voice seeming far sadder than he actually felt inside. "I assume Master Myrddin or Kim Le has informed you of how I came to be here."

The other man nodded. "I am aware of the unwanted burden you carry in your mind," he intoned, though Morgan noticed that he seemed to be trembling just a little. "I am also told that you have become somewhat proficient at blocking this Mizarian probe."

Morgan smiled faintly. "I'm not so sure about my proficiency," he replied, allowing himself to relax somewhat from the strict formality, "but I haven't been aware of it for about a week now."

The other seemed to consider that in momentary silence and, this time, Morgan was certain he saw the other man tremble. The night air was cool, yet the torch gave off enough warmth to heat their immediate vicinity, and he thought it unlikely that cold was entirely responsible. And yet, seeing no other reasonable explanation, he put the idea from his mind.

"Tomorrow," the Alfarian said at last, "we will begin your formal training. Tonight, however, it is important to discuss those things which are a source of trouble to you."

Morgan frowned, recalling a similar first-meeting conversation with Myrddin shortly after he'd broken the suspended tree limb. They'd talked for several hours – about his past, his hometown, the family dog, about everything and nothing at all. But at the very least, he conceded, he *did* need to talk. The subject matter wasn't terribly important.

Taking a deep breath, he met the other's eyes, smiling somewhat shyly. "I'd hate to be accused of boring you to death," he warned with a grin.

"Boredom is the result of an inattentive mind," Master Lucien said presently. "I am most interested in anything you may wish to say."

Morgan found himself at a momentary loss for words. At least Myrddin and Kim Le had been constantly prodding, questioning, demanding. This soft-spoken master seemed far more reserved, even distant. And yet, there was something compelling in that distance, a challenge which, illogically, he found himself hard-pressed to ignore.

He shrugged again, almost nervously. "I'm not sure what you want me to say," he ventured, trying to lure the other into making the first dangerous move.

"If I am to teach you," Lucien murmured softly, "it would be helpful to know those things which distract you from your studies. I am told by Master Myrddin that, at times, your anger is great."

At that, despite his expected reverence, Morgan laughed aloud. "Told you that, did he?" he said with a grin. But he sobered quickly, noting the other's confused expression. "Let's just say that I had a life, a career, and friends that were very important to me. I very much want those things back. And... well... yes: I *do* get angry when I think about it."

"Why?" the Alfarian asked in a deep, soft voice.

Morgan shrugged, ignoring the inexplicable goosebumps which prickled along his arms. "I'm not sure," he said, then quickly rephrased. "What I mean is that I'm not sure why my anger comes *out* like it does." Recalling the incidents Myrddin had obviously spoken of, he added: "When it happens, it's as if I strike out at the nearest target. Sometimes the people closest to me get in the way."

"Or become the target," Master Lucien commented.

Morgan glanced up sharply. "Yeah," he conceded, not liking that part of himself. "I guess so."

Once more, Master Lucien was silent. Then, looking up, he held Morgan's eyes with an intensity which caused the human to shudder inside. Something told him he would not be able to hide even the most insignificant detail from this man.

"Many times," the master said at last, "it is important to establish priorities before long-term goals may be set. By defining what causes your anger, it may be possible to control it more adequately, to internalize it effectively."

Morgan considered that, choosing his response carefully. It wasn't easy to discuss his weaknesses so openly, yet he reminded himself that this man was here to help him, that this man might well hold the key to his answer if not the answer itself. "I guess the biggest part of the anger comes from being used," he said finally, "from knowing that the Mizarians are playing some mental hide-and-seek game inside my head, using *me* to keep the Empire in line."

"What else?" Lucien questioned softly.

Morgan shrugged, realizing that the very anger they spoke of was dangerously close to the surface merely as a result of the conversation. He wanted very much to deny that anything at all was out of the ordinary, wanted to convince himself that it was a nightmare from which he would soon awaken. And yet, as he recalled the eight months and some odd days of waking each morning, only to have the nightmare continue, he conceded that denial would play no part in the answer.

He sighed heavily, running the fingers of one hand over the knobby texture of the woven grass mat upon which he knelt. Then, looking up, he met the probing dark eyes, suddenly uncomfortable with the conversation.

"Morgan?"

He nodded, battling the urge to lash out at invisible demons as he thought once more of everything that had been left behind. The *Starling*. Lucien. Vanya. His entire past, his entire life. His jaw tightened almost imperceptibly and, shaking his head, he felt the old familiar frustration bend its powerful arms around him.

"Maybe we should talk about this later, Master Lucien," he said, the word feeling wrong on his tongue when spoken to a comparative stranger. Then, trying to soften the impact of that implied rejection, he offered a smile which came only from his lips, never passing near his heart. "I wouldn't want *you* to get in the way of my anger, too."

Instead of the argument Morgan had fully expected, the other merely inclined his head in agreement, then rose gracefully to his feet in a single fluid movement. "Come," he said, extending one hand down in an offer of help. "Walk with me."

142

For a reason Morgan couldn't pinpoint, he immediately reached out to accept the other's hand, feeling an odd sense of comfort pour through him as the Alfarian pulled him effortlessly to his feet. He wanted very much to please this man – not only for his own satisfaction, but so that he *could* eventually beat the Mizarians at their own game. And yet, he couldn't deny the emotions which rampaged, unchecked, so close to the surface.

But before he had time to analyze it further, he found himself walking at his teacher's side as they left the meditation area and began a slow, deliberate stroll through the center of the garden. Morgan noticed that neither spoke even as they entered the temple building and proceeded down the long curved corridors. Eventually, with his teacher a half-step in the lead, they came to another door on the outer wall, went through it, and emerged in the outer grounds.

Here, Morgan noted by the light of the moon now directly overhead, the trees grew somewhat taller; the low-lying shrubbery was less carefully trimmed to perfection, and the scent of tea roses hung lightly on the air. Nearby, the creek which cut through the temple grounds bubbled and rushed, creating a soft background melody which soothed some of his frustration away. He wondered briefly why the Alfarian had brought him here, but resigned himself to wait for an answer.

They continued walking for a few minutes more, then stopped as they drew up alongside the creek. On the bank, a large stone boulder provided a slight buffer against the light breeze and, leaning against it, Morgan took a deep breath, surprised at the sudden serenity which replaced his previous frustration.

"It's so peaceful here," he said, as much to himself as to the other man.

In the moonlight, Master Lucien's lips seemed to curve upward just a little. "I had felt that perhaps you would be more comfortable away from the formal gardens, Morgan," he commented. "You prefer chaos to order."

Despite himself, Morgan chuckled. "Yeah, I guess you're right. When I was a kid, I was always happier splashing around in the creek at my grandmother's than swimming in the back-yard pool."

He shrugged, somehow comforted by the memories of home. "My mom never did understand why, and back then I didn't know how to tell her."

"Why *did* you prefer the creek?" Master Lucien inquired with a seemingly genuine interest.

Again, Morgan smiled. "I think it had something to do with the fact that it was... I dunno... *alive*. It was filled with stones and moss and probably even a snake or two."

"And with dangers," Master Lucien commented.

Morgan considered that. "Yeah, I suppose so." He shook his head, laughing lightly, fondly. "But it was... *real*. The pool always seemed so... impersonal." He smiled again, pulling himself abruptly back to reality. "I know it doesn't make much sense."

"On the contrary," the Alfarian disagreed. "It is always preferable to follow one's instincts rather than to agree with the majority simply because they *are* the majority. In your case, it's obvious that you were more comfortable within nature."

Morgan found himself relaxing considerably as he saw the Alfarian's wisdom demonstrated in more than one fashion. His teacher *was* correct; he was far more at ease here than he had been in the formal gardens. Taking a moment to simply appreciate the beauty surrounding him, he studied the creek in the moonlight, listening to the chirp of crickets and the occasional twitter of a nightbird crying in its sleep.

He glanced from time to time at his quiet instructor, studying the sharp outline of the angular features, watching the controlled rise and fall of the black-clad chest.

"*You* seem more relaxed here, too," he commented presently.

Long brows formed a question mark.

Morgan grinned warmly. "You've stopped trembling," he observed. "While we were in the garden, you seemed... uncomfortable."

For a moment, the Alfarian seemed to falter. Then, taking a noticeably deep breath, he quickly regained his composure. "I have been... ill recently," he said.

For a moment, Morgan felt decidedly guilty for keeping the other man out in the cold. "Maybe we should go back inside," he

144

offered. "The air *is* awfully cool. I know your people prefer the warmer climates."

But instead of accepting his suggestion, the other man shook his head. "I was not aware that you knew so much about Alfarian physiology."

Morgan's smile slowly faded. "I had a very good friend who was Alfarian," he said, his mind filling again with memories of Lucien.

For a long second, the other man didn't reply. Then, taking a step closer, he spoke very softly. "It is apparent that you miss him very much, Morgan," he said.

Morgan's mouth opened to deny that gentle accusation, but when he remembered where he was and why he was there, he abandoned the ludicrous attempt and settled instead for the truth. "I do," he said, his voice very quiet as he looked once more toward the sky and a terrible aching thought struck him. "I don't even know where he is now."

"Perhaps," the Alfarian master murmured, "he is closer than you think."

Morgan sighed softly, ignoring the wistful comment, wishing he could reach that place deep within himself where all his memories of his friend dwelled. But somehow, even that seemed distant, unreachable, leaving him filled with an awful sadness which threatened to tear his heart from his chest.

"You know what hurts the most?" he whispered, the pain suddenly overwhelming him in its bright intensity.

"Please tell me."

Morgan took a deep breath, swallowing the anguish which rose unbidden in his throat as he continued gazing up at the moon, the light scattering of clouds and the stars hidden from view. On the *Dreaming Bird*, he'd had little time to think, to dwell on the past. But here, it came back to him with a sudden, unforgiving vengeance. "What hurts the most," he said, feeling strangely near to his former friend, yet terribly far away, "is remembering all the things I *should* have said to him, all the things we should have done, all the things we may never have a chance to do again."

He didn't notice that Master Lucien inhaled sharply as he

spoke, didn't notice the warmth glistening in the bright-dark eyes. Instead, he listened only to the silence between each second, saw only the mist of stars glittering so far from his reach. His very soul ached, the wounds re-opening as he touched them with his thoughts.

"Once you have completed your training," the deep voice said at last, "perhaps the opportunity will come again."

Somehow, Morgan couldn't share that optimism and, sighing heavily, he slid down the supporting rock until he sat on the ground with his knees pulled tight to his chest. "I don't even know if he's dead or alive," he repeated, that thought haunting him until he clenched his eyes tightly shut and tried to swallow the pain which strangled his throat. Space was a vicious mistress. There were no guarantees.

"You would know, Morgan, if he were not alive," the other man said with absolute certainty.

Morgan looked up, meeting the dark gaze in the moonlight. The Alfarian's eyes seemed far too bright, his expression somehow too fearful. And though he tried to accept the offered solace, he found it difficult to internalize as he gazed wordlessly at the man standing before him. His emotions surged, leaving him with a sense of desperation which was almost as familiar now as breathing. For a moment, he found himself wishing hopelessly for Lucien – *his* Lucien – or even for the comforting embrace of Myrddin.

His throat ached; his heart pounded; tears brimmed, unshed, in his eyes. He had nowhere to turn, nowhere left to run. And his strength seemed more like a past memory rather than a part of him now.

"Damn," he swore in a hoarse whisper. "*Damn....*"

He was only peripherally aware of the Alfarian kneeling next to him, and of the hand which reached out to rest supportively on his shoulder.

"Come," the gentle voice entreated as his master tried to help him to his feet. "Your journey to the temple has been a difficult one. I will see you to your room."

Morgan didn't even bother to protest or try to argue. Instead, he allowed himself to be pulled to his feet, almost grateful despite his embarrassment for the arm which remained strong and supportive around his shoulder. As they walked the short distance back toward the temple building, he found himself leaning into the other's strength, accepting for once in his life the solace of another when his own reserves faltered.

When they entered the building through the secluded doorway, Morgan noticed absently that the corridors were empty, the lights dimmed for evening. Torches burned low in their stone holders, and the scent of a gentle incense filled the air.

As they reached his assigned room, Morgan made an effort to right himself, growing self-conscious as reality struggled to return him to full awareness. He had met this man for the first time only hours before, and now, spiritually broken and sick with a love he might never fulfill, he was allowing himself to be comforted in the arms of a stranger. He came close to hating himself for that weakness – for he was beginning to see it as a pattern rather than an occasional fluke.

He was a broken man, though acknowledging that fact was far more difficult than he had ever imagined it might be.

And yet, as the Alfarian opened the door to his room and followed him inside, Morgan felt his lofty ideals float away, scattering through the cut-away window against the far wall. He wanted very much to explain the seeming weakness of his actions, yet his experiences with Kim Le and Myrddin reminded him that, in all probability, this compassionate master probably understood without lengthy verbalizations of the obvious.

With an effort, he extricated himself from the other's supportive embrace, standing in the center of the room as he lifted his eyes respectfully. "I ask forgiveness, Master Lucien," he said quietly. Then, remembering the traditional phrases, he added: "If you will have me as your student, I will study to master the art by your teachings."

The master's eyes glistened, but he inclined his head formally. Then, holding Morgan's gaze, the formalities were concluded. "No forgiveness is necessary for honesty, Morgan," he murmured. "And... I will not only have you as my student, Morgan, but I would be honored to claim you as my friend."

There was something in the Alfarian's demeanor that caused Morgan to tremble, something in the deep voice which made him want to weep. He held on with his last ounce of control. Then, remembering the discipline of his training, he bowed gracefully to show acceptance of the other's proposal. "I seem to need all the friends I can get, Master Lucien," he said, not finding it as difficult as he'd thought it might be to admit his needs aloud.

Master Lucien smiled easily, then stepped back toward the corridor nonetheless. "My door is open to you at all times, Morgan," he stated quietly.

Again, Morgan nodded, fighting the overwhelming urge to take the Alfarian up on that offer, to sleep just once in the other's arms in order to gather his own strength back again. But he resisted that temptation with discipline alone, determined to rely on inner resources rather than on fleeting physical gratification.

You're starting to piss me off, The Little Voice complained, his own personal devil. *There was a time when you would've had this guy in bed so fast it would make his shiny head spin! He's hot. You're hot. What's the problem? Why all the analysis and none of the action?*

"Shut up," Morgan muttered under his breath, horrified an instant later to realize he'd spoken aloud.

"I'm sorry?" Master Lucien said with a quizzical expression.

Morgan waved his own words aside. "I – I'm sorry, Master Lucien," he said, struggling to recover, making a mental note to strangle The Little Voice first chance he got. "I was just thinking out loud."

To his relief, the other man didn't pry, just nodded with a reassuring smile.

But the moment the door closed behind the Alfarian, Morgan flopped onto the edge of his bed, curling onto his side with his feet still on the floor. A thousand new questions raged through his mind; a thousand possible answers brought only a new barrage of questions. He wondered if his first assumption had been correct – if he were losing his grip on reality, losing the strength he had always possessed so naturally. Clearly, The Little Voice thought so – and in many ways, that nasty little pest was right. In the entire course of his life, he had never felt so helpless, so lost, and so utterly analytical. In the past, everything had simply flowed – one action into the next, like a well-oiled machine. Now, it seemed, that sense of instinct had been reduced to the need for constant questioning, perpetual thinking.

It occurred to him only briefly that perhaps that was simply part of the process. If learning to block the Mizarian probe required temporarily relinquishing his instinct, maybe it stood to reason that he would be forced to replace instinct with reasoning, impulse with analysis.

You're doing it again, The Little Voice commented.

He sighed, a snort of annoyance.

First, Myrddin had rattled his control, shaking it loose with results which could easily have been devastating. Now, less than a week later, his new teacher – a man who carried the same beloved name as his treasured friend – tore those re-built controls loose again, leaving him trembling and terrified and filled with loneliness in the middle of his small bed.

He clenched his eyes tightly shut, his hands clamped into fists on the pillow as he tried to drive the images of three Alfarians from his mind. It would have been a relatively simple matter, he thought, to go to Myrddin's bed chamber, to rest in the Alfarian's arms and allow himself to think of Lucien as they made love.

But what terrified him was the thought that it would have been equally as simple to have asked his new master to stay with him as he slept. At the very least, he thought mournfully, if he whispered the Alfarian's name, if he cried out in his sleep, the name on his lips would be the correct one.

He drove the thought from his mind, telling himself it was only his weariness which prompted the insane ideas. He had been alone before; he could be alone now.

I'll keep you company, The Little Voice offered. *Till death do us part.*

It wasn't exactly what Morgan had in mind.

~

Closing the door behind him as he left, Lucien leaned hard

against the stone wall, his mind spinning in too many divergent directions for normal methods of control to be effective. He had expected his first encounter with Morgan after so long a period of separation to be a difficult one; he had not, however, been prepared for the degree of difficulty he had faced.

Irrationally, he had allowed himself to believe that his own not-completely-defined feelings had been brought under control, that the time of separation on the *Starling* and at Earthbase One had given him an adequate perspective.

Now, with his heart pattering much too quickly and the blood pounding in his ears, he realized the crucial error. And yet, it was too late to turn back, too late to abandon the task to those with stricter controls and more effective training.

He thought instantly of Myrddin, of the other man's gently worded threat. *'If you cannot bring yourself to do what must be done, I shall have no choice but to act in your stead'*. What irritated Lucien was that, realistically, it wasn't a threat at all.

Clasping his hands tightly together, he gathered as much of his failing composure as he could manage, then began a slow and weary walk back to his own sleeping quarters. When he had spoken with Myrddin earlier in the evening, he had thought the other master to have over-stated the seriousness of the problem. Yet now, after seeing Morgan again, it was clear to see that, if anything, Myrddin had underestimated the depth of the human's despair.

Never had Lucien known his friend to project such an aura of aloneness, of desperation, of hopelessness. And though he understood that Morgan's intentions to overcome the Mizarian probe were honest ones, he also knew that another old Earth proverb was completely applicable. No man was an island – including Morgan Diego.

As Myrddin had discreetly predicted, Lucien witnessed symptoms in the human which foretold his eventual downfall. Sooner or later, he realized, Morgan would become unable to block the probe as his unchecked emotions ate away at the disciplines and controls he had only recently begun to learn. On the *Starling*, his commander would have vented those frustrations in the form of physical aggressions – strenuous work-outs in the gym, lap after lap around the large pool, or an occasional encounter with some nameless woman on some backwater planet.

Here, however, that final option was no longer available; and though the exercise and exertion required of Morgan in his physical training were of some benefit, Lucien began to understand that it alone was not sufficient to counter the mounting despair in the human's spirit. In the past, if he had been required to state the one attribute which made Morgan unique unto himself, Lucien would have replied without hesitation. It was his sense of freedom – not only a freedom of spirit, but a freedom of flesh as well. It was a freedom which, on occasion, he had envied.

Now, in the Temple of Ho Ling, he realized, it was a freedom he must seek to master if Morgan were ever to regain all that he had been, if he was to become all he was capable of being.

As he walked through the curved corridor of the temple, he passed by his own door more than once, continuing his thoughtful trek in silence and contemplation. The torches had burned low as the early morning solitude took him around the circular building repeatedly, depositing him at last back at his starting point outside the human's door.

He listened for a moment, hearing no sounds of movement from within. Apparently, Morgan's exhaustion had finally won out over human stubbornness, and sleep was the only possible outcome.

Feeling somewhat relieved at that fact, he hesitated only a moment longer, then moved along once more through the dim stone hallway, attempting to cope with the dichotomy which burned deep within himself. His own feelings were oddly mixed, his ability to make decisions rattled by the events of the evening.

He wanted very much to follow the instincts which had driven him to Ho Ling in the first place. He wanted to take Morgan to him as brother and mate, to speak of unspoken things, to couple mind and flesh to the one person in all the galaxy who could awaken such feelings. And yet, he wanted that for *himself* – not in the guise of some stranger, not with his heart crying out to take what his mind dared not trespass. For until Morgan mastered the art, Lucien realized, any coupling they may enter would be consigned to a half-

151

fulfilling physical level alone.

And yet, as that thought manifested, it was countered by
another. Regardless of what *he* wanted, what *he* desired, it seemed
that *Morgan* required that physical joining, the comfort of touch, the
renowned ecstasy of sexual release. It was, after all, human nature.
Deny it at one's own peril. And if Myrddin's insinuations were in
any way accurate, the human's *mind* would provide some
convenient fantasy to alleviate the fact that the joining was
accomplished on a physical level alone.

His mind reeled, spinning, his head aching down to the base of
his neck. And he understood with a sense of overwhelming pride
that it was *himself* that Morgan desired. Now, with so many months
of separation and so much anguish in the human's heart, the
reasons scarcely seemed to matter. And Lucien also understood that
Morgan *had* recaptured the memories which *he* had once taken
away. What surprised him was the fact that his friend's reaction had
been one of physical need and emotional desire rather than one of
anger or rejection.

He felt terribly unworthy.

Drawing up at last in front of his own door, he entered his
room quietly, and went to lean on the sill of the cut-away window,
his eyes fixed on a glimmering silver creek which bubbled
pleasantly under the setting moon. The serenity filled him with a
sense of peacefulness despite his inner turmoil, and he remained
that way for a very long time, listening to the sounds of animals in
the night, inhaling the delicate scent of tea roses and wild lemon
grass.

Weariness from his journey to the temple eventually drove him
to his bed, and after undressing, he stretched full-length beneath the
soft cotton sheets. In the morning, he told himself, his controls
would be better. After he had slept, coherency would return to his
mind. And by the afternoon, he would once again be reunited with
Morgan Diego – this time in the training arena where they would
spar with flesh and possibly even with words. In that, Myrddin was
once again correct: Morgan's anger was as a great ball of emotional
infection burning hot just beneath the skin.

But as sleep crept nearer, it wasn't the human's anger which filled Lucien's thoughts. Rather, it was Morgan's profound ability to love so deeply and so desperately even after all that had occurred. What he couldn't completely comprehend was *why* – of all the lifeforms in the galaxy, of all the lovers Morgan had taken to his bed and the few he had taken into his heart – why *he* should have become the object of that overwhelming human love.

It scared him half to death.

CHAPTER TWELVE

Following the morning meal – at which he saw neither Myrddin nor Master Lucien – and his required meditation prior to his formal studies, Morgan walked to the training area where Jahan had said he was to report. Remembering Myrddin's words, he realized that his morning hours would be spent with his first Alfarian instructor, while his afternoons would be assigned to Master Lucien.

With a night's sleep under his belt, and a meditation which had consisted of nothing spectacular, he felt somewhat more confident than he had the evening before and as he stopped just outside the door, he took a moment to study his surroundings, mentally comparing the facilities here with those on the *Dreaming Bird.*

The door in front of him was painted with the same symbols he had seen on the ship: the human-toned fist and empty hand, the Alfarian-inspired clasped hands with steepled fingers. And as he remembered Jahan's history of the temple, he recalled with an odd sense of pride that an identical temple had been constructed in Mother Forest, near the organic city where Lucien had grown up. There, he was told, students and masters performed identical training exercises, though amongst a more typically forest-inspired garden, and in a much cooler clime. Before complete mastery of the art, he had been told, a student might be required to study with the instructors on Alfarian as well.

He sighed to himself, wondering fleetingly just how long this training and mastery would require. And yet, when he recalled that he had little else to do and no place else to go, a small measure of the frustration dispersed.

He closed his eyes for just a moment, focusing his energies as he had learned to do before entering the training arena. Then, squaring his shoulders almost unconsciously, he stepped into the sanctuary of the room.

What instantly surprised him was to find Myrddin standing before a class of at least two dozen children – boys and girls ranging in age from no more than three up to possibly six. The children were dressed in initiates' robes of varying colors and as Morgan perused them with a profound and sudden sense of respect, he saw Jahan in the middle of the back row, performing the elaborate, difficult moves of the ancient Leopard Set with ease and grace. This class of children flowed together as a single body, each movement of hands, fingers, arms, legs and even eyes timed to perfection. To a layman, it would look very much like a dance of sorts, yet with even the sparse knowledge Morgan had acquired, he understood that each movement was part of a greater technique of defense and counter-attack.

For a moment, he felt profoundly embarrassed, recalling his own stumbling efforts to master the Leopard Set as he had trained with Myrddin on board the *Dreaming Bird*.

He was so absorbed in observing the children in their lesson that he was only vaguely aware of the door opening once more, and of another presence coming to rest at his side. Glancing briefly, he found Kim Le standing next to him, still attired in the pale blue robes which marked him as the Supreme Master of Ho Ling.

Almost by second nature now, Morgan bowed his head in respect.

Kim Le repeated the gesture and, with a wrinkled smile of weathered flesh, he gestured toward the class. "These are the future Masters of Ho Ling," he explained with an obviously great sense of pride.

"They make it look so easy," Morgan commented with a grin. "Makes me realize just how awkward *I* am."

Kim Le regarded him quietly for a moment, his dark eyes sparkling as he spoke. "There are always advantages in youth. There is agility and great desire to learn." He paused, his eyes returning once more to the class as it continued in unison through the moves which Myrddin performed in the front of the room. "But with age comes increased strength," the old man pointed out, "as well as a tighter focus and – hopefully – greater wisdom."

Morgan considered that, feeling somewhat less self-conscious as he watched the children and their master. In another few seconds, the class completed the Leopard Set in unison, all returning to the familiar ready position and bowing respectfully as Myrddin dismissed them in a quiet voice.

Immediately, the children filed from the room in an orderly fashion, hardly seeming to notice Morgan and Kim Le as they stood by the door. When the last child had left and the door swung shut, Myrddin straightened to a natural stance, turning his head in their direction. Despite his firm resolves, Morgan's stomach knotted, recalling the strange out-of-synch experience he'd shared with this mysterious master on board the *Dreaming Bird*. But he held his silence respectfully, waiting to be addressed before speaking.

"Morgan," Myrddin said warmly, coming to stand with them. "We will begin your lesson at once."

Morgan was somewhat surprised that his Alfarian instructor apparently didn't intend to take even a short break between classes. He looked expectantly around the room, his eyes grazing the door. "Am I too early?" he asked, noting that he, Kim Le and Myrddin were the only ones present.

Myrddin's brows narrowed, but before he could speak, Kim Le replied.

"Since yours is a special case, Morgan," the old man stated, "you will normally train alone with your masters. It is recommended, however, that you attend each morning and evening exercise session held in the outer gardens."

Morgan blinked, not knowing whether to be mildly insulted or extremely honored. "But... what about the other students," he said at last. "I wouldn't want to be responsible for–."

"Ta ta ta!" Kim Le scolded with just a hint of impatience. "Remember, Morgan, that the stone is more wise than the blade. You, are the blade – bright and swift and sometimes too sure. Your masters are the stone: rooted, eternal, wise."

Morgan digested that with a slight smile of humility. "In other words," he translated, "I should trust you to know what's best for me." With his past experiences and his commanding nature working against him, it was seldom easy to do.

Kim Le's head inclined in the affirmative. Then, turning his attention to Myrddin, he spoke again. "Instruct Morgan in the Plight of the Blind Man and the Cliff today, Master Myrddin," he commanded. "It is time for his training to progress beyond the level of a First Initiate."

But as Morgan watched Myrddin's face, he saw a faint expression of disapproval there. "Master Le," he replied, "with due respect to both yourself and Morgan, the student has not yet perfected the more basic principles of the art."

Morgan's eyes widened and, without thinking, he opened his mouth to protest. "I'm ready to advance," he argued.

"Ta ta ta!" Kim Le repeated, waving him to silence with a quick gesture of his right hand. "That decision is not yours to make." He turned once more to Myrddin. "Remember, my friend, that Morgan is not here entirely by choice or by his own design. He does not have a lifetime to devote to mastery, but must be made proficient in those areas which will serve his own needs best."

Without even so much as a hint of argument, Myrddin inclined his head graciously. "Of course, Master," he said humbly.

Kim Le bowed gracefully from the waist. Then, turning to the door, he stopped with his hand resting on the smooth wooden surface, glancing back and forth between Myrddin and Morgan. "In the training arena, it would be wise for both student and master to remember their goals."

Then, without further explanation, he bowed once more and slipped soundlessly through the door, leaving it to swing shut behind him.

When he had gone, Morgan stood with his mouth slightly agape as he looked up to meet Myrddin's dark gaze. "What did he mean by *that*?" he asked as much of himself as of the other man.

Not surprisingly, however, Myrddin had an answer. "His words were directed primarily to me," he stated quietly. "He is aware that, at times, my methods can be somewhat unconventional. In the training arena, such deviations are seldom permitted, though Kim Le has occasionally encouraged such unconventionality during personal time."

At that, despite himself, Morgan's face darkened and he swallowed hard. "You mean he... uh... knows about... what happened on the ship?"

Myrddin's eyes smiled very slightly, almost mischievously. "He also knows that no man, regardless of his intentions or discipline, is ever truly a priest."

Morgan frowned, perplexed. He changed the subject quickly. "I met your son last night," he said, recalling the insight Jahan had revealed to him regarding his father. "You must be very proud of him."

Instead of the surprise Morgan had half-way expected, Myrddin merely nodded. "He is of exceptional character."

Morgan bit his tongue, almost letting his automatic response slip through undisciplined lips. *So is his father*, he thought fondly. But then, remembering his commitment not to fall deeper into a mire of emotional involvements, he forced himself to concentrate on his purpose for being in the room.

"What, exactly," he asked, "is the 'Plight of the Blind Man and the Cliff'?"

Myrddin's lips curved up just a little, but he pointedly ignored the query. "You have great aspirations, Morgan," he noted. "But why do you continuously aspire to deny those feelings which are a so much a part of your human nature?"

Face deepening to crimson, Morgan felt himself start to bristle. "I don't know what you're talking about," he protested.

Myrddin remained dubious, then sighed softly. "The first step toward mastery of any art is to examine oneself and to subsequently define one's strengths and weaknesses. Your nature as a ram is a great strength – but it also carries certain burdens."

Morgan frowned, thinking as he often did when in the presence of Myrddin or Kim Le, that he'd missed something. "I don't understand," he said, the bristles smoothing just a little as he was forced to think in another direction.

"A wise man does not attempt to geld the ram, Morgan," Myrddin replied. "For he understands that one does not gain a docile sheep in the process – only a gelded ram. The fire does not leave the ram's eyes nor its heart; and in the end, the ram becomes useless to all, including itself."

Morgan caught himself hoping that Myrddin was speaking strictly in metaphorical terms. It also occurred to him that he *still* didn't know what in all the worlds the Alfarian was talking about. "What do you mean?"

Myrddin smiled just a little. "Simply that the fire which burns in your blood is a strength, Morgan, not a weakness. There is no power greater than the ability to give life, to create with the seed of your body a new lifeform. As with any force in the universe, this power must be used before it is useful. The blade must be constantly sharpened if the knife is to hold any value."

For a single moment, Morgan seriously considered passing out cold. He'd never heard anyone speak of sex in such unusual terms, and though the analogies were peculiar, he had to admit that the basic philosophy seemed correct. He *had* used sex to his advantage – not only as a weapon, but as a tool. Now, if he understood his fiery Alfarian master, he was being instructed to continue along that same path. He squirmed, suddenly uncomfortable with the whole subject.

Oh, don't puss out now, Cap'n Morgan, The Little Voice nagged. *Get a hold of yourself!* And then it laughed at its own unintentional double entendre. Fortunately, however, Morgan was growing accustomed to ignoring it, and merely filed its running commentary for future reference.

"Do not misunderstand me, Morgan," Myrddin said before he could gather his wits to speak. "Your sexual power is not something to be used *against* another or against yourself as a form of self-punishment. Instead, if you use it wisely, it will bring incredible strength to you through the gathering of power."

Morgan tried not to take the conversation personally, though he understood that that was *exactly* what he was supposed to be doing. He faltered uncomfortably, no longer certain whether Myrddin's words were intended as intellectual instruction or as a personal invitation. And for himself, he was no longer certain which he wanted it to be.

Then, relying on some inner intuition, he met and held the other's eyes steadily. "What about you?" he asked pointedly. "From what you seem to be saying, that little episode on the ship a few nights ago was for *you*? Or for me?"

Myrddin never blinked, never faltered. "It was intended for mutual benefit, Morgan, a symbiotic joining to nurture understanding and to instill strength for both." He paused, his eyes intense. "If I was unsuccessful in that attempt, I rely on your honor

159

to tell me now."

Morgan's mouth opened, then closed again. He lost the staring match and glanced absently to the floor. "It was... beneficial," he said at last.

"And?" Myrddin inquired when he fell silent.

"And?" Morgan repeated, genuinely confused. "I'm not sure what you want me to say, *or* what you want me to do, for that matter."

Taking a step forward and reaching out until one hand rested lightly on Morgan's arm, Myrddin spoke very gently. "I want you to survive, Morgan," he stated. "Not only spiritually and physically, but emotionally as well. Without that balance, you will not be whole."

Morgan tried to digest that as impersonally as possible. But too many questions rampaged unchecked through his mind. Myrddin's hand was warm and possibly even suggestive as it rested on his arm, and despite his unspoken vows, it was a comfort he was hard-pressed to ignore. He felt himself tremble inside, then looked up into the other's face.

"For once," he said, "why don't you just tell me what you want?"

Myrddin didn't flinch. "First," he countered, "*you* must tell *me*."

Morgan unconsciously straightened. "I want to learn," he stated. "And I want to survive. But *most* of all, I want my goddamn equilibrium back." Well, there it was. Right there in front of him, blurted out like a confession at the altar of rum. Problem was, he hadn't had a drop to drink in months. He stammered, faltered, then took a deep breath and spewed out the rest of it. "I'm tired of always feeling torn right down the middle, tired of thinking everything to death, and *really* tired of trying to second-guess what everybody *else* seems to want! So if you're asking me what *I* want, I just want to be *me* again!"

Myrddin seemed definitely pleased with that response. "Good," he said with a little smile. "At least you have defined the goal. Then obviously you are aware that in order to *be* yourself, you must be willing to follow your nature as opposed to trying to deny it?"

160

Morgan's heart threatened to stop in light of the conversation they'd just had. And yet, Kim Le's round-about words came back to him. *'You must trust your Masters to know what is best for you'.* It took the hot air right out of his sails, leaving him humbled.

"I – um – yes, " he mumbled, not at all sure what he was agreeing to, feeling that every conversation with Myrddin took him deeper down the rabbit hole. He had no doubt that that was precisely what the other man intended, but it didn't make the fall any less turbulent. "It's just that... *sometimes*... I have to understand the question before I can give you an answer."

Myrddin squeezed his arm reassuringly, then released him and took a step back, smiling openly. "I shall endeavor to remember that, Morgan." Then, moving to the front of the room, he brought his hands together in the symbol of the fist and the empty hand. "Ready position," he commanded.

Stunned and completely confused, Morgan blinked once more. "Wh-what?"

"Ready position, Morgan," Myrddin repeated. "We must begin your lesson."

Not knowing what else to do, Morgan moved to stand before his teacher, assuming the beginning stance which was the basis of all subsequent moves. Somehow, he'd thought that the conversation alone was more than enough for one day's lesson. What bothered him was not knowing what he had learned, not *really* knowing whether Myrddin's concerns were spoken from master to student... or from one lonely man to another.

~

Physically sore and emotionally exhausted from the lesson consisting of the Plight of the Blind Man and the Cliff, Morgan was relieved when the training session at last came to an end and the sleek black blind-fold was finally removed by deft Alfarian fingers.

Myrddin gave his usual commentary concerning his progress, pointing out areas where additional practice was required, outlining the formal steps and further explaining how they were applied to practical situations. Throughout the lecture, Morgan listened dutifully, though he realized with a sense of frustration that, once again, his mind wasn't entirely focused on the points of his lesson. And though Myrddin was undoubtedly aware of his lack of concentration, he said nothing of it.

When he was finished, Myrddin returned to his position at the front of the room, performing the ritualistic salute and dismissal of the student as Morgan followed in unison. Then, with the formalities concluded, the Alfarian returned to a relaxed stance.

"After your mid-day meal, Morgan," he said quietly, "you will continue your studies with Master Lucien in the outer gardens of the temple." He paused, then took a step forward to denote that the formal lesson was completed. "I trust your consultation with your new master last evening was beneficial?"

Too tired to read any hidden meaning into that question, Morgan answered it straightforward, still somewhat shaken by that meeting nonetheless. "We didn't exactly talk very much," he said, only then realizing it, "but yes, it was beneficial." He paused, then continued more slowly. "You said he would be teaching me techniques of defense as well as wholistic awareness," he recalled. "The first, I can figure out. But just exactly what does wholistic awareness *mean*?"

Myrddin took another step forward until master and student stood side by side. "It is a complex term for a relatively simple thing," he replied. "It is the acquisition of knowledge and balance as applied to the lifeform – in this case, yourself – as a whole being, a complete unit. You will learn how to more effectively balance the needs of the spirit with the demands of the flesh, for example, and to control the flesh in order to increase the power of the spirit."

For a moment, Morgan was confused all over again. "But... I thought you just got through saying an hour ago that I was supposed to... uh... well... give in to the needs of the flesh once in awhile."

Again, Myrddin smiled very gently. "There is a difference between control and starvation. If the flesh is starved when it cries out for fulfillment, the spirit will wither. But if the flesh is overly indulged, the spirit grows lazy, weak. Again, as with all things, it is a matter of proper balance."

162

For the first time, it was beginning to make sense, and Morgan sighed inwardly, feeling some small degree of relief. In the back of his mind, he thought abruptly of Lucien – *his* Lucien – and an odd sense of melancholy came over him. "I once had a friend," he ventured as much to himself as to Myrddin, "who could have profited very much by that lesson."

Myrddin's brows lifted with interest. "Lucien?"

Only then realizing he'd spoken his thoughts out loud, Morgan shook himself from his reverie, looking up into the other's dark eyes. "Yes," he admitted, "Lucien." He shook his head, suddenly saddened. "Sometimes I think it was more important to him to be *Alfarian* than to be... *himself.*" They'd had the stars and a potential forever in the palm of their hands... and Alfarian fingertips had taken it all away in a flash of telepathic sorcery. "Unfortunately, I didn't know then what I know now."

"Which is?" Myrddin questioned.

Morgan shrugged with a wistful smile. "What you've taught me," he said. "That being Alfarian doesn't have to mean living strictly by some code of ethics written a long time ago and a long ways away." He wondered fleetingly where the sudden philosophical meanderings had come from, but dismissed that consideration as irrelevant. "Anyway," he said, drawing himself back to reality with firm determination, "if I get through all of this, and if I ever *do* see him again, I plan on passing along some of your wisdom."

Myrddin smiled very gently. "As for 'getting through all of this', Morgan," he said, "I have no doubts that you will succeed. And as for the reunion with your beloved, it is my impression that it will come much sooner than you might think."

Morgan allowed himself to smile, feeling more at ease with the intense work-out behind him. "I hope you're right."

Myrddin's answer was succinct and profoundly applicable. "Trust me, Morgan," he requested with a distinctively mischievous glint in his eye.

Morgan grinned. "Now how did I *know* you were going to say that?"

CHAPTER THIRTEEN

Lucien arrived at the secluded training arena in the temple's outer gardens more than an hour before his student was scheduled to appear, taking advantage of the time of solitude to gather his thoughts. He realized with a sense of dismay that he had come painfully close to jeopardizing the entire scenario the night before, that his own unexplored feelings had almost caused him to reveal more than circumstances would permit. If Morgan recognized him for who and what he really was, their relationship would end quickly – quite possibly right along with life as the Empire had come to know it.

Now, with a few hours of rest, time and distance, his priorities righted themselves once again, though he was left with an odd tingling in the pit of his stomach as he recalled Myrddin's words once more. *'If you cannot bring yourself to do what must be done, I shall have no alternative but to act in your stead'.*

He knew the other would do it, and that possibility caused him to tremble whenever he considered it. Myrddin did have the advantage; Morgan knew him considerably better – or, Lucien amended, the human *thought* he did. His dilemma was further complicated by the fact that, without seeming to push too quickly, he had no genuine idea of how to make the move which would bring Morgan to his side... and to his bed.

At that thought, a surge of adrenaline tightened the muscles in his stomach, causing his eyes to close with a sudden rush of feeling. He had accepted that he *did* desire this man – mind, body and spirit. And yet, the fine art of courtship was one he had never thought to master. Contrapuntally, he realized the impending danger with Myrddin, knowing that Morgan could easily be attracted to the other's wisdom, even to his physical strength and the aura of power which surrounded any true master of the art.

With that knowledge, he stiffened just a little. Somehow, within the next few minutes, he knew he must lay aside his pre-existing beliefs, his inherent and inexplicable fear of matters sexual. He must become, as Myrddin already was, a master.

There was, however, only one fallacy in that plan.

164

Lucien knew within himself that he was not a master at all. His training on Alfar, though intense in his youth, had taken him only to the level of an adept. One small matter had kept him from mastery even then.

A true master lived in balance. Flesh and spirit moved as one. There was no fear to fly nor to fall as a result.

His heart threatened to break. Myrddin had no such fears. He, on the other hand, had been their slave for longer than he cared to remember – and his own fears had taken the ultimate possibility from his grasp when he had stolen dangerous and delightful memories from Morgan's mind years ago. What bothered him now was knowing he hadn't *really* done it for Morgan or for the good of the galaxy. He had done it as a result of his own gut-wrenching fear – a fear that had been awakened in the heat of a stolen kiss when he had come dangerously close to killing the only person he had ever truly loved. No, he hadn't done it out of nobility.

He was a coward – terrified to face the possibility of this thing every species in the known galaxy craved and dreaded in equal amounts. Love.

Now, he conceded, was his time of penance for that fatal fear.

~

After finishing his noon meal, Morgan returned to his living quarters for a few moments, taking the time to shower and gather his thoughts into a tighter focus before proceeding to his next lesson. It occurred to him that, when he was distanced from Myrddin, thoughts of Lucien once again filled his mind, leaving him to wonder how a momentary need for physical satisfaction could even temporarily overshadow the love he felt for his former second-in-command and friend.

And yet, the answer was plain. Myrddin was a *fact*: real and close and obviously willing to share the warmth of his bed. Lucien, on the other hand, remained a memory, a distant dream for the future, an almost painful hope for a tomorrow he might never realistically see. And even if he *did* fulfill that goal, if he *did* learn to efficiently block the Mizarian probe enough to one day return to his former life, there were no promises made or even implied. Lucien had rejected him once; he could easily do it again.

Oh woe is you! The Little Voice commented in response to his reverie. *Have you actually looked in the mirror lately? And I don't just mean the one on the wall. Jeezus, Cap'n Morgan... you two have been in love since before either one of you was a nasty sparkle in your daddy's eye. You want your power back, then take it and stop acting like a scared little kid.*

"I wish it were that easy," Morgan mumbled to himself.

Sighing heavily as he pondered that thought, he quickly pulled on a clean uniform, trying hard to ignore the rampaging emotions which followed him as he made his way through the temple building and eventually emerged in the outer gardens. His frustration was compounded by the fact that he didn't know quite what to expect from his new teacher and master who would be waiting for him amongst the tea roses and the serenity of the stream's light lullaby.

And, whether he cared to admit it or not, he was still shaken by his reaction to Master Lucien the night before.

Without understanding why then or now, he had given serious thought to asking the Alfarian to remain with him as he slept. In his thoughts, he had imagined being enfolded in the other's arms, held safe and secure from harm, protected by the wisdom and power of a master. Myrddin had shown him that kindness once, and would easily do so again if asked. That much he was certain of. And Master Lucien, without ever voicing it, had obviously been open to the idea as well. Or, Morgan amended, his imagination was working double-time, right along with his overly-flattered ego.

Not knowing what else to do, he put it down to imagination alone, telling himself that he was here to learn, that his masters were here to teach, and that each moment would simply have to reveal itself at the proper time.

Then, taking a deep breath, he quickened his stride, setting his sights on the secluded outdoor training arena and enjoying the feel of the sun on his face. For the moment, *that* seemed the easiest thing to do.

~

Standing in the center of the circle of stones, Lucien looked up as he sensed another presence entering the arena, his heart pattering more quickly as he found Morgan Diego standing only a few feet away. What startled him most was the human's profound beauty in the natural lighting. The sun was at an approximate 90 degree angle on the westward horizon, illuminating the bright face and causing the gold-bronze hair which had grown to almost shoulder length to glisten. In the white robes of a First Initiate, his musculature was highlighted to perfection, causing Lucien to tremble as he realized that this prize *could* be his, causing him to shudder as he realized Morgan could just as easily turn to Myrddin.

He took a deep breath, inclining his head with controlled precision. "Morgan," he intoned deeply, "I trust you are well rested."

Morgan managed a faintly sheepish smile, recalling their parting conversation of the evening before. "Yes," he said. "Thank you." He noted that the Alfarian also appeared more relaxed, that the youthful face seemed more at ease and unlined than it had when they'd first met. Still, he couldn't help noticing the underling tension which resided just beneath the calm exterior. "And you?" he asked leadingly.

Again, Lucien's head inclined in agreement. "The solitude of sleep is always helpful in alleviating anxieties," he said, wanting to say much, much more, but uncertain how or where to begin. He settled, logically, for the beginning, hoping he hadn't already said too much with his single statement. "Are you ready to begin today's lesson?" he inquired, allowing himself to hope that the formality of teaching might open some avenue down which he could proceed.

After only a moment's hesitation, Morgan nodded, though he couldn't deny the disappointment which whispered without apparent cause through his mind. Somehow, he'd wanted to talk, though about what he wasn't certain. Despite his resolve not to, he couldn't help comparing Master Lucien with Myrddin. Whereas Myrddin seemed open and almost overwhelming in his intensity, this man was far more reserved, almost as if he kept some great secret close to his heart. And though Morgan had always been challenged by the task of gently chipping away at barriers with *his* Lucien, he wasn't certain he was up to it again now – was even less certain that this apparently stern master would tolerate it. Nonetheless, he was intrigued by the dark fire which burned beneath this man's surface.

"I'm ready," he said at last, making a silent reaffirmation of his previous vow. He would take each moment as it presented itself, living it only then rather than attempting to predict the future like some self-appointed mystic. "Where do we start?" he asked when the other didn't immediately respond.

Gathering his control, re-defining his priorities, Lucien chose his answer carefully. "Kim Le has instructed that I am to further your education in the areas of physical defense," he stated. "By learning to shield against any possible attack against the body, the mind will likewise begin to function accordingly." And he also admitted to himself that the physical contact *would* bring them closer. "To begin, we will spar. Once I am aware of your strengths and weaknesses, it will be simpler to plan your training."

Morgan blinked as a half-smile teased along his lips. He looked pointedly at the other man, noticing the lithe musculature which was a common trait among Alfarians – a trait which effectively caused many humans to misjudge their strength. "I don't stand a chance, you know," he pointed out, wondering briefly why the idea of sparring with this man caused his nerves to jangle.

But Lucien merely smiled reassuringly. Despite his own shields, he easily detected Morgan's nervous rush of adrenaline. "This is not intended as a combat, nor as a test. It is merely a method to discern which techniques you have already perfected, and which still require further instruction."

Morgan took a deep breath, still unnerved by the idea of fighting with this man even under controlled conditions. But he nodded his agreement nonetheless, once again recalling Kim Le's words. *'Trust your masters to know what is best'.*

Then, meeting and holding the other's gaze, trying very hard not to be intimidated by the power he sensed there, he stepped into the ready position, indicating his ability to defend.

Summoning up every ounce of control and using it to

168

temporarily abolish his fears, Lucien gave a curt nod to his opponent. "We will spar at combat speed, but with proper control to guard against injury. Is that understood?"

Morgan nodded, adrenaline surging through him as every muscle tightened in preparation for the attack. His sole focus became one of defense and counter-maneuvers and, without effort, he put all other thoughts from his mind. "Understood, Master Lucien," he acknowledged, then dropped back instantly into a well-practiced fighting stance.

Recalling the times they had fought together on the *Starling*, Lucien deliberately altered the pattern of his attack, moving warily to circle his human opponent, noting the fact that Morgan had indeed gained new knowledge in his studies with Myrddin. The human moved with the grace of a cat, his fingers poised in the Leopard's Claw position, his legs crouched and low to the ground. His eyes never wavered, and their gazes remained locked together as they moved around one another with a combination of wariness and respect.

Initially, Lucien attempted a series of two controlled kicks, not surprised when Morgan easily deflected his leg and instantly step-dragged forward with a controlled elbow strike to body and face. And yet, even the fight, the slightest physical contact caused his heart rate to increase, his breath coming more quickly as he dropped back, calculating his next attack, preparing for Morgan's offensive.

Seeing a momentary distraction in his opponent, Morgan took immediate advantage of his opportunity, countering with a controlled roundhouse kick which the Alfarian easily deflected, then following up with a series of rapid open-handed strikes – only one of which found a target, glancing harmlessly off the other's shoulder as the master side-stepped. Determined not to be so easily dissuaded, Morgan followed the other's momentum, catching his right arm and attempting to hammerlock it behind his teacher's back.

Surprised by the human's quickness, Lucien followed through instantly, going with the angle of the attack as he allowed the attempted hammerlock to spin him around until they faced one

169

another once more, his arm slipping free of the intended pin. Again, they stood eye to eye, less than a foot apart, each looking intensely for weakness in the other.

Seeing none, yet realizing he dared not declare a draw so soon, Lucien feigned to the left with a checked kick, then immediately pivoted in place, one long leg sweeping backward and making contact with the human's knee. Slipping his foot behind his target, his ankle locked, throwing his opponent off balance and causing him to drop to the mats which completely covered the ground inside the training arena.

Momentarily stunned by the quickness with which it happened, Morgan fell forward, landing awkwardly, but recovering his composure almost at once. He went into a forward shoulder roll, springing to his feet in a well-practiced maneuver, yet when he turned to follow through with a kick to the Alfarian's mid-section, a sense of profound horror greeted him as he realized his opponent had already circled around behind him.

Attempting to duck out of the way of whatever attack his master intended to launch, he doubled over, trying to unpivot in place, then stopping when he found himself caught from behind in a forearm choke hold that snapped him upright and brought his back flush against the Alfarian's chest. He gasped in surprise, struggling futilely in the other's more powerful grasp.

For a brief instant, it was no longer a game. It was terribly, eternally real. Abruptly, his feet were on the floor of Mother Forest again, his lungs constricting as he tried unsuccessfully to breathe, his heart racing wildly as the memory of that life-altering kiss flooded his mind. The images whipped through him at light-speed; but as he fought for control, reminding himself of exactly where he was, the horror diminished, replaced instead with renewed determination. But despite that knowledge, he was nonetheless shaken, and the proper counter-maneuver to break the hold eluded him.

Sensing the human's confusion and disorientation, Lucien loosened his hold just a little, indicating a temporary pause as he lifted two fingers in front of the human's face. He did not, however, release Morgan entirely. Instead, reminding himself of why he had

170

chosen to spar in the first place, he merely remained in the superior position with his right forearm pressing loosely against the human's throat. His own heart thundered as the gentle scent of Morgan's shampoo came to his nostrils, and when he felt the other man relax against him, he thought he might drop to the ground and begin to babble incoherently. He was holding in his arms the manifest power of the universe, the reason for all existence. And it was a drug like no other, instantly addictive, enslaving him as it had enslaved him when this sorcerer human had unexpectedly and unashamedly kissed him on the floor of Mother Forest some three years in the past.

Only with extreme discipline did he manage to remain standing. Only with intense determination did he manage to continue the charade.

"Can you break free?" he asked, attempting to play his role as instructor rather than give in to his sudden desire to abandon the pose entirely.

Morgan took a deep breath, coming slowly back to reality. He wondered momentarily if he'd blacked out, yet his conscious mind seemed to have recorded every second of their feigned combat. What unnerved him was the sharp scent of myrrh and musk which pressed against his nostrils, the overwhelming warmth of the Alfarian's body pressed tightly against his back. Despite his predicament, despite his sworn resolve, his stomach knotted with the intensity of a thousand butterflies, causing him to lean heavily against the other man. For an instant, he felt like the ultimate hard-luck-case, soaking up a few moments of physical gratification in the safe sanctuary of his own mind. And yet, he couldn't deny the wave of power which engulfed him when he realized he was completely at the mercy of another being, another man, another Alfarian. It was a sensation which, with a little practice, he could learn to crave.

Took you long enough to figure that out.

"Morgan?" A moment of panic caused Lucien to wonder if he had applied the hold too efficiently.

But finally, Morgan shook his head, a smile which Lucien couldn't see toying with his lips. And yet, it faded abruptly as he enforced his own reality, reminding himself with firm authority that fleeting moments of unrequited gratification would hardly serve his long-term goals. He sighed heavily, his body stiffening away from the other.

"I'm sorry, Master," he said formally. "The match is yours."

Feeling a strange sense of defeat in his 'victory', Lucien reluctantly released him, taking a step back as they came face to face. His own emotions were under careful control, yet clamoring close to the surface – a condition which was heightened as he noted the unexpected expression of anger blazing in the human's eyes. Fear filled him, causing him to falter.

"Are you injured, Morgan?" he inquired.

Morgan's jaw tightened. He didn't know *where* the anger came from; he only knew that, suddenly, it was there. He shook his head, trying desperately to control it, reminding himself that this man wasn't to blame for his own human shortcomings, nor the annoying human fantasies which sprang to the surface at the most inconvenient times.

"I'm fine," he said, realizing it to be true only on a physical level, and perhaps not even there. But as he looked at his master's eyes, he knew he could not fight again so soon. Inwardly, he damned himself for what Myrddin had delicately referred to as the burden of the ram. In plain, simple English, he translated it to mean the uncontrollable passions which drove him to lust when love was unavailable. His face darkened and, shamefully, he dropped his eyes. That morning, he had contemplated going to Myrddin's bed. Now, in the afternoon, he was given to similar thoughts with a man whom he'd met only the day before. He hated himself. And he hated the laughing god with the questionable sense of irony who had placed him in a seeming thicket of Alfarians – none of whom, he thought, were completely satisfactory. It was *his* Lucien he wanted, *his* Lucien he needed, *only* Lucien he would accept. His mind continued to recite that, yet his body threatened to betray him at any moment.

What would it really hurt if you just gave in? The Little Voice tempted, a perennial devil on his shoulder.

Everything. Every goddamn thing in the galaxy. That's what it would hurt, Morgan thought, suddenly outraged at the fact that *nothing* was simple anymore.

"Morgan?" the deep voice intoned, interrupting his reverie. Through the short distance which separated them, even through his own self-imposed shields, Lucien could easily interpret the turmoil which raged within the other man. And, without thinking, he reached out to rest one hand gently on Morgan's arm. "It was not my intention to cause you distress of any kind. Please, tell me what troubles you."

Glancing up sharply into the other's eyes, Morgan found himself amazed at the coolness with which the Alfarian spoke. His control faltered, leaving him at the mercy of dangerous feelings. "What 'troubles me'," he repeated, "is that I don't belong here!" He pulled his arm roughly away from the other's touch, dropping his hand to his side. "I keep saying that, and instead of getting better, it's getting worse! How in all collective hells am I supposed to control the Mizarians when I can't even control myself?" It was a rhetorical question, and he expected no answer. He turned abruptly, ready to abandon the entire discipline when, suddenly, he felt a restraining hand on his arm and he was halted in his retreat.

"Controlling the actions of others is a relatively simple matter, Morgan," Lucien said, though the fear in his chest constricted his voice, causing it to quaver. "Controlling oneself is another matter entirely."

But Morgan didn't want to hear it. He continued staring at the ground, unwilling to meet the Alfarian's eyes. In that moment, he felt strangely free, as if he had absolutely nothing else in the universe to lose. And that knowledge caused him to speak. "I feel like a goddamn yo-yo!" he snapped, then suddenly looked up to meet the penetrating stare of his Master. "I can't turn my feelings on and off like a light! I don't want to!"

"Then don't," Lucien casually suggested, though the turmoil burning within him was anything but casual.

Morgan stared at the other man. "If you knew what you were saying, you'd change your mind," he quipped sarcastically, not liking himself very much in that moment.

I don't like you much either.

Lucien was hard-pressed to understand the abrupt mood

swings. He didn't even stop to consider the possible consequences of his actions. Instead, knowing only that he had to reach the other man before the opportunity evaded him, he tightened his grip, struggling to maintain his pose as a master. "You would be wise to understand, Morgan, that your instincts have served you well in the past. If you will stop resisting them now, your path will be much easier."

Morgan blinked, wincing at the sudden pressure from the other's restraining grasp. "In case you hadn't noticed, there's no such thing as an easy path!"

But Lucien wasn't dissuaded by the stubborn denial residing in the fiery eyes. Knowing what lay in the balance, keenly aware of Myrddin's presence in Morgan's life, he held the human more tightly, refusing to let go despite the dynamic tension strung taut between them. "At some time in your life, you will come to understand that no path is carved solely by your own footsteps. Others have walked it before you, and more will follow when you are gone. It stands to reason, therefore, that you need not walk the road alone. Despite the momentary glory you may experience as a result, the joys you deny far outnumber the fleeting moments of pride."

Something in the other man's tone, something in the undeniable wisdom caused Morgan to falter; yet the anger he felt was already too intense to control so easily. It surged once more, causing him to gasp as he tried to break the Alfarian's hold, failing once again. "You know," he snapped harshly, "between you and Myrddin, I'm starting to get the impression that all Alfarians have it firmly imbedded in their thick skulls that a quick fuck will cure all ills for us poor helpless humans! That *does* seem to be what you're trying to say!"

Despite the pain which rattled through Lucien's shocked system, he held onto his control with the last ounce of strength he possessed, reminding himself that Morgan was shouting at a strange Alfarian master, that the human's words weren't directed at him personally. "There is no cure for the love you feel, Morgan, except to experience it fully."

The words only infuriated Morgan despite the fact that he

recognized them to be true – perhaps *because* he recognized them to be true. "You're so certain, aren't you?" he returned sharply. Then, as an odd feeling of rebellion settled squarely in the center of his chest, his eyes narrowed as he continued to study the Alfarian. "Would you be every bit as certain if I took you up on that? Would you still stand there reciting profundities if I just gave in and threw myself on the ground right here and now?"

Can we? Please?

Lucien found himself momentarily at a loss for words. He thought harder and faster than he'd ever done before, and eventually came up with the only possible response. "I would say, Morgan," he murmured levelly, though he trembled within at the thought, "that my door is always open to you."

At that, Morgan was abruptly and painfully jolted back to reality. He stood staring at the other man with his jaw agape and his face darkening to a deep shade of crimson. But he squelched the moment of sanity, replacing it instead with another bitter test. "And if I said that I plan on going to Myrddin for the same act of mercy?" he demanded, his voice tight and hoarse with pain. He wondered briefly why he'd even said such a thing, why he felt such an overwhelming need to rattle the control of every Alfarian with whom he came into contact. And yet, that unanswered question didn't soften his attack. "What then?" he wanted to know.

Lucien stifled the sharp stab of pain which impacted against his mind, abruptly dropping Morgan's arm as if it suddenly turned hot. He *had* to give the honorable response which only a master of the art would be capable of giving

"I would wish you well, Morgan," he intoned, though he wanted at that moment to throw himself from the highest mountain and fall without screaming to his own death. But he did what he had to do, gave the only response Morgan would accept. "Master Myrddin is as aware of your needs as I," he stated, his very soul aching. "Go to him if it will alleviate this suffering you feel inside."

Morgan stood there for a very long time, staring blindly at the man before him. He wanted to rant and rave and tell the world that he didn't need anything or anyone. He wanted to write an edict and sent it to Alfar, telling the whole damned planet that their philosophies were fucked up and their philosophers fucking crazy – governed by some high fallutin' notion of inner peace when it was a well-known fact that Alfarian passions were among the most fierce in the galaxy. Like trying to put out the fires of a volcano with a jug of gasoline.

Independently, Lucien was having much the same revelation, though on a slightly different wavelength. On the one hand, he was telling Morgan to let go of *his* controls, while at the same time, struggling to maintain his own. It was no wonder the human was angry and confused.

And Lucien's own expectations were as fucked up as anything he had ever encountered. So, in that moment of self-realization, what he came to realize was that he had never *really* known himself at all. He, like Morgan, had been playing a role for so long that he had forgotten who Lucien of Alfar really *was* behind all the masks. And now the masks were falling, leaving him face to face with the stranger he had become.

There was something he should say. Something he should do. Yet he faltered utterly, and could only stare at the defiant human who had frayed his proverbial last nerve with seemingly very little effort when all was said and done.

That, of course, was the legacy of Morgan Diego – his stock in trade, his claim to fame. It shouldn't have surprised Lucien that even *he* could fall prey to it.

As for Morgan, his weaknesses lay exposed and bleeding and, whether he liked it or not, both Myrddin and Master Lucien were correct: he *did* need something more. He needed to shield himself in the strength of another, he needed an Alfarian sheath for the blade of his anger, he needed Alfarian control to soothe his faltering human emotions.

He *needed* Lucien.

And yet, as he turned abruptly and walked away, he couldn't help wondering if Lucien needed him... or ever truly had.

With a dark cauldron of frustrated rage burning hot in his eyes, he made his way back to the sanctuary of the temple walls, secluding himself in his room and shouting his self-hatred into the safety of his own pillow. He gave serious thought to packing his

176

bags and fleeing the temple once and for all.

And yet, one inescapable fact stopped him: he had no bags no pack, no place left to go.

~

Lucien stood stunned and terrified in the center of the training arena for a long time, watching the human's retreating form until it disappeared back into the temple. And though every instinct he possessed urged him to follow, he was forced to accept that such an action would only worsen an already dreadful situation.

He felt as if every nerve in his body had been severed, leaving his flesh numbed, his mind oddly anesthetized. Only when dizziness overwhelmed him did he remember to breathe, though even that action caught in his throat, causing him to gasp with unexpected pain.

The sun had fallen low on the horizon, and the cool air caused him to shiver uncontrollably as he dropped to sit cross-legged on the mats.

"Your only mistake was in not finishing him when you sparred, Lucien," an unexpected voice said, interrupting his misery and causing him to wince as he looked up to find Myrddin standing a few feet away.

"Leave me," he commanded, barely able to look on the other without wanting to weep or to kill – both new experiences for him. He was too weary to even be surprised by the fact that Myrddin had apparently witnessed most if not all of his confrontation with Morgan.

But Myrddin didn't back down to the firm authority in Lucien's voice. Instead, taking a few steps closer, he knelt in front of the other man. "If you are going to play the role of a master," he said with extreme gentleness, "you must learn to act like one." He paused, then added: "Had you finished him when you sparred, he would not have lost respect. He must *feel* your authority if he is to respect it."

Wrapped in a tight ball of misery, Lucien took a deep breath, looking up at last to meet Myrddin's penetrating gaze. "What you say may well be true of another man," he said, wondering why he was bothering to say anything at all, "but not of *him*. Had I 'finished him', he would have felt defeated. And since Alfarian strength is a factor to be considered, there would have been no honor in such a victory."

In the early evening coolness, Myrddin sighed softly. "Why do you fight me?" he asked unexpectedly, ignoring Lucien's comment altogether. "I am not your rival. Surely you realize that the seduction of your beloved is not my goal."

Despite the fact that Lucien knew Myrddin to be incapable of lying, he found himself doubting the other man's words – perhaps, he conceded, because he *wanted* to doubt them. "But if he came to you, you would not turn him away," he countered, suddenly determined to confront the other man, to put an end to their rivalry one way or another.

Myrddin's lips curved very slightly. "Nor would you," he reminded his kinsman. Then, reaching out, he laid one hand supportively on Lucien's arm. "But you must know that, when this difficult journey is ended, Morgan will belong only to you."

Lucien's brows lifted. "Can you be so certain? Do not forget that he is capable of great feelings. If he should begin to love you–."

"He would quickly come to understand that I am nothing more than a temporary diversion from his anger," Myrddin countered. "His *spirit* is already sworn to *you*, my friend."

Lucien didn't completely accept the seeming words of comforting wisdom. "Perhaps," he conceded, "but he is a man capable of great change. Our lifelink is unconsummated. If he turns to you before–."

"Lucien," Myrddin interrupted with overwhelming tenderness, "do not misjudge Morgan to be so indecisive and weak. And do not underestimate your own influence in his thoughts. He thinks of no other."

"He thinks of *you*."

"*And* of Master Lucien," Myrddin countered quickly. "Do not forget that he sees only your outer self now. He does not know who you are behind your masks. To him, you *are* Master Lucien – a man whom he met only last night. That does not diminish his feelings,

178

however."

Lucien was hard-pressed to admit it, but it *was* something he hadn't yet had time to consider. And, in many ways, it was almost as disturbing as his realization that Morgan desired Myrddin in some fashion. His eyes closed and, wearily, he dropped his head into his hands. Never in all his years of being alive had he felt so entirely helpless, his reason and his sanity ripped to shreds by the soft and dainty state of love. It was no wonder it had driven poets and philosophers to madness since time created itself out of the Nothing.

What surprised him was when he felt Myrddin maneuver around behind him and powerful fingers began a slow and deliberate massage of the muscles which cramped and ached in his back and neck. At first, he leaned forward, attempting to evade the other's touch, but when the firm hands seized him in a commanding grip which transmitted the full power of this mysterious master, Lucien halted his retreat, knowing he was no match for the other, and having little doubt that Myrddin would force the issue if pressed..

"Relax, Lucien," Myrddin commanded. "This struggle between us is pointless."

Lucien gave serious thought to launching a well-placed elbow to the other's ribs, even more serious thought to picking up a nearby stone and using it to end Myrddin's life. And yet, with reverence for life firmly imbedded in his subconscious even if not in his coherent mind, he was forced once again to accept the other's position of authority. And, keenly aware of his own vulnerability, he willed himself to relax physically even if not mentally.

"You seem to enjoy taking risks, Myrddin," he commented darkly.

"Risks?" the other repeated, his hands once again resuming their well-practiced massage. "You would profit well to internalize one of Kim Le's favorite expressions."

Despite himself, Lucien couldn't help asking: "Precisely what expression is that?" But even he could easily discern the note of sarcasm which crept into his voice.

Myrddin's fingers dug deeper into sore muscles, soothing away a small part of the physical discomfort even though they did nothing to alleviate Lucien's mental anguish. "Trust your masters to know what is best for you at times when your own judgment may be clouded."

Lucien's eyes closed and he fought hard not to let the other's surface arrogance provoke him further. On a strictly intellectual level, he couldn't help agreeing with that statement. But where Morgan Diego was concerned, it was a matter not open to discussion.

"Leave me," he commanded again, overwhelmed with the need to be as alone as he felt inside.

Myrddin seemed not to hear, his hands never missing a stroke in their healing massage. "Lie down," he instructed, pushing lightly on Lucien's shoulder. "Your body is tight; by morning, you will be as crippled as an old man."

Amazed by the other's stubborn determination, Lucien turned slightly until their eyes met in the thickening twilight. "Leave me!" he repeated.

At that, Myrddin merely chuckled – a warm and melodic sound. Then, with surprising quickness and strength, he slid one leg around Lucien's hips, upsetting his balance and causing him to pitch forward. Following through, Myrddin wrestled him easily to the ground. His right hand seized Lucien's wrist, bringing his arm up behind his back.

"Apparently you do not understand what is at stake, Lucien," he said quietly, his tone an amazingly calm contrast to the abruptness of his actions. "Unless you learn control – and quickly – everything we have done will be undone by morning." He paused as if to let that penetrate stubborn resistance, then added: "Now, will you permit me to help you, or do you wish to engage in meaningless combat?"

With his cheek pressed against the mat, Lucien's eyes closed. He wondered fleetingly if this were Myrddin's way of *showing* him how to command the respect of another rather than merely telling him. But at that moment, he didn't bother to ask. Instead, knowing he had no alternative other than unconsciousness, he gave in, willing his body to relax despite the turmoil which burned hot just beneath the surface.

In a few moments, Myrddin's skilled hands resumed their massage, drawing the soreness from his body, replacing it with a lingering sense of heat and well-being.

"Why do you do this?" Lucien wondered aloud, more to himself than to the other man.

"Sometimes," Myrddin replied gently, his hands punctuating his statement, "it is necessary to start a fire in order to prevent another." He paused, fingers digging deep with compassionate concern. "Only when you realize that I am not your enemy will you be able to give Morgan the instruction he requires – *and* the affection."

Despite his inner conflict, Lucien couldn't maintain his anger with Myrddin. It, too, was taken away by the skilled hands, the soft and gentle voice. "And if he seeks affection only from you?" he inquired nonetheless.

"If that should happen," Myrddin said gently, "I believe you will survive."

Lucien's eyes closed and he realized with a terrible pang that Myrddin wouldn't make the concession he had hoped for, wouldn't make some vow of words to deny Morgan should the human seek him out. Rather, his distant kinsman gave him the truth, relying on his Lucien's own strength to see him through the pain. It didn't help knowing that, in all probability, Myrddin was correct in his actions, honorable in his intent.

Lucien only wished he could summon that same strength within himself. And, for just a moment, he allowed himself to do as Myrddin had suggested; he permitted himself to trust.

"I... am... afraid," he said, speaking the words of truth for the first time, relying on Myrddin's honor as a master not to use those words against him now or in the future.

Myrddin's hands slowed only for a moment, then resumed their therapeutic massage. "So is Morgan," he pointed out. "But surely you must realize that it is pointless for each of you to fear the other."

Lucien started to protest. And yet, lying under the weight of a man he'd tried to make into his rival as the twilight deepened to night, he was confronted with the fact that he *was* afraid – not only of his own feelings, but of Morgan's as well. Terrified was more like it. And he couldn't deny the spark of fear he'd seen in the human's eyes just minutes before.

He sighed heavily, trying to find a solution. "How can I control this fear when I do not even understand it?" he asked, realizing abstractly that his mind was drifting against his will toward sleep.

"Control may not be possible, Lucien," Myrddin warned with gentle authority. "In this case, you will have to defeat your fear by facing it."

Lucien heard the answer only distantly. He had no recollection of being carried back to his own room and placed gently in his bed when his own mental exhaustion dropped him at last into a deep, undisturbed sleep.

~

Despite his exhaustion, Lucien slept less than an hour, and awoke with a profound sense of disorientation as he opened his eyes to discover himself in his own bed. The room was dark, and through the cut-away window, the waning moon cast a silhouette of leafy shadows on the stone walls while the scent of delicate jasmine and honeysuckle lingered on the air.

For an instant, he felt completely at peace, the lethargy of sleep creating a pleasant amnesia which momentarily blocked the memories of his confrontation with Morgan, his secondary confrontation with Myrddin.

But as full awareness returned, he winced painfully at the images which settled in his mind. Having lost his time sense somewhere in the afternoon, he sat up straight in the bed, a thousand imagined horrors claiming him as he wondered simultaneously where Myrddin had gone and if his kinsman's destination had led him to Morgan's room. Despite his conversation with Myrddin, he felt no better.

You will have to defeat your fear by facing it.

But as his feet slapped the floor and he fumbled awkwardly for the lamp switch above his bed, he caught a shadow which did not

182

belong in the room from the corner of his eye. Still somewhat disoriented and filled with emotions, his control faltered, allowing a choked gasp to escape his lips before he could call it back.

His hand missed the light switch entirely, his knuckles scraping against the stone wall and causing him to flinch with the stinging pain. Whirling instantly on his intruder, however, he was able to discern by the moon's pale glow that the silhouette standing near the window was Myrddin.

For a single instant, all traces of civility flew from Lucien's mind, causing every muscle to tense in preparation for battle. But then, sensing more than seeing another presence in the room, he held himself in check, squinting through the darkness to discover a second silhouette sitting in the straight-backed chair against the wall.

"Be at peace, Lucien," a soft-spoken human voice intoned gently.

Lucien blinked, poised in a cat-crouched position ready to spring, as he recognized the voice as belonging to Kim Le. With an effort, he commanded his muscles to relax, drawing a wary breath as he rose to a natural stance and stood peering into the darkness.

At once, he heard the scratch of a wooden match, saw a brief flicker of flame, then breathed somewhat easier as Kim Le lit the white meditation candle and placed it the sill of the open window. In the dim light, Lucien noted with some sense of dismay that the old man's features were pressed into a frown, and that an aura of sadness surrounded his slight frame. He knew instantly, intuitively, that *he* was the cause.

Standing near the candle, Kim Le studied him compassionately for a moment before speaking. Then, when he did, his voice was filled with an undeniable tenderness. "Master Myrddin has informed me of the turmoil which consumes you, Lucien," he said, not mincing his words with delicate softeners. "As you undoubtedly know what is in the balance here, then you also know that some step must be taken to remedy this."

Lucien stared at the other man for an extended moment, then glanced toward Myrddin, his eyes narrowing slightly as he felt unaccountably betrayed. Then, returning his attention to Kim Le, remembering that this man was also a master of the art, he lowered his head in accordance with tradition. "With all possible respect, Master," he said, holding his voice in firm control, "Master Myrddin came to my training arena unannounced and uninvited. It was my understanding that I was to work with Morgan in my own manner and according to my knowledge of him."

Kim Le was silent for only a moment. "In the temple, it is written that no master shall usurp the authority of another. However," he hastened to add, "I must remind you, Lucien, that your lifetime has not been spent within these walls. You are not yet a master of the art." He paused as if to let that sink in, then continued in the same gentle tone. "Please understand, my friend, that my respect for you is immense, and that I am aware of your accomplishments within your own chosen field. If not, I would not have allowed Admiral Bryse to convince me that you should come here."

At that, Lucien felt his hopes sinking as he mentally prepared himself for the next blow. Here, he realized, Kim Le was the final authority; arguing – even rationally – would serve no purpose. He held his breath, awaiting the expulsion which seemed imminent on the old man's lips.

"It is not my desire that you should leave us, Lucien," Kim Le said, surprising Lucien not only with his insight, but with a statement completely contradictory to what he had expected. "It is plain to see that you do have an effect on Morgan – a most positive effect. The fact that you can touch his anger speaks well of your concern for him; the fact that you struggle so hard to contain your own anguish tells me that you are a man of honor. However," the old man continued, "any man can only be the sum of his previous experiences, the finished product of his former training. Most of your life has been spent with the Galaxy Corps; and though you have mastered certain disciplines through your own efforts and by your training on Alfar, you cannot become overnight what it has taken the masters a lifetime to achieve."

Slightly confused by the seemingly contradictory observations, Lucien lifted his head to study the other's face in an attempt to read the time-weathered features. They revealed nothing, and his own inner conflict caused his heart to wrench. He wished fleetingly that Myrddin had not been in the room, that he could have spoken more freely with the old man. His own knowledge of the fact that Myrddin was sworn to mastery, that his distant kinsman *couldn't* use his words or his feelings against him and still remain a master did little to calm the hurricane which rampaged through his mind.

"What would you have me do, Kim Le?" he asked at last. Then, taking a deep breath, he said what he knew he had to say. "If you feel that my presence is a detriment to Morgan, I will leave here at once." His heart almost stopped waiting for the answer.

"I have already stated that I have no desire to see you leave us," Kim Le said presently. "However, I also have no desire to see you torn apart by the knowledge of things over which you possess no control." He paused thoughtfully, then added: "If we were given all the time in this world, I would recommend only that you study with the masters here at the same time you serve as instructor to Morgan. However," he continued, "because of the uniqueness of our circumstances, and because Morgan will eventually see through your facade if your controls continue to falter, I am forced to make a decision which will undoubtedly set poorly with you."

Lucien's stomach knotted. "A decision?"

Kim Le's head inclined in agreement. "Since you are here, and since you are of value to Morgan," he began almost evasively, "it is my hope that you will agree to what I shall momentarily propose. If you do not," he added with a definite sadness, "then I shall have no alternative but to request that you do leave the temple at once."

Heart pounding, Lucien tried to control the blind terror which lashed through his mind. It was not uncommon for the Supreme Master to occasionally design a test; and he was left to wonder if he would be required to sleep on some ancient bed of nails or to walk barefooted through a bed of glowing embers. Somehow, though, he doubted it would be so simple.

"On your honor, Lucien," the old man said at last, "I ask you to tell me now what it is that is the source of your trouble."

Lucien blinked. "That is all?"

Kim Le smiled faintly. "No," he said. "I will hear your answer first, then I will tell you what must be done."

Lucien fought the emotions which churned and boiled within his mind, wishing illogically that he had never been born. He knew exactly what the 'source of his trouble' was, yet attempting to voice it without sounding like an infant fighting its twin for the mother's breast was no easy task.

"Lucien?" Kim Le said when he didn't reply. "I must have your answer now. Our time is short. It will be morning soon, and Morgan must not be made suspicious because of our hesitations."

Fully realizing that it was no idle threat, Lucien looked up at last, meeting and holding Kim Le's gaze, trying to convince himself that Myrddin was anywhere else. "The source, Kim Le," he said very quietly, "is Master Myrddin."

Kim Le's brows lifted. "Why?" he asked as if already knowing the answer.

Lucien's jaw tightened and despite the fact that he hadn't been able to make himself actively dislike his kinsman, he adopted a false sense of inner anger to mask that fact. "It is my opinion that he seeks to take from me that which is rightfully mine," he said at last, choosing the ancient words to express himself.

But Kim Le only smiled, deflating Lucien's assumed airs instantly. "That is not your true opinion, Lucien," the old man said gently, "for you know it to be untrue. It is instead what you choose to *believe*. And it is a belief which will not only be your undoing, but Morgan's as well. Now," he continued without hesitation, "you must extinguish the light of that belief if you are to remain here at the temple with your beloved."

Lucien drew back. And though he knew that putting that belief to rest would be no simple task, knowing that, in all probability, he would be too rattled to even try, he nonetheless inclined his head in acknowledgement. "I accept that, Master," he intoned correctly. "Through meditation, I will–."

"Ta ta ta!" Kim Le interrupted, waving Lucien to silence with a quick slicing gesture of one hand. "Do not believe that the fire has gone out in this old man's head simply because the eyes have grown dim with age, Lucien!" he chastised. "You are not a master; you do not yet possess the disciplines to merely turn your beliefs off like blowing out a candle!"

Lucien held his breath. Kim Le *was* going to make him walk on hot coals. Or worse. "What then?" he asked, dreading the answer before it ever manifested in the air.

The old man glanced back and forth between Myrddin and Lucien. Then, moving toward the door at a slow shuffling walk, he stopped just before his hand touched the knob. "Only by taking your enemy into your Self will that enemy become a friend, Lucien," he said. Then, without further explanation, he bowed to dismiss himself from the room. "By morning, I expect this matter to be resolved."

And with that ultimatum hanging in the air, the old man disappeared into the corridor, leaving Lucien standing in the middle of the room with his jaw dropped and his eyes unblinking as they stared at Myrddin. His stomach turned over, threatening him with nausea as the full meaning of Kim Le's 'decision' smacked him in the face. He felt remarkably as if he'd 'been had', as Morgan might have said.

In his own inimitable way, Kim Le had suggested – no, Lucien corrected, he had *demanded* – that he join minds with Myrddin. And in that moment, he was forced to admit he would rather swap slobber with a rattlesnake, as Vanya was fond of saying. To join thoughts with another was the most intimate exchange in all the galaxy. Even sex paled in comparison.

He swallowed with difficulty, the color draining from his face. He couldn't speak, his mind recoiling in horror as he looked at the other man through the haze of candle-lit darkness. He felt shamefully naked, and the mere idea of another – especially Myrddin – entering his mind left him shaken and trembling and utterly terrified.

Not surprisingly, Myrddin offered a gentle smile. "Though you may not believe me, Lucien," he said quietly, "I attempted to change Kim Le's mind." He shrugged casually. "Unfortunately, he is correct. Until you have *seen* my intentions, you will continue to doubt them."

Shocked at last into speaking, Lucien launched a weak protest. "I do not doubt your honor, Myrddin," he said quietly. "Meditation will suffice to regain control of my feelings."

"For myself, I would agree with you, Lucien," Myrddin said with a soft-spoken sigh. "However, Kim Le's instructions were explicit despite their vagueness. If you do not permit me to touch your thoughts, you will be expelled from the temple by morning."

Lucien's heart wrenched, temporarily overshadowing his blind, unreasonable terror. He wondered fleetingly how he'd gotten himself into such a complex maze of problems, wondered if perhaps Myrddin had *created* that maze in order to lead him to his downfall.

"You would like that, wouldn't you?" he asked, hating himself the moment the words were out of his mouth. They sounded so completely, utterly, awfully *human*.

Myrddin took no offense. "No," he said quietly, taking a step forward until they stood less than a foot apart. "Your loss would be keenly felt by Morgan. And though you obviously do not believe me, I have also grown somewhat fond of the fire which keeps you burning so brightly. I would like, very much, to be your friend rather than your rival." He paused, then moved around Lucien and went to sit on the edge of the bed. "The decision is yours, my friend," he concluded finally. "I hope it will be a wise one."

Lucien barely heard the other's words. Instead, he stood staring out the window, listening to the gentle chirp of crickets, the sound of the wind in the trees. It was a serenity he no longer felt within his own life. "I... cannot join with you," he said, as much to himself as to Myrddin.

And, behind him, the other released a soft, melancholy sigh. "Would it help," Myrddin asked, "if I reminded you that you have only one alternative?"

You will have to defeat your fear by facing it. He didn't like the sound of it now anymore than he had earlier.

Lucien's eyes closed and, for a moment, he thought of what it would be like to leave the Temple of Ho Ling now. He would leave in disgrace – if not with Kim Le, then certainly with himself. The entire journey would end in failure and, ultimately, Morgan *would* turn to Myrddin. The fact that he might anyway was no help. He said nothing, hating himself for the unbidden jealousy which had created the situation, hating even more the fact that reason alone

188

was insufficient to chase that awful feeling away.

He trembled, his eyes clenched tightly shut. He knew that, ultimately, he did not wish to leave; and with that conviction his only form of guidance, he turned at last to face the other man. Once again, as he actually *looked* at Myrddin, he was forced to realize that it was only in his mind that his kinsman had become a monster, a threat, an enemy. But it *was* in the mind, he conceded, that all wars began. And yet, the idea of turning his thoughts – his very Self – over to the other left him faltering and horrified.

"I... cannot," he repeated.

Still sitting on the edge of Lucien's own bed, Myrddin seemed to contemplate that for a silent moment. Then, with a gentle smile, he made a quiet confession. "It is not an easy matter for me either, Lucien," he murmured. "I have learned to live without the touch of another's thoughts for so long that I am forced to admit my own reticence as well." But as he spoke, he held out one hand, palm up. "If it will make it less painful for you, however," he said at last, "I will do what is necessary. The only thing I must have from you is your consent."

Lucien couldn't breathe. Blood pounded in his ears and he thought for a moment that he might simply drop dead and save everyone a lot of trouble. He didn't want this, was actively set against it. And yet, he couldn't deny the aura of warmth and compassion which emanated from the man sitting on his bed. He looked at the other's outstretched hand, weighing that against the images in his mind – images of himself leaving the temple, leaving Morgan, leaving everything he had fought for.

Then, without ever realizing he'd made the move, he felt his own hand slide into Myrddin's, felt himself gently pulled forward until he knelt, head bowed, at the other's side. In some corner of himself, he was reminded of the time he'd been required to give his thoughts to Dunwillow on the day of his betrothal to Shalice, and of the impersonal touch of the old shaman's mind. And yet, as Myrddin's hands embraced his face with a warmth that was surprising, he was overcome with a profound sense of calmness, even of well-being.

He was somewhat surprised that Myrddin hesitated for an

extended moment, almost as if allowing him to adjust and accept before proceeding further. Then, as he released the breath he'd been holding for what felt like minutes, he experienced the full intensity of the joining as it opened like a delicate blossom into his mind.

In some vague and insignificant reality, Lucien heard himself gasp, felt his body tremble as he became One with the other. Myrddin was not, he discovered, given to treachery or subversion. Nor was he inclined to take his position as a master of the art lightly. His thoughts were ordered and surprisingly gentle despite the exterior mask of occasional mischievousness. And as the joining grew more stable, Lucien was shown more – more of Myrddin, more of Morgan Diego, more than he had thought he could bear to know.

In the mind, he saw confirmation of what he had already suspected: Myrddin *had* joined with his beloved. Their flesh had coupled as Morgan slept, restless and dreaming, in his bunk on an alien ship.

For a moment, Lucien struggled to turn away, but a tender suggestion from Myrddin's unverbalized thoughts encouraged him to further his knowledge. With an effort which required all discipline not to pull away, Lucien quieted the pain which rose in his chest, attempting to study the private images with a cool, dispassionate attitude.

And what he found in Myrddin's memories of the incident left him aching with an unexpected, unwanted tenderness for his kinsman. While it was true that Myrddin had taken Morgan as a lover, it was also true that the human had thought only of Lucien – of *him*. In their joining, Morgan had cried out, his lips forming a single name time and again. *'Lucien'*, the human murmured, gasping. *'Lucien....'*

Hearing his own name spoken in such a fashion by Morgan, even though he 'heard' it only in the context of Myrddin's memories, softened his heart, causing him to understand that, in those moments of passion, Myrddin had tried to *be* what Morgan needed most: he had tried to become Lucien himself. Not with any sense of intrusion, not as an intention to invade or usurp, but for *Morgan* he had laid aside his own passions, allowing the human to

190

fill his thoughts with memories of Lucien. Then, having taken those memories unto himself, he had lived the role for a short time, slipping silently back to his own lonely bed when the human eventually drifted into a restful sleep.

The memories of the incident passed quickly, and Lucien found himself irrationally longing to study them more closely, to garner a greater understanding of the motives – and the disciplines – which had permitted Myrddin to abandon his own wishes or desires and to deny his ultimate Self in order to bring comfort to another's suffering.

But even as Lucien longed to know more, it came to him with surprising tenderness, offered to him as Myrddin's intimate gift. And, not knowing how to refuse, no longer certain he wanted to refuse, Lucien accepted that gesture and allowed himself to drift further into the other's essence.

If you wish it, Lucien, the other man whispered in his mind, *I can offer you the Knowledge of Mastery. With it, your own controls will increase, and the pain which drives you to despair will eventually begin to lessen.*

Despite the fact that Lucien had previously wanted – very much – to find reason to dislike Myrddin, that tender offering shattered his final coldness. And, in the serene sanctuary of the joining, he came to understand that his only hope of accomplishing that goal lay in his ability to master his weaknesses, to harness the power of his currently undisciplined fear. And the means to that end – even if had to be Myrddin, he conceded – scarcely seemed important.

With a humility which was no longer painful, he projected his acceptance of Myrddin's proposal, vaguely aware of his head dropping to rest on the other's leg as the intensity of their joining drained his physical energy.

I would be honored to receive such Knowledge, he agreed, wondering vaguely if his mind were capable of absorbing so much in such a short span of time. *If you have the compassion to make such an offer,* he added, choosing the ancient and formal words, *then I am humbled to accept... Master.* Even his acknowledgement of Myrddin as his present master didn't diminish the determination he suddenly felt, the overpowering, all-encompassing need to become more than he had been before.

For a few moments, nothing at all happened. Then, in a vaguely distant reality, Lucien felt himself urged up onto the bed, felt Myrddin's hands pushing him gently back against the physical support of the mattress. It occurred to him that the other's hands had left his face, yet the joining remained firm and intact between them – an accomplishment which even the masters at the temple on Alfar would have been hard-pressed to equal. But instead of questioning methods or comparing his own admittedly limited abilities to those of a recognized master, he merely allowed himself to accept as he had sworn to do.

In another moment, he felt Myrddin's weight settle next to him, and though the implications left him trembling, he closed his mind to unwanted and impossible unlikelihoods.

Then, as the other's hands settled once again on his face, he held himself open and waiting, feeling very much like some sacrificial virgin.

At first, there was nothing other than a vague awareness of what was to come. But then, as he took a deep breath to steady the trembling in his body, his mind suddenly came alive with the Knowledge Myrddin had promised. In the span of minutes, he studied with Kim Le of Earth and Elmoon of Alfar. In the span of moments, he accumulated the wisdom of a thousand worlds, filing it in his memory as efficiently as possible under the circumstances. He realized with a detached sense of melancholy that he would never be able to grasp all of it; Myrddin had spent a lifetime gathering the wisdom and the knowledge which now marked him as a master. And even through the duality of the joining, Lucien understood that a total transfer of such knowledge was impossible.

The most he could hope for was to internalize the basics, to grasp the control and the disciplines and the ability to sacrifice which had previously held him checked in an emotional turmoil.

It will be enough, my friend, Myrddin promised gently, reading Lucien's stray thoughts with ease.

For a moment, Lucien was shamed by his own previous misconceptions concerning this man, for it was obvious in the Total

Truth which resounded between them that Myrddin was incapable of placing his own needs above those of others. What saddened Lucien most was the inescapable knowledge that this distant brother *did* care for Morgan: as a student, as a friend, as a man. But he knew now with utter certainty that Myrddin was no threat – for he came to understand that the other's primary dedication was to the art and to the Knowledge. He had cared for other students in the past, had even taken them to his bed and joined with them as he had joined with Morgan. He had wept with them when they wept, laughed when they laughed, rejoiced with them when they rejoiced.

He *was*, Lucien now realized, a true master.

And though that thought would have terrified him an hour before, he felt it settle gently into him now. Myrddin had earned the right to teach, the right even to love more than a single being, despite his Alfarian heritage which placed such strong emphasis on biological monogamy. He had earned the right to side-step useless disciplines which served only to bring misery to the disciple – including, Lucien realized, the Alfarian discipline which, on the surface, seemed to teach the negation of most passionate feelings.

And yet, seeing it in Myrddin's thoughts, he began to realize that abolishment of a part of the self was no less than murder. To smother passion was to take away the possibility of a future life; to stifle the power which was a natural by-product of loving sexual contact was to deny to the Self the ability to create – not only the ability to create offspring, but the ability to create Life itself. It was no wonder, Lucien suddenly realized, that even Alfarian biology had become so twisted that it forced his people into what amounted to an unnatural Calling – undoubtedly nature's way of attempting to keep the species alive when it seemed so hell-bent on its own annihilation – not through war or disease, but through a plethora of bizarre belief systems which taught reverence for all life… *except* its own.

For if left to their own devices, he now understood that most Alfarians would go through their lives hugging the trees and talking to the four winds – because that was what their culture had programmed them to do, to be – yet they would 'love' only in vague and intellectual terms, if at all. Certainly, he realized, his own

193

parents – the renowned Xander and Katrice – had never really been 'in love'. That very state of being was alien to them – not by their nature, but by their programming which stressed harmony above passion, reason above creativity, discipline above the natural fire which burned so brightly in the heart, but was stifled by a well-meaning philosophy which had somehow gone so terribly, terribly wrong.

Every living thing was simply *meant* to love, Lucien knew. And yet... how could real love even exist in a culture that still practiced the ancient and altogether foolish ritual of arranged marriage?

Suddenly, he felt reborn, rekindled, reawakened. He felt, simply, *alive*.

Thou art God, Lucien, Myrddin's mind-voice said with a gentle smile. A Terran philosophy made popular in Earth's 20th Century, but nonetheless applicable now.[1]

Lucien didn't have the strength to argue. Instead, he felt the concept take root in his thoughts, filling him with a sense of infinite power he had not possessed before. And as the joining began to slowly dissolve, he felt himself drifting in a sense of complete wellness, wholistic balance, spiritual freedom.

He remained that way for more than an hour, allowing new philosophies to settle into his subconscious thought patterns, to become a part of his Whole Self. At some point, he returned to enough awareness to realize that Myrddin had left his bed and, commanding himself back to reality, he opened his eyes to find the other standing at his side, looking down at him with an oddly contented expression.

No longer bound by meaningless dogma, Lucien allowed himself a faint smile, not surprised that it felt right and good. Then, getting to his feet, he stood facing the other man as he reached out to place one hand on each of Myrddin's arms. The second half of their allegiance was all that remained necessary to bind them to a single goal. He leaned forward willingly, placing his lips against the other's left cheek.

---

[1] Robert A. Heinlein; *Stranger In A Strange Land*

"That is for strength," he intoned in the ancient words, then moved to kiss the opposite cheek in identical fashion. "That is for *chi*." Then, holding the other's dark gaze for a long and meaningful moment, Lucien pressed his lips to Myrddin's mouth, leaving a warm kiss in his path. "And that is for you." He was slightly surprised that the difficult gesture filled him with a pleasant warmth, a feeling of completing something left previously undone.

Myrddin smiled gently, then reached up to smooth Lucien's disheveled bangs back into place. "I am honored... Master," he said quietly.

But Lucien shook his head. "I see now that mastery is not within my destiny, Myrddin," he murmured. "But with your help, perhaps I will fall somewhat closer to the level of an adept."

Myrddin's smile grew and, in accordance with tradition, he stepped back until they were once again two separate beings. "Do not underestimate yourself, Lucien," he said softly. "You have great strength."

Lucien accepted the compliment graciously. "But never enough wisdom," he realized.

Myrddin's head inclined in acknowledgement. "That is a truth we must all endeavor to internalize," he agreed. "No life is ever long enough to gather too much wisdom – for if it were, Death itself would become a thing of the past."

Lucien contemplated that in thoughtful silence, realizing as he glanced momentarily at the window that the horizon was growing progressively lighter, the sky now a deep silver-gray rather than the black of evening. "You must rest, Myrddin," he stated quietly. "The new day is with us already."

Myrddin likewise gazed through the open window, his face highlighted by the coming dawn. Then, with a courteous bow of his dark head, he moved to the door. "Sleep well, Lucien," he intoned, then disappeared into the corridor to face the morning.

Lucien stared at the door long after it had closed behind the other man, finding a strange feeling of aloneness deep within himself. And yet, he accepted it as a part of his Self, a new challenge which must be met with the strength and stamina of an adept even if not with the full knowledge of a master.

He lay down at last on the bed, closing his eyes as the new serenity filled him. At the very least, he now understood what Morgan saw in Myrddin. Now that he had dismissed his jealousy and dealt with his inexperienced passions, *he* was hard-pressed not to see it himself.

But he knew that his first and foremost duty was to his friend, his beloved. And with that priority to strengthen him, he realized that he could accept whatever obstacles might come his way before that final goal was realized.

He could even cope with the possibility that, very soon, Morgan might choose to join again with Myrddin.

It wasn't what he would have wanted, certainly not what he would have chosen; yet he couldn't deny the fact that, for Morgan's sanity, it could easily become a necessity. Morgan needed tenderness, affection, the warmth of another's touch to assuage the loneliness which had followed him throughout his life. And he needed to touch the power before he would be able to instill it within himself.

What amazed Lucien was that he had almost deliberately ignored that fact before. Now, with serenity as a part of himself, he began to accept that, *whatever* Morgan needed, he would have. Even if that need turned out to be Myrddin rather than himself – for he understood that, in the end, the human would belong solely to him, just as he would bind his life only to Morgan's.

Whatever might occur in the meantime was merely a diversion.

Still, he couldn't help hoping that Morgan would choose *him* – *now* as well as forever.

CHAPTER FOURTEEN

Standing in the center of the training arena as the morning's lesson concluded, Morgan bowed according to tradition, then stepped into the relaxed natural stance, raising his eyes to meet his teacher's penetrating dark gaze. A thin sheen of perspiration stood beaded on his forehead, and his muscles quivered from the intense work-out. But despite his accomplishments of the day, he felt unaccountably dissatisfied.

"You appear troubled, Morgan," Myrddin noted, taking a step forward. "Did you not sleep well?"

Morgan sighed softly, his face darkening as he glanced at the floor, the memories of the previous afternoon filling his mind. To say he hadn't slept well would be an understatement; he'd barely slept at all. "I think I made a few serious mistakes yesterday, Master," he said, feeling a sudden need to express the anger which had burned even in his restless dreams. "I'm afraid I might have completely alienated Master Lucien."

Myrddin's face showed no outward change of expression. "In what manner?"

Morgan shrugged. "We had an argument." But on second thought he rephrased that statement more truthfully. "Actually," he corrected, "_I_ had an argument... with myself, I guess."

Myrddin smiled very gently. Then, moving toward the door of the arena, he motioned Morgan to follow. "Come and walk with me," he instructed. "Let us see if we cannot quiet your anger and calm your spirit."

For a reason Morgan couldn't pinpoint, he froze for an instant, his nerves jangling as he recalled the last time he'd met with Myrddin outside the formality of the training arena. But then, realizing that his current predicament was anything but acceptable, he closed his eyes briefly, his lips pressing tightly together as he forced himself once again to trust.

They walked for several minutes in silence, passing through the temple building and emerging in the outer gardens. Once outside, Morgan took the time to appreciate the beauty of his surroundings once again, inhaling the delicate scent of honeysuckle and jasmine, listening to the creek's gentle lullaby as it rushed toward some distant ocean.

Instinctively, he was drawn toward the water, and within another few moments, he found himself sitting on the coarse sand of the creek's shore, his bare feet soothed in the coolness of the stream. He was filled with a sense of well-being, inner warmth.

"You know," he mused, "when I'm *here*, I don't feel the anger."

Myrddin knelt by his side, dipping his hands into the clear water and letting it run through his fingers. "Is it the location which softens your emotions, Morgan," he questioned, "or is it only that, here, you feel alone?"

Morgan frowned thoughtfully. "I'm not sure I understand."

Dipping his hands again into the water, Myrddin replied with a tenderness which left Morgan's heart aching. "Many times, with sufficient beauty to distract the mind from its daily pursuits, the emotions we feel are softened, made to seem insignificant against the greater power of nature. Here," he added, indicating the stream and the weeping willows which bent low over the water, "your mind is filled with thoughts of creation, of the majesty of a single blade of grass or the mystery of where this water goes once it passes through our fingers. There is no time or reason to trouble oneself with anger."

Morgan considered that, the stillness growing more profound within him as he accepted the other's words as truth. Overhead, the sun was bright, casting a spray of shadows on the ground, warming his face as he lifted it skyward. He laughed lightly, feeling a burden lift from his shoulders. "When I was a kid, I used to go swimming in the creek that ran through my grandmother's farm," he recalled fondly. "There was a place where the water was deeper, and I often thought that I could take all my troubles there and drown them in the river."

Myrddin's brows lifted. "Perhaps you were correct to think in such terms," he commented. Then, rising to his feet, he motioned once more for Morgan to follow. "There is a place near the temple's outer wall where the stream's waters run deep," he explained. "It is a short walk, but the serenity to be found there is well worth the journey."

198

Decidedly unconcerned about the length of the journey, Morgan also rose and walked at his master's side through the lush green gardens. They followed the stream's course along what appeared to be a seldom-used path, and had it not been for occasional memories of what he had left behind, he could easily have believed that all was well with the world.

For a moment, those memories threatened to surface, to drive the serenity from his spirit; and yet, relying on the disciplines he'd learned over the past weeks in the company of Kim Le and the masters, he set those thoughts temporarily aside, realizing the uselessness of dwelling on impossibilities.

"For what it's worth," he commented when the silence grew lengthy, "I haven't been aware of the Mizarian probe for quite awhile now." He smiled wistfully. "Sometimes, if I just don't think about it, it's like it doesn't exist, almost as if the whole thing never really happened." He shrugged. "With a little imagination, I can almost believe that I *do* belong here."

Myrddin was silent as he pondered that. "Yet you still wish to return to your former life," he commented.

Morgan nodded, listening to the stream as its waters rushed more loudly, leaving him to assume they were nearing the deeper part of the tributary. "Yes," he confirmed without hesitation. Then, remembering his recent difficulties, he allowed a sheepish grin to press his lips. "I just wish I could remember how *much* I want to go back when my temper gets out of control." He paused thoughtfully, then added: "Like yesterday.... I didn't even know at the time why I *was* angry. Master Lucien and I had been sparring, and we came to a point where everything just... well... flew out of my mind. I couldn't, for the life of me, remember how to break a hold he had me in. And then, the next thing I knew, I was at his throat." That thought saddened him greatly.

Myrddin inclined his head in understanding. "Perhaps you were angry because, in your sparring, he emerged the victor," he suggested.

Morgan shook his head. "No... I don't think so," he countered, reveling in the sensation of cool green grass on his bare feet. "I've been defeated before," he added, a stray and unbidden thought reminding him of his combat with Lucien on the floor of Mother Forest. "And I'm not stupid enough to think I could win in *any* fight with a Alfarian." He frowned thoughtfully, trying to make sense of the unexplained reaction. "I dunno. It was as if I was... well... testing him."

Myrddin's brows lifted. "Do you know why?"

Morgan shrugged. "Not really," he admitted. "It's just that... he gets to me."

Myrddin stopped walking, and turned to face him, curiosity written in the dark eyes. "He effects you," he translated. "Is this effect positive or negative?"

Morgan blinked, also stopping to stand with Myrddin beneath the low-spread limbs of a huge weeping willow tree. He hadn't thought about it in those terms. "Well... positive," he decided presently, recalling the unusual feelings which had inundated him after his initial meeting with Master Lucien. His face darkened.

And, not surprisingly, Myrddin noticed. "You are embarrassed," he pointed out with a gentle smile which robbed the words of any sting.

Again, a light laugh parted Morgan's lips – perhaps, he conceded, to conceal the discomfort he felt inside.

"Sometimes," he ventured cautiously, "human nature has a nasty habit of rearing its ugly head at the worst possible times." Then, as he caught the double-edged meaning of that, he quickly rephrased, trying to pry his foot loose from his teeth. "I mean... well...."

Myrddin's lips curved upward just a little. "You are attracted to your master," he deduced.

Morgan's mouth opened to protest. Then, realizing that he probably needed to justify himself to Myrddin least of all, he merely shrugged, wondering how he'd gotten himself into the discussion in the first place. "But I *shouldn't* be!" he decided abruptly. "I mean, I don't even know him! Granted, I may have the reputation of being the so-called Galactic Stud, but I'm not in the habit of jumping into bed with anyone I might happen to be attracted to. I'm not like that," he repeated, his words coming more quickly. "If I *were*, you and I would have ended up together again--."

Who are you trying to convince, Cap'n Morgan? The Little Voice wanted to know, laughing at him as his embarrassment deepened in direct proportion to the foot in his mouth. *And for that matter, do you think this guy cares? The only one judging you is you.*

Myrddin studied him with a detached yet warm compassion. "You know from experience that you will not fall in love with me. Perhaps you do not have that same certainty where Master Lucien is concerned," he suggested casually.

Morgan blinked. "Love?" he repeated incredulously. But even as his mouth opened to argue, he closed it again, realizing with an abruptness which slapped him in the fact that, once more, Myrddin was correct. His heart pounded furiously, leaving him silently angry with the fact that his emotions were so unpredictable even to himself. Then, looking more closely at Myrddin, he said what had been on his mind for days, possibly even weeks. "But... I *do* love you." Saying it made him realize just how true it was and, deep within himself, the pain lessened just a little despite the complications his statement awakened.

The other man smiled very gently, then reached out to place one arm around Morgan's shoulders as they began walking once more. "I have no doubt of that," he said quietly. "But do not forget that there is a difference between loving someone from a safe distance and being eternally dedicated to that love with equal dedication in return."

Listening to the pounding of his heart as it kept rhythm with the stream's rushing waters, Morgan struggled to translate that into English. "Then... what you're saying is that... *you* don't love *me*."

If I had a hand, I'd smack you stupid, The Little Voice threatened. *Are you really that dense or are you just jackin' off at the mouth again?*

But Myrddin shook his head. "I do, in fact, love you, Morgan. But my love for you will be confined always to levels which would be insufficient to serve you well over an extended period of time."

Somehow, that explanation left Morgan feeling just a little more at ease. And he also understood something about himself as well. "We can love without being *in* love." For some reason, though that little fact was common knowledge among every lifeform in the galaxy, he'd never felt it applied so appropriately to his own life.

Morgan allowed himself the luxury of mulling those thoughts over in his mind like some newly-discovered jewel. Sure, it was nothing new. But somehow, it was the missing corner piece he'd been searching for in his own life for longer than he could remember. It was one reason he had sated himself with the distant pleasures of distant women – no danger of falling in love, no long-term responsibility, no strings. And until very recently, that lifestyle had served him well – *so* well, in fact, he had never really troubled himself with the introspections which now flooded him and caused The Little Voice to threaten a variety of violent atrocities.

"The love you feel for your masters is normal, Morgan," Myrddin explained as they suddenly emerged from underneath the overhang of trees and stood at the edge of the stream where the waters ran still and deep, "as is the love a master nurtures for those he teaches. And so long as each understands that the other is sworn to a different goal, destined to walk a different life path, then even the *expression* of such love is to be considered as an aspect of learning, as a thing of profound beauty."

Morgan felt the words settle deep within himself. It left him more at ease, less confused, and with considerably less guilt nipping at his heels. He realized with an odd sense of chagrin that Myrddin had led him to this secluded spot for reasons other than to appreciate the serenity of the sun and the stream. And he also understood that he'd permitted himself to be lead – something he'd seldom been able to do in his lifetime as a ram.

Now, standing at the water's edge as the morning sun climbed high in the cloudless blue sky, feeling his humanity surround him with need and longing and a strange desire to alleviate the frustrations of flesh and spirit, he lifted his eyes to his teacher, his heart pounding in his chest. In the other's steady gaze, he saw no fear, no threat, no possibility of a lifetime together.

Ultimately, that made his decision easier.

He knew only that he was tired of fighting – not only with the memories of a life to which he no longer belonged, but with his own needs, his own desires, his own human nature. He was weary of battling invisible demons and sparring with distant windmills, especially weary of hurling his bitterness in the face of those who

202

sought only to help and comfort.

And, realizing that, internalizing it, he gave in to the terrible need which had brought him to the creek's deeper waters. With fingers that trembled, he slowly unfastened the white sash which marked him as an initiate, dropping it to the grass growing along the creek's sloping bank.

In another few moments, he stood naked and unselfconscious before the other man, his need burning in his eyes, reflected in his body as his flesh swelled and yearned.

Then, with a smile of concession, he turned and stepped into the cool stream, the waters rising to chest-height as he edged his way down the steep incline of the creek-bed. Without looking back, he crossed to the other side, closing his eyes and bracing his chest against the smooth warmth of a stone boulder which rested half-in, half-out of the water.

In another moment, he was aware of a familiar presence at his back, and of Myrddin's long and powerful arms closing around him from behind. He held his breath in silent anticipation, waiting for completion. Here, in this sacred place, he did not want to be in command as he had always been in that past life he'd left behind. Here, he was not Commander Diego. Here, if he would only allow it, he could let down his guard and simply *be* the man and not the roles that man had been required to play.

He breathed softly, waiting, and then, abruptly, he was filled with another's presence, the swift and powerful thrust causing him to gasp and bite his lip in an effort not to cry out.

He came instantly, painfully, the frustration and anger forced to the surface in a blinding explosion which almost blotted consciousness from his mind. He was aware of Myrddin thrusting twice more, and then of an alien seed spreading deep within him.

The lean arms remained locked about his waist for a long time, the stream's waters providing an odd contrast to Myrddin's cool flesh as a thousand divergent thoughts and realizations rattled through Morgan's mind.

Physically, he felt relieved and decidedly more relaxed than he had been for days. Emotionally, he was secure in the knowledge that this brief encounter was strictly what it had been labeled only minutes before: a method of expressing love without sharing the infinite responsibilities of love.

But spiritually... he was left with a profound emptiness inside.

Never satisfied, are you?

He didn't like that about himself.

~

Lucien sat half-lotus in the center of the outdoor training arena, glancing at the sun's position in the sky and realizing with anticipation that Morgan was due to arrive momentarily. Following his joining with Myrddin and a morning spent in private meditation – which, surprisingly, came with ease – he was left with an inner peace that alleviated much of his previous anxiety. It was, he conceded, a peace which came with a high price – though he had not yet had time to sufficiently contemplate what the end result might be of his new insights into his own heritage, his own people, the culture which had shaped him. He wondered fleetingly why he hadn't seen it before, yet the answer was painfully written on the fabric of the universe itself. One could not see the maze while trapped inside it, so it stood to reason that false belief systems could only be seen as false once one had moved beyond them. The fact that he now recognized that 99.9% of *all* cultures, religions and belief systems were false brought little solace. Instead, it only reinforced his resolve to find his own path, to follow his own heart. He would no longer be Alfarian. He could *only* be Lucien.

The danger, he knew, resided in the fact that he had been Alfarian for so long that he wasn't entirely sure who Lucien was.

And yet, as he looked up to see a white-clad figure approaching the training area, he felt just a hint of fear whisper through his mind. He stood, hands clasped neatly behind his back, waiting for his student to enter, wondering if today would lead to the same difficult confrontation he had faced with the human the day before.

But as Morgan stopped momentarily at the training arena's edge, bowing from the waist to show proper respect for the art, Lucien's brows lifted in surprise.

He couldn't help noticing the relaxed set of the other man's shoulders, the fluidity of his movements, the lack of tension in his facial muscles. For an instant, he attempted to pass it off to nothing more than a good night's sleep; but as he observed more closely, almost visualizing the deep blue of a sated aura, he felt the Knowledge inundate him with truth.

Sometime between the morning and now, Morgan and Myrddin had made love.

His heart thudded noisily, his controls threatening to falter. But then, calling up some ancient discipline which had no name, he felt the anger leave him to be replaced with an odd sense of acceptance. His anger would do nothing to alter the past, he realized. His frustration would only serve to destroy everything he had fought for the evening before. His jealousy was nothing more than a role – an extension of one of those false belief systems. *And*, he knew, if he failed his controls once more, Kim Le would expel him from the Temple of Ho Ling once and for all. Then, he would forfeit everything – including, he realized, the man standing before him.

Closing his eyes for a fraction of a second, he inhaled slowly through his nostrils, summoning up the power of Knowledge and relying on the wisdom Myrddin had given him to overcome fleeting feelings of possessiveness.

And with that thought, he realized something utterly profound: Myrddin had joined mind to mind with *him*, heart to heart, soul to soul. Surely, Lucien thought, he could live with the fact that his distant kinsman had only joined flesh to flesh with Morgan.

"Morgan," he intoned, opening his eyes and gesturing the human into the training area. "I presume you are ready to begin today's lesson."

But as Morgan moved to stand face-to-face with his master, he looked up into the dark eyes, his lips pressed together in a moment of silent decision. Then, lowering his head, he bent to one knee in a gesture of humility.

"Master Lucien," he said very quietly, "I have no excuse for my behavior yesterday. But I'm hopeful you'll see fit to forgive my rudeness, and continue to have me as your student."

Lucien stood for a long moment staring at the kneeling form before him, realizing with an odd sense of surprise that the Morgan

Diego he had known in the past would have been very hard-pressed to offer such an apology in such a form to *anyone*. It occurred to him that his commander *had* changed – out of necessity and circumstances, perhaps, but he had nonetheless changed. He had grown spiritually stronger.

Lucien reached out to place his right hand on the humbly bowed head, trembling internally at the soft silkiness of the other's hair. "What did you learn from the experience, Morgan?" he inquired, likewise asking the proper question at the proper time.

Morgan's eyes closed and he contemplated his answer for only a moment. "I have learned, Master, that the ram who butts his head against the wall usually wakes up with a headache in the morning." Then, wondering if his humor would be wasted on the stern Alfarian, he grew more serious. "I have also learned that... it's necessary to accept one's nature rather than trying to pretend it doesn't exist."

Morgan's statement was almost certainly a reference to the interlude with Myrddin. Still, he followed his kinsman's instructions, prying deeper and leaving no room for doubt. "Elaborate," he entreated, his hand still holding Morgan's head in a bowed position.

Morgan tried not to tremble under the intense scrutiny of this man's questions. He realized that, if he truly wanted to master his own controls, if he actually did want to master the Mizarians' probe and hold any hope of regaining his former life, he could not afford to hold back even a small measure of the truth. And, with that knowledge, he offered his explanation carefully, not wanting to offend.

"Through Master Myrddin's guidance, I have... dealt with my anger," he said, hoping that would be sufficient. "Now, if you will teach, I am ready to learn."

Lucien considered that response with a faint smile which went unnoticed by his student. 'Guidance' was one of the most clever euphemisms he had ever encountered, yet he was forced to acknowledge Morgan's repeated attempts to spare him the truth. It made him rest just a little easier, however, realizing that at least the human had regained his controls, his sense of emotional balance.

"Very well," he said presently, releasing his hold on the human's head and taking a step back. "Face me." But then, as the other rose, Lucien caught himself wondering if his acceptance had come too easily, if he should, as Myrddin had suggested the evening before, do something more severe to regain Morgan's respect. Somehow, between the two men they were *now*, it almost seemed a foregone necessity and, understanding that, realizing that it would serve Morgan's needs as well as his own, he selected his lesson carefully.

"To demonstrate your sincerity to learn all that is possible, Morgan," he intoned levelly, "we will spar once again."

Morgan's brows narrowed; it wouldn't be that simple. "And?" he prompted, reading the unspoken challenge in the other's eyes, finding it to be a challenge he could live with despite the sudden rush of butterflies in his stomach.

"This time," Lucien concluded, "it is a fight to the finish."

Morgan blinked, feeling a measure of the color drain from his face as he perused his opponent. "You *do* realize that I don't stand a chance."

Lucien merely inclined his head in acknowledgement. "You may utilize all training within your sphere of knowledge, Morgan," he stated. "Techniques of defense and attack are recommended but not required. This is not a test on form or stamina, but an exercise to more accurately determine your strengths and weaknesses when more than points are at stake."

Morgan actually caught himself grinning, feeling a sudden enthusiasm overcome him. "What about you?" he asked. "Are you playing by the rules of an initiate, or with the knowledge of a master?"

Lucien considered his response briefly. "I will control my speed and agility to match your level of accomplishment," he agreed, putting a degree more fairness into their fight. "Other than that, I make no promises."

Morgan realized he wouldn't gain any points by arguing; and, feeling suddenly as if he could conquer the galaxy again, he bowed his head in agreement to the terms. Despite his previous difficulty with this man – and perhaps *because* of it – he was determined to do everything within his power to regain the other's respect. Even, he thought, if that included getting himself beaten to a pulp as a result.

~

Lucien was surprised that the human evaded moves which, in the past, would have taken him to the mat and made him an easy mark to finish. Now, with several weeks of training with Myrddin and Kim Le, Morgan had clearly gained extreme speed and a cunning which any opponent would have been hard-pressed to match.

Already, Lucien found his own breathing elevated, his heart-rate increased dramatically. In the intensity of their combat, he had little time to contemplate Morgan's nearness, and was grateful for the temporary distraction.

Taking a moment to judge his distance, the Alfarian launched a series of kicks, connecting only with one glancing blow to the smaller man's leg. Under other circumstances, it would have been sufficient to score a fall; but now, Morgan merely side-stepped with grace and agility, his knee touching the mat only for a moment.

Pleased with himself for lasting as long as he had, Morgan grinned as he pivoted in place, turning once more to face his attacker. Then, relying on a trick which had served him well in the past, he locked his eyes on the other's chest, hoping to distract his teacher from his intended point of attack at the leg.

He cross-stepped forward, holding the other's gaze, making a point of glancing occasionally at the chest. Quickly, he feigned a punch toward the other's solar plexus, then dropped to a close kneel and launched his intended flurry of open-handed strikes to his master's lower leg, attempting to knock the taller man off balance and drive him to the mat.

But with equal quickness, Lucien evaded the intended strikes, maneuvering into a sliding leg sweep which, when matched against Morgan's close kneel stance finally succeeded in usurping the human's balance and dumping him awkwardly to the ground.

With an "*Oof!*" of surprise, Morgan landed heavily on his butt, his hands only marginally breaking the fall. Then, anticipating the other's next move, he instantly launched himself into a backward roll, clamoring to his feet and ascertaining Lucien's position despite his momentary disadvantage. He stepped instantly into the customary fighting stance, drawing a heavy breath to steady the trembling in his tired, abused muscles.

Lucien contemplated his adversary with a combination of surprise and a deep feeling of accomplishment. Once again, a maneuver which would have finished Morgan in the past had succeeded only in a momentary set-back. Now, with both of them breathing raggedly, trembling with exhaustion, they squared off again.

Despite the seriousness of the circumstances, Morgan couldn't help noticing the bedraggled appearance of his opponent. The formerly sleek hair had been disheveled and was now mussed into a feathered array of individual strands. The once-crisp black robes were rumpled, the purple belt almost completely untied and hanging loosely about the slim waist.

"Had enough?" the human asked with a lop-sided grin.

"This fight, Morgan," Lucien reminded, "is to the finish." But he allowed a faint smile to press his lips, realizing the danger of being misunderstood to be severe and unbending. "Unless, of course, you wish to surrender now and award the match to me."

Morgan's smile grew. "Not on your life, Master!" he said, feigning forward with another series of jabs, kicks and punches, connecting with less than half. Still, when he remembered the object of the day's lesson, he knew he couldn't quit; respect was a two-way commitment.

And yet, even as he recovered from his unsuccessful attack and dropped back into position to defend against the other man's counter, he caught a quick flurry of motion out the corner of one eye. Instinctively, wired to defend against all possible attacks, he jerked his head in the direction of that disturbance, and was momentarily horrified to find only a hawk pursuing some unseen prey through the tall green grass.

Instantly trying to recover from his fatal distraction, he jerked his head back in Lucien's direction – or, he realized a fraction of a second too late, in the direction of where his master *had* been a moment before.

It was then, with a sense of futile frustration that he felt himself wrenched into the dangerous choke-hold. And somehow, given the rules of the match, he wasn't surprised that Master Lucien didn't even allow him the time required to defend himself.

A moment later, his world grew dark while the hawk took to flight, its cry sounding almost like a victorious laugh as it rang in his ears.

~

For a few long minutes, Lucien remained utterly still, gazing down at the unconscious man in his arms. His heart pounded, as much from the sudden surprise of what he had done as from the combat itself. His breath came in quick, ragged gasps.

When he could think straight again, he gently lowered the human to the mats, resisting the unnecessary urge to strip off his own tunic and use it as a blanket. The late afternoon air was cool but not cold, and he realized with a sense of profound tenderness that he had always sought to shield this man even from imaginary harm. Still, he couldn't help wondering what would await him when Morgan regained consciousness, if the human would react with anger or bitterness, respect or an attitude of defeat.

But as he lowered himself to sit at the other's side, he was distracted by the sound of approaching footsteps. And, glancing up toward the entrance to the training arena, he wasn't surprised to find Myrddin observing him with an oddly pleased smile residing on the angular features, reflecting in the dark eyes.

"Better," the master commented lightly. "Your solution shows wisdom which Morgan will undoubtedly respect."

But Lucien wasn't paying attention. Rather, he was attempting to control the surprise which threatened to drop his jaw. "It was my impression, Myrddin," he intoned levelly, "that you were here at this temple to teach. Surely your students require your presence at *some* time." He wasn't angry, only somewhat confused by his kinsman's constant supervision.

But Myrddin remained unruffled, his smile becoming more

pronounced. "You must understand, Lucien, that Kim Le would not accept – even on *my* word – that you had mastered the basics required to teach another," he explained gently. "Now I will be able to inform our master that you are indeed an accomplished adept... well on the way to even higher accomplishments."

Lucien blinked, not knowing where to begin with Myrddin, knowing he had precious little time to say anything at all. He remembered his own humility, however, and reminded himself again that Myrddin had earned the right to be called a master. "Then... I presume you will inform Kim Le that I will be remaining here at the temple."

Myrddin's head inclined in agreement. "Of course, my friend," he acknowledged. Then, indicating Morgan with a gesture of one hand, he commented, "He fought well. Do not forget to stress that when he regains consciousness."

Lucien glanced at the unmoving man on the ground, then up to Myrddin. He took a deep breath, trying once again to resolve the fact that, sometime in the cool of the morning, they had made love. "He appeared more focused," he said presently. "I presume you had something to do with that?"

And, not surprisingly, Myrddin's head bowed once more. Then, meeting Lucien's eyes, he spoke very gently and very deliberately. "Please understand, Lucien, that no attempt has been made to usurp what you share with Morgan. However," he added quietly, "it became obvious to me as we talked together that his nature could not be too long denied. It is possible that he would have come to you soon enough, yet it seemed more likely that he would continue to resist his own needs, eventually condemning himself to fail the discipline completely. In this manner, it is my hope that I have given you a somewhat more receptive student, a more wholistically balanced man." He paused, then smiled with extreme tenderness. "And... if I may be so bold, I would say to you that I envy you the future you will certainly share with Morgan."

Lucien considered that with remarkable detachment, but when he looked up to respond, he discovered only the trees and the wind and the setting sun. Distantly, moving as a silhouette against the horizon, Myrddin had returned to the temple.

But Lucien had no time to contemplate it further, for as he returned his attention to Morgan, he realized with a sense of anticipation that the human had begun to stir.

~

Morgan returned to consciousness gradually, his hand automatically moving for the sore spot in his neck. But by the time he reached it, he found Master Lucien's fingers already there, massaging away the stiffness which had settled as he slept.

For a moment, a trace of the old anger threatened to return, but as he looked up into the expectant face of the other man, an odd sensation of amusement overwhelmed him.

"Well, other than the fact that I lost, how did I do?" But then, not really wanting to hear the answer, he waved his own words aside with a gesture of his hand, struggling to sit up, accomplishing it only with the assistance of the arm which slid automatically around his back. "No, let me guess. The whole match is rendered null and void because this lowly student forgot to bow properly before he fell flat on his face."

Lucien's lips curved upward just a little and he continued his healing massage by maneuvering around behind him. "You didn't fall," he commented. "I caught you."

For some strange and admittedly perverse reason, Morgan felt a deep sense of satisfaction in that, his stomach knotting pleasantly as the lethargy lingered in both body and mind. "I would say thanks," he said with a groan as he stretched his right arm out to alleviate the cramp in his muscle, "but under the circumstances, that seems rather lame."

Lucien smiled once more; a few minutes before, when Myrddin had spoken in such elegantly logical terms of seducing Morgan, *he* had felt exactly the same way. He continued to massage the other's back and neck, however, becoming almost mesmerized by the flowing motion of his own hands. "Are you recovered?"

Morgan grimaced, playing it for all it was worth. "I'll live," he decided at last. "But if I had a blaster, I wouldn't make the same prognosis for that damned buzzard!"

212

"Hawk," Lucien corrected automatically.

Morgan rolled his eyes; the response was nothing less than what he'd expected. But as he fully realized what had happened, he felt an odd sense of accomplishment settle in to mingle with his admitted defeat. "Well?"

Lucien was genuinely perplexed. "What?"

Morgan shrugged, wincing only slightly at the remaining soreness. "Aren't you going to give me the standard lecture about how my own distraction was my downfall?"

Lucien considered that. "I do not feel that such a 'lecture' is necessary, Morgan," he said. "However, if it would please you to hear it, I shall be pleased to point out your errors and how they led to your defeat."

Taking a deep breath, Morgan waved the other to silence with a gesture which had carried over from his days as a commander. In that moment, it didn't even occur to him that he was silencing his master. "You were right the first time," he said. "It's *not* necessary." Then, stifling an unbidden yawn, he added: "I lost my concentration and you took advantage of it. It can't get much more fair than that."

Lucien was mildly surprised by the ease with which Morgan accepted defeat. "Then... you feel no anger?"

Morgan frowned thoughtfully. "No," he said, only then realizing it. "I guess I don't." A faint, gentle smile pressed his lips upward. Then, with an air of mischievousness which had evaded him since his exile he added: "But if you'd like, I'll see what I can do."

Lucien actually laughed softly, a rare occurrence which seemed to stretch his diaphragm with a distinctly pleasant sensation. He hadn't expected such a relaxed humor so soon, and fleetingly wondered if one morning spent with Myrddin had made this much difference. He also wondered if, when he and Morgan *did* eventually come together, *he* would be able to leave the human with this obviously profound sense of well-being.

But he didn't take the time to make foolish comparisons then. Instead, he got to his feet, urging the human to stand by a touch on his arm.

"Come, Morgan," he said, indicating the temple with a gesture of his hand. "The sun is leaving us, and you are undoubtedly hungry."

Morgan allowed himself to be pulled up. His stomach growled; his muscles ached. And yet, feeling strangely at ease with this man, he didn't wish to be parted so soon. Looking at his master, an odd thought struck him.

"Considering your strategy in a fight, how would you feel about a game of chess after dinner?" he inquired impulsively. Then, on second thought, he added: "Or are games even allowed inside the temple?"

Lucien's stomach did an elaborate dance which left him momentarily dizzy with a rush of feeling. "Since chess has traditionally been a game of strategy and skill which heightens one's awareness, it is not only permitted but encouraged at Ho Ling." He paused, realizing that, if it *wasn't*, he'd change the rules and carve a chess set from stone within the hour if necessary. "And, in answer to your question, I would be honored to play."

Morgan grinned warmly. For the first time since his exile, he was beginning to feel like himself again, beginning to believe that, one day soon, he *would* demand his old life back, even if that meant doing battle with every Mizarian in their Empire. He thought momentarily of *his* Lucien, experiencing a pang of regret that it wouldn't be *his* Alfarian with whom he sparred on the chess board... *or* in the sanctuary of a shared bed.

Then, telling himself that Time must be his friend rather than his enemy, he lifted his chin a little higher, making a silent vow to learn all that was within his power to grasp. And when he *did* return to his own beloved, he would take that knowledge with him, use it to convince even the cool and aloof Captain Lucien that the ram would always need the stalwart support of his shepherd.

Some way, he vowed, they *would* have that life together.

But he drew his attention back to the present, remembering that, for the moment, he had no alternative but to rely on the alliances he had formed within the sacred walls of Ho Ling.

"So... where can we set up the board?" he asked, suddenly aware of his teacher's silence as they walked together toward the

214

temple.

Lucien managed to control the rush which once again sent shivers darting along his spine. He smiled faintly, remembering his promise of the day before. "My door is always open, Morgan," he reminded the other as he projected a deliberate aura of mystique and suspense which would have been right at home on Myrddin. "If you wish to engage in a game, come to my room after you have eaten and dressed."

Morgan blinked. Then, looking down at himself, he realized that his uniform was torn, his chest streaked with runnels of dirt and sweat – the trophies and colognes of his accomplishments. He smiled to himself, not entirely certain that the reference to a 'game' was intended to refer solely to chess.

CHAPTER FIFTEEN

Lucien studied his sleeping quarters carefully, making certain that any article which might have betrayed his true identity had been removed to the temple's storage facility and safely locked away. Now, as with the quarters of the other masters, his room held only a small single bed, two straight-backed chairs which faced the large cut-away window, a night-stand with two drawers holding clean uniforms and an assortment of healing herbs and oils, and a small round marble table which, under normal circumstances, held only a single meditation candle. Now, the candle had been removed to the window sill, and a hastily borrowed chess set waited in its place.

The board was cut from colored marble, the pieces carved from pale oak and dark rose wood. Each piece was intricately and individually formed, with no two being the same. The pawns represented ill-clad and weary soldiers, and were carved with such precision that even the tears in their eyes were easy to distinguish. Kings and queens were elaborately dressed and painted to represent the ancient Chinese royalty of Earth; the bishops and knights were attired in delicately carved finery, and the rooks had been designed to represent in detail the royal palaces of two opposing clans.

As Lucien sat at last on the edge of his bed gazing at the game, however, he began to wonder if indeed Morgan would come at all. The human was impulsive and had been known on more than one occasion to speak before he thought. It was entirely possible, Lucien conceded that, with time and distance between them, he could easily change his mind or come to some decision which would keep him away.

But even as those thoughts came to trouble him, they were interrupted by a faint sound of footsteps which stopped just outside his door. He waited expectantly, his nerves jangling through his stomach until, finally, a somewhat hesitant knock broke the spell which had bound him.

Rising, he stood in the center of the small room, mentally re-checking his attire, confirming that the voice module was firmly in place and secured. Then, taking a deep breath as his eyes closed in a silent moment of self-centering, he spoke very softly.

"The door is open, Morgan," he said, fully realizing and intending the double meaning of his statement.

But as the wooden door opened slowly, Lucien's brows lifted, expressing his surprise at finding Kim Le standing there instead. The old man moved quietly into the room, closing the door behind him as he bowed graciously from the waist.

"Lucien," he intoned with a gentle smile in his dark, deep-set eyes.

Lucien wondered, if in direct contradiction to his promises, Myrddin had recommended his expulsion. He waited, then remembered at last to bow his head in respect before lifting his eyes again to the Supreme Master of Ho Ling.

"Kim Le," he acknowledged presently, holding his breath despite his attempt to remain calm and unflustered. Then, abruptly, another thought struck him. "Is Commander Diego all right?"

The old man smiled once more, then gestured toward the two empty chairs by the window. "Morgan is quite well indeed, Lucien," he assured, going to sit down with his gaze fixed on the rising moon on the Eastward horizon. "Come," he said when Lucien remained standing in the middle of the room, "sit with me while we talk."

Lucien glanced briefly at the door, his mouth opening to speak.

"Not to worry about Morgan," Kim Le said as if reading his thoughts. "I have sent him to light the Candle of his Existence with the other initiates. Following the ceremony, he will return to you for your scheduled game."

Trying to process the sudden change, Lucien moved at last to take the empty chair, turning his attention to the old man.

Kim Le was silent for a moment, his gaze distant as he continued to observe the rising moon. Then, turning at last to face Lucien, he responded succinctly. "I have spoken with your friend, Bryse," he revealed quietly.

Lucien blinked, trying to comprehend why and when. "And?"

Kim Le sighed softly. "Though I am not aware of every detail, I am told that a Mizarian vessel is on its way to Earth at this moment. It will be here within three days. It is my understanding from the admiral that an agreement of some type has been reached between our empire and theirs."

Lucien's heart almost stopped. "So soon?"

Kim Le seemed equally as surprised. "Apparently Morgan has been more successful in blocking the probe than even we had believed possible. Bryse revealed to me that their ambassador has formally declared a nullification of the previous Directive once their ambassador reaches Earth, and that new terms are being negotiated."

Despite what should have been good news, Lucien felt an odd sense of disappointment which mingled with his confusion. "I do not understand," he murmured, as much to himself as to Kim Le. "It was stated that any future negotiations between the Empire and the Mizarians would not concern the existing Directive."

Kim Le smiled once more, almost wistfully. "Many times, Lucien, an enemy is forced to realize that his weapons are inferior to those of his opponent, his shields less sturdy. At that time, the enemy must make peace, or live in fear of his own destruction." He paused, then clarified that statement into more conventional terms. "Apparently, the Mizarians are a technologically poor race; they do not possess the fire power to engage in a real battle with the Empire, thus they must endeavor to negotiate peace."

At that, Lucien's brows lifted. "With all due respect, Kim Le, I have seen a Mizarian battleship. It alone could have defeated an entire fleet of star cruisers."

But Kim Le shook his head with a slight laugh. "Did you *see* it, Lucien?" he asked quietly. "Or did you only *believe* you did?"

Lucien blinked. "Regardless of my own perceptions, Master," he said after a moment's hesitation, "it registered and was recorded and subsequently analyzed by sensors and computers. It *does* exist."

Kim Le's brows lifted. "It exists in your mind," he pointed out, "therefore it exists in your reality. However, it is my understanding from speaking with Bryse that the Mizarians have been discovered to rely almost totally on telepathic suggestion. Their minds are disciplined and tightly focused. And because of that, should they choose to use it as a weapon, it is conceivable that they could obliterate all life in the Empire simply by creating a *belief* that a state

218

of war existed. And as for the matter of your sensors and computers, it is my understanding that the Mizarians are capable of projecting – for a short period of time perhaps -- an illusion of sufficient force that it can be recorded on instruments." He paused, then added again: "You *believed* the ship to be real, and the fact that it registered on your sensors confirmed that belief, resulting in a state of Knowledge. The ship was real, but its grandness was exaggerated through the power of projection."

Lucien contemplated that silently. It wasn't such an alien concept. Even on Homeworld Alfar, sorcerers and shamans such as Dunwillow and others were capable of projecting what amounted to 3-D 'hallucinations' commonly referred to as tulpas on Earth. It wasn't such a stretch to consider that the Mizarians possessed the same ability.

"When a consensus of belief exists within a large group of people, 'reality' has very little to do with it, Lucien," Kim Le said as if reading his every thought. "What matters now," he stressed, "is that Morgan must remain distracted by his studies until the final arrangements have been made."

Lucien's head was starting to ache with the abrupt, lightning-fast changes of subject. "Sir?"

Kim Le's smile remained wistful and knowing. "At this moment," he explained, "the Mizarians have agreed to negotiate further because they have been made to believe we have the ability to shield against their powers of deception. However," he hastened to add, "should Morgan falter before their vessel reaches Earth, should their seer be able to locate him through the probe-link, they will subsequently know that they, too, have been deceived. And if that should happen, all we have accomplished would be quickly undone."

Lucien made a valiant attempt to digest all of that without losing track of the details. "Then... would it not be wise to simply take steps to insure that Morgan *cannot* be reached by the probe?" He didn't wait for an answer. "There are life suspension devices available at Galaxy Corps Headquarters, and I am certain Commander Diego would agree to such a solution on a temporary basis."

But Kim Le shook his head. "Too risky," he countered. "Should he lose consciousness for an extended period of time – even three days – it is possible that the Mizarians would be able to detect the change. Only his continued discipline will accomplish our goal safely."

Lucien sighed softly. An hour before, three days had seemed such a short and cosmically insignificant span of time. Now, with so much hanging in the balance, it stretched out before him like a private eternity. Still, another thought struck him, leaving him decidedly uncomfortable. "If the Mizarians believe that all humans are capable of blocking their probe," he began, "then–."

"They hold no such beliefs, Lucien," Kim Le interrupted gently. "They know only that one man of great power – your commander – has this ability. At this point in time, Morgan represents an unknown factor to the Mizarians – a factor which, hopefully, will bring them to negotiate a lasting peace between our Empire and theirs."

It seemed such a minor point that Lucien wondered for a moment how one man could make such a difference to the fateful outcome of the galaxy itself. And yet, when he remembered just *who* that man was, he was led to a more easy acceptance. Morgan Diego had toppled governments and created them, he had bent the rules and slammed his fist through Galaxy Corps regulations on more than one occasion. It stood to reason that now, without ever fully realizing it, he would be the one man to hold the destiny of the galaxy in the palm of his hand.

Finally, Lucien looked up again to Kim Le, trying to absorb as much as possible. "It seems... so soon," he said when other, more appropriate words failed.

But Kim Le smiled knowingly. "If you knew your enemy had it within his power to destroy you as you slept, would you then lay yourself down to sleep at all, Lucien?"

Lucien considered that, his lips pressing into a gentle smile. "Perhaps not," he agreed. "What I fail to understand, is what will occur between the Empire and the Mizarians once the truth is known. When the Mizarians discover that my commander is not representative of most others within the Empire, they will certainly

220

realize the deception. Is not war a certainty at that point, Master?"

Kim Le shook his head. "You forget, Lucien, that the Mizarians are possessed of honor. They will respect the man who bettered them, and it is the hope of your Galaxy Corps that they will desire to learn rather than to fight."

Lucien blinked. But when he recalled Morgan's brief recorded account of his experiences within their Empire, he was forced to concede that the Mizarians sought to gain knowledge more than territory, to harness the power of the mind rather than the fleeting power of more conventional weapons. And, for the moment, he could only permit himself to hope that the Mizarians would *remember* their honor during the next three days.

"If I understand you correctly, Kim Le," he said at last, "the exile which has been placed on my commander will be lifted once the Mizarian vessel reaches Earth." He paused, wondering how such a sudden and dramatic change would affect both himself and the human as well. "Since that is the case, I see no reason to continue this charade any further."

Kim Le gave him a quiet, scolding look. "Ta ta ta!" he reprimanded. "Do not seek to live life in such a hurry, Lucien! While I understand your need to reveal your true self to your commander, remember that *he* is the one who has been through the greatest trial. If you permit your own wishes to take precedence now, the shock of the truth may be sufficient to distract him from all he has learned. If the block he has placed in his mind should fail him before he *allows* it to drop at a time of his own choosing, the Mizarians would quickly realize that we are not so dangerous as we must now appear to them."

Lucien couldn't help smiling to himself as the full implications of it all slowly began to penetrate his mind. In another three days, if all went according to Kim Le's plan, it would all be over. Within seventy-two short hours, he and Morgan would be able to return to the lives they had known, to the ship which was their home, even to the safe and distant sanctuary of the stars. And though Lucien realized with a certain sense of melancholy that he would miss the serenity of the temple, he also understood that he must follow his own destiny. That destiny, he knew, was to be the ram's first shepherd, to follow the ram's footsteps, and occasionally untangle his horns when they became caught in some dangerous thicket of thorns.

It was enough, he conceded, to know that it *would* end soon; and though he was left with a sense of anticipation as he pondered the course of the upcoming three days, he sought solace in the knowledge that they probably wouldn't be too different from the three days which had just passed.

He sighed again. Then, realizing he'd been gazing fixedly through the window, listening to the wind and the stream and watching the moon on her journey, he returned his attention once more to Kim Le.

"What would you have me do, Master?" he inquired, realizing the critical importance of the next seventy two hours, looking to Kim Le's greater wisdom for guidance and support as he bowed his head in a gesture of reconciliation and respect.

Kim Le's answer was succinct, to the point. "The ram is quick and clever, Lucien," he pointed out. "He will immediately smell a change in the air or react to a difference in his environment. For the next three days," he clarified, translating, "you must give him something to react *to* so that the scent of change never reaches his nostrils. His routine must be upset, and what he has believed to be true must be challenged." He paused only for a moment, then continued. "You must become the second ram, my friend. Be as clever and as quick as he is – *and* as unpredictable."

Lucien felt an instant of protest building in his chest. But as he reminded himself that his entire future was hanging in the balance, he inclined his head in acceptance.

And with the Knowledge Myrddin had given him, he already had a few ideas in mind.

~

Kim Le had only been gone for a few moments when another knock sounded at Lucien's door, and though he had hoped for a few additional minutes to contemplate his strategy and digest the full impact of the new knowledge, he stood at once, turning as the door opened.

"Morgan," he said softly, only then realizing that whenever he spoke the human's name, it was with a tone of reverence.

Coming into the room and pushing the door shut behind him, Morgan faced him with a smile. "Sorry I'm late, Master Lucien," he said quietly. "I didn't realize that Kim Le had elaborate after-dinner plans when I suggested a game." He paused, realizing absently that he was slightly out of breath from the long run through the maze of corridors, and that he was speaking more quickly than usual. "Am I too late?"

Lucien considered the other man's obvious enthusiasm with a smile which lit his eyes. "No," he said quietly, then gestured toward the two chairs which now sat on opposite sides of the table. "Please be comfortable."

Morgan hesitated for only a moment, realizing that the typical formalities of bowing had been ignored. And yet, as he remembered that they weren't in the training arena, weren't under the scrutiny and supervision of Kim Le or any other masters, he allowed himself to relax, moving across the room and sliding into the chair behind the darker chess pieces.

Lucien considered that. Normally, with every game they had played in the past, Morgan had chosen the white. But, passing it off to nothing more than chance, he concealed the insignificant reaction and moved into the opposing chair.

They played for more than two hours in almost total silence until, finally, Lucien succeeded in cornering the human's king and checkmating it with his last remaining bishop. He had deliberately altered the strategy he normally employed when they'd played on the *Starling*, and the changes resulted in a more lengthy match.

"Checkmate," he said at last

Shaking his head with a slightly disbelieving laugh, Morgan studied the board for only a moment longer, then showed his concession by toppling his assigned king on its side. Looking up, he sighed softly, his gaze going automatically to the window and the calm serenity of the outer gardens beyond.

Lucien frowned, somewhat surprised that the other man had said nothing at all regarding the game's outcome. "Morgan?"

After another moment, Morgan returned his attention to his teacher as a deep sense of unbidden sadness settled within him. "Sorry," he murmured. Then, feeling suddenly uncomfortable, he got to his feet and stood for a moment beside the chair before pushing it back beneath the table. "It's late," he offered with a wistful smile. "I'm sure you could use a break from your students once in awhile. Thank you for the game." He started toward the door.

Confusion and sudden surprise jolting him into action, Lucien rose, determined not to let some unspoken turmoil rob him of the moment. "Wait," he said quietly, yet with firm authority. He moved quickly from behind the table, going to stand at the human's side, attempting to decipher the meaning of the bowed golden head – not a bow of respect, he knew intuitively, but a posture of sadness. "Has something happened to trouble you, Morgan?"

Morgan sighed softly to himself, then looked up at last to meet the other's eyes. "It's nothing," he said, trying to make himself believe it. But as the melancholy probed deeper, he realized with a pang that he at least owed this man an explanation. "Actually," he tried again, "it's just that... I used to play chess or poker back on the *Starling*... with someone I care about very much."

Lucien's heart wrenched, and he wanted desperately to end the charade then and there, to spill the truth in Morgan's lap and leave the galaxy at the mercy of whatever invaders may come. And yet, understanding the short-sighted selfishness of such a desire, he held his control firmly in check. "Lucien," he murmured, his own name sounding alien on the tongue of the master he had attempted to become.

Morgan glanced up. "Yes," he said, very quietly. "Lucien." He shook his head sadly, the memories pouring into him with a sudden vengeance. "I haven't seen him in almost a year," he said, barely able to believe that statement himself. "And... well... I'm just afraid that if I ever *do* get back, if we ever *do* meet again... there might be... someone else." It seemed such a silly, possessive, childish fear; yet it was one that had haunted him since the moment of his exile.

Someone else? The Little Voice chimed in. *Do you enjoy torturing yourself with these wild hairs or are you just a certifiable worry wart?*

With an effort, Morgan ignored his inner critic, though he had to admit it may have a point.

Lucien's eyes closed; it was a fear he well understood, particularly after the incidents with Myrddin. He plotted his response carefully, feeling the cool breeze blow the scent of tea roses past his nostrils. "I would seriously doubt, that any other could replace you in his heart or in his mind," he said, aching awfully to say more, knowing that now wasn't the time. He glanced again toward the open window, a sudden thought taking shape in his mind. He put it into action quickly, before the other man's impulsive nature could drive a deeper distance between them.

"Come," Lucien murmured, heading for the door with a touch on the human's arm to urge him to follow. "It is obvious that your spirit is restless, your heart heavy. Let us walk together by the stream and talk of those things which trouble you."

For a moment, Morgan stiffened, recalling the last time he'd walked in the gardens with this man. His emotions had become suddenly, inexplicably, dangerously explosive, and he had spent the night alone in his small bed weeping over things he had lost and might never regain. And yet, as he looked at his master now, as he sensed the compassion within the other's spirit, he loosened his firm resolve just a little, allowing himself to be ushered from the small room.

~

As they left the temple and moved into the outer gardens, Morgan took a deep breath of the gentle night air, realizing absently that a change in the weather had left the temperature somewhat warmer, the air a bit more humid. To the east, a bank of thunderclouds completely covered half the sky, and an occasional flash of distant lightning was followed by a low, ominous rumbling.

Too far away to prove any danger, Morgan allowed himself to simply appreciate the beauty of it, the power which was inherent in any storm. He walked for some distance without even thinking to speak, his ultimate destination becoming the creek.

Lucien allowed the human his solitude, keeping pace as they

moved through the trees, the roses and the low-lying shrubs which bloomed close to the ground. He, too, was aware of the building storm.

He did not know precisely what he planned to do or even to say, and had it not been for the knowledge Kim Le had given him earlier in the evening, he could easily have made a silent pact to simply enjoy their time together. But now, feeling that Time itself was pressing against him, he quickened his pace until he walked at Morgan's side rather than a half-step behind.

Finally reaching his destination, Morgan stopped at the edge of the creek and stood for a long time doing nothing more than looking up through the trees, watching the leaves turn to black silhouettes against the backdrop of distant lightning. The scent of rain was in the air, and he closed his eyes, inhaling deeply as the serenity he sought came a step closer to being within his reach.

And yet, the frustration continued to nudge him in the ribs, making even the peacefulness of his surroundings insufficient to quiet the fire inside. "Sometimes," he mused almost to himself, "I just wonder if this is ever going to end."

Lucien considered that. He realized they were standing less than a foot apart. Morgan stood just at the edge of the creek, his feet half-in, half-out of the water. Lucien dropped slightly behind and to his left. The nearness made him ache once again and, reaching out, he rested one hand on Morgan's's shoulder.

"Have you been dissatisfied here at the temple?" he inquired presently, choosing for a moment to discuss less personal topics.

Morgan shrugged, keenly aware of the hand which touched him. "Not really," he said quietly. "But this isn't what I'm supposed to be doing with my life." He smiled wistfully, running his toes through the cool comfort of the stream. "When I first met Kim Le and Master Myrddin, I thought they were mercenaries. And while I'm not much for selling my skills to the highest bidder, I have to admit that I was intrigued with the possibilities."

Lucien's brows narrowed. "I was not aware of the misconception that your masters were mercenaries," he commented. "How did this come about?"

Laughing lightly, Morgan quickly explained the scenario, then

226

concluded with: "I guess Kim Le figured he couldn't very well just walk up to me on Calipri, spout a few lines of wisdom, and tell me that I had to come back to Earth to Ho Ling so that I could make some crazy attempt to free every living thing in the Empire from the Mizarian threat." He shrugged again, his amusement quickly fading. "Anyway, by the time I found out we were going to Earth, it was too late to change my mind."

"Would you have done so?" Lucien inquired curiously.

The human's lips formed a faint smile. "Probably not," he responded. "I wasn't doing very well living in the streets and trying to steal a meal now and again from the supply stock slated for a shuttle."

Lucien tried hard to control the pain which twisted his heart at that image. "But the wisdom you have gained from the experience will be with you always, Morgan. It is said that each minor incident we encounter throughout a lifetime occurs for a reason – either as a lesson through which we learn, or as an avenue through which we teach others."

Morgan considered that quietly. "All I know is that it was one hell of a lesson. – one I wouldn't care to repeat in this lifetime or any other." He looked again at his surroundings, the temple building not far away. "Oh, I suppose I could stay here for the rest of my life if necessary, but... no matter how much I may learn or how close I might become to you or Myrddin or Kim Le... I'd always know something very important to me was missing."

Almost without thinking of it on a conscious level, Lucien took a step closer, allowing the hand which had rested on Morgan's shoulder to slide across the human's back until his arm formed a protective support for the other's anguish. He noted that Morgan didn't flinch, didn't pull away, didn't even seem to really notice.

"Many times, Morgan," he said quietly, "we do not have an understanding of those things which occur in our lives. It is only when the happening is done that we can look back with wisdom and gain some small comprehension of the intended lesson."

Despite the pain burning in his mind, Morgan closed his eyes, leaning very slightly on the other man's arm. "The one thing this has taught me, is that I'll never trust a bureaucrat again." But he waved his words aside with a quick gesture. "And, hopefully, *if* I ever get back to where I belong, I'll have learned that it's sometimes better to say what's on your mind rather than trying to keep it hidden away inside."

At that, Lucien's brows lifted. "You are speaking of your beloved," he concluded, his heart beating a little faster with that knowledge. And it was in that moment that he understood precisely what he had to do. "Tell me, Morgan," he murmured gently, "when you *do* see him again, what will you say?"

Morgan blinked, taken off guard by the question. In the distance toward the east, the lightning flashed again, and the thunder sounded more quickly. The storm was coming closer, and that fact gave him an odd sense of comfort to mingle with his exhilaration. And for a reason he couldn't have defined, he found himself feeling oddly at ease with the other's question.

And yet, speaking of it openly, even with his master, didn't come easily.

Sensing that shy hesitation, Lucien tightened his arm very slightly, pulling the human closer to him, trying not to tremble as their bodies pressed side-to-side together. "You have nothing to fear in speaking of it, Morgan," he said gently, quietly.

Despite his momentary hesitation, Morgan felt an odd sense of truth echo throughout his being as those words penetrated his resistance. And, suddenly, he understood why it was that lovers everywhere felt that *their* love was the most unique, the most perfect, the most eternal. He knew at last why lovers seemed to glow with an aura of gold, why they did not sleep and could not eat and never seemed to suffer from the lack of rest and nourishment. And, in accordance with his teacher's words, he suddenly knew why lovers talked of nothing else but love. It *was* a part of the power and, realizing that, coming alive with it, he felt a sudden need to express himself, to understand his love by stating it aloud like a vow of marriage.

With his heart beating a little faster, he turned his head very slightly, looking up into the warm bright eyes of his master. "You... sure you don't mind talking about this?" he asked, not wanting to make another uncomfortable with his ramblings.

228

Lucien took a deep breath to steady himself, and allowed his lips to press upward into a smile. "I would be honored to talk with you on any subject," he assured, "particularly one which obviously is a source of pleasure to you."

Sensing the genuine interest which emanated from his master, Morgan drew a deep breath, fighting the shy smile which threatened to break out on his face. "*If* I ever return to his side," he said, not permitting his hopes to outweigh his realistic assessment of the situation, "the first thing I plan on doing is putting in for a month's leave on some planet somewhere – some place that's secluded enough that Lucien'll want to come along."

Lucien considered that. "Why do you believe he would not wish to accompany you?"

Morgan shrugged, skimming the bottom of his foot over the top of the water as he found himself settling into a quiet, restful fantasy which he hoped one day to fulfill, though doubted he ever would. "Oh... if you knew him, you wouldn't ask that." A tender smile touched his lips. "I've tried to get him to go with me on leave at least a hundred times that I can remember. But... after that incident on Alfar a couple years back, it just seems like he... like he decided to keep his distance." He paused thoughtfully, solemnly. "I dunno," he sighed at last. "Maybe he's really afraid of what would happen... or maybe he just isn't interested in having *anything* happen."

Lucien's lips pressed together to control the pain those words awakened within himself. "Perhaps," he suggested, "after this time of separation is ended, his fears will no longer control his actions to such an extent." He wondered fleetingly if he were even making sense, and attempted to clarify his meaning. "Many times, a man must first lose something before he can fully appreciate its value."

Morgan considered that in thoughtful silence, grateful for the warm and supportive arm which rested on his shoulder. "All I know is that *I* don't ever want to be separated from him again. It's as if I've lost a part of myself – maybe the *only* part of me that's real."

Spirit aching, Lucien began to wonder if he'd gotten himself in over his head; but with a discipline which required supreme control, he held onto his sanity for a few moments longer. Distantly, the lightning flashed, illuminating the entire sky and turning the deep black to an odd shade of silver-blue. Thunder caused the ground to tremble, its power leaving him to feel insignificant in comparison.

"Morgan," he murmured at last, "you must trust me when I tell you that you have it within your ability to do anything you wish to do, to be anything you wish to be... and to have at your side whomever you choose as your companion." He paused only for a moment, noting the doubtful/hopeful expression in the human's eyes. His own heart was breaking with love and, unable to completely deny his own needs, he reached out with his free hand, gripped Morgan's opposite arm, and turned the other man toward him until they stood face to face. Then, with a tenderness he hadn't realized himself capable of, he lifted his hand to the human's face, gently brushing back the unruly gold-bronzed hair, running the back of his fingers over the planes of cheekbone and jawline. "You are an extraordinary being, both in body and in spirit," he stressed. "And I am quite certain that your beloved longs for you as much as you long for him."

Morgan felt himself trembling inside. He felt inexplicably close to Lucien – *his* Lucien – as if this Alfarian master's insight were based on Knowledge rather than on simple conjecture. And in that moment, with that feeling pounding in his heart, he didn't have the strength to resist what he somehow knew to be right. Lowering his head to the other's shoulder, closing his eyes, and taking a deep breath, he gave in to a sudden instinct which left him physically weak but spiritually filled.

He was only vaguely aware of lifting his head, imagining in his sudden desperate fantasy that he was in *his* Lucien's arms, sheltered and protected from the storm which raged within as well as the storm which had slowly crept upon their environment. It occurred to some half-sane corner of his mind that, once again, this man had shaken his controls and rattled his convictions; but with a distant, heady scent of myrrh coming to his nostrils as if in a dream, he collapsed into his teacher's arms, losing himself in a fantasy which suddenly flew out of his ability to control.

In another moment, he stretched upward on his toes, his lips tingling even before they met the other, cooler ones. And as he kissed this strange-yet-familiar Alfarian, he knew he was utterly lost.

Lucien experienced a similar reaction, his legs going weak and threatening to drop both himself and his human companion to the ground. But relying on some inner reserve of strength he had thought exhausted, he braced himself against the sudden onslaught of feelings, returning the first shy kiss with an intensity which no longer surprised him. Morgan was warm and wonderfully alive in his arms, and though he realized that the human's love was for his alternate self rather than for 'Master Lucien', the petty details scarcely seemed important.

He seized the man to him in a fierce embrace, his arms convulsing around the other's back as his lips pressed more tightly into their first private and utterly genuine kiss. After a few moments of the shy, dry-lips-to-dry-lips touch, he began to think he might survive; yet when he felt the human's tongue trace the outline of his lower lip then delve abruptly into his mouth, he was overwhelmed by an all-encompassing dizziness which caused his knees to buckle.

Lowering himself with as much control as he could manage to the grassy shore of the rushing creek, he found himself on his knees in front of the other man, their lips still pressed together in a life-giving embrace.

Morgan intentionally lost himself in the physical sensations of their kiss, lost himself even deeper in the fantasy which rose around him with the strength of Alfarian arms. His entire reality was one of need and desperation. His body swelled with an aching desire, causing him to cry out as his erection pressed tight against the soft fabric of his pants. And as he instinctively arched his back and his pelvis thrust gently against the man in his arms, he was thrilled to discover the same yearning hardness reflected in the other's lean form.

No longer even completely aware of what he was doing, consumed instead by the fires of need, he unfastened the belt which marked him as an initiate, letting it drop unnoticed to the ground.

Then, a moment later, he felt skillful hands burrowing beneath his tunic, urging it over his head as he leaned forward. Catching the bottom of his teacher's tunic, he removed it quickly, tossing it aside and noticing by the lightning's glare that the master's black and the student's white mingled on the grass, landing in such a manner that their configuration oddly resembled the ancient yin/yang symbol.

It seemed strangely appropriate, Morgan thought, then put the matter from his mind as the cooler-than-human hands circled his waist, traveling around to cup his buttocks, then returning to untie the suddenly restrictive drawstring pants.

As Lucien slid the final article of clothing down the human's hips, he threw it aside with an irreverence which might have made Kim Le pass out cold. But somehow, in the frenzy of that moment, he wouldn't have cared if the Supreme Master himself had walked up. Nothing, he decreed, would keep him from his beloved.

In some distant reality, Lucien was aware of Morgan's hands touching him, cupping his buttocks, kneading the flesh of his thighs and back, then quickly untying his pants and slipping them down and away. He was not surprised to feel his fully engorged cock bob up toward his belly, thick with the proof of his own painful need.

Morgan took a moment to fully appreciate the Alfarian's beauty in the intermittent flashes of lightning. In a far-away corner of his mind, he realized that the fantasy had become complete. Here, in the darkness, the master *became* Lucien for him – down to the smooth, hairless chest and the powerful abs. The other's penis was long and generously thick – lightly veined and rigid; and, with a thought that caused Morgan to grin, he realized that even the thick ridge had started to flare with need, a peculiar but altogether delightful aspect of elven physiology.

Unable to deny himself any longer, he bent to press his lips once again to the other's mouth, lingering there briefly, then breathlessly moving down the long slender neck, over the jeweled collar, across collarbone and sternum, and down the center of the tightly-muscled stomach. Then, closing his eyes, he knelt lower, placing a delicate kiss on the tight testicles, and finally beginning a slow and deliberately reverent line of dry kisses up the straining shaft of the proud cock.

232

Head arching back onto the cool green grass, Lucien clenched his hands into the ground, bracing himself against the unexpectedly intense stimulation with which Morgan worshipped him. He felt his cock kissed and cupped, stroked and teased. Then, when the knowing mouth drew away for a moment and he thought he might be able to breathe, he was thrown back into ecstasy as it descended suddenly to cover him. The hot tongue bathed him in delight, and powerful lips began a suckling motion which caused his hips to thrust upward.

Morgan went with the sudden thrust, opening himself fully and allowing his fantasized beloved to take shelter within his mouth. He sucked gently, then powerfully, then gently again, reveling in the soft smoothness of the other's skin, becoming intoxicated with the scent of elven musk – a scent which was uniquely Lucien.

He didn't question, didn't analyze. Instead, lost to sensation, he merely continued his ministrations until, breathless, he raised his head and kissed his way back up the other man's body, coming to rest at last on the open, eager lips.

Instantly overwhelmed by the kiss which bore his own taste and scent, Lucien realized that he could not hold onto sanity or mental controls much longer. And if those failed, he knew, the charade would be revealed; and Morgan would know the truth.

Acting quickly to forego such an outcome, he pulled the human into his arms, urging the lighter body on top of him until they were perfectly matched – chest to chest, mouth to mouth, blade to blade. Then, continuing in the same direction, he slid Morgan off the opposite side of his body, leaving the human flat on his back. Lucien rose to his knees, running his fingers through the silky softness of the golden hair, then beginning his own predestined journey down the beloved body. He kissed and licked the proud jawline, sampled the delightful flavor of each nipple, and continued on down the smooth, almost hairless body until his cheek pressed against the straining hardness of his beloved's erection.

Closing his eyes in reverence, he extended his tongue slowly, touching it to the rounded tip which quivered in ecstatic response. He was rewarded by a slightly salty flavor that only served to ignite his own desires further. Parting his lips, forming a sanctuary with his mouth, he lowered it gently onto the other's flesh, his tongue swirling about the firm hardness, leaving a slippery sheen in his wake.

Morgan's head tossed wildly from side to side on the ground, his hips arching instinctively as he fought for the completion he knew was waiting for him. Then, commanding just enough control to lift his eyes to the other, he saw the other man draw back, their gazes locking in the reflection of lightning, under the scrutiny of thunder.

As a wordless agreement passed between them, Lucien bent once more to his task, suckling the large maleness into his mouth, lubricating the trembling shaft with his own moisture. Then, satisfied with the glistening results, he lifted his head away, returning to place a kiss on the receptive mouth as he straddled the needful human body.

For a brief instant, Morgan fought the urge to thrust and, with a control he summoned through strength of will alone, he reached down to take his own cock in his hand, positioning it carefully against the entrance to the other's body. As the lightning flashed, their eyes met again and, in his teacher's gaze, Morgan read the acceptance and approval he so desperately needed.

Closing his eyes, he gave himself over to his fantasies entirely, his hips lifting even as the man above him slowly lowered his weight onto the waiting shaft. It was a slow, forbidden entry, and though Morgan realized the discomfort he was undoubtedly bestowing on the other, he had no strength left to stop.

Lucien accepted the human into him willingly, biting his lower lip to ease the precious pain of the joining. He felt the smooth, round head penetrate him at last and, releasing the breath he'd been holding, took a moment to adjust to the burn of that initial shock. But as he opened his eyes and looked down into the enraptured face of his beloved, he fully accepted that any amount of anguish would be a price well paid.

With that knowledge, he steadied the trembling in his legs, summoning up the control necessary to continue his downward journey. Then, focusing only on the bright intensity of the moment, he pressed his weight lower, forcing the thick shaft to enter him even as a swift gasp was torn from his throat.

Morgan held himself still, realizing with a profound sense of tenderness the importance of the gift he was receiving. This was *Lucien*. If not in physical reality, then certainly within the sanctuary of his own mind. And that thought gave him the discipline not to thrust, not to take, but instead to wait for the ultimate gift which was their shared reward.

It came with agonizing slowness and, as Morgan stiffened his hips and pressed upward with just enough pressure to make the other's task easier, he felt the trembling buttocks finally settle against his hipbones. His cock was surrounded by a burning tightness, a sanctuary he had never thought to find. And, reaching up to take the other man's hands, he pulled him down until their lips met again.

Then, with a slow and deliberate precision, he began to thrust, placing his hands on the prominent hipbones and using the strength of his arms to aid in establishing a calm, undemanding rhythm.

Lucien went with it, his body gently buffeted by the human's thrusts, his entire being filled with the hard, needful flesh. In the back of his mind, he was distantly aware of the pain, the stinging reminder of his gift – a pain he realized he very much wanted to experience. It was, he realized, extremely *real*, perhaps even a symbol of their past, a crossroad on their path toward the future.

His own cock had swollen even more as Morgan took him, and as he looked down to see it resting lightly on the human's abdomen, he was filled with a sensation of aching tenderness.

Seeing that expression cross Lucien's face, Morgan reached out to take the hard alien maleness between his fingers, stroking it with a precision he had perfected on his own flesh in times of solitude and loneliness. He knew how to give pleasure even in the face of pain and, relying on that comfort, he quickened his thrusts as the need built to a bright crescendo within him.

His mind took control, taking him back to the *Starling* and dumping him into the security of his own bed. But now, in spite of all that had gone before, he was no longer alone. Instead, as he opened his eyes and looked up into the serene face which hovered above him, he realized he would never be alone again.

And it was with that echoing in his mind that he thrust upward, impaling his fantasy lover even as he impaled his master. The fire which had built in his mind was expelled in a sudden explosion, his seed boiling up like hot lava to flow deep within the other's flesh.

Lucien sensed the spasms of his beloved's climax, and the knowledge that he could give such pleasure to another caused his own long-denied flesh to respond, releasing his love in the form of a moist wetness which spread over the bare, sweat-moistened chest. He heard his own voice crying out with relief, a wordless sound like that of an animal calling its long-lost mate. His cock spasmed, pulsed, spasmed again, and as he collapsed onto the body beneath him, he felt his fall broken by a desperate, needful embrace.

For a very long time, Morgan didn't move, didn't even dare to breathe. Overhead, the lightning flashed, ionizing the air with electricity even as the thunder spoke again. But despite the imminent danger, he was filled with a strange sense of peace.

Instead of the guilt he had expected as his fantasy dematerialized, he was left only with a feeling of well-being, of serenity, of wonder. He realized absently that his hands were stroking a series of comforting circles on the Alfarian's back even as his cock softened within the other's body.

For a few moments he had been home – back on the *Starling*, safe in the sanctuary of his own bed with his beloved at his side. And *that*, he knew, was the ultimate sacrifice any teacher had ever made for any student throughout the history of the galaxy. Myrddin had soothed his loneliness for a time, had even filled him with the power of sexual pleasure. But this kind, caring master who called himself Lucien had given him the gift of future sight.

He wasn't entirely certain what that meant, yet the Knowledge inundated him like some bottomless well-spring of certainty.

"You... took me home," he whispered, awed.

Lucien's eyes remained closed, and the sensation of Morgan's softening cock still buried deep within him left him lethargic and wonderfully completed. "The journey was pleasant for me as well, Morgan," he promised. Then, lifting his head very slightly, he pressed his lips to the other's mouth. "There must be no guilt, my friend," he whispered gently, "and no regret."

Filled as he was with peace, Morgan only smiled, running one hand reverently down the angular planes of the other's face. "The only regret I could ever have is if it never happened again, Lucien."

For a brief moment, Lucien's nerves jangled. It was the first time the human had referred to him as anything other than Master or Master Lucien. And yet, as he studied the relaxed features more closely, he realized that it was Morgan's 'fantasy' to whom he spoke now.

"I promise you, Morgan," he vowed, "that this experience will be repeated as often as you like... now and quite probably forever."

Morgan sighed pleasantly, enjoying the burden of the other's weight pressed to his chest. "If only...," he whispered almost to himself.

"'If only'?" Lucien repeated, bending to kiss the warm lips once more.

Morgan smiled very softly. "If only you *were* my Lucien."
Don't start.

Almost directly overhead, the thunder spoke its ominous agreement; lightning split the clouds and opened the sky. The night began to weep with warm, delicate tears.

CHAPTER SIXTEEN

Morgan awoke in his own bed the next day, a smile lingering on his face as he realized it was still raining. The distant patter created a lethargy in his mind, lulling him back toward sleep, yet the odd sense of satisfaction which had settled in the pit of his stomach informed him that he was more lazy than tired.

It occurred to the rational part of his mind that he should be decidedly uncomfortable with the memories of the previous evening, yet as he recalled Master Lucien's gentle request – no guilt, no regrets – he was overwhelmed instead with a deep feeling of accomplishment. Not the same male chest-pounding sensation he might have experienced following the conquest of some beautiful woman or the seduction of an adversary in the line of duty, but a personal satisfaction, as if he had somehow overcome a great obstacle in his own life.

Snuggling deeper down into the warm nest of covers, he wanted very much to remain that way forever, to let the rain wash away the last of his sorrows, to allow himself to really believe it *had* been his own beloved Lucien with whom he'd made love the night before.

But even as his eyes started to close, pulling his body closer to sleep, he was interrupted by a faint knocking at his door.

Snapping instantly alert, he sat up in the small bed, squinting toward the brightness of the open window. With the sun obscured by clouds and his own time sense disrupted by the persistently falling rain, he realized with a sudden flash of horror that it was sometime in the middle of the afternoon. He'd slept all through the night and more than half-way through the next day and, without ever trying to visualize it, he could already hear Myrddin's reprimand, could already see the stern expression on the face of Master Lucien. Even though they had made love, he reminded himself, they were *still*, first and foremost, his masters.

His feet hit the floor and, dragging a white robe on to cover his nakedness, he stood facing the door. "Come in," he called, with an added, "Shit!" muttered under his breath.

The door opened to reveal both Myrddin and Master Lucien

238

standing on the other side, and for a moment, Morgan wondered if he'd end up tending the candles in the meditation room for the next week. And yet, despite his momentary shock at realizing he'd overslept terribly, he couldn't help the reaction which overwhelmed him at seeing the two of them together for the first time. Though they were dressed in identical black robes and pants, though both wore the same deep purple sash and both had very similar hair cuts, Morgan realized for the first time the distinct differences between the two.

Myrddin stood almost three inches shorter than Master Lucien, his shoulders slightly broader, the musculature in his legs somewhat more pronounced. Master Lucien, with the added height, was leaner and more lanky, his eyes slightly lighter than Myrddin's, his posture somewhat more relaxed than the formal grace with which Myrddin always seemed to move.

Despite himself, Morgan grinned, noting the deep sparkle in Master Lucien's eyes, seeing that same affection reflected in Myrddin's dark gaze. It occurred to him that he'd been privileged to study with what were quite probably two of the most intelligent – *and* the most handsome – men of Alfar; and though he longed desperately to see his own Lucien, he was forced to admit that he'd had extremely good fortune.

But as he remembered the training he'd sought to master, he lowered his head in a gesture of respect. "My pardon to you both, Masters," he said, wondering if either knew of his entanglement with the other, wondering if indeed it would have made any difference. "I have no reason for my tardiness other than the weakness of the body."

"The student overslept," Myrddin translated.

Morgan lifted his eyes at last to find a smile pressed against the thin lips and, despite the implications of his own predicament, he couldn't help allowing it to mirror on his own face. He shrugged sheepishly, trading glances with Master Lucien. "Yes," he said, not ashamed of it. "The student overslept."

But instead of the gentle reprimand he'd half-way expected, Myrddin seemed decidedly pleased. "It is good that at last the body is at peace, Morgan," he pointed out, causing Morgan's face to darken with the implied meaning. "However, we have not come to discuss such matters now. I am informed by Kim Le that the fo ti herb which grows in the mountains near the temple is ripe and in need of picking. It is his wish that you, as the newest initiate, should accompany Master Lucien into the mountains today to secure sufficient quantities of the herb to last until the next season."

Morgan blinked, only then realizing that he hadn't been outside the temple walls since his arrival almost a week before. He smiled pleasantly, bowing his head in acknowledgement. Then, after trading glances with Master Lucien, he turned his attention once more to Myrddin.

"I suppose this is considered punishment to the student who overslept," he commented with amusement, realizing full well that any herb, no matter how rare, could easily be secured through less complicated methods.

Myrddin smiled warmly, easily. "You will be required to spend this night in the foothills, and the journey is to be considered as any other part of your training." He paused, then added: "It is said that the mountains are a source of great spiritual power, thus it is a tradition for new initiates to gather the fo ti herb, thereby accomplishing two goals with a single journey."

Morgan smiled faintly to himself. "Killing two birds with one stone," he translated, not entirely disliking the idea of spending additional time alone with Master Lucien. If nothing else, he decided, it would give them both time to accept the reality of what had happened between them the night before, time to perhaps let it happen again.

Now that's the spirit! The Little Voice chimed in, yawning just a little.

Morgan ignored the persistent little pain in the neck, forcing his attention to the matter at hand, meeting Myrddin's gaze once more. "What about you?" he asked with a grin. "Aren't you going to come along to keep an eye on my temper?"

Once more, Myrddin gave smile. "I am confident that Master Lucien is quite capable of handling any situation which might arise. I am required to remain here at the temple to further the knowledge and training of my students," he added quietly. "When you return

240

tomorrow, we shall resume your lessons."

Morgan's stomach knotted pleasantly, and he couldn't help wondering if there was more of an invitation in the dark eyes than the soft-spoken words implied. He couldn't deny his attraction to Myrddin, yet he was beginning to understand that it was consigned to a single level – a deep respect, a haunting physical yearning, a security in the knowledge that Myrddin *was* sworn first and forever to the temple and the Knowledge therein. Put another way, Myrddin was completely safe.

He looked up once more, glancing back and forth between the two of them, only then realizing that Master Lucien hadn't spoke a word the entire time. And yet, there was something strangely compelling in the pale brown eyes – something which said more than words could ever express.

That something left him with a feeling of great inner peace, an all-encompassing strength which took his fears of loneliness away. Until he was reunited with his own beloved, this man seemed sworn to stand at his side... and to lie down with him in the soft sanctuary of his bed.

He only hoped that, when and if the time ever came, he would be able to say his goodbyes and return to the life he had left behind.

And yet, as he realized how far away that time might be, he squared his shoulders and took a deep, steady breath, grateful for the good fortune he had been shown in both these men.

"When do we leave?" he asked with a new sense of enthusiasm living deep within him.

"You will depart the temple walls as soon as you are dressed and equipped for the journey, Morgan," Myrddin explained. "As the nights are sufficiently warm, you will travel light." Then, turning and bowing with respect toward the other Alfarian, he bowed once more before disappearing into the long corridor beyond the door.

For an extended moment, Morgan stood looking at the man left standing before him, barely able to suppress the unbidden feelings which caused his stomach to tighten with unexpected anticipation. He considered attempting to control the automatic reaction, then abruptly decided that it was anything but unpleasant. He smiled faintly.

"So," he mused, allowing himself to relax in the other's calming presence. "How far away is it that we're headed?"

At that moment, Lucien didn't tell him that their journey together would, if successful, lead them home to the stars.

~

As they walked together along the ancient stone path which led away from the temple's outer wall, Lucien took a few moments to appreciate the beauty of the surrounding land. Far in the distance, snow-capped mountains reflected the faint glimmer of sun which had started to shine late in the afternoon when the rain had finally ended. The scent in the air was fresh and clean, and as he looked again at Morgan, he was filled with a sense of deep longing.

With his sense of time-keeping firmly intact once more, he calculated that only another twenty two hours, seven minutes and nineteen seconds remained before the Mizarian vessel would reach Earth. And in accordance with the terms of the pre-agreement which he'd studied at length on the terminal in Kim Le's private office, he knew that Morgan Diego would once again be a free man when the Mizarian representative and Ambassador Martell of the Empire clasped hands in the ancient gesture of concession.

He allowed hope to fill him.

The one thing which continued to trouble him, however, was how he would tell Morgan that, at last, the time of exile was ended, that the year of the ram should terminate with celebration rather than sadness. For though he fully understood his friend's desire to return to his former life, he was also filled with the knowledge that Morgan had made deep ties at the temple – both with Myrddin and Kim Le, and with the illusion of Master Lucien as well.

But as they drew closer to the foothills, having walked for more than an hour in companionable silence, he attempted to put those thoughts from his mind, determining to deal with them when the time came, making a silent vow to insure that nothing intervened to destroy the freedom which seemed suddenly so near to becoming a reality.

Looking again at the man at his side, a smile tugged at his lips, reflecting in his eyes as he spoke. "You appear quite intrigued by your surroundings, Morgan," he noted conversationally.

Pulling himself back to reality, Morgan blinked. The scent of the earth after a cleansing rain was light on the breeze, and the harmony of a dozen different varieties of songbirds had lulled him into some pleasant fantasy wherein he and Lucien were once more together, walking an ancient path of stone, climbing higher into the foothills of the eternal mountains of China. At their present altitude, the temple was little more than a mark of color in the distance and, closing his eyes, he understood just how alone they really were.

"It's so peaceful here," he commented, following his teacher's lead and depositing his shoulder pack to the ground as he stretched his muscles.

Lucien lowered himself to the ground and curled his legs into a half-lotus position. Morgan also sat, though in a more casual position, leaning back on his hands, legs stretched out in front of him. "I am pleased to have this time away from the order of temple life," he ventured quietly.

Surprised by that revelation, Morgan looked to the other's expressive face. "I thought the temple *was* life to the masters," he replied. "I... hope I haven't done anything to... uh... disturb your serenity."

Again, Lucien's lips pressed upward. "No, Morgan," he assured. "Indeed, you have deepened my serenity by allowing me to serve you as teacher and friend." He paused, gazing down the foothills to where the temple's walls created a round mark on the terrain. "It is only that here, there are no formalities. There is only the wind and the sky and the earth upon which we walk. It is a simpler life."

Morgan considered that in thoughtful silence. He'd caught himself wondering from time to time how life could be any simpler than that within the temple walls; for despite the rigorous training and the constant mental challenges, it was a peaceful, ancient way of existence which had taught him much. And yet, contemplating the Alfarian's words more carefully, he felt a gradual understanding dawn within him.

"I know what you mean," he commented at last, a wistful smile pressing at his lips. "When I was on the *Starling*, there were times that I thought I'd die for lack of seeing a sunrise, or breathing real air." He laughed lightly, shaking his head with fond remembrances. "Then, when I *did* finally get a week of leave on some nice quiet planet, I was ready to go back to the ship after about the second day."

"It is wisely said," Lucien recalled, "that a man's serenity is not dependent on his environment, but on the peace he finds within his own spirit."

Morgan nodded. "Yeah," he sighed quietly. "I can see that now." He thought again of Lucien, fighting the pang of loneliness which tugged at his soul despite the comfort he found with his Alfarian master. "I just can't help wishing that I'd known that a long time ago."

"Please elaborate."

Toying with a blade of grass, skimming his fingers through the raindrops which lingered on the ground, Morgan took a deep breath, attempting to put into words a feeling which defied explanation. "I dunno," he said at last. "I just feel that if I'd been more secure in my own abilities, more comfortable with *myself*... maybe things could have been different with Lucien." Then, realizing that not even a master was impervious to hurt, he quickly added: "You've given me something that I never thought I'd find, something I honestly didn't think myself capable of."

"What is that, Morgan?" Lucien asked with genuine curiosity.

Morgan was gazing out over the distant horizon, watching the sun slip at last behind the high peak of a mountain toward the west. "You've shown me that I'm usually not a bad person," he explained to the best of his ability. Then, realizing how easily that could be misinterpreted as arrogance, he sought to clarify. "What I mean is that, before I came to Ho Ling, I sometimes wondered if I ever *could* really care for someone, if I could love someone for reasons other than... well... sexual gratification." But he waved his own words aside with a quick gesture. "Oh, I've occasionally thought I was in love with someone, but... once the initial magic wore off, I started to fall right back into my old bad habits. You know," he said, looking up with a grin, "the old wandering-eye-syndrome."

244

Lucien considered that, attempting to internalize the full impact of this revelation. "And you feel that this has changed now?"

Morgan's expression was one of tender determination. "*I've* changed," he said quietly. "Maybe I've finally learned to tell the difference between a physical attraction and a spiritual bonding," he decided. Then, realizing to whom he was speaking, he again sought to clarify his meaning. "What I mean is that I'm ready to make a commitment to someone now. I've never felt that way before... and maybe that's what kept Lucien from ever pursuing a different part of our friendship."

"Perhaps he, too, was unready to commit," Lucien suggested, realizing that truth within himself as it was verbalized by the other man. "But when you meet again, I am confident that you will find his attitudes changed, that you will both be able to explore those things which, previously, were kept from you through your own fears." Now, after separation and a partial reunion, he couldn't envision a life without this man at his side. And so he was compelled to add, "One function of the teachings of Knowledge is to peel away the false belief systems and the inauthentic roles we all adhere to until we become aware of them. Put another way, what you have learned here is hopefully the first step toward a true personal freedom."

Morgan sighed softly, realizing for the first time just how true those words really were. When he had first encountered Kim Le, he was a broken man – yet only now did he see that it wasn't the Mizarians who had broken him. It was, instead, an *idea* of himself that had to die before the essence of the real Morgan Diego could ever take his first breath. Yes, he was changed. More than he could verbalize even to himself, he had embraced himself in the mirror when he found his wholeness.

And yet, one fear lingered. "But... what if I *can't* go back?" he asked, trembling internally at the very real possibility.

Very gently, Lucien reached out to slip one arm around the human's back, holding him close in a gesture of tenderness and reassurance. And in that moment, he, too, came to a profound decision. "In that eventuality, Morgan," he murmured, "I would be honored to ask you to remain with me at the temple for as long as we both draw breath." He paused, not wishing to push the other too quickly, yet realizing that he *would* remain forever in the guise of Master Lucien, that he *would* abandon the stars and even his own identity if necessary to remain with this man.

Morgan's eyes closed and he took a deep breath, leaning into the supportive strength of the man at his side. "If... if I *can't* go back," he said at last, listening to the distant cry of a songbird, "then... I... I will...."

Lucien placed one finger against his lips, silencing the other's words with a touch. "Is it not enough, Morgan, to know that we have been given this time together now?" But he didn't wait for a response, didn't remove his hand from the other's face as his own lips pressed upward into a smile. "Let us simply agree to be to one another what the fates have destined."

Morgan relaxed just a little, overwhelmed as usual by this man's tenderness, his wisdom, his strength. He realized abstractly that the sun had slipped beneath the distant horizon, and that twilight was already upon them. He glanced forlornly at the empty herb sack which lay on the ground, then returned his attention to his master when a gentle hand caught his chin and caused him to turn.

"The fo ti will not blow away on the wind by morning, Morgan," Lucien promised, not wanting to break the sanctuary of the closeness between them. Then, taking the human's hand and drawing him to his feet as he stood, he cast about the immediate vicinity, finding a slight windbreak against an outcropping of rock. "Come," he intoned, not releasing the other's hand as he picked up their packs and started toward it. "We will gather wood for a small fire, and then it will be time to rest."

Feeling a mild amusement at the other's easy attitude concerning Kim Le's prized healing herb, he felt a small amount of the burden lift from his shoulders. They slept in front of the fire that night, pressed chest to chest, with Morgan's head pillowed on Lucien's firm shoulder.

They didn't make love. It seemed somehow unnecessary.

~

Lucien was awakened the following morning by the sound of fast-approaching footsteps and, instantly alert and aware of the openness of their surroundings, he slipped gracefully to his feet, dropping into a defensive stance as his vision cleared from sleep.

But instead of any danger, he found himself face to face – or, more accurately, he corrected – waist-to-face with the small boy he recognized as Myrddin's son, Jahan.

"Master Lucien," the youth began, barely winded from what had obviously been an extended period of running. "Kim Le has requested this humble initiate to bring a message for you."

Glancing automatically over his shoulder, Lucien wasn't surprised to find Morgan already at his side; and, almost on a sub-psychic level, he knew the contents of the message. His stomach tightened.

"What is the message, Jahan?" he inquired nonetheless, trading cautious glances with Morgan.

Jahan bowed formally, then lifted his eyes once more to Lucien. "You are requested to return at once to the temple," he explained. Then, looking to Morgan, he added: "I have been instructed to remain here with you and to gather the fo ti herb." He smiled just a little despite his seriousness. "It was my impression that Kim Le wished to speak alone with you, Master Lucien, and that Morgan and I are to follow you back to the temple within the hour."

Mentally re-checking his time-sense, Lucien was fully aware of the possibilities awaiting him at the temple. And yet, as he turned to see Morgan's confused and somewhat disappointed expression, he bowed formally to Jahan, asking him to take the herb sack and busy himself further along the trail.

As soon as the child scampered quickly away, Lucien turned once more to face the human, attempting to quiet the sudden nervousness which rose in his spirit. "Morgan," he murmured, stunned by the beauty of the other's face in the distantly rising sun. "I must leave you for a short time now, in accordance with Kim Le's wishes." He wondered fleetingly why he was stating the obvious, and decided it must have had something to do with the fact that he was afraid of dealing with the unknown at that moment. He reached out, placing the back of his hand against the human's cheek as he offered a reassuring smile.

Morgan experienced an odd sense of sadness which came from no identifiable source. Something seemed different, distant; and though he realized nothing had changed since the evening before, he was unnerved by the thought of being so abruptly parted from his master.

And yet, relying on the strength and discipline of his training, he squared his shoulders just a little, taking a deep breath to quiet the unbidden melancholy as he stood gazing up into the other's soft eyes. "I'll be along in awhile," he said, not knowing what else he could say. Then, summoning up the humor which had often seen him through difficult situations, he smiled faintly. "I assume everything'll be back to normal by this afternoon," he ventured with a growing grin. "You up to another sparring match?"

Lucien's lips pressed upward gently. "Are *you*?"

Morgan perused the other man quietly, appreciating the strength, agility and power. "I was born ready," he challenged with a grin.

Lucien allowed himself to rest a little easier, though he was hard-pressed to ignore the fact that Kim Le had been correct: the ram *did* sense the change in the air. But as he drew himself back to reality, he stepped back slightly, allowing his hand to drop to his side as he bowed from the waist.

"Kim Le does not like to be kept waiting," he said, straightening again to his full height.

Morgan caught himself holding his breath and, for a moment, he almost forgot the courtesy of bowing. Remembering it at last, he did so with as much grace as he could muster, then rose to look again into the compelling dark eyes. Then, not knowing why he was compelled to do it, he took a hesitant step forward, placing his hands abruptly on each of the Alfarian's arms as they stood face to face. His brows tightened; his mouth opened to speak, yet words wouldn't come. Finally, his face darkened and, after a gentle squeeze of reassurance, he forced himself to step back without ever saying a word.

But as he watched the other's dark-clad form walking away on

248

the ancient path of stones, he was overwhelmed with a terrible, aching sense of loss and regret.

He had the distinct feeling he would never see his master again.

~

Lucien entered Kim Le's private office immediately upon returning to the temple, and after the courtesy of bowing, stood facing the Supreme Master of Ho Ling, who remained seated behind an ancient rosewood desk.

"Jahan delivered your message, Master," Lucien said, struggling with every ounce of control to remain calm.

Kim Le perused him for only a moment, then gestured for him to sit in an ornately carved chair. Doing so, Lucien waited, his heart rate elevated as much from the nervous anticipation as from the strenuous journey back to the temple.

Finally, the old man's lips curved upward into a gentle, contemplative smile. "I have again spoken with your friend, Bryse," he revealed at last. "The Mizarian ambassador has arrived at your Empire Council Building in San Diego. Apparently their vessel was somewhat swifter than expected – they arrived yesterday, I am told."

Lucien blinked, holding his breath. "And?" He was grateful to be sitting down.

Kim Le held his hands open in a gesture of having nothing to hide. "Your task here is completed, Lucien," he said quietly. "Bryse informed me that the ambassadors spoke throughout the night, and that the morning brought news of a new treaty between the Empire and the Mizarians."

Drawing a cautious half-breath, Lucien didn't move. "Then... my commander is released from his exile," he presumed hopefully.

Kim Le inclined his head in agreement. "It has been requested that, when Morgan has been informed of this, he be transported at once to San Diego, where he must formally accept this declaration from Tashkeeln himself." He smiled again, seemingly relieved. "Following that, my friend, he is to be immediately reinstated as the commander of his vessel, and the two of you will undoubtedly begin your new life together."

Stunned to silence, Lucien found himself wondering how it could have been accomplished so easily. Ambassadors were not miracle-workers; and the Mizarians had gained a reputation for being deliberately difficult. "But... *how*?" he asked presently, as much of himself as of Kim Le.

The old man shook his head with a knowing smile. "I am not fully aware of all the details, but Bryse intimated to me that the Mizarians wish to gain the Knowledge which has enabled Morgan to defeat them in their cruel game. It is my further understanding that they have agreed to full diplomatic relations between their Empire and ours, and that an exchange of sorts is being negotiated."

Despite the calmness with which Kim Le spoke, Lucien felt himself stiffen at the implications. "They wish Commander Diego to return to their Empire in order to give them the knowledge which has resulted from his training here at the temple," he surmised, prepared to fight that decision if necessary.

But much to Lucien's surprise, Kim Le began a low, throaty chuckle. "The Mizarians have no desire to deal with Commander Diego any further," he said. "He has defeated them with honor, but he *has* defeated them."

Lucien blinked, feeling properly put in his place. "What then?"

Kim Le's smile slowly faded to be replaced with a look of quiet determination. "They have requested to be taught the discipline of the art," he revealed at last. "And I have agreed to Bryse's proposal: soon, several of their most promising youths will be here within the walls of Ho Ling. Additionally," he continued slowly, "a few of our masters will journey to Mizar – where a *new* temple, identical to this one, will be constructed within the year."

Lucien absorbed that with a combination of surprise, relief and a sudden sadness. "Yourself and Master Myrddin?"

Kim Le's lips pressed upward. "As I am an old man who, despite his experiences, is often set in his ways, I shall be remaining here at Ho Ling," he said quietly. "But it is Master Myrddin's wish to journey with Ambassador Tashkeeln back to Mizar. There, he will oversee the construction of the temple; and when it is completed, he will serve as Supreme Master." He paused, perusing Lucien quietly, respectfully. "Though I know you probably could not accept such an offer, I am confident that you would be welcomed as a master there as well as here."

Lucien's lips pressed together gently. "I am honored that you would think me worthy, Kim Le," he said quietly, "but my destiny lies in another direction." He thought briefly of Morgan, still high in the mountains. Then, taking a deep breath, he offered a smile. "If, however, I may ever be of service to you in any manner, you have only to ask."

Kim Le inclined his head in acknowledgement, then stood slowly and crossed around the desk to stand at his side. "I wish we had the time to walk together in the gardens and discuss the future, Lucien," he said with a degree of sadness, "yet I feel it is wise that you should leave here before Jahan returns with Morgan."

Lucien blinked, a protest building automatically.

"Ta ta ta!" Kim Le scolded with extreme gentleness, laying one hand on his shoulder. "A wise man does not attempt to say painful farewells to those he will see again tomorrow," he pointed out. "Bryse has requested that you return to Galaxy Corps at once in order that the *Starling* may be properly prepared for the tour by Ambassador Tashkeeln. You must trust me to tell Morgan of these great changes, and to see to his safe return to you by the morning."

Things were happening too quickly, and Lucien found his head reeling with the sudden clamor which had returned to his life. For a fleeting moment, he gave serious thought to Kim Le's offer, gave thought to the possibility of remaining forever at the temple, even asking Morgan to remain at his side in that serenity. It occurred to him that he still had unresolved issues of his own – though he conceded that taking on the entire cultural programming of his Homeworld would have to wait, at least for a little while.

For now, he knew that his duty was as it had always been: shepherd to the ram. He stood at last, bowing in respect to Kim Le for what would quite probably be the last time. "I shall miss you, my friend," he said, meaning it. "I owe you a great debt – for Commander Diego and for myself as well."

Kim Le likewise bowed, then returned to his full height as a wistful smile brightened his weathered features. "It is my hope that the temple will be here always, long after I am gone, Lucien. Please," he entreated, "return to these walls whenever you are in need of serenity. This is your home now, too."

Touched by the kindness of that gesture, Lucien merely nodded, his throat suddenly too tight to speak. Then, knowing he dared not look back, he walked quietly from the room, following the curved stone corridor until he found himself once more in his sleeping quarters.

After securing his few personal belongings from the storage facility nearby and packing the shipping case in silence, he retrieved the communication chip which had been stowed securely in the lid. But as he prepared to transmit his transporter coordinates to the technician on board the *Starling*, he was stopped by a faint knock at the door.

For a moment, he almost didn't answer it, fearing that it might be Morgan, knowing he couldn't contain the suddenly dangerous emotions which clamored at his mind. But the decision was taken from him as the door slowly pushed open and Myrddin glided into the room with his lips pressed into a tender, wistful smile.

"I wanted to see you off, Lucien," the other Alfarian explained without the customary formality.

Lucien took a deep breath, acutely aware of the unbidden pain which continued to constrict in his throat; despite his victory, despite the fact that he was at last returning home, despite the fact that, quite probably, he would share his mind and body with Morgan very soon, he was torn inside. He turned slowly away, gazing through the cut-away window to the eternal serenity of the gardens beyond.

"I... did not know how to say farewell to you, Myrddin," he confessed with a sudden, desperate honesty. Then, gathering his faltering controls more tightly to his chest, he turned to meet the other's gaze. "I am told you will be the Supreme Master at the new temple on Mizar. My congratulations." It sounded hollow even to his own ears despite the fact that he intended it sincerely.

But Myrddin shook his head, taking a step nearer. "It is a long journey, and a lifetime commitment," he said, almost to himself, "yet I am eager to begin this new challenge." Then, sighing very softly,

252

he reached out to place one hand on Lucien's arm. "You will, of course, become One with Morgan."

Lucien nodded, hearing the curiosity and the concern in the other's voice. "We are already One," he realized quietly. "It only remains to formalize our union, to lay aside the people we have been here and to embrace what destiny has chosen for us."

Myrddin smiled, squeezing Lucien's arm very gently. "If I may be so bold, Lucien," he said softly, "do not attempt to 'lay aside' the Knowledge you have both acquired here. Rather, integrate it into your lives, make it a part of your union... and I am confident that no force in the universe will be able to tear you asunder."

Absorbing that, Lucien nodded his agreement. Then, lifting his head to meet the other's eyes, he was compelled to ask one unanswered question. "You... love him... don't you?"

Myrddin's brows lifted and he reached out to place one hand on each of Lucien's arms, a wistful smile lingering in his eyes. "Almost as much as I love you, Lucien."

For a moment, Lucien was taken aback by the other's response. And yet, as he considered it, he came to understand that Myrddin's commitment to the art would always overshadow his own needs. His love was for his students, for the challenges they brought to him, and for the Knowledge he sought to teach.

At last understanding that fully, Lucien found his own love rushing to the surface. Closing his eyes, he bent his head lower until it rested on Myrddin's shoulder in a gesture of humility and respect. "I am honored, my friend, to have known you." Then, stepping back, he met the other's gaze one last time, knowing that his own new challenge could wait no longer. "May the blessings of Mother Forest follow you always, Myrddin," he murmured. "I shall miss the pleasure of your company."

Myrddin bowed low at the waist, then straightened and embraced Lucien warmly. "And you, my friend," he returned. "And know that you and your beloved are always welcomed in my home."

Unable to respond with words, Lucien merely returned the heartfelt embrace. Then, taking a deep breath, he took a step back and activated the long-dormant communication channel. But as he felt the energy beam engage, he closed his eyes, wanting to remember the beauty and the serenity of the temple, wanting to remember Myrddin's gifts to him rather than their moment of parting.

A few seconds later, he found himself in back on board the *Starling*, his emotions tight as he realized that, through the instantaneous technology of the matter scrambler, he was no longer a master at the Temple of Ho Ling.

Instead, despite his robes and the purple sash and the assumed physical identity, he was once again a member of the Galaxy Corps, technically still in command of the Fleet's most illustrious star cruiser.

Still, the transfer didn't come easily and, needing a few minutes to adjust to the abruptness of the changes, he made his way through the deserted corridors of the ship until he came at last to his cabin. Then, setting the small shipping case aside, he went to the dormant cauldron and tried to make peace between the two lives he had led.

Soon, he knew, Morgan would return to the ship. And despite everything they had shared at the temple, Lucien couldn't help wondering how the human would react to the truth.

CHAPTER SEVENTEEN

As Morgan neared the temple's outer wall and allowed Jahan to run on ahead, he noticed instantly that Myrddin stood between the great stone arches, his silhouette unmistakable in the mid-day sun. The human's heart pattered faster and, quickening his pace, he fought the urge to run forward as a thousand divergent thoughts coalesced in his mind.

Reaching the gate at last, he took a deep breath, trying with every ounce of his acquired discipline not to give credence to the rising state of panic. "Master Myrddin," he said, going through the quick formality of bowing. He proffered the sack of gathered herbs, then noted with a sense of dismay that the Alfarian merely tucked it under one arm.

"Come, Morgan," Myrddin said quietly, "walk with me for awhile."

For a reason he still couldn't identify, Morgan felt his heart pound as a cold chill raised gooseflesh on his arms. "Something's wrong, isn't it?" he asked, recalling the sensations he'd experienced that morning when he'd been suddenly separated from Master Lucien.

But Myrddin gave no indication that he heard the question, continuing his leisurely pace as they started off on a path which Morgan remembered would take them in a complete circle around the temple building – a long walk through the outer gardens.

"There is much to discuss, Morgan," the other said presently. "But I am confident that what I have to say to you will be reason for rejoicing."

At that, Morgan stopped cold in his tracks, reaching out to place one restraining hand on his Master's arm. "What *is* it?" he demanded, his tone more clipped than he'd intended, his arm trembling as it halted Myrddin's steps.

Myrddin's brows lifted as he gazed at the hand resting on his arm. Then, covering it with his own long fingers and squeezing reassuringly, he seemed to come to some private conclusion. "Much has happened within the Empire during your exile, Morgan," he revealed at last. "In the interest of conserving the commodity of time, it is only important for you to know that you have been successful in your studies." He paused as if to let that revelation sink in. "The Mizarians have agreed to revoke the Directive which was responsible for your expulsion from the life you knew before you were taken into their Empire."

For a very long time, Morgan stood stone-still, his jaw slightly slack, his mind reeling with shock. "Wh-what?" he said at last.

Myrddin smiled very faintly, squeezing his hand as if to remind him of reality. "As I am not a diplomat, I do not possess an awareness of the details. I do understand, however, that the Directive has been revoked by the authority of the Mizarian Ambassador, Tashkeeln." He smiled faintly. "And, after a brief ceremony at the Headquarters of your Galaxy Corps, you will be free to return to your former life – *and to your beloved.*"

Could you have him repeat that? I think I missed something.

For some reason, none of it registered in Morgan's mind. He blinked, squinting against the noonday sun and feeling somewhat stupid as well as pole-axed. "I - I don't understand," he stammered, shaking his head to clear it, but with few results. "I mean - I thought - I thought I was still learning to block the probe. I'm not *ready!*"

Myrddin's brows lifted. He smiled openly. "Ready? For what, Morgan?" But he didn't wait for an answer. "You have succeeded in your task, my friend. Now, as soon as you have made your peace with yourself and said your farewells to the friends you have made here, it is time for you to go."

Morgan felt himself swaying with a sudden, inexplicable dizziness. "But... what about–."

Myrddin silenced him with one finger pressed against his lips. "I am told that Admiral Bryse will answer your questions on the terminal in Kim Le's office," he said. "However, as I, too, must prepare to leave Ho Ling, I wished to speak with you in private, to tell you of this triumph before you depart on your journey."

Morgan blinked again, not knowing which way to turn first. But as Myrddin's words registered on his mind, he looked more closely at the Alfarian. "Leaving Ho Ling?" he repeated. "Where will you go?" He hadn't even considered the possibility of *himself* departing, much less the idea that his Alfarian master would ever be anywhere other than the sanctuary of Ho Ling.

Reaching up very gently, Myrddin smoothed Morgan's hair back from his eyes with a tender smile. "As part of the agreement, I am to oversee the construction of a new temple on Mizar."

Morgan realized with an odd sense of detachment that this couldn't be happening. Not so quickly. Not with such a degree of neat finality. He faltered. "But... I... I thought your home was *here*," he stressed, indicating the temple with a gesture of his eyes. "I thought...."

Again, Myrddin silenced him with a finger against his mouth. "Would it not serve the student better to concern himself with his own immediate affairs, Morgan?" he asked with a soft smile that robbed the words of any sting. "You have accomplished a great task. Now, as your reward, you will soon be going home." He paused for only a moment, then added: "I am quite pleased with the opportunity which awaits me on Mizar – for, as a teacher, what greater challenge than to work with those who so influenced the life of one of my favorite students?"

In some distant, practically insane reality, Morgan realized he'd been paid a deep compliment and, forcing himself to respond with some answer, he took a slow, ragged breath and tried to get his priorities firmly in hand. Still, it wasn't an easy task. "Will I - will we ever meet again?" he wanted to know, emotion threatening to choke him in the midst of what *should* logically have been a celebration.

Myrddin offered a gentle smile as his response. "How could we not, Morgan? It is said that no man's journey progresses in a straight line. At some point, my friend, our paths will overlap once more." Then, running his fingertips over the human's face, he added: "And even if they do not, then we must both find peace in the Knowledge that destiny permitted us to meet at all." Then, stepping back, he bowed gracefully from the waist.

Realizing abruptly that this was goodbye, Morgan found his eyes wet, his throat suddenly tight. And though he was torn with the need to stay, he understood that this man would not permit him to forfeit all he had fought for on the basis of an impulsive decision. He couldn't think straight, didn't know what to say, what to do, even what to believe.

But then, as if it came from some mystical well-spring of inner strength, he thought again of Lucien – his own Lucien; and he knew, in order to gain that ultimate reward, he would have to sacrifice other alliances formed along the way. At least temporarily.

He took a hesitant step forward, glanced over his shoulder to the temple, then reached out impulsively to place his hands on each of Myrddin's powerful arms. "Aren't you... coming inside?"

But the Alfarian shook his head. "Understand, Morgan, that this parting is not easy for me either," he murmured gently. "A part of being a teacher is accepting that one's students eventually leave the temple and return to this world or some other in accordance with their individual destiny. But sometimes," he added very quietly, "the day of parting comes too quickly, and even in the face of great victory, there is a sadness which can only be internalized through solitude." He smiled faintly. "As I am certain you do, my friend, I require time alone now."

Morgan tried very hard to accept that, then nodded his agreement as he attempted a smile of reassurance. "We *will* meet again, Myrddin," he promised. "If I have to go all the way to Mizar and knock down the temple walls, we *will* meet again."

But the Alfarian's response was a faintly lifted brow. "Surely the ram has learned that it need not butt its head against an unyielding structure," he said with tender affection. "The gates will open to your command at any time... as will my door... and my heart."

Morgan's lips pressed tightly together as he fought to contain the bittersweet pain which rose in his throat. Then, taking a deep breath, he stepped back, allowing each of them to once again embark on their separate paths. "Thank you, Master," he murmured, meaning it to the core of his being. "For everything."

Myrddin's head inclined in acknowledgement. Then, gesturing toward the temple building, he offered a final tender smile, though Morgan couldn't help noticing that his eyes were brighter than usual. "Go now, Morgan," he commanded, "before we both forget our dignity."

Knowing at last that he *had* to go, that Myrddin's life and his own were of two divergent realities, Morgan turned and walked slowly away, unashamed of the salty-sweet tears which traveled soundlessly down his cheeks. But as he neared the temple wall, he turned and looked back over his shoulder, needing to find one last memory to press in the pages of his mind.

Somehow, he wasn't surprised to see Myrddin walking the path with his son at his side. And, as Morgan watched for only a moment longer, he saw his stern master lift the boy high into the air, and finally deposit him on his shoulders.

Distantly, carried to him on the wind, Morgan heard him speaking to his son about the new temple they would build together on Mizar.

~

Long after his conversation with Bryse, Morgan sat in the sanctuary of his own room as the sun slipped below the horizon and the light evening breeze brought the scent of tea roses and jasmine to his nostrils. And yet, instead of the serenity that pleasant odor had inspired the night before, he was left with a deep ache of loneliness that threatened to shatter his last remaining controls.

In the face of what should have been a celebration, he felt remarkably miserable, as if he were making plans to attend his own wake rather than a ceremony marking his resurrection.

Bryse had been his usual calm and succinct self, rattling on about treaties and negotiations and even spilling the beans about how he'd been responsible for Kim Le scraping him up off the floor of the spaceport on Calipri. The admiral had spoken in glowing terms of the treaty between the Empire and the Mizarians, had babbled on about how the *Starling* would be ready to receive him back as her commander within another few hours. After the ceremony at Earthbase One which Bryse promised repeatedly would be brief, he was to simply walk back onto the bridge of his ship and sail once more toward the stars on some new mission. The Old Man had answered his questions and explained every detail more than once; but when it was all over, Morgan was left feeling as if he hadn't heard a word

Now, sitting on the edge of a bed in which he would never sleep again, he stared out the cut-away window, fighting the urge to kick himself for the misery he felt inside, fighting even more the thought which made him long to stay at the temple, forever forsaking the clamor and hassle of life in the Corps.

But his reverie was interrupted by a faint knock at the door and, after murmuring permission to enter, it swung open to reveal Kim Le. The Supreme Master came quickly into the room, then sat by his side on the small, lonely bed, neither of them speaking for several silent minutes.

"Your trouble reaches me even in the serenity of meditation, Morgan," Kim Le revealed presently. "Should this not be a time for rejoicing?"

Morgan's eyes closed, then slowly opened again. "It should be, but...." He shook his head with a slightly embittered laugh. "Even though it's been almost nine months since this all began... since I went into the Mizarian Empire, I mean... I just didn't think it would be over so... so *soon*."

Kim Le contemplated that in silence for a moment. "Many times, the thing we long for the most is the source of the greatest anxiety when at last we achieve it," he said at last. "Even though you are filled with hopes and dreams for the future, you cannot help but grieve for the past." He smiled softly, knowingly. "No student at Ho Ling has ever left these walls without wanting very much to stay."

Morgan smiled wistfully. "I just wish... I wish I could have at least said goodbye to Master Lucien," he said quietly. Then, remembering his strange foreboding on the mountain that morning – which now seemed more like weeks in the past – he shook his head once more, filled with an odd sense of regret. "But... you know... when Jahan called him back to the temple... I knew then that I'd never see him again."

Very gently, Kim Le reached out to rest one hand on Diego's clenched fist, carefully unfolding the knitted fingers. "The matter which took him from the temple was of utmost importance to his family – and to his future, Morgan," he explained. "I am certain, however, that he would wish for you to complete your journey, to claim the reward for which you have labored. Then, later, if you wish to return here to say your farewells, I know you will both be well received."

Again, Morgan's eyes closed. "The road to Hell is paved with good intentions, Kim Le," he said realistically. "We make plans we know we'll never complete, fully intending to go back and finish things we started. But... in the end... does it ever really happen?" He didn't expect an answer, and waved the question aside with a quick gesture. "I just hope that I have a life to go back *to*," he said then, laying his sudden fear in the air.

Kim Le's gray brows tightened. "You fear that your beloved has taken another path," he surmised with tender understanding.

Morgan shrugged, sighing heavily. "I don't know," he said, recalling one of the first conversations he'd ever had with the old man. "I always thought that when the time came to go back to the *Starling*, I'd just fall right back into it as if I'd never been away. And I guess I was idealistic enough to let myself believe Lucien would be there – not just as my second-in-command and my friend, but...." His voice trailed off.

"If you take nothing else with you away from these walls, Morgan," the old man said when he faltered, "take with you the certainty that the ram's destiny is to cut his own trail through a thicket of thorns. And remember, my friend, that all is not as it seems. Once you have returned to the life you have known, the blocks you have employed to defeat the Mizarians will begin to fall away. You will begin to see more clearly, to understand that which may now seem vague."

Morgan considered that in silence, only listening with half his heart. The other half, he realized, was breaking.

And yet, as he glanced once again through the open window and noted that the sky had fallen into darkness, he understood that, at last, it was time for him to go.

It would soon be dawn in San Diego, and the responsibilities which had returned to his shoulders wouldn't wait.

At last standing up, he straightened the white initiate's garments, trying to quell the pain which rose in his chest as he looked once more at Kim Le, knowing intuitively that it may be the last time.

The old man stood, bowing from the waist as his lips pressed upward into a smile. "Remember, Morgan, that all things are within your grasp, all Knowledge within your reach." Then, dipping one weathered hand into the folds of his own robe, he withdrew a familiar purple sash which, without explanation, he tied quickly around Morgan's waist. "Wear this in honor, my friend," he said quietly, "with the certainty that you are a master of your own destiny."

Too touched for words, Morgan seized the old man to his chest, hugging him fiercely as his eyes misted with tears of parting. "You've given me back my life, Kim Le," he said. "I just hope I can live it with one tenth of your wisdom."

Finally, however, the old man stepped back, his pale lips pressed to a smile. "If you find your path too difficult, there will always be another to guide you. There is no shame in turning to others for strength, my friend... *or* for love. Remember that always." Then, with a final bow of respect, he turned and disappeared back into the torch-lit corridor, leaving Morgan suddenly alone with his joys and with his sorrows.

He looked down at the purple sash about his waist, touching it reverently with his fingertips. Without completely understanding the hows and whys of it all, his battle was suddenly won; his primary reason for being at Ho Ling had been nullified.

Taking a deep breath, he tried not to tremble with the knowledge that, once again, he was leaving a familiar home behind. The infamous Cap'n Morgan was going home.

~

Morgan made it through the formal ceremony with Tashkeeln feeling numb and cold, hearing little of the elaborate speeches delivered by Bryse, Ambassador Martell of the Empire and the Mizarian Ambassador. He was only peripherally aware of the formal declarations of peace, the announcement that a Temple of Knowledge was to be constructed on Mizar. And what troubled him more than his own numbness was the fact that, save for a very few, none of the stiff and proper onlookers would ever understand what any of it meant. They would continue with their daily lives, their military or political careers, their desk jobs and their proper family lives.

They would never really live, never know what it meant to face exile or to walk through the gardens at the Temple of Ho Ling.

When the ceremony finally ended, Morgan was vaguely aware of being ushered into the press conference, and though he realized from the patter of occasional applause that his responses must have been proper in some manner or another, he had little recollection of delivering them. Without the sun as his marker, without the scent of jasmine and tea roses on the wind, he was suddenly and inexplicably lost; the clock's red digital numbers seemed alien and out of place, and the stale odor of cologne in the press room left him silently nauseous.

At some point, he remembered Bryse's private welcome-home-Morgan speech, the admiral slapping him on the back, telling him that the cultural shock would eventually wear off, and apologizing time and again for dragging him through the added stress of the ceremony and press conference.

And yet, despite repeated assurances from the admiral, Morgan's first *real* awareness came when, at last, he slipped through a private doorway and into the uncluttered back corridors of the base. Alone at last after several hours of intense pomp and circumstance with no sleep to soften the shock, he drew a deep, ragged breath, closing his eyes as he struggled to regain the perspective which seemed suddenly, impossibly lost.

But as he opened his eyes, squaring his shoulders as he prepared for the short walk to the transport, he looked up to find himself face to face with Liam Vanya.

For a moment, Morgan's heart stopped, skipped several beats, then started forward once again. He blinked, a slow smile starting up his lips as he saw the doctor squirm almost imperceptibly in the formal dress uniform.

"Doc?" he stammered, not daring to breathe.

The other man stood a few feet away, looking him up and down. Then, abruptly moving forward, he grabbed Morgan into a fierce bear-hug, holding on desperately for a very long time without saying a word. Finally, he took a step back, but continued to hold him at arms' length nonetheless.

"Morgan!" he practically shouted, his face brightening with a broad smile. "For the life of me, I don't believe this is happening! But it's about time this exile nonsense ended so we can all get on with our lives!" He paused, then grinned broadly, shaking his head as he looked Morgan up and down. "Damn! I just can't believe it's finally over!"

Feeling just a trace of the man he had once been return to the surface, Morgan returned his old friend's smile, reaching up to place his hands on the doctor's arms, mirroring the other's embrace. Then, not knowing what else to say, he opted for the truth. "To be perfectly honest, Doc, I can't believe it either." He looked down the long corridor, watching two young cadets disappear around the bend. Some unsettled corner of his mind wondered why they wore such uncomfortable attire, why they weren't dressed in the white robes of initiates. For himself, he had no intention of climbing back into the stiff uniform. A white pirate shirt seemed far more appealing, and as far as *he* was concerned, the brass could kiss his ass if they didn't like it. They owed him, after all.

But as he struggled with the balance, he was forced back to the reality of his surroundings. He shook his head, rubbing his brow with one hand as he offered a small smile. "I dunno," he ventured, trying without much success to let it all settle back into place, "maybe Bryse is right. Maybe it *is* just a bad case of cultural shock. But... it all seems so... *alien*."

At that, Vanya held him further out at arms' length, perusing him cautiously. "Well, you look a little leaner and maybe a little shaggy around the edges," he said quietly, "but I 'd say the prognosis for a full recovery seems pretty good."

Morgan allowed himself to smile once more, knowing Vanya needed it even if *he* didn't completely feel it inside. Then, meeting the other's intense blue eyes, he steeled himself mentally. "Where's... Lucien?" he asked, his heart quickening despite his resolve to take each moment as a separate entity.

Automatically, Vanya inclined his head toward the ceiling.

"He's still up on the ship playing tour guide to a bunch of four-foot-high Mizarians," he revealed. Then, his brows tightening to a frown, he added: "If you ask me, I think he's using that as a good excuse not to transport down into this hooplah. You know how he is about the press and bureaucrats." He seemed almost apologetic, definitely uncomfortable with the question.

Morgan relaxed a little, realizing that at least that much hadn't changed where Lucien was concerned. Then, knowing he could procrastinate no further, he inclined his head toward the long corridor and the transport waiting beyond. "Well," he sighed, "I don't know about you, but I could use a decent night's sleep in my own bed."

But as he started off once more down the corridor, he was halted by Vanya's restraining grasp on his arm and, turning, he found a familiar look of concern residing on the other's features. "Are you sure you're all right, Morgan?"

Morgan tried to project an air of self-confidence and security which he was far from feeling inside. He manufactured a perfect replica of a somewhat piratical smile. "You should know by now that I'm not much better than Lucien when it comes to the press and the bureaucracy." He tapped a point between his brows with one finger. "Headache."

~

An hour after being accompanied to his quarters by Vanya, Morgan lay on top of his bed, his eyes closed as he listened to the ship gearing down for simulated night. He realized with a pang that Lucien had not yet answered his summons, and despite the fact that he was well aware of protocol and diplomacy where visiting dignitaries were concerned, he couldn't help wondering if indeed the Alfarian would come at all.

He had deliberately not spoken much about Lucien with Vanya, too weary from his journey and the sense of lingering shock to stand up to a long-winded conversation. But now, exhausted but unable to sleep, home once more in his own bed, he found himself wishing he'd pressed the doctor for more information. For all he *really* knew, the past eight months had been nothing more than a minor inconvenience to Lucien. All he really *knew*, he reminded himself, was the depth of his own feelings; and despite a thousand rehearsed speeches in his own mind, it occurred to him that he had no genuine idea of how he was going to impress that Knowledge onto Lucien. It seemed a distinct possibility that, considering the Alfarian's aloofness, he might just as soon prefer to keep a safe and professional distance.

You worry more than a virgin in a whorehouse, The Little Voice informed him, though with more amusement than accusation.

He sighed softly, then reached up to wave the light sensor for total darkness, knowing that, ultimately, he would sleep whether he wanted to or not. The events of the twenty-four-hour-long day left him weary and drained, and more than a little dissatisfied.

Somehow, the coming home seemed anti-climactic; and he realized with an almost constant pang that he was already missing certain aspects of the life to which he'd grown accustomed at the temple. Rationally, he understood that Myrddin had achieved his ultimate goal – that of mastery of a new temple, that of meeting new challenges and taking new students to teach. And Kim Le had obviously been intrigued with the possibilities of teaching the Mizarian students who would come to dwell at Ho Ling. Life at the temple would continue as it always had – ordered, preserved, simple.

And yet, as Morgan thought once more of Master Lucien, he couldn't help sighing heavily as a terrible, aching sense of loss overwhelmed him. It occurred to him that he could very easily go to the desk terminal, punch in the code which would connect him with Kim Le's private office, and ask to speak with his former master, to at least make some effort to say a proper farewell before the *Starling* launched on her new mission in the morning.

But as he considered the impersonal coldness of the communication console, he sank back down in his own bed, knowing that *that* wasn't the way he wanted to say goodbye. It should have been different, he told himself. Master Lucien should have been there to share the happiness of his regained freedom and to gently tell him that it was all right to go... or possibly even ask

266

him to stay.

As it was now, he was filled with the awful feeling of something left undone, something which would gnaw forever at his mind. And though he had sworn to return to Ho Ling at some later date to meet with his former master, he well understood the dangers inherent in his chosen profession. He could die tomorrow; or he could return to Earth in a month to discover that the Alfarian had departed the temple never to come back.

And suddenly, he was filled with the same gut-wrenching fear which had overwhelmed him as they'd parted in the foothills of the high mountains: he would never see Master Lucien again.

Feeling a profound sense of loss and regret, he found himself wondering if he'd made a mistake in returning to the *Starling*, if his priorities and attitudes had changed so drastically that he was no longer fit for command. And yet, he couldn't deny the fact that he'd had no other alternative. Once he had learned of his regained freedom, he could no more have stayed at Ho Ling than he could have jumped up and touched the moon. It was, as Myrddin, Kim Le and Master Lucien had said: his destiny.

~

Lucien stood gazing down at the sleeping human for a very long time, easily reading the tension in the other's body, even more easily interpreting the turmoil and sadness which boiled like lava just beneath the surface. It occurred to him that perhaps he had made a mistake in not permitting Vanya to reverse the minor cosmetic surgery, and in not shaving off the light beard or coloring the gold-bleached streak which ran through his hair. What surprised him was that he found he had no desire to have the ship's barber cut his hair back into the familiar regulation-length style. Instead, he determined, he would keep the longer locks as a tribute to the year of the ram. And the brass could kiss *his* ass, too.

It was, he discovered, freeing to embrace his own inner pirate, just as Morgan had always done. On a vessel such as the *Starling*, which would often be months away from any military base, it hardly seemed reasonable to truss oneself up in an uncomfortable uniform, or cut one's hair to suit somebody's notion of decorum.

False belief systems. Inauthentic roles. Yes, that was all going to change, even if it meant going against all the edicts of Galaxy Corps and the known worlds, even if it meant single-handedly changing the universe. And *that*, Lucien knew, was *his* destiny.

But now, standing at the side of the human's bed, still dressed in the familiar black garments of a master of Ho Ling, he knew he must remain as Master Lucien for a few minutes longer, relying on *his* strength to give Morgan the truth which Captain Lucien still had not learned to speak of.

Taking a deep breath, he knelt on one knee, reaching out through the near darkness to place his hand in the center of the human's back. His heart pounded, rushing blood through his ears and causing him to tremble as he realized that, finally, he had arrived at his own moment of truth as well. He must confront the question of whether *he* could be all things to Morgan, or if that Knowledge and ability rested solely in the persona of Master Lucien.

~

Aware only of someone touching him, Morgan opened his eyes slowly, disoriented as he looked for the moon through the cut-away window. And yet, hearing the distant purr of the ship's engines, he recognized with an ache of aloneness that he was no longer at the temple. Reality returned slowly and only after running through a quick checklist did he realize that the hand touching him was part of his physical existence rather than an extension of some already-forgotten dream.

He blinked into the darkness, his body jolting as he caught just a glimpse of the intruder by the faint crack of light which came through at the bottom of his door. Then, sitting bolt-upright in the small bed, he gasped aloud, instantly recognizing the other's dark silhouette.

"Master Lucien!" he half-whispered, believing himself for a moment to be completely mad. And yet, if he had gained nothing else from his training, it was the certainty that his own sanity and perceptions were still at least somewhat intact. "Wh-what – I mean *how*?" He shook his head, trying to rattle the sleep from his mind. It didn't even occur to him in that moment to ask how the Alfarian had gotten onto the *Starling*. Without waiting for an answer, he reached out impulsively, afraid to let go for fear of shattering the moment as he grasped the other man's hand, squeezing it with a sudden desperation.

With every ounce of control he could muster, Lucien reached up to cover the human's hand with both of his own, only then realizing that he had no pre-prepared speech, no well-rehearsed lines. He was at the mercy of his own feelings and, relying solely on them, he bowed his head until it rested on the top of his own hand. He was afraid, yet he captured the power of that fear to motivate his actions.

"It is time, Morgan," he murmured, "that you know the truth." Feeling the other man tremble, he lifted his head at last, both wanting and not wanting to wave the lights up to a dim glow. He resisted, realizing that some things were best said in the darkness. "I regret that I have not had the courage to tell you before."

Morgan held his breath. It was enough that this man had come to him to say his goodbyes; and the details of how and why scarcely seemed to matter. He swallowed the hard lump in his throat, wetting his suddenly dry lips with his tongue as he struggled to breathe.

"The... truth?" he managed, not daring to even think what that might mean. "What truth, Master?"

Lucien's eyes closed and, taking a deep breath, he steadied himself as best he could. "My truth," he said presently. Then, knowing no other way to say it, he laid the words in the air, relying on Morgan's kindness to treat them gently. "The truth that I wish to be with you always, that I wish our lives to join, that I wish for us to be all things to one another." With his heart open, his soul bared, he began to tremble, waiting an eternity for the human's response.

Morgan felt his heart threaten to stop as he was overwhelmed with a sudden dizziness, the words penetrating his exhaustion and snapping him instantly alert. In his body and mind, he wanted nothing more than to say yes. But in the deepest part of his spirit, he held the Knowledge that he was already sworn to another – to his own Lucien. And even if that love never flourished between them, he understood suddenly that he could not give only half of his heart to any man. Master Lucien deserved far better than that.

Closing his eyes, he bit his lower lip until the pain caused him to speak. "Master Lucien, you... honor me more than I can express." But, knowing it had to be said, he laid his own truth in the air. "But... I... I have to at least *try* to find the life I should have had before... before this all began." He squeezed the other man's hands desperately, not wanting to cause his teacher any emotional pain, yet knowing suddenly that it was inevitable. "I... have to stay *here*... with *Lucien... my* Lucien."

Knowing and internalizing only then that Morgan was indeed committed to him *now*, even after all that had happened and after months of separation; and feeling that same depth of commitment within his own aching spirit, Lucien let out the breath he'd been holding and very slowly reached up to unfasten the jeweled choker collar, dropping it to the floor at the side of the bed. Morgan loved *him*, and that Knowledge was sufficient to take his own worst fear away.

"Is there any reason, Morgan," he began, his own deep voice penetrating the silence in the room and sounding vaguely alien even to his own ears, "that we can not *all* share that life together?"

For a fraction of a second which lasted several lifetimes, Morgan had the insane idea that his *own* Lucien had somehow crept into the shadows of his room, and that now some unholy trinity was being proposed even as *he* sat stunned and slightly horrified in the center of his bed. But suddenly, as the shock of hearing Lucien's voice rattled him with a long list of impossible possibilities, he felt just a portion of the shields he'd so carefully constructed slip away, realizing that the voice – *Lucien's* voice – was also the voice of his master.

It was then, in that same fraction of a second that he jolted to action, one hand flying instantly toward the light sensor. He caught only the edge of the beam, however, causing the illumination to raise slightly, but still remaining less than that of a single candle.

He stared at the other man until his eyes stung from not

blinking, his jaw somewhat slack as he noted the Alfarian's appearance. Dressed in the familiar robes of a master, with angular features and a light growth of beard, he *looked* very much like Master Lucien – except for the aura which he only then began to really see. That aura, however, was one he couldn't have mistaken even in a room filled with a thousand others. With the Mizarian probe now terminated, his shields faltered, allowing a faint glimmer of light to penetrate the darkness he'd imposed on his mind. And as the blocks he'd instilled began to slowly crumble, he felt himself inundated with the majesty of Lucien's presence, with the beauty of the words his beloved had spoken to him, the life-time request he had uttered.

He couldn't speak, his mind turning in on itself with too many questions, leaving him mute and on the verge of actual shock.

Sensing that danger, Lucien reacted more from instinct than from any real knowledge of what he was doing. He drew the disheveled blanket up around the bare shoulders, then took his hand once more, squeezing it with firm authority as he realized they had safely navigated the most dangerous point in their journey toward Oneness.

"I did not know how else to tell you, Morgan," he murmured, feeling suddenly guilty for the shock he'd perpetrated upon the person he loved most in all the universe. "And... I was not certain you would have believed me if I had told you only with words."

Morgan barely heard it. Instead, he remained transfixed, staring at the Alfarian's face until he grew mesmerized. "Lucien?" he whispered.

Lucien nodded, releasing the breath he'd been holding. Then, knowing only that he had to somehow quiet the storm in the other's heart, he rose from his kneeling position and sat on the edge of the bed, slipping his arm around the human as Master Lucien had often done. The difference, he noted, was that Captain Lucien trembled openly in response.

"*Lucien?*" Morgan said again, shivering as the other held him close.

Lucien drew the golden head down against his shoulder. "I am here, Morgan," he promised. "And if you will have me, it is here that

I wish to always remain."

Within another few minutes during which neither spoke, the shock had lessened somewhat in Morgan's mind, though his thoughts remained filled with questions. Most of them, he discovered, he could easily answer on his own. He chiseled away at them, baring the bones of the truth until the skeletal remains stared up at him from the grave in which he'd temporarily hidden them.

"You... it was you all along," he murmured. Then, turning slightly to meet the other's tender expression, he wondered aloud: "How could I not have known, Lucien?" He recalled in a flash of horror the intimacy he had shared with the Alfarian, thinking him to be another, the words he'd hurled in anger, the hurt he'd undoubtedly caused. "By all the pagan gods, you must hate me."

Somewhat surprised by that conclusion, Lucien's brows lifted. "How could I find fault with the fact that you loved another aspect of myself?" he asked. Then, running one hand gently up and down the human's trembling back, he leaned his cheek against the soft silkiness of the other man's hair. "What we shared at the temple, Morgan, was the most we could share under the circumstances. And yet, it has shown me that Kim Le was correct in his wisdom." He paused for a moment, pulling the human closer as he felt the muscular body tremble. "We are destined to be together in whatever guise we assume, in whatever lives we may lead." He shook his head to reaffirm his own commitment. "There should be no shame in the fact that we have loved before, but only if we do not now begin to harvest the rewards of our labor."

As Morgan listened to the inescapable reason and the undeniable passion in the Alfarian's words, he felt himself breathing just a little easier. He realized that the shock would be with him for awhile, yet as he mentally replayed Lucien's eloquent speech, trying to superimpose those words onto *his* Lucien, he was struck with a sudden revelation.

Filled with awe, he reached up to touch the other's face, his fingertips skimming over the angular features, mentally stripping away the surgery and the beard until he was once again with his old friend. "You've changed, too, haven't you?" he asked gently, realizing with a deep sense of Knowledge that *he* had helped to

272

bring those changes about.

Lucien considered that, then slowly inclined his head in acknowledgement, feeling himself shiver at the lightly skimming fingers which brushed his face. "It is my hope that I have grown in wisdom and spiritual strength," he ventured, recalling the possessiveness he had overcome, the loneliness he had learned to accept as an unnecessary burden. "The experience at Ho Ling has taught me many things," he added, then smiled with his lips as well as his eyes, "not the least of which is that I have loved you... since the day we first met." He hadn't intended to say it in just that manner, nor so quickly, but once done, he had no desire to pull the truth back.

Morgan's eyes closed and he rested his head on the Alfarian's shoulder as he had done when they had slept together high in the mountains near the temple. "I... I thought I'd never see you again," he mused, uncertain whether he was referring to his own Lucien, to Master Lucien or to both. In the end, it didn't matter; they were and always had been one in the same. Then, knowing he had to offer the same commitment the Alfarian had already verbalized, he lifted his head until their eyes met in the dim darkness. "But now that we're together," he vowed, "I don't ever want to lose you again... I don't ever want to be apart."

Finally allowing himself to breathe again, Lucien could not contain the bright grin that burst forth. "*That*," he promised, placing a lingering kiss on the human's jawline, "can quite easily be arranged, Morgan." He continued to surprise himself with his own actions, yet he knew he couldn't have stopped if every life in the galaxy had depended on it. It *was*, he now understood, his personal journey – not only to love this man, but to love him with some degree of openness. No longer would he remain mute and terrified of his own feelings. No longer would he risk losing what he had fought so desperately to regain. No longer would he be held prisoner by false beliefs or inauthentic roles.

Deep within himself, Morgan felt the old burdens slowly starting to lift and, turning to face the man who could awaken such a trembling within his spirit, he offered a gentle, heart-felt smile. "*Now*," he pointed out, "you sound like the Lucien I know." But then, realizing the possibilities for misinterpretation of such a general statement, he hastened to clarify. "Of course," he added with just a hint of mischievousness, "I could spend a lifetime getting to know both sides."

Lucien's brows lifted simultaneously with the corners of his lips. "I would not find that too long to be together," he decided, easily following Morgan's lighter, gentler mood. "Indeed, if you wish it, we can begin your lessons at once," he added in the familiar tone of the Master he had been, of the man he had now become.

Morgan's smile reflected all the way through to his spirit. "Then... you'll join us into One," he said, needing that confirmation, that assurance, that promise of forever. And as usual, he wanted it *now*.

But Lucien only smiled as he leaned closer and pressed his lips to the welcoming mouth. "Ta ta ta," he scolded in a deep-throated, seductive whisper. "Let us save at least *one* mystery for tomorrow, Morgan." Then, gently pushing the human back onto the bed and covering him with his weight, he gazed deeply into the bright green-gold eyes. "For tonight," he added, "is it not enough to love?"

Morgan's eyes closed and he sighed pleasantly, his body quickening in response to the deep velvet voice, to the sensation of feeling his beloved pressed tightly against him. His arms came up around the other man's back, pulling him even closer as one hand strayed through the black-silk hair, lingering on the spray of gold which streaked the sleek bangs.

"Tonight," he agreed, "you're still the Master, Lucien." Then, feeling a little more of his old command presence return as he realized he had no remaining desire to resist his chosen path, he arched his hips delicately upward, pressing their bodies together until a familiar stirring began. "But tomorrow," he warned softly, "the ram might just come back to life."

Lucien's brows lifted and, bending down to kiss the beloved mouth once more, he was filled with a sudden aching tenderness. "In that event," he promised, stating his commitment aloud, "I shall be your shepherd, Morgan... for as long as you wish me at your side."

Morgan sighed softly, opening his lips to the gently probing kiss. Already, the ram was beginning to stir. But he was inundated with the Knowledge that, as the night deepened, the shepherd's presence would comfort him until he slept.

In the morning, they would become One. But for now, for the thick and eternal serenity of the night, it was enough to love.

Tonight, he vowed joyfully, they would master *that* art together.

THE END

About the Author...

Della Van Hise is a native of Florida, transplanted to California at the age of 21, who has subsequently sunk her roots into the high desert near Joshua Tree National Park. She has not personally seen any aliens since around 1992, but there is rumored to be a secret UFO base underneath her house.

Della's writing started around age 11, when she would bang out some of the very earliest "fan fiction" on an old Smith Corona typewriter. No, not an electric one. A real antique, made of metal and heavier than a wet coffin. Her first professional novel was *Killing Time* - the controversial *Star Trek* book which was recalled and re-edited in 1984.

Della has written extensively in the non-fiction genre, with titles such *as Quantum Shaman: Diary of a Nagual Woman* and *Scrawls On the Walls of the Soul. Quantum Shaman* focuses heavily on the author's metaphysical explorations and experiences, while *Scrawls* is a continuation of those journeys many years later. If you enjoyed the works of Carlos Castaneda or Don Miguel Ruiz, you'll enjoy the non-fiction works of Della Van Hise.

In addition, Della has written professionally for *Tomorrow Magazine* and other prominent science fiction publications. Her fiction works include *Sons of Neverlands* (an award-winning vampire novel); *Year of the Ram, No Forwarding Address*, and *Coyote*.

All of the titles mentioned here are available through Amazon, or through Amazon or www.eyescrypublications.com

Other fiction titles from Eye Scry Publications...

SONS OF NEVERLAND
an erotic vampyre novel
by Della Van Hise

"The virtuosity shown here is only the beginning of a pyrotechnic talent unfolding into the hidden dimensions of the human and nonhuman spirit."
                        Jacqueline Lichtenberg

"What Sons of Neverland resembled to me was the creative hagiographies of Nikos Kazantzakis, where a few stylized characters deliver a message that goes way beyond the parameter of the characters themselves. And much like Kazantzakis, this book zones on the question of immortality. However, this is not just the decadent historical immortality of the long-lived vampire, it is immortality as a change in one's perception. This is the story behind the story, delivered by characters that are hyper-real - each one loaded with symbolism. Sons of Neverland will have you filled, even brimming over with the sense of Mysterium Tremendum et Fascinans. Go there for a full helping of the numinous." (A Reviewer on Amazon!)

_____

Set against a backdrop of contemporary culture, SONS OF NEVERLAND explores the universal questions of life & death, sex & love - the most crucial challenges every human being faces - through the eyes of the immortal vampire.

_____

The novella "Kiss of the Black Angel" is available for free on Kindle – a preview to SONS OF NEVERLAND.

NO FORWARDING ADDRESS
Della Van Hise

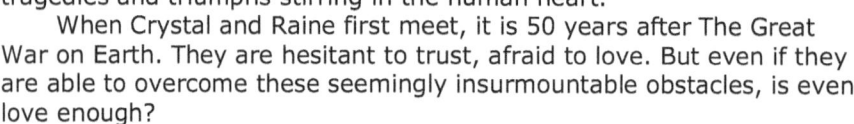

When Terrans came to sail dark seas,
And see what stars might be...
Heaven moved with no forwarding address,
And left this void to me.
(Children's song from Lazali)

_____

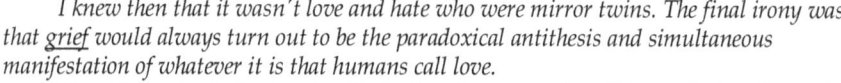

A literary science fiction novel told in the voice of an empath, *No Forwarding Address* explores the lures and the dangers of love, the tragedies and triumphs stirring in the human heart.

When Crystal and Raine first meet, it is 50 years after The Great War on Earth. They are hesitant to trust, afraid to love. But even if they are able to overcome these seemingly insurmountable obstacles, is even love enough?

When a man has the stars in his eyes, legend says he must serve them above all others.

_____

I knew then that it wasn't love and hate who were mirror twins. The final irony was that <u>grief</u> would always turn out to be the paradoxical antithesis and simultaneous manifestation of whatever it is that humans call love.

Crystal remained silent and walked a few steps away from Raine – further down the shoreline, until she stood under the wing of one fallen Phantom. She thought of the ship she had seen from the balcony of our home, and though it had long since disappeared over the dark and treacherous abyss of the ocean, its image lingered clearly in her thoughts. On that ship was a man, she thought. A terribly lonely man who made no great difference to the flow of time or the memory of the galaxy. A man who, like Raine, was compelled to keep moving and look only ahead and never behind. A man who could not afford the luxury of waving goodbye to friends on shore.

At last, she turned toward her beloved and watched him watching the darkness. He stood only a few feet away, yet the images in my mind said he might as well have been a million light years off in the void. He was lost to her in that instant out-of-time, just as lost and impossible to find as the light from that ship which had vanished over the horizon...

www.eyescrypublications.com
http://www.amazon.com/Forwarding-Address-Della-Van-Hise-ebook/dp/B00PEOSKJ0/

COYOTE
Della Van Hise

*A Novel of Love, Honor
and Personal Sacrifice...*

When River Willows is accused of a murder
she didn't commit, her life takes a turn
toward the sanctuary of a world existing at
right-angles to our own. Combining the
mysticism of martial arts and the romantic
conflict of a young woman torn between two
powerful men, COYOTE takes the reader on
an epic journey of dangerous secrets,
military cover-ups, and the infinite heart of
the peaceful warrior.

_____

"So who's Coyote?" I asked, trying to ignore the effect he was
having on me. "You?"

Steale laughed easily, though it did little to hide the torment behind
that mask of indifference he wore so well.

"Coyote's a scavenger, Jack of all trades. The Native Americans call
him the trickster - the one who brought chaos down on the world." He
shrugged as if altogether unconcerned. "Original sin."

"Is that what you are?" I asked, keeping it light despite the growing
knot my stomach. "Original sin?"

He kept his profile to me, eyes straight ahead as he drove. "Sure
you want to know?"

I couldn't help wondering if I had cornered the coyote, or if the
clever trickster had cornered me.

_____

By the author of **KILLING TIME** – without a doubt the most
controversial **STAR TREK** novel ever published!

From the author:
www.eyescrypublications.com

On Amazon
http://www.amazon.com/Coyote-Della-Van-
Hise/dp/0976689782/

YEAR OF THE RAM
Della Van Hise

Year of the Ram was described by one reviewer as... "A spacefaring gay romance full of love, angst, and longing."

Only after Star Commander Morgan Diego becomes an exile as a result of a Galaxy Corps political blunder does he begin to realize how much he valued the companionship of his second in command - the mysterious Lucien, an Alfarian who is more elven than human, with peculiar powers & abilities which begin to unfold as he, too, realizes what he has lost.

Separated by circumstance from his former life, Morgan is thrust into a world where he must survive by his wits. When he meets a peculiar little old man calling himself Kim Le, Morgan finds himself in a situation where he is required to master The Art - not only a form of human & extraterrestrial martial arts, but a way of living and being that will alter his life forever.

At the temple, he is introduced to his new teacher, another Alfarian who begins to steal his heart - a heart which is already promised to Lucien. Torn and conflicted, Morgan struggles with the world he left behind and the world he now inhabits.

Beginning to believe he may never again return to his ship and to the friends and loved ones he left behind, he is all the more frustrated and heartbroken when a new Master arrives at the temple: a man to whom Morgan is immediately drawn both mentally and physically, a man who is strikingly familiar... yet utterly alien.

Year of the Ram is a fully-fleshed novel, approximately 97000 words, with a focus on the love story and romance angle. Set against a science fiction milieu, it explores the infinite possibilities of the human and alien heart. Sexual content is explicit, though is not the primary focus of the novel.

For those who like a romance that forces its characters to contemplate the ecstasies AND the agonies of love... you will enjoy *Year of the Ram* immensely.

FROM THE AUTHOR:
www.eyescrypublications.com

ON AMAZON:
http://www.amazon.com/Year-Ram-Della-Van-Hise/dp/0989693813/

LETTERS TO AN ANDROID
Wendy Rathbone

Cobalt is a created human, vat grown and born adult, with no human rights and indentured to serve others for the duration of his life. Liyan is a young man with wanderlust in his eyes, embarking on a career that takes him to the furthest regions of space. The two become unlikely friends and create a memorable long-distance correspondence. Through Liyan, Cobalt gets to explore the universe, living vicariously through his friend's wave transmissions. A strong bond develops between them that not even the stars can put asunder.

_____

Now you know an android who writes poetry.

This is all your fault. Did you not read my last wave telling you extracurricular activities for my kind are discouraged? Of course this is harmless and strangely enjoyable and does not necessarily require me to leave the hotel. Pel would not care if I wrote lines of equations or nonsensical juxtaposed words. As long as the act does not bring my mental state into question.

However, in history, poetry is often written by the rebels.

So we can keep this to ourselves.

Let me know about your lieutenant's test.

And to give you peace of mind, I never believed you observed me as anything other than human.

Some people are and always will be hateful bigots. Most people are simply uncomfortable in speaking to "property." And anyway, friendship, like poetry, is also discouraged.

Your friend,
Cobalt

FROM THE AUTHOR:
www.eyescrypublications.com

ON AMAZON:
http://www.amazon.com/Letters-Android-Wendy-Rathbone/dp/0989693872/

PALE ZENITH
Wendy Rathbone
A Science Fiction Novel

On a far-flung "Earth" in a parallel universe, two factions are fighting a decades-long psychic war. Young talented psychics are being temporarily kidnapped from present day Earth, seemingly at random, to serve as part of one side's psychic army. They are put under the control of spychiatrists, mysterious machines with many limbs that have a programmed ability to travel time and space and universes to kidnap and control carefully selected humans. The humans never know they are being used; when their missions are completed they are brought back to their universe through time and placed back in their beds, their memories wiped.

———————————

The shadows wound the tall corridor in muted gold, varnished brown. It seemed as though they were in the bowels of a giant serpent coiled outside time, outside space.

When they left the palace, a familiar sun flourished in a clear, blue sky. But this wasn't their sun. Not Zack's sun. It was an alien star burning within a different galaxy in an all too distant universe. Zack looked up squinting, trying to see if he could peer beyond the sky, beyond the pale of midday and into his own timespace, but there was nothing. Only sunlight. Only the thin atmosphere of an Earth not his own.

His back knotted again. Leo's presence was a gelid space inside his chest, empty. Always before he'd felt a warmth there, a sort of pressure like someone's hand pressed gently to his heart. He'd taken Leo for granted knowing, the way a shadow falls when you block the sun, that he was there around him, inside him: blood, air, salt, brain, soul. They were genetic duplicates, twins, spiritual halves. Without him, Zack knew the first icy tugs of panic.

FROM THE AUTHOR
www.eyescrypublications.com

ON AMAZON
http://www.amazon.com/Pale-Zenith-Wendy-Rathbone/dp/0976689790/

The Foundling
by Wendy Rathbone

Diego is a powerful man with a tragic past. Out on the expansive ocean in his private yacht, he discovers a beautiful and mysterious man adrift on a raft, near death. The bond that forms between them in the aftermath of Alec's rescue is one of fierce passion, though lacking in trust. Can they make it work, or will Alec's amnesia bring forth secrets so disturbing as to tear them apart? A passionately erotic love story of desire and darkness, exquisite and explicit.

_____

I can see his struggle between gratitude and uneasiness. He is buffeted by all things new and strange. He does not know where he is from, who he is or what happened to him. He does not know me. There has not been enough time to transition between strangers and friendship.

This isolation of his is something I can identify with, but it is also a feeling no one can help him with until or unless he gets his own life back. And his memory.

If that doesn't happen, then it will take time for him to build a new life. He is polite to me, even friendly, but even a night together during a storm with his arms wrapped tight around my waist doesn't calm the surge I see inside him, the emptiness, the loss, possibly even panic. That night may have reinforced some trust in me, but so far not enough for him to completely relax.

He seeks me out, though. That's something. He sits by me at dinner when he can have any seat of his choosing. I watch him closely when he does not realize it. At dinner the following night after we had only 'slept' together, and before we go to bed again in separate rooms, I notice everything about him, how he moves, the way the air warms when he is closer to me, the dry sheen of his lips as they part for more air when he is reacting to something, or speaking, or eating.

His hands still shake. Anyone else might not notice because he keeps them clasped into fists at his sides or, while sitting, pressed tight to his lap.

I spend another fretful night alone. I dream restlessly, wild, loud and colorful visions I cannot recall at all as soon as my eyes open. All I know is the dreams leave me unfulfilled, impatient.

www.eyescry.com/html/publications.htm

None Can Hold the Dark
Wendy Rathbone

In Book 2 of "The Foundling" trilogy, Diego and Alec meet new challenges in private and from the outside world. Diego is being investigated by the local police for murder. Meanwhile, Alec's amnesia and the trauma of his kidnapping by white slavers continue to plague him. And the danger to Alec is not yet over.

Distracted by their new love, both men fail to see certain threats until it is almost too late.

"Why do you keep doing this illegal business?" Now Alec's gaze turned toward him, open as the day and lit with a sad frenzy, a challenge. "You could go anywhere, do anything, be anyone."

Diego had asked himself that question on rare occasions. In truth, he got used to what he was, what he did. Even a dangerous known was perhaps preferable to the unknown. "People depend on me."

Alec shook his head, but smiled a little as he said, "That's so weak." He leaned forward, over the arm of the chair, and put his shaking hand on the back of Diego's head. The kiss was cool, lingering, moist with salt. When Alec pulled back, he said almost matter of factly, "It's like there's sharks and there's goldfish and one can't decide to become the other."

Diego was still stunned by the kiss. But the words hit him hard. In them was the unfair conjecture of a locked fate. He believed in making his own fate...or luck. Did Alec think only one kind of man lived inside him and that was all there was to it? To life? It hurt. Badly.

Diego sat back on his heels, catching himself with his hands on the smooth floor. "So, Alec, which am I?"

Alec frowned.

Diego said, "I made choices in my life. I made them No one made them for me. If I need to be strong I'm strong. If I need to be vicious I can be that too. So what? I'm stuck there? In a pattern, a role...with no free will?"

Alec watched him inquisitively now.

"Because," Diego went on, "I'm solely responsible for my actions. Me. Could you say the same of the shark?"

They both waited, the silence covering them in muggy discomfort.

"You think you understand me?" Diego finally asked.

284

The Lostling: Alec's Story
Book Three in The Foundling
by *Wendy Rathbone*

The Lostling takes place directly after *None Can Hold the Dark*, as Alec and Diego relocate to San Francisco. There, amid salty winter wind and fog, Alec's lost memories slowly return and he must relive some of his most painful and terrifying moments to regain his forgotten self. In agonizing dreams and flashes of memory, he finally remembers what happened to him... and why.

Excerpt: *Putting a hand on his arm or leg, I can always feel the tremor of Diego even through his clothes, an innate wildness, a life-power.*

I always believed, from the first day Diego found me unconscious and dying, floating in the middle of a sapphire Caribbean ocean, there was a core of me unhidden, unforgotten, that cried out silently to the air and everything around me communicating who I am, what I am.

I can't remember it myself. Not that core, not anything up to the day I awoke in Diego's bed, sick and panicked. In that moment, I remembered nothing more than my first name, and even that memory is suspect. But this core of me demands to take things into its own hands to be seen, to make sure it remains "I am."

I believe Diego saw it, the urgent desperation in me wanting to be witnessed, and he made a promise to that essence of me, to that heart of me, that he would see me through anything that came my way. Something in me reached up and latched onto him, a clasping energy, and Diego clasped back.

It caught and held him. He was moved. He was compelled. He was mesmerized.

http://www.eyescrypublications.com

http://www.amazon.com/Lostling-Alecs-Story-Foundling-Book-ebook/dp/B00RO8GSUW/

My House Is Full of Whispers
Wendy Rathbone

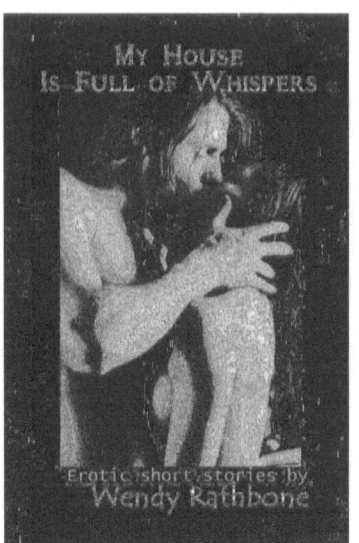

Ten erotica short stories by Wendy Rathbone - former winner of the prestigious WRITERS OF THE FUTURE contest!

Leda has not one beautiful man, but two. Kale enters a secret world in a wealthy man's basement. Noah is in love with a man who hates sex. Dina lives next door to a famous Hollywood director she secretly loves. Dorian has a sixteen year old female student coming onto him. Tara is haunted by an erotic ghost. Young Dimitri is kidnapped by lecherous men. And more.

Author's Preface

When I wrote these stories, I deliberately set out to gently break down certain barriers, and I've certainly broken taboos. Do I care? No. This is fantasy at its purest level. The stories are never meant to be political statements, nor do they make any attempt at political correctness, and there is little consideration for safe sex. While I definitely condone safe sex, my stories come from fictional realities in my head where safe sex is not much of a concern because, well, it's imaginary and it's fiction!

For me, these stories are meant as little poetic erotic ramblings merely to stir the flames of desire, nothing more. They are pure fantasy and therefore to be enjoyed as such. Every story is erotic in nature, meant to titillate, some more explicit than others. Some of the stories are light, some are darker. I invite the reader to a feast of diversity and delight.

One reader commented: *"...some of the most beautifully written erotica since Anais Nin!"*

FROM THE AUTHOR: www.eyescrypublications.com

ON AMAZON:

http://www.amazon.com/House-Full-Whispers-Wendy-Rathbone-ebook/dp/B00IJK3G04/

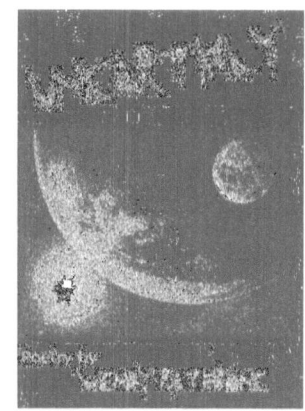

UNEARTHLY
by Wendy Rathbone

A Collection of Award-Winning Poetry

Intro by the Author: This book contains all my out of print chapbooks (mini-collections of an author's work usually published by smaller presses.)

The chapbooks published within include:
Moon Canoes, published by Dark Regions Press, 1994
(Im)mortal, published by Shadowfire Press, 1996
Scrying The River Styx, published by Anamnesis Press, 1999
Autumn Phantoms, published by Flesh and Blood Press, 2000
Dreams of Decadence Presents: Wendy Rathbone, published by DNA Publications 2002
Dancing in the Haunted Woodlands, published by Yellow Bat Review, 2003
Vampyria, published by Eye Scry Publications, 2005

She Sleeps With Vampires
She sleeps with vampires
courting velvet breaths
poem-dreams
chill-stopped hearts

Wrapped in her arms
like teddy bear thoughts
purple lips trembling
at her quiet throat
they love her more than
somber rain
more than autumn
more than ash-soft hearths of night.

FROM THE AUTHOR
www.eyescrypublications.com

ON AMAZON
http://www.amazon.com/Unearthly-Wendy-Rathbone-ebook/dp/B00B0MTIZK/

287

Non-fiction titles from Eye Scry Publications...

TEACHINGS OF THE IMMORTALS
by Mikal Nyght

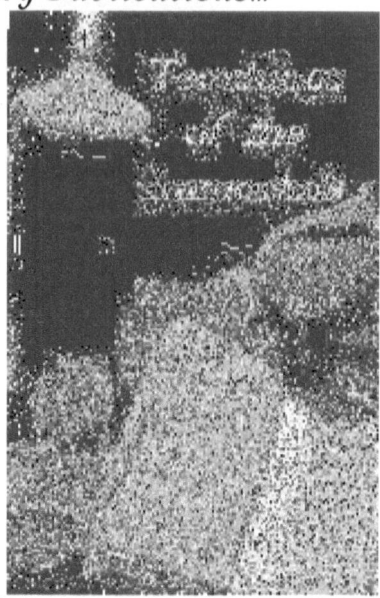

So... You Want To Live Forever?

The teachings are presented as brief vignettes in no particular order of importance. This is not a book you read from start to finish in a single night. It is a grimoire of self-creation, intended to be contemplated slowly so as to be assimilated wholly. Pick it up and turn to a page at random. Where your eyes come to rest on the page is your lesson for the day. Go no further until you have assimilated the lesson totally.

The teachings are seduction as much as instruction. This is the way of The Dark Evolution.

Two Brief Excerpts...

The Ruby Slippers

The danger of the consensual continuum is that its natural gravity exists at the lowest common denominator of human experience, and because of this it will automatically make you forget those elusive truths you've fought to learn, and before you know it you're lost in petty dramas again, sinking into the mire of old familiar scripts.

The only way to overcome this is to be continually cavorting with worlds and events beyond human experience, journeying into the unknown so that it can become known, expanding knowledge and awareness to become more than you were, bringing back from the Dreaming those secrets which will teach you how to use the ruby slippers to transport yourself over the rainbow to the vampyre wizard's secret lair.

Perception

This is the nature of reality: to be precisely what perception dictates, as solid and whole as your interpretation of it, or as changeable and eternal as you permit it to be.

It wasn't knowledge god tried to keep from Man, you see. It was perception, for perception alone has the power to destroy god and obliterate comfortable consensual realities to create unending immortality.

Take the apple, my embryonic children. Nibble its red red flesh. Open your vampyre eyes so you may finally begin to *See*.

FROM THE AUTHOR
www.immortalis-animus.com
www.eyescrypublications.com

ON AMAZON
http://www.amazon.com/Teachings-Immortals-Mikal-Nyght-ebook/dp/B00C2HY5WS/

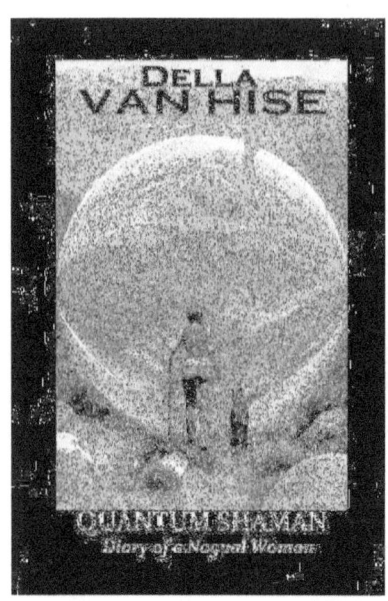

Quantum Shaman: Diary of a Nagual Woman
Della Van Hise

"Diary of a Nagual Woman brings a quantum understanding to what has traditionally been believed to be a mystical path alone. This book picks up where Carlos Castaneda left off to take us on a roller coaster ride of our own forgotten power..."
- Michael Grove, Reviewer

When I asked how Orlando had known I would come to this remote location, and how he himself had gotten there, he only smiled a little, stretched out his long legs, and slouched down on that cold metal bench to stare up at the stars.

"You're predictable," he said. "I'm here because this is where you always come when you're mad at the world."

I attempted to engage him in a conversation of just exactly how he knew I was mad at the world, since I'd had no direct contact with him in quite some time. But even as I began spelling all of that out to him, he brushed my words aside with an easy gesture.

"Do you want to talk or do you want to waste time looking for logical explanations for every magical thing that ever happens?" he asked. "That's what's wrong with the world, you know. Instead of embracing the mysteries and trying to determine how they might open a crack in an otherwise humdrum, pre-programmed existence, people waste their entire lives explaining it all away, attaching labels to it, filing and categorizing it until it loses any meaning."

He had a point. *'Magic is only science not yet understood'*. Words Orlando had written more than a year before rattled through my mind up there in the middle of the night, in the middle of nowhere, looking down on a distant world that seemed far more unreal to me at that moment than the world he had been trying to teach me to *see*.

He was there – whether physically or in some spirit-form manifestation is ultimately of no importance, for in the sorcerer's world there is no difference between body and spirit, and in any world, perception is reality.

www.quantumshaman.com
www.eyescrypublications.com

Scrawls on the Walls of the Soul
Della Van Hise

The long-awaited follow-up to Quantum Shaman: Diary of a Nagual Woman. **Stands alone, or order together!**

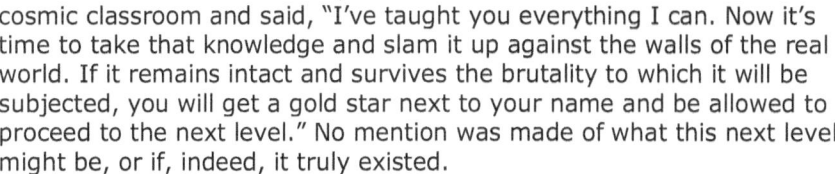

"If you've ever felt like a stranger in a strange land, this book is your road map to survival in the spiritual wilderness!" (Michael Grove)

~

It was May of 2000 when my mentor threw me out of the quantum cosmic classroom and said, "I've taught you everything I can. Now it's time to take that knowledge and slam it up against the walls of the real world. If it remains intact and survives the brutality to which it will be subjected, you will get a gold star next to your name and be allowed to proceed to the next level." No mention was made of what this next level might be, or if, indeed, it truly existed.

Go ahead – try to explain this all-consuming path to your friends and relatives. They will smile politely, squirm uncomfortably, and eventually they will stop returning your phone calls and look the other way when they see you coming. And who can blame them? They live in the real world with their office jobs and nuclear families and a host of mindless sitcoms waiting on the propaganda box at the end of their busy day. In direct contrast, it could be observed that anyone who has dedicated themselves to the pursuit of forbidden knowledge really doesn't live in that world at all. Not for lack of wanting, perhaps, but because the real world is quickly seen to be little more than a series of programs and illusions – not unlike The Matrix. And not surprisingly, the people who populate that world may begin to take on a peculiar zombie-like quality.

You find yourself alone in a world of jesters, jokers and jackasses. Now what?

FROM THE AUTHOR
www.quantumshaman.com
ON AMAZON
http://www.amazon.com/Scrawls-Walls-Soul-Della-Hise-ebook/dp/B008CUKH6C/

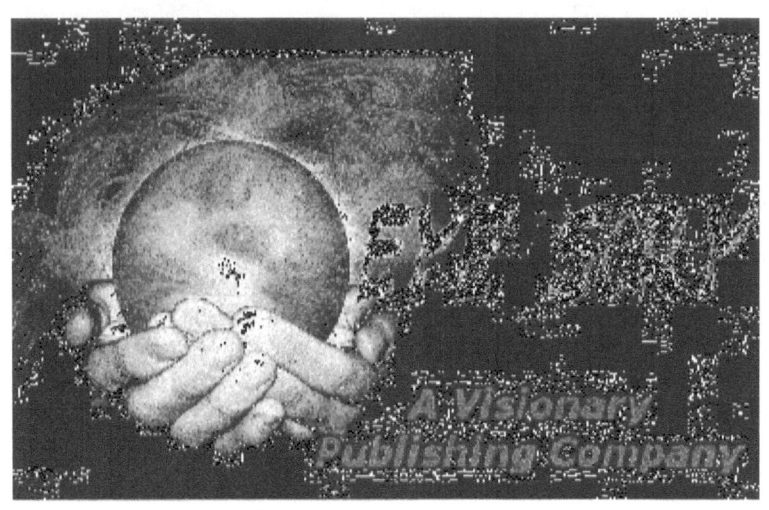

Eye Scry Publications
A Visionary Publishing Company

www.eyescrypublications.com
www.fanzinesplus.com
www.quantumshaman.com
www.immortalis-animus.com

www.ingramcontent.com/pod-product-compliance
Lightning Source LLC
Chambersburg PA
CBHW020602260626
47157CB00003B/828